A Woman's Place

Also by Barbara Delinsky

FICTION
The Secret Between Us
Family Tree
Looking for Peyton Place
The Summer I Dared
Flirting with Pete
An Accidental Woman
The Woman Next Door
The Vineyard
Lake News
Coast Road
Three Wishes
Suddenly
Shades of Grace
Together Alone
For My Daughters
More than Friends
The Passions of Chelsea Kane
A Woman Betrayed
Within Reach
Variation on a Theme
Finger Prints
Moment to Moment
The Carpenter's Lady
Fast Courting
An Irresistible Impulse
Gemstone
Passion and Illusion
Search for a New Dawn
A Time to Love
Sensuous Burgundy
Sweet Ember
Rekindled

NONFICTION
Uplift: Secrets from the Sisterhood of Breast Cancer Survivors
Does a Lobsterman Wear Pants?

A Woman's Place

BARBARA DELINSKY

AVON

An Imprint of HarperCollins*Publishers*

FIRST EDITION

Designed by Rhea Braunstein

Library of Congress Cataloging-in-Publication Data is available upon request.

ISBN 978-0-06-173528-8

09 10 11 12 13   WBC/RRD 10 9 8 7 6 5 4 3 2 1

Acknowledgments

I never fail to be humbled by the willingness of very busy people to give of their precious time and expertise so that my books may have a ring of truth. In writing *A Woman's Place*, I was particularly blessed. For her legal advice, I thank one of Boston's leading family law specialists, Margaret Travers. For her keen insight as owner of The Wicker Lady, I thank Charlie Wagner. For help in countless other little ways, I thank Fay Shapiro, Melanie Gargus, Regina Hurley, Ashley Brown Ahearn, and Peter Carr. If there are technical errors in *A Woman's Place*, the fault is mine.

Thanks, also, to my own lawyers—my husband, Steve, and my son, Eric, for deflecting their minds from their own cases to brainstorm on behalf of mine. Not that the twins did nothing. They listened and reacted and gave valued opinions on everything from title to plot line to cover.

Finally, huge thanks to my agent, Amy Berkower, who went above and beyond with this one.

One

Had I been a superstitious sort, I would have taken the smell as an omen. I had wanted the morning of our leaving to be smooth and now it was down to the wire. The last thing I needed was Dennis annoyed.

But I was a trusting soul. Entering the kitchen that October Friday, I sensed nothing of the broader picture. All I knew was that something had gone bad. A rank smell sullied what should have been the sweetness of fall—the scent of crisp leaves drifting in from the backyard, cranberry candles on the glass tabletop, a basket of newly picked Macouns.

I checked under the sink for fishy paper from last night's scrod, but the air there was fine. Same with the inside of the oven. Nothing hit me when I opened the refrigerator, still I checked the milk that my daughter too often left on the counter, the chicken that was ready for Dennis to eat while we were gone, the cheese bin where plastic wrap might hide something fuzzy and blue.

Nothing.

But the odor remained, offensive and strong, another glitch in a godawful week of glitches. With a husband, two young children, and a career to juggle, preparing to go away for more than two days was always a challenge, but I was going away for eleven days this time, in part on a dreaded mission. My mother was dying. My equilibrium was shaky, even without complicating glitches.

Having ruled out the obvious, I was beginning to wonder if something wasn't rotting under the two-hundred-year-old floorboards of the house, when my son padded in in his stockinged feet. He looked more sober than any nine year old with mussed hair, an authentic Red Sox baseball shirt, and battered jeans should look, but he was a serious child under any conditions, and perceptive. Much as I had tried to minimize the meaning of our trip, I suspected he knew.

"I can't find my sneakers, Mom. They're not in my room, and if I can't find them, I don't know what I'll wear at Grandma's. They were my best pair."

"'Were' being the operative word." I draped my arms over his shoulders. The top of his head reached my chest. "I had to scrape mud from the bottoms last night. What were you up to, Johnny? We agreed you wouldn't wear good sneaks to play football."

"It was basketball. Jordan's dad put in a hoop, but nothing's paved yet." He made a face. "Peewww. What stinks?"

I slid a despairing glance around the kitchen. "Good question. Any ideas?"

"Don't ask me. Ask Kikit. She's the one always leaving things lying around. Are you sure I'll be home in time for practice Tuesday?"

"The plane lands at one. Practice isn't until five."

"If I miss practice, I'll be benched."

I took his face in my hands. His cheeks were boy-smooth, deep into the lean and cool of preadolescent limbo. "The only way you'll miss practice is if the flight is delayed, in which case Daddy or I will talk with the man—"

"It's a rule," Johnny broke in and took a step back. "No practice, no play. Where are my sneakers?"

"On the landing in the garage." My voice rose to follow him there. "Want something to eat? Brody will be here in forty-five minutes. They'll feed us on the plane, but I can't guarantee you'll like it. Unless you want some of Kikit's food." Silence. He was through the mudroom and into the garage. I used the pause to shout upstairs for my youngest. *"Kikit?"*

"She changed her mind again and is moving the menagerie from her bedroom to the den," my husband announced, tossing the morning *Globe*, minus the business section, which he held, onto the table. "I have never seen so many stuffed things in my life. Does she really *need* all those things?" He sniffed and screwed up his face. "What's that?"

The question was more damning coming from Dennis. In the overall scheme of our marriage, the house was my responsibility.

But I couldn't hunt more now, just didn't have the time. "It may be a rat. The exterminator had to rebait some of the basement traps, which means some of the poison was eaten, which means something may have died before it reached the outside."

Johnny ran through with a pithy, *"Gross."*

His sneakers left a trail of dried dirt, but there wasn't time for remopping, either. "Eggs, Dennis?"

"Maybe. I don't know. Coffee first." He sat down with the paper.

I put on the coffee and, ignoring the heebie-jeebies inside that cried, *Come on, come on, let's get this show on the road*, said gently, "Eggs, yes or no? I have forty minutes to be cleaned up, packed, and gone."

"What about that smell? I can't live with this for eleven days."

"It may go away on its own," I prayed. "If not, give the exterminator a call. His number is on the board."

"But I won't be here to let him in. I'm leaving right after you do to meet the Ferguson group in the Berkshires. That was the whole problem with driving you to the airport." He shot me a disparaging look. "I can't believe you messed up with the service."

"I *didn't*. I don't know what happened, Dennis. I booked the airport run two weeks ago and have the confirmation number to prove it. They say I called and canceled last week. But I didn't. If I hadn't called to check a little while ago, we'd be waiting an hour from now for a ride that isn't coming. Lucky thing Brody can take us. And as for the smell," I tried to keep calm, "have the exterminator come when you get back. I don't know what else to do, Dennis. It's a holiday weekend. Flights are booked solid. I can't just decide to fly later." There was more to be said, more about his being sensitive, what with my mother's illness preying heavily on me, but he was already taking care of the kids so that I could fly on for a week's work after Cleveland. I wasn't ungrateful, just feeling frayed around the edges. It was getting later by the minute.

Just as I took out the egg tray, skipping footsteps came from behind, then the voice of seven-year-old Clara Kate. "Mommy, I'm taking Travis, Michael, and Joy, okay?" She gazed up at me with her cheek at my waist, an angel's face framed by a barretted mass of chestnut curls. My own hair was the same color, though the curl had long since fallen prey to scissors and a blow-dryer.

Hooking an arm around her neck, I held her close while I beat eggs. "I thought we agreed you'd only bring two."

Her cheek moved against my arm. "Well, I said I would, but which one can I leave? I'm the only one who knows what'll make Travis sick if he eats it, and Michael has nightmares if he isn't with me, and Joy'll cry the whole time because they're always together, those three. Besides, I want them to see Auntie Rona, and they'll cheer Grandma up. What's her hospital like?"

"I don't know. I haven't seen it."

She waved a small hand, fingers splayed. "Is it all shiny and noisy, like mine?"

"Only the parts that treat little girls who have allergic reactions to things they're not supposed to eat. Grandma's floor will be shiny and quiet."

"Will she be sleeping?"

"Not all the time."

"Some of the time?"

"Maybe some. Probably not while you're there, though. She'll want to be awake for every minute of that."

"Can she talk?"

"Of course she can."

"Not if she has tubes in her throat. Will she have tubes in her throat?"

"No, sweetie." I opened a pack of shredded cheddar and offered it to her.

She took a fistful. "Will she have tubes in her nose?"

"No. I told you that last night."

"Well, things change sometimes." She put the fist to her mouth and, nibbling cheese, ducked free of my arm. "Daddy, why aren't you coming with us?"

"You know why," he said from behind the paper. "I have to work."

"If you have to work," she asked, climbing up a chair to the table top and sitting on its edge so that her legs swung, "why'd you put your golf clubs in the car?"

I whisked together shredded cheddar and eggs, but softly.

"Because," Dennis said, "I'm playing golf after I work. After," he emphasized.

"We're missing school to see Grandma. I think you should come."

"I went with you in August."

Her legs swish-swished against the paper's edge. "When's she getting out of the hospital?"

"I don't know."

"Is she *ever*?"

"Good God, Kikit," he said with a tight laugh and the abrupt rustle of newsprint set aside, "I can't read when you bump the paper like that. You're getting cheese *all over* the place. Get off the table."

"Are you meeting us at the plane on Tuesday?"

"Yes."

"The airport's really big, so how will you know where to go?"

"I'll know where to go. Off the table," he ordered and flipped the paper back up the instant she complied.

"He'll be there to meet you," I called as she hopped from the room. I poured the egg mixture into a sizzling skillet, pushed the toaster down, and reached for a plate. "The flight information is on the board," I told Dennis, "along with the number you can call to find out if the plane is on time. The Cleveland numbers are there, too, and, after the kids get back, who's taking who where on what day, with phone numbers."

The newspaper went down again, his chair scraped back. He went to the board by the phone, stood a minute, made a grunting sound.

"What?" I asked.

"What else? Same old, same old. We need a nanny."

"We had a nanny. She monopolized the phone, drove like a maniac, and kept offering Kikit peanut butter no matter how many times I told her it was lethal."

"She was French. French nannies are frivolous. We need a Swedish nanny. I know, I know. You say we do better without," he tossed an impatient hand at the board, "but that list of who's taking who where and when is a joke. Even when you're home, things get hairy. Remember last week?"

How could I forget? I had kept Kikit and her friends waiting an hour after ballet, when the store in Essex, where I had been working at the time, lost electricity and the clocks stopped. I had felt awful.

"Why didn't you look at your watch?" he asked for the umpteenth time.

"I was distracted trying to get the computers up again."

"You're overextended," said the die-hard pessimist.

"I'm not," said the die-hard optimist. "I do fine, as long as you help."

"It'd be simpler just to hire someone to drive the kids around."

"They would hate it," I said, scrambling the eggs. "They want us. *I* want us. Besides, we have a sitter for emergencies. Mrs. Gimble."

"She doesn't drive."

"She lives two doors away and loves the kids. Dennis?" I waited for him to look up from the paper. "You'll be at Johnny's game Saturday, won't you?"

"If I can."

Oh, he could. The issue was whether he would. "He'll be heartbroken if you aren't there."

"If something comes up and I can't be there, I can't. I'm running a business, too, Claire."

I couldn't forget that either, not with him reminding me so often. Nor could I point out that, with his business a shadow of its former self, he had time to parent if he chose, because that would put him on the defensive. We had been down that road before. This wasn't the time to travel it again. I simply needed to know that the children would have Dennis's full attention while I was gone.

"How many in the Ferguson group?" I asked.

"It varies."

I turned the eggs again. "What is it they make, exactly?"

"Plastic things."

I turned the eggs once more. "For commercial displays?"

He grunted, yes or no, I didn't know.

The toast popped up. I buttered both slices, cornered them on the plate, slid the eggs in the center, and slipped the plate into the gap between the paper and Dennis. Then I set to scrubbing the skillet.

"The game is at ten Saturday morning. Plan business around it. Please? Johnny needs one of us to see him play. Besides, he loves it when you're there. He was crushed when you missed his touchdown last week. He's convinced he'll never score another one. Even if he doesn't, he needs to know that you want to see him play."

"I said I'd try," Dennis warned, "but if work interferes, I may only make it to the last half. What *is* that smell?" He shoved the paper aside with the most unruly rustle, pushed back his chair, and started banging cabinets open and shut. "Your mind has been everywhere but here lately. You must have put something where it didn't belong."

It was possible. But I didn't expect him to find anything in the cabinets. They had been thoroughly cleaned the week before.

"Here," he said with disgust. "Get rid of this."

A reeking baggy landed in the sink. It contained half of a decaying onion. I had no idea how it had ended up in a cabinet with refolded grocery bags, but when I looked questioningly at Dennis, he was backing away from the stench and returning to his breakfast.

I disposed of the onion, grabbed the air freshener, and gave a spray. "See?" I said on an up note. "You're good at finding things. Much better than me."

He shot me an irritated look before returning to the stock market report.

Brody arrived thirty minutes later. He helped himself to a cup of coffee and talked business with Dennis while I finished packing our bags, made the beds, and slipped into a suit. It had soft gray pants, an ivory vest, and an apricot jacket, and would be perfect for the work following Cleveland. More, my mother would love it. She loved fine things, loved the feel of them against her skin and the sight of them on her daughters, and understandably so. She had known hard times and was pleased they were past.

Once everything was in the car and Dennis had been hugged and kissed and left waving on the front porch of our Cape Cod Georgian, which wasn't on the Cape at all but in a small township just north of Gloucester, we joined the Boston commuters and headed for Logan.

Settling into the seat of Brody's Range Rover, I exhaled.

"Tired?" he asked softly.

I smiled and shook my head, then moved my hand in a way that contradicted the headshake. Yes, I was tired. And worried. I was also, at that moment, relieved to have Dennis behind me. He hated my traveling, saw it as an imposition on our lives, even in spite of my attempts to minimize the inconvenience. Actually, he hadn't been too difficult this time, more grumpy than belligerent. Maybe he was mellowing. Or feeling bad about my mother. Whatever, there hadn't been any major explosions.

Now, with Brody at the wheel, I could relinquish responsibility for the hour it would take us to reach the airport. "You're a peach to do this," I said, turning my head against the headrest. He was as easy on the eye as he was on the mind—light brown hair, wire-rimmed glasses over deeper brown eyes still soft from sleep. He was loose and laid-back, a welcome balm.

"My pleasure," he said. "By the way, I think Dennis is onto something with the Ferguson thing. The company has suffered some bad breaks, but it has solid management and mega-brains. It just needs a little money to work with. If Dennis can arrange that, he may have a winner."

I hoped so. He had had too few of them of late, which made my own success with WickerWise more difficult for him. Not that he worked that hard. Not that he wanted to work that hard. But it wouldn't bother me if he hit a bonanza. My own ego needs were small.

"I should get the St. Louis franchise contracts back today," Brody went on in his quietly competent way. "Once the franchisee is locked in, I can finalize a deal with a builder for the renovation work. I'll have that information faxed to the hotel by the time you get there Wednesday. He'll handle the subs. Do you have the design plans?"

I touched the briefcase by my leg. "Hard to believe this is number twenty-eight."

It had been twelve years since the first WickerWise had opened. That flagship store still operated out of an abandoned fire station in Essex, a short fifteen-minute drive from the house. It had become the model for a chain of stores that stretched from Nantucket to Seattle. We kept a tight rein on our franchises, Brody and I. All were in freestanding buildings—old schoolhouses, abandoned bars, service stations, general stores, even a retired church or two. That was part of the charm. The rest came from the internal design, based on our central plan, and the presentation of the wicker furniture we sold. Brody and I controlled that, too. All ordering went through us. One of us directed the opening of each franchise and revisited twice yearly.

Twenty-eight franchises, another dozen boutiques in upscale department stores, a wicker plant in central Pennsylvania, rooms in numerous charity show houses—it boggled my mind, when I stopped to think about it. So much in so little time, nearly serendipitous. I had potted a tiny plant and it was blooming wildly.

"Know where we're going?" Kikit asked Brody. She had come up from behind to lean around the side of his seat with one little sweatered arm hooked around his large leather sleeve. She should have been sitting back, belted in like Johnny was, but I didn't have the heart to insist when the flight attendants would do it soon enough. Besides, Brody was a good driver, and he loved my kids. If there were an accident, that large leather sleeve would be cinching Kikit to his seat back in no time flat.

"Cleveland, I believe," he answered, ever so patient, though we both knew what was to come.

"You ever been there?"

"You know I have, Clara Kate."

"Well, tell me anyway."

"I went to college in Cleveland," Brody dutifully said. "That's where I met your dad."

"And my mom."

"And your mom. But first your dad. We were fraternity brothers." He paused. It was part of the game.

Kikit prompted, "You raised all kinds of hell."

"We were into all kinds of mischief, was what I was going to say," he corrected, prim enough to win one of Kikit's sweet little laughs. "Then we graduated and went to business school in different places and didn't see each other for a while."

"Six years."

"You know the story better than me."

I closed my eyes, rested my head back, and smiled. She did, indeed. Brody had continued telling it to her long after Dennis had tired of the repetition.

"You and Daddy talked about it a while, then went into business together, but not in Cleveland. Did you know my grandma in Cleveland?"

"Nope. Didn't meet her until I was living out here."

"Is she gonna die?"

My eyes flew open. I looked back at Kikit, about to scold her for suggesting such a thing. Then my gaze slid to Johnny's alert face, and I realized that she was only saying what they were both thinking. She did that a lot—and I loved her for it, even when it demanded answers I wasn't ready to give.

"Not today or tomorrow," Brody answered for me.

"But soon?" Kikit asked.

"Maybe. She's been sick for a while. Her body's getting pretty tired."

"I get tired sometimes."

The final *s* had a faint *th* sound to it, the remnant of a lisp that only appeared at moments of stress. The mention of sickness would do it.

"Not the same," Brody said. "Not the same at all."

"Are you sure?"

"Absolutely, positively. You get tired like we all get tired. With your grandma, it's her age, and the sickness she has."

"Cancer."

"Cancer."

Kikit took a loud breath. I steeled myself for a deepening of the onslaught, only to hear a long-suffering, "Brody, are we going to the circus this year? You promised me we would, but I haven't heard anything about it. My friend Lily's going. So's Alexander Bly. I want to go, too."

"I have tickets."

She lit up. "You *do*? When? Are we sitting in the middle like we did last year? That was where all the elephants did that climbing thing, remember that, Brody? It. Was. So. Cool. Joy," Brody's daughter, as distinguished from Kikit's doll, "is coming, too, isn't she, because it wouldn't be right if we went without her. I want another alligator like Hector, can I get one, Mommy? A *purple* one this time? I don't care what Daddy says, alligators need to be with other alligators. Can I, *please*?"

Connie Grant had always been a small woman, but everything about her seemed to have shrunk even more in the few weeks since I had seen her last. Size, color, energy—all diminished. She was heavily medicated. Her eyes focused only in spurts. The immediate problem, the doctor had explained during one of my calls, wasn't the cancer but her heart. Repair work was out of the question. She was too weak.

She must have called on every last bit of strength she had to be alert for the children, because as soon as Johnny and Kikit took off with my sister, leaving us alone for a spell, she closed her eyes and lay silent.

Heavy-hearted, I sat close by her side. After a few minutes, I began to hum and was rewarded enough by her weak grin to put words to the tune. Connie loved Streisand. Starting with "Evergreen," I sang softly until she was rested enough to open her eyes. I finished the last few bars of "The Way We Were" and smiled.

Her own smile was brief and wan. The look that followed was adult, woman to woman, startlingly acute. It held the truth that I feared, and made me say a fast, "Don't even think it."

"How not to?" she asked in a frail voice. "I'm not able to do much but lie here and think. Ironic. So much idle time." She closed her eyes, sighed. "I was always busy. So busy, with so little to show." Her eyes opened, begging my understanding. "It's frustrating, all I wanted to do in life and didn't."

"You did *tons*," I said, "starting way back when Daddy died. You were the one who kept us afloat. You held two jobs, worked night and day."

"I chased my tail, was what I did. Couldn't seem to get ahead. Like now. I get a handle on the pain, then it hits me again. I'm tired, Claire."

It frightened me to hear despair, made me angry, too, because Connie Grant didn't deserve to be dying at sixty-three. She had fought long and hard for a better life, fought even harder when things wouldn't come easy. "Oh, Mom. There have been positive things. Lots of them."

"You, certainly." She sighed. "Rona, I don't know."

"You did just fine with Rona."

"She's thirty-eight going on twelve."

"Well, then, for a twelve year old, she's a whiz. She's been here for you, Mom. Much more than I have. I wish I lived closer."

"Even if you did, you have a family. You have a business. Rona has nothing."

"She has friends."

"They're as lost as she is. Not a one of them has direction, other than to the beauty shop for a manicure. What would Rona do if she didn't have me to hover over? Two husbands have come and gone, she has no children, no career. I worry about her."

"She's just a little lost. She'll find herself."

"Will you watch out for her, Claire?" Connie pleaded, more pale than ever. "Once I'm gone, Rona will have no one but you."

"I'll do what I can."

"Offer her a franchise."

"I have. She won't take it."

"Offer it again. She'll go through Harold's money in no time. Poor thing, she's nearly as dependent as I was when your father died. Maybe she needs a scare, like I had. Sad, how history repeats itself. You try to save your children from making the same mistakes you did . . ." The ardor that had been holding her up let her down. She sank deeper into the pillows. "At least I succeeded with you. Talk to me. Where is this newest franchise?"

Content to be distracted, I told her about the St. Louis store and about the International Home Furnishings show in North Carolina. She smiled and nodded, though I sensed her floating in and out. Still, WickerWise pleased her. So, while she lay there with her head turned my way, I told her about the flood damage to be assessed at our franchise in New Orleans, the possible expansion of our franchise in Denver, the franchisee to be interviewed, and potential locations to be visited in Atlanta.

"Good," she said at one point, and at another, "The more cities the better—visibility is important," and finally, predictably, "and New York?"

We had a store in East Hampton that was thriving, but East Hampton wasn't Manhattan, as far as Mother was concerned. She wanted a WickerWise on Fifth Avenue.

"Not yet," I said. "Maybe in a few years."

"Now *that* would be success. Don't you think so?"

"I don't know, Mom. Manhattan's tough. The overhead alone would be a killer. Maybe a boutique in a department store—"

"All by itself on Fifth Avenue. No less. Now. Tell me everything the children didn't."

I told her about Johnny singing with the church choir, about Kikit's Brownie troop's flower sale, about their teachers and friends. I talked until she wilted again. She seemed angry this time, resentful of wasting my visit. So I left her to her rest, promising to be back at dinnertime.

Rona was a scant two years my junior. We had grown up sharing a bedroom, clothes, even friends, and we should have been close. That we weren't stemmed from the fact that we also shared Connie. Sharing her wasn't hard for me. Connie and I were so much alike that I always came out on top when comparisons were made. Rona was the different one, the one out of sync, the one who wanted Mom's approval and tried so hard that she bombed every time. Still she came back for more, determined to get it right.

Thinking to rescue us all from poverty, at twenty she had rushed into marriage to the richest, most eligible bachelor she could find. Three years and two mistresses later, Jerry became her ex. Not to be discouraged, particularly since I was on the verge of marriage, she found husband number two. Harold was the richest, *oldest* eligible bachelor she could find, and he didn't cheat on her. He died.

My children loved Rona, and she them. While I visited with Mom, she took them to movies, to toy stores, to the science museum, to restaurants where anyone who was anyone in greater Cleveland took their kids. The need to be moving that came across as restlessness when she was with adults, came across as stamina when she was with children. And why not? She was a child herself when she was with them, albeit the one with the open wallet. There was defiance in what she did with Kikit and Johnny, as though the goal wasn't so much to do one thing or another, but simply to do what I wouldn't. Rona might live to please Connie, but she loved challenging me. I was the Scrooge, the disciplinarian. I was, when all was said and done, the cause of her deepest angst.

I was also the one in charge of answering questions, of which there was a nonstop stream. Rona was suspicious, demanding to know what the doctors had told me, convinced they weren't telling her half as much. Johnny was evasive, asking about the fate of his grandmother's cat when he couldn't ask about that of his grandmother, but Kikit had no such qualms. If it wasn't, "What was in that shot?" it was, "Did you see her hand shaking?" or, "Why is the machine beeping that way?" or, "I heard her *cry* when they were turning her to the side. Why was she *crying*, Mommy?"

The children joined me at the hospital twice each day, short visits designed to be light and cheery, but they were upset by their grandmother's frailty. So Rona, quite happily, took off with them. My arrival was her escape, which she made no effort to hide. Sometimes she said a dry, "Good luck," or a teasing, "We'll be thinking of you." Other times there was only a look of satisfaction that said it was payback time.

And she was right. Not only was she in the hospital all those days when I wasn't, but she saw a different, more judgmental side of Connie. She was the one who bore the brunt of Connie's frustration.

No, I didn't blame her for wanting time off. Given a choice, I'd have been anywhere else, too, because it was painful watching my mother die. No matter how often I visited the hospital, each time I turned into that room and saw her suffering, it hit me like the first time. No matter how long I sat studying her pallor, the next visit I was shocked to find her so pale. No matter how deftly I distracted my mind when I wasn't with her or how tired I was climbing into bed, I lay awake grieving.

The children stayed until Tuesday. Saying good-bye to their grand-mother was only the first of our trials. We arrived at the airport to learn that incoming planes had been delayed by hurricane rains whipping up the East Coast. Departure times were moved back, and back, and back. I called Dennis—at work, at home, once, twice, three times—and left messages when he didn't answer.

Johnny started worrying about missing practice.

Kikit started worrying about Dennis missing their plane.

Their departure time was delayed yet again. I left new mes-sages for Dennis.

Johnny cried that he *really* didn't want to be benched, because the team they were playing that Saturday sucked, so his had *the* best chance of winning.

Kikit cried—repeatedly—that Michael, Travis, and Joy were in her suitcase and scared to death of getting lost, and what *did* happen to luggage during delays?

I wasn't any happier than the children. I didn't like them fly-ing alone to begin with, but when I suggested they wait for better weather the next morning, Johnny got so upset about missing practice that I relented. The airline finally rerouted them through Baltimore, which made Johnny even more nervous, which had him poking at Kikit, who came crying to me, and all I could do was to leave another message for Dennis and put the children on the plane with lingering hugs and the sworn word of the flight attendant that she would hand-deliver them to Dennis at Logan.

I returned to the hospital with one eye on the clock and continued to try Dennis. Mostly, accessing the messages on our answering machine, I heard myself. It wasn't until shortly before their original flight would have landed that I reached him.

"You'll be there?" I asked, giving him the new information.

"Of course I'll be there," he answered.

But he wasn't. The children landed at Logan at six. Dennis didn't arrive until six-forty. He claimed that was the time I had told him.

It wasn't. But arguing was pointless. All I wanted to do was to calm the children as best I could long distance, then fall into bed. I hadn't slept well all week, never did when I was away from home. I was beat.

I put St. Louis off until Thursday to allow an extra day with my mother. One phone call to Brody, and the arrangements were made. Friday, he and I met at the International Home Furnishings show in High Point and put in twelve-hour days from then through Monday, moving from exhibit to exhibit, meeting with sales rep after sales rep. I knew which designs I liked and which would work in our shops. Brody knew which products were well-priced and which would complement our list.

Attuned to my worry about Connie, Brody did Denver and New Orleans for me. I did Atlanta, and, late Tuesday, returned to Cleveland. Rona was thrilled to have the added day off, but I didn't do it for Rona. I didn't even do it as much for Mom as for me. No matter that I was anxious to be home. Connie Grant was the only mother I would ever have. For too long I had lived too far away. Too soon it wouldn't matter.

The children were disappointed, but understanding. They were that way with most all of my traveling, but then, having spent their youngest years toddling around the shop, they felt personally involved in my career. They knew the merchandise, knew the jargon, knew a startling amount about each franchise as it opened. They also knew they could call me wherever I was.

In this instance, having just seen their grandmother, they knew how ill she was. If my being there could make her happier, Kikit vowed, I should stay, even if she *was* missing me to bits herself.

I wished their father had been half as gracious. He made me swear to be home on the Thursday afternoon flight.

That last Wednesday, Mother seemed stronger. She actually talked of coming east for Thanksgiving, and, while the doctors thought it improbable, I clung to the thought. Meeting Grandma at the airport had become standard holiday fare. The kids counted on her coming. So did I.

She insisted I call them so she could talk, and was disappointed when we got the answering machine. I figured that getting the machine was good news. "Dennis must have them out doing something good."

Mother's expression grew wistful. "So easy, with those two. They're wonderful children—articulate, mature—different from each other but so special. You're a better mother than I was."

"No, I'm not. I've been lucky, that's all."

"Luck has little to do with it. People make their luck."

"Maybe some of it. But not all. We *have* been lucky, Dennis, the kids, and me. Aside from Kikit's allergies, we've been healthy. The children have nice friends, they do well in school. Johnny worries me. He pressures himself to do well. But bless him, he does do well."

"Takes after his mother," mine said. "My friends see your stores all the time. They ask about buying stock." Her brows rose in question.

"No, no. No public offering."

"Why not?"

"No need. We're not expanding so fast. I like having control. I like being personally involved with my franchisees. Much bigger, and I'll lose that."

"But think of the money."

I already had plenty of money. Connie knew I thought so, since we'd had this discussion before. In the past she might have argued anyway. This time, looking weak, she let it ride.

"Well, anyway, I am proud of you, Claire."

I knew that. Not once, from my childhood to the present, had her faith in my competence wavered. She trusted me. She believed in me.

I leveled my shoulders. "I'm proud of me, too."

"Is Dennis?"

My shoulders didn't stay quite as level. "Hard to tell. He doesn't say so in as many words."

"How's his own work?"

"I wish I knew, but he doesn't say much about that, either." I hesitated. It seemed wrong to be complaining, what with Connie so sick. But she had always been my sounding board, and, damn it, she wasn't gone yet. "I don't understand it sometimes. You'd think he would want to toss ideas around. I may not have a business degree like he does, but I do have *some* sense of what works and what doesn't. But he keeps everything to himself. Like it's a power play. Like he won't risk my shooting him down. Fat chance of *that*. For years and *years* I've held my tongue when I doubted something he did."

"You should have spoken up."

"He would have hated it when I was right and blamed me when I was wrong, no winning for me, nothing for him but wounded male pride." I smiled. "Anyway, Brody thinks well of the group he met with last week. With any luck, Dennis will convince them he's the man who can gather the backers to keep them afloat."

Connie didn't argue with my reference to luck that time. Nor did she remind me that, while she wished ever more for me, I was already successful enough in my own right not to need a penny of what Dennis earned. We both took the kind of comfort from that that only people who had once been overboard without a life-jacket could feel.

"I do want to see Dennis succeed," she said.

"So do I."

"I'm not ready to die."

"I'm not ready to let you go."

She gave me another one of those woman-to-woman looks then, and, bound to her as I would never be to another living soul, I felt such a surge of love and grief that my eyes filled and my throat went tight. Beyond love and grief was admiration. Connie Grant was mulish. Hard as life had been, she had always pushed on. Often, now, she was so weak she could barely lift an arm, so nauseated she could barely eat, so riddled with pain she could barely think. Still she refused to die.

"You're a stubborn woman," I said when I could speak.

"Well, what choice do I have?" she countered. "The alternative is—what—defeatism? But then you end up worse. You don't put dinner on the table by walking away from the kitchen. Your sister never learned that. She could have made something of herself, if she hadn't been so bent on finding the quickest solution. Want a tan? Stand in a booth. Want money? Marry rich. I thought she would have seen me working hard and learned by example. Not Rona. She wants it bigger and better and faster. Well, sometimes that isn't possible. Sometimes the best you can do is the best you can do."

She sank back, momentarily spent. Her eyes were closed, her breathing shallow. While I watched, fearful at first, then calmer, she rested and regrouped. When she opened her eyes, she was mellow. "Claire, Claire, you're like my own mother Kate. She was resourceful. Determined." Her eyes took on a faraway cast, her mouth a fond quirk. "There was a story. I'd nearly forgotten. Sweet Kate and her pearls."

I had never heard about any pearls. "Grandmother Kate was dirt poor."

"Poor in things, not thoughts. Her pearls were moments—one beautiful one and another and another, strung together on a fine, strong thread. Bits of sand, well, she just brushed them aside and forgot them. Some people, she said, couldn't see the pearls through the sand, or only had the strength of character to push away sand from a few pearls and ended up with chokers. Your grandmother Kate's strand was quite long. Yours will be, too. Rona, well, Rona won't apply herself long enough to one thing to *create* a pearl. Me," she sighed, "I'm still working at it. Seeing the children, seeing you—they're good times, Claire. Better than morphine, you know? You'll come see me again soon, won't you, baby?"

The story of Grandmother Kate's pearls was one of the more philosophical ones my mother had shared. I thought about it through the flight home Thursday, thought of my own pearls— wonderful family moments, so many I couldn't count, moments of pleasure and pride at work—and suddenly the dislocation I had been feeling all week intensified. I couldn't get home fast enough.

My plane landed on time. The driver was there to meet me on time. Incredibly, my impatience grew. I had been away too long and needed to be home, needed to touch the children, needed to talk with Dennis. I needed to do all those hated things like washing dishes, folding laundry, vacuuming carpets, making beds. Home was my anchor. I needed to be moored.

When I arrived at the house, it was five-thirty, just when I had told the children to expect me. I was surprised that they weren't waiting outside—two beautiful little pearls of my own, Johnny hanging off the front porch rail, Kikit playing hopscotch along the gently curved walk. It was warm out and still light. Dennis should have had them picked up and home half an hour before.

Sure enough, his car was parked by the garage at the side of the house. I went to the front door with my luggage, and had to use my key, another surprise. Whoever arrived home first usually unlocked both doors for the children, who were then in and out until dusk.

"Hello?" I called.

I waited for the answering shrieks that usually hailed my arrival from the kitchen straight ahead, or the upstairs, but got none, and the silence was the least of what unsettled me. Aside from my own bags at the very bottom, the stairs leading to the second floor were clean. There were none of the sneakers, backpacks, sweaters, and other miscellaneous items that usually gathered while I was gone.

"Hey, you guys, I'm home."

"I hear," Dennis said, materializing in the doorway of the study on my right. He was holding a bourbon on-the-rocks. It looked to be his first, his eyes were that clear and focused.

Maternal instinct—personal instinct—no matter, I felt a fast unease. "What's wrong?" I asked into the silence, knowing that something was and fearing, fearing—Kikit sick, Johnny injured, Connie gone. "What's wrong?" I repeated, whispering this time.

Dennis put his shoulder to the door frame and studied his drink. When he looked back at me, his expression was odd.

"Is it my mother?"

He shook his head.

"Then the kids."

"They're fine."

"Where are they?"

"At my parents' house."

My in-laws lived just over the New Hampshire line, an easy thirty minutes away. I could understand their helping Dennis with the children while I was gone, though not at the very time I was coming home. Johnny and Kikit were as anxious to see me as I was to see them. "Should I go pick them up?"

"No." His voice was as odd as his expression, colder than usual, firmer than usual. I had a sudden flash to another discussion, one we'd had several months ago. That one had started with spit and fire before reaching the colder than usual, firmer than usual stage in which Dennis had suggested we separate.

"Why not?" I asked now, but cautiously.

He took a drink.

"Dennis?" I didn't like the things I was thinking or feeling. I had argued against a separation that last time, just as I had other times before that, but he looked more self-assured now.

The doorbell rang.

My eyes flew behind me to the door, then back to Dennis. "Who is it?" I asked when he showed no surprise.

He gestured with the glass for me to open the door, which I quickly did. A pleasant-looking, casually dressed, middle-aged man stood there.

"Claire Raphael?"

"Yes."

He handed me an ordinary business envelope. No sooner had I taken it when he turned and started back down the walk.

The envelope had my name on the front. The return address read the Office of the Constable of Essex County.

I closed the door. With an uneasy glance at Dennis, I opened the envelope.

Two

The heading proclaimed the paper a Temporary Order issued by the Probate and Family Court Department of the Commonwealth of Massachusetts, Essex Division. Dennis's name was typed in as the plaintiff, my name as the defendant.

Bewildered, I glanced up at him. He looked totally placid. I read on.

Pending a hearing on the merits or until further order of the court, it is ordered that:

The plaintiff/father is to have the temporary custody of John and Clara Kate Raphael, the minor children of the parties.

The wife is to vacate the marital premises for the weekend beginning forthwith and up until noon on Monday, October 28, at which time all parties are to appear to show cause why the order for temporary custody and vacate should or should not continue.

At said time a hearing will be held to deter-

mine temporary child custody and support pay-
ment in advance of a final divorce settlement.

The form was dated that day, Thursday, October 24, and
signed by E. Warren Selwey, Justice of the Probate and Family
Court.

I stared at the paper for the longest time. All I could think
was that Dennis was playing a sick joke to drive home the fact
that he hated my traveling. But the paper looked real—embossed
letterhead, blanks filled by an honest-to-goodness typewriter
that, I checked, left marks on the back—and Dennis wasn't
laughing.

"What is this?" I asked.

"It should be clear."

"It looks like a court order."

"Smart girl."

"A *court order*?"

"Right in one."

"*Dennis,*" I protested and held out the paper. "What *is* it?"

Dennis was a showman. What he lacked in business sense, he
made up for in good looks and charm and the kind of confident
smiles people gravitated toward. As his wife, I knew there was a
certain unsureness behind the facade.

At least, there usually was. This time the confidence seemed
real. It gave me a chill.

"I've filed for divorce," he said. "The court has given me temporary custody of the kids and ordered you out of this house."

Definitely a joke. "You're kidding."

"No. That paper makes it official."

I shook my head. It made no sense. "Why are the children at
your parents' house? It's a school night."

"My parents live close enough. Having supper with them is a

novelty for the kids, and it gives you time to be served and clear out. I don't want them upset."

"If you don't want them upset," I said with a hard swallow and held up the paper, "what is *this* all about?"

He pushed away from the doorjamb, less patient now. "For Christ's sake, Claire, it's *right there*. I'm suing you for divorce. I repeat. Suing you for divorce. Why won't that register?"

My voice rose. I was getting scared. "Because it isn't the way two rational people who have been married for fifteen good years behave. People like that approach each other and talk."

"I tried. You wouldn't listen. Three times I mentioned divorce. I'll tell you the exact dates if you want. The last time was in August. I said we should separate when the kids got back to school."

He had been upset. A deal he'd been working on had just fallen through. At the same time, compounding his humiliation, the second quarter figures for WickerWise had come through looking better than ever. So he had threatened to move out. He did that when he was upset, or humiliated, or frustrated. It was part of the pattern.

"I didn't think you were serious."

"I was. Very."

"*Dennis.*"

"*Claire,*" he mocked me and settled against the doorjamb, calm again. It was the calm that got to me, I think. It suggested that Dennis truly had the upper hand here. It put a distance between us, made his voice cold. "I want a divorce. Since you haven't been willing to hear me, I had to resort to this."

My thoughts were flying every which way—questions, fears, long-term meanings hitting each other. I struggled to slow them, to separate them, to think sentence by sentence, one step at a time. Even then I was breathless. "Okay. If you're serious about separating, we can talk about a trial something, but what is this about custody of Johnny and Kikit? And an order to *vacate*?"

"I want the house. I want alimony. I want sole custody of the kids."

"What?"

"You aren't a responsible mother."

"What?"

"Good *God*, Claire, do you want me to spell it out?"

"Yes, I want you to spell it out." I was getting angry. Enough was enough. "I'm a perfectly responsible mother. What in the world could you say to a judge to convince him I'm not?"

"Between your mother and your work, you're in a state of personal crisis. The children are suffering."

"Suffering *how*?"

"You're never here, for one thing. For another, when you are here, you're so preoccupied with your work you forget the kids."

"Kikit's ballet class. We've been over that a dozen times. The store lost electricity. The clocks stopped."

"What about the parent-teacher conference you missed?"

It was a minute before I realized what he meant. "The meeting with Mrs. Stanetti? I didn't miss it. We had to reschedule twice, and then we got our signals crossed."

He held up a hand. "She was waiting. You didn't show. And then there's the accident you had last month. The car was totaled. It was a miracle the kids weren't killed."

"Dennis, that accident wasn't my fault. I was hit by a man who was having a heart attack. The police agree. The insurance company agrees."

"The judge doesn't. He agrees with me that if you'd been more alert you could have swerved out of the way and not risked your kids' lives, speaking of which, Kikit had a whopper of an allergy attack while you were gone."

My insides lurched. "When? To what?"

"Tuesday night. To the frozen casserole you left. What did you put in it, Claire? If anyone is supposed to know what Kikit can and cannot eat, it's you—and that's not the worst of it. There was no Epi-pen. You must have left it in Cleveland."

"I didn't. I packed it. It was right in her bag."

"No, it wasn't. I looked. There was nothing there and nothing here. I had to rush her to the hospital. She was wheezing and swelling up the whole way. By the time we got there she was nearly blue."

I pressed my chest. More than anything else, this took my breath. Medicine or no medicine, any attack Kikit had was serious. "There was antihistamine and a spare Epi-pen. I always keep extras."

He shook his head. "We looked everywhere."

"It's in the basement refrigerator. I've told you that. Is she all right?"

"They stabilized her, but it took a while. She was crying for you, only you weren't there."

I felt a swift fury. "I was only as far away as the phone. Why wasn't I called?"

"I tried to call. You had the cell phone turned off, and your sister's line was busy."

"Then later. Or the next day. I used my phone. It was on. And Rona's line couldn't have been busy that whole time. The operator would have cut in if you'd said it was an emergency—or you could have called Connie's hospital room—or the nurses' station. I left all those numbers on the board. You could have reached me if you'd wanted to. I'd have flown home right away."

"Would you have? You've been gone thirty-four days of the last ninety. You love being on the road. Face it, you do."

"I *don't. Especially* not when one of the kids is sick. You actually counted how many days I've been gone? How many of those were spent visiting my mother?" I would have counted myself, if I hadn't been so upset. Poor Kikit. I knew how her attacks went. There would have been several hours of panic, followed by a swift physical recovery. The emotional one wouldn't be nearly so swift. Until we identified what had triggered the attack, she would be afraid to eat.

And I hadn't been there. She must have thought I had deserted her.

Furious at Dennis for keeping me in the dark, I ran into the kitchen and lifted the phone to call her at my in-laws. Dennis pressed the disconnect button before the call could go through.

"Don't." I tried to remove his hand. "I need to talk to Kikit."

"You need," he said with deadly slowness and fingers like lead, "to take your things and leave. That's a court order, Claire. If you resist it, I'll call the cops."

"You wouldn't."

"I would," he said, and what I saw in his face as I stood there, so close, made me believe him. He was my husband. He knew me more intimately than any other man. But his face held no warmth, no fondness, nothing to suggest I was special to him in any way. I could have been a stranger to whom he had taken an instant dislike, or someone who had offended him and against whom he was taking revenge.

Just then, he was a stranger to me, too. "You're scaring me, Dennis."

"Just leave."

"This is my home. Where am I supposed to go?"

"You'll figure something out," he said with an odd expectancy.

I waited for him to go on. When he didn't, I asked, "Like what?" It was like he knew something I didn't, like he really wanted to tell me what it was.

He raised an arm to the wall over the phone and gave me a slanted smile. "Kikit told me about your run-in with the window washer."

"Run-in?"

"When you came prancing in here in your prettiest Victoria's Secret bra and panties while he was doing that huge picture window over there."

I didn't know what that had to do with anything, still I said, "I turned around and ran back out the minute I saw him. I was mortified."

"You looked good and you knew it."

"You think I did it *on purpose*? Dennis, please. That boy is twenty years old."

"Young flesh. Hot flesh."

"He's the big brother of Johnny's best friend, which is why I hired him in the first place. He needed the money."

"And got a nice little thrill for a tip. Kikit thought it was funny as anything. Me, I think it's a lousy example to be setting for an impressionable little girl." He slid his arm down the wall. "I don't think it's funny about you and Brody, either."

I drew a blank. "Me and Brody what?"

"Screwing."

Screwing? Me and *Brody*?

It was a long minute before I could speak, and then it was in a level tone. I couldn't take the charge seriously, it was so absurd. "This is madness, Dennis. What's wrong with you?"

"The two of you, eating at my craw for months and months. Did you think I wouldn't notice? You touch him all the time."

"Touch him?"

"A hand here, an arm there. And even aside from touching, there's the way you look at each other, the way you talk to each other. Hell, you all but finish each other's sentences. You spend more time with him than you do with me or the kids any day."

"I doubt that's true, but if you're into counting hours there, too, consider that Brody is my CEO."

"A convenient arrangement. Like the office at his house."

"The office is at his house," I argued, "because you didn't want the office *here*. I wanted it in the attic, could have had a *perfect* office in the attic, but you said no, you didn't want phones ringing and people coming and going."

"I told you to rent space."

"That was five years ago. The business was smaller. Renting seemed extravagant. I'd have stayed here in the den if I could have, only I needed more space. So we put the office in Brody's garage. Not his house. His garage."

"You're in his house all the time. I've seen you. You use the kitchen. You use the bathroom. I'll bet you know his bedroom soup to nuts."

I nearly screamed, he made the picture so dark and dirty. "You're dead wrong. There is nothing going on between me and Brody that doesn't go on all the time with people who work together."

"And travel together. To wit, this week. Four nights in High Point."

"Working."

"Uh-huh. I have telephone records from other trips. For every call to us, there were three to him."

"He's my CEO," I repeated. "My *business* partner."

"So why weren't those calls made during business hours?"

"Because I was busy with *other* people during business hours. Calling home had to come before or after."

"Brody's calls sure were after. Nine-forty-five at night. Ten-thirty. Eleven-fifteen."

"That's right. By the time I was done talking with you and the kids, by the time I had something to eat and turned on my laptop and evaluated what I'd done that day and listed what my second in command needed to know and what I needed to ask him, and taking time differences into account, it was that late." I knew I sounded defensive, but Dennis's charges were so unfair that I couldn't let them stand.

"Nice that Brody didn't mind."

"He's a night owl like me."

"And how do you know that?"

"The same way *you* do. Because Brody is our closest friend!" I pushed a hand through my hair, like that would straighten everything out. My mind was jumbled up, not the least of it from the realization that Dennis had to have been planning all this, gathering arguments for a long time. Telephone records? *Brody and me?* "Brody was your college roommate. You've known him almost twenty-five years. He was your business partner long before he was mine. He was your *best man*. He's our kids' godfather, their favorite uncle, and, yes, okay, he's my best friend. If you're jealous of all that, I'm sorry—"

"Jealous? He can have you! Sex between you and me was mediocre at best!"

I felt I'd been hit in the stomach, actually bent at the middle. "You *never* complained about sex with me. You couldn't get enough."

"Damn right. It was like pulling teeth. Either you were exhausted, or up late working, or listening for one of the kids to be sick—"

"Hold it! I *rarely* put you off, and you *never* had sex without coming, so what is your complaint? Don't throw stereotypes at me, Dennis. No matter how busy I was, I made time. We had sex plenty."

"Quantity. Not quality."

I prayed to the ceiling. "Good *God*, what's going *on* here?"

"This," Dennis said, slapping the paper that hung from my hand. When I took a step back, he swung in front of the phone. I was too stunned to react when he put the receiver to his ear and punched in a call, then befuddled when he gave our address and said, "Get someone here fast." It wasn't until he hung up the phone that I realized what he'd done.

My husband, who had given me a hug and waved me off barely two weeks ago without a hint of his plans, had just called the police.

"Dennis." I fought panic. "My God, Dennis. You're burning bridges, here."

"Leave."

"What are you doing to our lives?"

"You've done it, not me."

"I need the children, they need me."

"They have me, now."

"Now? *Now?* All of a sudden? Where have you been for the last nine years? I *want* my children."

"Tell it to the judge on Monday. In the meantime, I want you out."

"But I'm your *wife.*"

"According to the court, we're formally separated."

I was having trouble breathing, felt more battered with each thing he said. And the way he said it. So uncaring? So blunt? So fixed? I didn't understand this Dennis. But I did understand that I was about to lose what meant more to me than anything in the world. So I pleaded, "There has to be a better way. For the children's sake. A gentler way. They knew I was coming home today. How will you explain my absence? How will *I* explain it? And when? I need to see them, Dennis. It can't wait until Monday."

"That court order—"

"I don't *care* about that court order, I care about *my kids*!" I was starting to cry, but I didn't care about that either, not even when the doorbell rang. I was on his heels all the way to the front. "They're terrific kids. They're well-adjusted and secure. They're *happy.* What you're doing—the way you're doing it—is going to screw them up, it can't *help* but screw them up. You're going to *ruin* them, Dennis!"

"She won't leave," Dennis told the police officer. It was Jack

Mulroy. We knew him and he knew us, ours was that small a town.

"I'm their mother," I told Jack through sniffles and swipes at tears that kept coming. "I love my children. They love me. Some judge I've never met can't just—just order me out of my own home, away from my own kids!"

Jack opened a hand for the court order that was crushed in my fist. I uncurled my fingers and gave it to him. He would understand, I reasoned. He had helped me once when Kikit had had a bad attack. He had helped me another time when Dennis had been away and our burglar alarm had sounded in the dead of night. He knew I was a decent person. He knew that I loved my children and wouldn't ever, *ever* do anything to hurt them. He knew that I didn't deserve to be booted out of my own home. He was a law enforcement officer. He believed in justice.

"I'm afraid you do have to leave," he said. "This is official. I can't nullify a court order."

"But it's wrong. I haven't done anything wrong."

"You'll have to say that in court on Monday."

"I can't wait until Monday. Don't you see? If I do, the damage will be done, the kids will be hurt." I looked at Dennis. "There has to be a better way."

He folded his arms on his chest.

"Dennis," I begged.

"Please, Mrs. Raphael," said Officer Mulroy. "Don't make this harder than it has to be. Are these your bags? Here, I'll carry them to your car."

I was half hysterical. "My car was totaled. I haven't bought a new one yet."

"There's a rental in the garage," Dennis told Jack. "The keys are there."

Jack took my arm. I took it back. "I returned the rental car before I left," I told Dennis.

"I rented another for you yesterday."

Jack touched my arm again. "I don't want to have to call for support," he said so quietly that I knew he was embarrassed, but the reality of the situation hit me then, good and well.

If I didn't leave, I would be removed.

If I had to be removed, Dennis would tell the judge.

If that happened, the judge might believe I was out of control, and if he believed that, I might lose my kids.

Arms, legs, insides—everything seemed to be shaking. I pulled a tissue from my pocket and pressed it to my nose, took a deep breath that was part sob, and thought of what my mother had said, incredibly, not twenty-four hours before. *Well, what choice do I have?* she had asked about having to deal with her body's betrayal.

My body wasn't betraying me. My husband was. *Well, what choice do I have?* I could panic. I could scream and yell and rail against a system that was making me do something I didn't want to do. Or I could seek a remedy.

Ignoring Dennis, I said to Jack in a small voice, "I'm not sure what to do. I've never been in this situation before."

"You need to leave here. That's the first thing. Car's in the garage?"

I nodded, pressing my lips together to keep them from trembling. I didn't want to cry anymore. Not in front of Dennis. Not in front of Jack.

I knelt to slip the strap of my carry-on to my shoulder. Jack took the larger bag. "Is this everything you'll need?" he asked.

Having lived out of these two bags for the past thirteen days, I could manage for another three. Besides, I couldn't have picked out and packed other clothes if my life had depended on it.

I didn't look at Dennis, didn't speak to Dennis, didn't trust myself not to cry or beg or snarl. Concentrating solely on reaching the car without falling apart, I led Jack through the kitchen and the mudroom to the garage.

The rental car was the burgundy color that I liked and Dennis hated. I found that ironic, along with the fact that he had rented another car rather than putting me in a cab. I had been planning to get a rental myself tomorrow, and buy something within the week.

Jack stowed the bags in the trunk. I slid behind the wheel and fumbled around for things like the ignition switch, the head-lights, the gear shift. Somehow I managed to back out. I pulled around until I was beside the police cruiser, rolled my window down, and waited for Jack to reach me.

When he did, he said, "You need to see a lawyer as soon as possible." His voice held greater sympathy now that we were out of the house. I wanted to believe he was on my side after all. "You have to put together a case by Monday to convince the judge you should be the one in the house with the children. Do you know of a good lawyer?"

A lawyer. I hadn't thought that far. A *divorce* lawyer. The thought shook me. A *family law specialist*. I wanted to cry.

The only lawyer I had experience with was the one who did the WickerWise contracts, but he didn't do this kind of work. I supposed he could recommend someone who did. But then I'd have to tell him why I needed it, and I didn't want to do that.

I did know of someone else, though. He was one of Boston's more prominent divorce lawyers. I had taken notice of him not because I knew anyone who had used him, but because he was the brother-in-law of my Philadelphia franchisee. Given the connec-tion, I was sure he would see me quickly.

First, though, I wanted to see my kids.

Jack nixed the idea. "I wouldn't. You're upset. They'll pick up on it. Besides, what'll you tell them?"

I opened my mouth, then shut it. I didn't know what I would say. It seemed important, for the children's sake, that Dennis and his parents and I coordinate our stories, but I had no idea what they had already said.

"It might be easier if I call them on the phone." I could fudge it, could say I was delayed in Cleveland or something. "Am I allowed to do that?"

"The court order doesn't forbid it, but if your husband doesn't want it, you may have trouble getting through. Things like phone calls and visitation rights will be spelled out next Monday."

Visitation rights? *Unreal.*

"Kikit has a birthday party on Saturday. I have to take her to buy a present. And what about Johnny's game? Am I allowed to go?"

"Talk that over with your lawyer. You're allowed. But maybe you ought to speak with Dennis first. Who's representing him?"

"I have no idea."

"Your lawyer can find that out pretty quick."

Panic was creeping in again. "I'm a responsible mother. I haven't put my kids at risk any more than any mother who lets them out of the house to play. This is crazy. So is talk of a divorce. Dennis didn't say *one word* when I left here a week ago last Friday. We were on perfectly good terms. We talked on the phone while I was away." I looked at the house, *my* house, the one from which I'd been banned. "This is mind boggling."

"See a lawyer. You have until Monday to appear in court. There's your chance to change things."

I headed north, toward New Hampshire and the children. It wasn't a conscious decision, just where my heart directed the car. My mind was preoccupied replaying what had happened at the house. It wasn't until I reached the highway that I came to the part where Jack Mulroy asked what I would say to the kids.

I pulled to the side of the road and ran through the possible scenarios. Each one ended with either the children crying or me crying or me yelling at their grandparents or their grandparents calling the police. The last seemed unlikely. I had always had an amicable relationship with my in-laws. But I thought I had with Dennis, too, and look what he had done. My faith was shaken. I couldn't be sure that the people I trusted would behave rationally.

But the kids were my first priority. What mattered most was that they wouldn't be traumatized before Dennis and I could work things out. I needed advice on that. Yes, I needed a lawyer.

I pulled the cellular phone from my purse, called information for the number of Lloyd Usher's law office, and dialed it. The office was closed for the day, of course. It was six-thirty. But I knew the kinds of hours I kept, knew the kinds of hours most successful people kept, and figured he was still there.

I rifled my Filofax and called my Philadelphia franchisee at home. Working to sound normal, I told her that I had an urgent question and needed to reach her brother-in-law. She gave me his private number. I dialed it.

Lloyd Usher answered with a grunt that said he was busy. Hurriedly, I gave him my name, that of his sister-in-law, and the bare bones of my situation. I should have known he wasn't the man for me when he offered to see me the following afternoon at two, but his was the only name I had, and I was desperate.

So I pleaded. I said it was an emergency, that I had concerns about my children that couldn't wait until the next day. He complained that *everyone* had concerns that couldn't wait, and that he had to leave the office by seven-thirty. I promised to be there before then and take only a few minutes. That was all I needed, really, a few minutes to ask a few questions. That would be a start. It would counter the awful helplessness I felt and give me a semblance of control.

I drove as fast as the rush-hour traffic would allow. After

having trouble finding parking, I didn't reach his office until seven-fifteen. He was glaring at his watch—it was a large gold thing—when he charged into the reception area to fetch me.

"I'll be quick," I assured him. I tried to sound calm and efficient, understanding of the time squeeze, and appreciative. I wanted him to think me mature and rational.

He hurried me down a corridor of offices. An interior designer by training, I would normally have noticed what I passed, but my mind was too clogged to conclude anything but that the decor was lavish and the clientele moneyed. Lloyd Usher and his office suggested more of the same. Imported carpet, rich woods, double-breasted suit, styled hair.

After gesturing me into a leather chair, he went behind the desk. He took off that large gold watch, held it in one palm for clear viewing, opened the other my way. "Let me see the court order."

I took it from my pocket and passed it over.

He read it and passed it back. "This is a drastic move. What brought it on?"

"I have no idea. I walked into the house after eleven days away. My husband was waiting for me. I hadn't been there ten minutes when the man arrived and handed me this."

"He served you," Lloyd Usher corrected. "But you didn't answer my question. An Order to Vacate is serious business. You must have done something to warrant it."

"I did nothing."

"Mrs. Raphael," he chided.

I was taken aback. This man was supposed to be my advocate. I didn't understand his accusing tone, or his disdain, or his watch, at the ready, keeping time.

But he was successful. He was in demand, the divorce lawyer's divorce lawyer. He had to know what he was doing. And I needed help.

So, calmly, I said, "My husband had a list of things. None was significant alone. As a group, they made me sound negligent."

"Are you?"

"No. I love my children."

"Many an abuser loves his children."

Either he was testing my mettle or playing devil's advocate for the sake of learning more about me. But staying calm was harder this time. "I am not an abuser. Not physically. Not verbally. My children and I have a good, strong, healthy relationship."

"How can that be, what with your business?"

"Excuse me?"

"Juggling everything. I've heard my sister-in-law talk about you. She thinks you're a role model for everything women can be. Me, I think she's naive in her awe. I remember when my kids were younger. Thank God my wife didn't work. I can't imagine she could have done half of what she did for the kids if she had. So how do you do it? You can't be *there* for them and *there* for your business, and what about your husband, what about his needs?"

I drew myself straighter in the chair. "What about them?"

"Who's meeting them, if you're working double-time mothering the kids and running the business?"

I had pleaded for a last-minute appointment and driven like a madwoman to get here on time, yes, for answers, but also to put a lid on my panic. Only Lloyd Usher wasn't making me feel better. He wasn't giving me any sense of relief, any sense of having an ally. He certainly wasn't making me like him. I couldn't imagine telling him the details of my life.

I took a slower breath, puzzled now. "Is this the way you approach all your cases? Or is it just me?"

There was an arrogant quirk at the edge of his mouth. "Most of the women I represent have been seriously wronged—cheated on, lied to, manipulated. Most of them have been held down—no life outside the marriage, no career. Many of them face a severe loss in lifestyle if I don't negotiate a good settlement. You aren't like those women. You have everything."

"Not everything," I said quietly. "I don't have my kids. I don't have my home. I don't have the husband I thought I did two hours ago. So maybe there were problems with my marriage that I didn't pay attention to when I should have, but this court order is a travesty. I've done for my husband and I've done for my kids, and in the time that was left, I built a business. I make good use of my time. Is there anything wrong with that? I don't see how anyone can remove me from my own home and my own children this way."

"The court can and did. It has every right. You say you've done it all. Your husband says you haven't, and the court agreed."

"It sounds like you do, too."

"Let's just say that I'm wary of professional women."

"Guilty until proven innocent?" I asked and saw him check his watch. "Look, Mr. Usher. The reason I had to see you tonight is that I'm worried about my children. I don't know what they've been told, and I don't know how I'm supposed to find out, whether I'm supposed to call Dennis or call Dennis's lawyer, and I don't even know who that is. I understand that I have to work with a lawyer of my own to put together a counter-argument to Dennis's, and I understand that that takes time. I also understand that you're busy, and that you can't just put aside everything else you're working on to work on my case, but that brings me back to the beginning. I'm worried about my children. I'm worried about doing anything to make things worse—both for them and my case. How much freedom does this court order give me?"

He was strapping the large gold watch back on his wrist. "Not a hell of a lot. I'd make myself scarce from the family home until Monday."

That wasn't the answer I wanted. "What about seeing the kids at my in-laws' house? Or at my son's football game?"

He rose and began putting files into his briefcase. "Will that be in their best interest? Or will it be more upsetting for them?"

"I don't know."

"Well, if you don't, who will? You're their mother. If anyone knows them, you do. I certainly don't. I can only talk legal strategy. A court order is a court order. If I were you, I would heed it until you talk with the judge. Monday at noon?" He flipped pages on his daily calendar. "I have a hearing in Barnstable at eleven. I won't be back until two or three. We can get it continued for a couple of days. Or one of my associates can stand in for me. In any case, given my impression of your business and the fact that your husband seems to want to make things difficult, I'll need a retainer of ten thousand dollars."

"Ten thousand dollars." For *what*? Getting a continuance that would keep me away from my children even longer? Letting an associate handle my case? Barraging me with accusations at a time when I already felt skinned?

"Well, I'm not running a charity here," he growled in a playful way that I found distinctly condescending. "Come on. You know how things work. You're a successful businesswoman, calm, cool as a cuke—"

"Cool as a cuke, well, what choice do I have?" I cried in anger. "It's either be calm and cool, or lose it and panic."

"I dare say you aren't one to panic. Calm, cool, and ballsy. Your husband must have had his hands full with you."

I stood. "Thanks for your time, Mr. Usher, but this isn't a good match."

"I'm only saying what any judge will be thinking. Times have changed, Mrs. Raphael. Women like you aren't helpless. They aren't vulnerable. They don't inspire sympathy. Women like you are often the ones who've broken the marriage contract. So I'm saying you may face an uphill battle. If you are the major bread-winner, if your husband has more time to give to the kids, if you travel a lot—well, it may be better to let your husband keep the kids. Think about it and give me a call when you're ready to talk."

I wasn't wasting the energy. Gathering what little was left of my dignity, I put it together with my fear and my pride, and walked out the door.

Panic hit ten minutes later. I was sitting in another traffic jam, going nowhere fast. The court order lay crumpled on the passenger seat, beside the parking ticket that had been put under my wiper while I was in Lloyd Usher's office at an hour that didn't require meter money. I didn't understand either one, didn't have a lawyer to explain either one. I didn't have my kids, didn't have my home, didn't have a place to spend the night, or a clue about how to restore sanity to my life.

I was suddenly sweating, shaking, not knowing where to turn or what to do.

The car behind me honked. I let up on the brake and rolled forward. "Okay," I whispered. "Okay. Okay."

So I wasn't perfect. I had kept the kids waiting, had missed a parent conference. I had been in an accident with the kids in the car. I may even have messed up with the plane times, or forgotten to tell Dennis where I kept Kikit's spare medicine. But I tried my best.

Was I being punished for earning more than Dennis? Well, damn it, he had once had everything going for him—great business, impressive client list, name recognition—and he blew it. Was I supposed to sabotage my own career, just because he had screwed up?

The car behind me honked again. I released the brake and rolled ahead.

As soon as we were at another stand-still, I snatched up the phone, dialed home, heard my own message. That meant Dennis hadn't brought the kids home yet, because Kikit loved answering the phone. She would reach it before anyone else could and talk as long as possible with whoever would listen. Unwanted solicitors usually gave up before she did. I had often threatened to market her.

Was that crude? Abusive? Dennis knew I was kidding. Kikit knew I was kidding. She loved it, actually, said she could have her own business, just like mine—not that mine was helping me now. Just the opposite. My husband was using it against me.

I started to shake again. This time, when it seemed that the line of cars hadn't moved in an age, I was the one to honk. Nothing happened. But I felt better.

I snatched up the phone again and started to punch out the number of the Cleveland Clinic, but canceled the call before it went through. I couldn't tell my mother about this, not with her heart so weak.

Had Rona and I been close, I might have called her. As things stood, I couldn't risk her delight.

I dialed home again, but hung up after one ring. I couldn't talk to the kids, either. Not until I knew what to say.

What to do, what to do. I had always approached life as a challenge to be faced, but this was a biggie. It had the power to affect my entire future and that of my children.

"Help," I cried, but softly because suddenly, in a darkness riddled with dashboard green, taillight red, and neon on either side, I knew where I wanted to go. There was only one place where I could be sure of a haven, only one person I knew I could trust.

Three

I remembered when Brody bought his house. He had been living in the east for four years, the last three as Dennis's partner. The novelty of being divorced had worn off, along with the excitement of being a swinging single. He was tired of his high-rise condo, tired of first dates, hungry glances aimed his way, inane chatter. He wanted privacy. He wanted air. He wanted a cozy place for the times when his daughter, Joy, who was six then, came to visit.

The house was a neat three-bedroom Cape built of cedar shakes that had weathered to gray. It sat on the shore, a gentle fifty-foot climb over sand and rocks from the water's edge at high tide. He had taken me to see it before putting in his bid. I didn't even have to go inside. One look from the pebbled drive, one sniff of the ocean air, one crash and swoosh of water and foam, and I felt the peace he craved.

Remarkable, given how upset I was now, but, turning in off the main road, I caught a glimpse of that peace. It was a conditioned response triggered by the first crunch of pebbles under my tires. I'd had only positive experiences here, first visiting Brody, later coming daily to work. I loved what I did and the people I did it with. This place represented comfort, challenge, and success.

The office was closed now. The windows and skylights—I was of the never-too-much-light school of thought and had insisted on putting in as many as the physical structure would allow—reflected the moon in silver blocks. The only other outside light came from antique sconces flanking the door.

Brody was home, though. My headlights picked out the Range Rover in the carport. The lights pouring from the house spoke for themselves.

A little something eased up in my chest and unclenched in my stomach. Stepping from the car into the moist ocean air, I felt more grounded than I had seconds before.

He didn't answer the bell. I rang a second time. I didn't recall his having plans, but he might easily have gone out with a friend and left the Range Rover here. He wasn't expecting me. We hadn't planned on meeting until morning. We had both assumed I would be busy with the children and Dennis until then.

The thought of that brought pain, the rushing return of reality, disbelief. Quickly, before I started to cry right there on Brody's side steps, I singled out his house key from the others on my ring and let myself into the kitchen. The warmth hit me first, welcome against the cooling night air. Then I caught the smell of a stew simmering on the stove. That was good news indeed. If Brody had left something cooking, with the lights on and the Range Rover in the carport, he was out running.

He ran six miles, five times a week. At eight minutes a mile, give or take, depending on the condition of the knee he had shattered years before in a cycling accident, his run would take some forty-eight minutes.

Praying he was nearly done, I went to the eating alcove and slipped into a chair. It was rattan and matched the pedestal base of the round, glass-topped table. The set was the only concession

Brody had allowed me in this room, his preference being a scarred trestle table with benches on either side. He wanted hominess, warmth without frills, a kitchen where a man wasn't embarrassed to work. So I had cushioned the rattan in a warm brown and gray plaid that went with the dark wood of the cabinets and the black of the iron pots hanging in a bunch over the stovetop island. He had found the accessories himself—Brody was big on nostalgia. The duck decoy was from his grandfather's cabin in the woods, the earthen bowl was one over which he had cracked walnuts as a child, the rooster weathervane was from the barn where he had worked mucking out stalls. I wasn't wild about the sculpture that stood on a low stool under the phone. It was made of two plain stones, the smaller on top, and had carvings that resembled a face if you squinted a little. I saw a Neanderthal who gave me the willies. Brody saw a simpleton who reminded him that even when he was feeling low, he had a lot more than most.

Brody was compassionate. He was humble. He was a man of his own mind, and I loved him for it.

Yes, loved him. Of *course*, I loved Brody. Had we ever had sex? Absolutely not. I had been faithful to Dennis to a fault and was hurt that he would think otherwise.

Leaving the chair, I went to the stovetop and gave the stew a hard stir. Bits and pieces of things came and went in the eddy—chicken, carrots, onions, green peppers, mushrooms, all in a red sauce that smelled decidedly of burgundy and was sure to taste good. Brody could take a pot, throw in most anything he found lying around the kitchen, and make it work. Many a meal he had made for himself became leftovers for lunch for the two of us and—yes, Dennis—for whoever else was around.

Dinners I always ate with the children. Dennis joined us when he wasn't off doing his own thing. Brody joined us every week or two. I had been looking forward to eating with the children tonight. Now I didn't even know when I would see them again.

I refused to panic. Still, my stomach started to churn.

But fate was with me. Just when my emotions were threatening a revolt, I heard Brody thumping up the wood steps. He opened the door and entered the kitchen, a tall, slightly winded, very sweaty athlete wearing running shorts, a T-shirt, and a broad smile. "Hey—*terrific*—I didn't expect you tonight," he said in short breaths, but the last word was barely out when the smile faded.

I didn't have to wonder why. Hair, makeup, clothing—I hadn't done a thing with any of them since Cleveland, and that was worlds and worlds away. I was scared. I was worried. I hadn't eaten since breakfast. I hadn't had a good night's sleep in two weeks. I must have looked like death warmed over.

But I felt relieved, suddenly, acutely relieved that Brody was home. Pulling the crumpled court order from my pocket, I gave it to him, then stood close while he read. His face was flushed. His breathing remained rapid. Sweat dripped down his cheek, down his chest, I was sure, down his spine to the small of his back, all those places where his T-shirt was darker. I felt his warmth, even smelled him, but it was a healthy smell, that of heated male. In a day of incredible turns, that smell was reassuringly honest.

Dennis, who worked at looking good, had cause to be wary of Brody. Brody wore glasses, wire-rims which he had taken from the counter and put on as soon as I handed him the court order. He had straight hair that was a mild pecan shade and receding at the part, had scars all over one knee and a pinkie that was permanently crooked. Twice a year he went into Boston's finest men's specialty store, bought a suit or two, a casual outfit or two, but he didn't agonize. On his time off, he wore old jeans and older plaid shirts. He was one of the least vain, most gorgeous men I knew.

But I hadn't slept with him. So help me, God, I hadn't. Nor had I ever, *ever* lorded Brody's looks over Dennis. Did I touch Brody more than I touched Dennis? If so, it wasn't intentional.

Brody's face was blank at first. He was mopping sweat from

his forehead with his sleeve when a frown appeared. He left the arm suspended, shot me a puzzled look, read on. Then he held the paper up and, less winded now, said in the deep voice that was his alone, "This is a joke, isn't it?"

I had thought it at first, too. So we were alike, Brody and I, but that wasn't a crime. It was common sense. We both knew I was responsible. We both knew I loved my kids. We both knew I had been an attentive wife.

"He wants a divorce," I said, calmer now that I wasn't alone. "He wants the house, he wants alimony, he wants the kids."

Brody looked so stunned that I nearly hugged him. His disbelief validated mine.

"Since when?" he charged.

"God knows, but he's been planning it for a while. The kids are with Howard and Elizabeth."

He stared blankly at the court order. "What judge in his right mind would issue this?"

"One who has been read a list of my sins."

"*What* sins?"

I told him the ones to do with the children. "Dennis says I'm in a state of personal crisis that is interfering with my parenting, but you haven't heard the best. He says you and I are having an affair."

Brody jerked his head back. I couldn't tell if his cheeks grew redder, what with the color already there, but I could have sworn there was something, maybe in his eyes, an intimate twinge. I felt it, myself. Embarrassed, almost.

He didn't say anything at first. Then he swallowed. "Dennis said that?"

I nodded.

Again he pushed his sleeve across his forehead.

"I need help, Brody. He's making arguments based on circumstance and supposition, and the bottom line is that I've been barred from my home and ordered away from my own kids, *from my own kids*. When I tried to reason with him, he called the cops, and one actually came. Right to the house. Because of *me*," I thumped my chest, "like I have a history of violence. He said I had to leave. He actually walked me out."

Brody reread the court order. "What is Dennis thinking? I thought court orders were a last resort. He hasn't ever talked divorce."

"Separation, he has. He does it when he's feeling low. I always argued against it. Our marriage may not be made in heaven, but it's better than most." Or was I kidding myself. "Isn't it?"

Brody didn't answer. Bending over the sink, he drank straight from the faucet, then straightened, wiping his mouth with the back of his hand. His eyes were dark. "So he says we're having an affair. That's priceless," he muttered. "What kind of fuckin' evidence does he have?"

"Stupid stuff. Working together, traveling together."

"He's crazy. *Damn* it." He looked stricken. "I know about the pain of divorce. I never wanted it for you. Never wanted it for Johnny and Kikit." He swore softly.

"I want my kids back, Brody."

"You need a lawyer."

"Well, that's the next problem. I just came from seeing Lloyd Usher. Talk about mistakes. He made me feel like I'm getting what I deserve. Am I? How did I do wrong by trying to do everything right?"

Brody started to put an arm around me but stopped and looked down at himself in disgust.

So I did it myself, slipped my arm around his waist. I didn't care if he was sweaty. I wanted the comfort. And it was innocent. *Despite* what Dennis would have made of it.

Pulling me closer, Brody said a vehement, "You didn't do anything wrong. You've worn three hats at the same time and worn them well. You deserve a medal. Dennis knows that. What in the hell's got into him?"

"I don't know."

"Did you give Usher a retainer?"

"No."

"Good. He isn't a nice guy, Claire. The greatest thing he has going for him is name recognition. His clientele is mostly women. Helpless women. They go to him because they think he's tough and they need someone tough. They don't object when he demands a huge retainer because they think that'll guarantee his attentiveness. Then they go home and assume he's working on their cases, only he isn't. He's taking them for a ride. They find that out when things don't happen. When they complain, he acts insulted and pawns them off on associates. By then, they've invested too much time and money and are feeling too vulnerable to start over again with someone new."

I could identify with those women, with the helplessness, the vulnerability. I wanted someone tough, too, and had gone for reputation, with little knowledge of substance—not that I would have conducted my business like that in a million years. But the circumstances were extenuating.

"His was the only name I had. I need someone fast. I have to be in court on Monday to answer this charge."

"You don't want to work with Lloyd Usher."

I looked up at him, feeling a twinge of hysteria. "Who do I want to work with?"

"Carmen Niko."

The hysteria stalled. Here was a name. I had heard it before, but not in the context of law. "Is that a man or a woman?"

"A woman. She's about your age—thirty-nine, forty—very smart, passionate about her work."

I was trying to place the name. "Have I ever met her? Is she a customer?"

"I dated her."

"Oh God, I do remember. That was a long time ago." But hot and heavy for a time, if memory served, though I wasn't sure how I knew that. It wouldn't have been from Brody. His love life was one of the few things that was off limits between us. While he might mention in passing that he was taking someone to a particular restaurant or show, I learned more from Hillary Howard's column in the local weekly. Hillary kept track of North Shore movers and shakers. She had a vivid imagination and a weakness for gossip. Brody, who was often out and about, was fair game. Hillary had always had her eye on him. She still did, and she wasn't alone. He could deny it all he wanted, but women looked when he passed.

I knew. I traveled with him.

He was currently seeing a woman named Ellen McKenzie. She was an artist with a loft in Boston's South End and was a knock-out in an unconventional way, if the picture of them Hillary had run several months back was anything to go by. He didn't see her every week. I doubted he had long-term designs on her. The sex was probably great. Brody was virile.

But we weren't talking about Ellen McKenzie. We were talking about Carmen Niko. "How did it end?" I asked, because if there had been angst, and if Carmen associated me with Brody, there might be trouble.

But he said, "Amicably. I was working with Dennis at the time, and things were hairy there. Carmen's career was taking off, one case coming in after another. We were both preoccupied. It got so the relationship was more trouble than it was worth. We're better friends than lovers. She may not have the name recognition of Lloyd Usher, but she's a better lawyer any day."

That was enough of a recommendation for me. "How do I reach her?"

Brody pulled free, crossed to the phone, and dialed the number. After a minute, he said, "Carmen? It's Brody. I need to talk with you. If you're there, pick up the phone."

I held my breath. It was nearly nine. I didn't expect a lawyer to meet with me at this hour, but I had to see someone tomorrow. If Carmen Niko was on trial, out of town, or otherwise indisposed, I was back to square one.

"Carmen," Brody chanted, "come on, Carmen. This is a professional call. A *great* case."

I must have looked like I was dying inside, because he came back to me, phone and all. He took my hand, brought it to his mouth, and kissed it—all of which made me feel cared for and loved, which was what I desperately needed after Dennis and Lloyd Usher—but what really helped was when he said, in response to what I assumed was a dry greeting from Carmen, "It *is* a great case. Right down your alley. Successful woman being sued for divorce by a less-successful man, who wants to boost his ego by milking her dry. We're talking money, possessions, and two young kids who love her to bits and, p.s., have spent far more time with her than with him. She got back a few hours ago from Cleveland, where she was visiting her mother, who's dying, and he had her served with an Order to Vacate. She has until Monday to answer it. So she needs to see someone fast. I told her you were the best."

He paused, listening, still holding my hand, for which I was grateful. This was foreign ground for me. If someone had told me, twenty-four hours ago, that I would be embroiled in a custody suit, much less a cold-turkey divorce, I would have laughed and said, "Me? No way. My husband would *never* do anything like that."

How little I knew him after fifteen years. That was as jarring a thought as the others.

"Eight-thirty tomorrow morning?" Brody asked me.

I nodded vigorously.

"She'll be there," he said into the phone. "Her name is Claire Raphael."

"Can I call the kids?" I whispered.

He related the question, listened to Carmen's answer, nodded to me. "Anything else tonight?" he asked me.

Oh, yes. There certainly was. I reached for the phone.

"Hold on, Carmen. Here's Claire."

"Hi," I said. "I am really, really grateful for this. Brody says you're the best."

The voice that came back to me was throaty and amused. "Brody is biased. But your case sounds interesting."

"I want it to go away. I wasn't expecting any of this."

"The good guys never are. It's the bad guys who scheme."

"Can he win?"

"I won't know that until I know more about the case."

"Can we get a reversal of the Order to Vacate on Monday?"

"Same answer."

"You said I can call the kids, but can I see them, too? My son has a football game on Saturday. I want to watch. My daughter will be there. She had an allergy attack while I was gone that I knew nothing about until today. I want to talk to her and make sure she's all right."

"What do your kids know about the situation?"

"I don't know."

"Find out, if you can. You don't want to upset them. Phone calls are easy. The kids don't have to know where you're calling from. But if you show up at a football game and then don't go home with them afterward, there's more to answer for."

"Is there any way to reverse this order before Monday? Can we go to court tomorrow to get an emergency order of our own?"

"Only if your husband suddenly does something to put the children in danger. Will he?"

I wanted to say yes. He claimed I was a distracted parent, but if so, I learned it from him. Dennis was a master of evasion. Without blinking an eye, he could manufacture scheduling conflicts, I swear had a list of excuses ready for why he couldn't do this or that. He had missed Johnny's games and Kikit's recitals. He had missed back-to-school nights. He had missed a few birthday parties, and more dinners than I had by a long shot.

But would he put the children in danger? I sighed. "I don't think so."

"Then be patient. Come see me tomorrow. We'll strategize then."

Howard and Elizabeth Raphael were in their late sixties. They had their wits, their health, and the luxury of a retirement fund amassed during Howard's forty years as a regional manager for Granite Savings and Trust. While Elizabeth could be flighty, Howard was solid. He would have been the one to insist that the bank manage his retirement account, rather than handing it over to Dennis, and a good thing that was. As a venture capitalist, Dennis was like his mother, zealous in his causes but too easily taken in.

The Raphaels liked me. I had often suspected they trusted my career more than Dennis's. Even if they felt guilty for that, even if they felt it was time to be more loyal to their son, they knew what I felt for and meant to my kids. I didn't know what Dennis had told them about our separation, but I refused to believe they would hang up on me.

As it happened, they didn't have a chance. The voice answering the phone belonged to my baby. "Hello?"

My heart beat up a storm, eyes filled with tears. The sound of her was heaven. "Hi, sweetie."

"Mommy," she squealed, then her voice left the mouthpiece to yell, "It's Mommy, Grammy Bess. I *told* you she'd call. Where *are*

you, Mommy? Daddy said you had to go places after you saw Grandma, but you didn't tell me about it. Mommy, I had the *worst* allergy attack the other night, but I don't know what I ate. Daddy said it was something in the casserole, but I *always* eat that casserole. He had to take me to the hospital. Johnny kept saying we should call you, but Daddy said he wasn't leaving me alone to go do it, and by the time we got home and he tried, he couldn't get through, and then I fell asleep. Where was my medicine, Mommy?"

I brushed at tears with the heel of my hand, then took the tissue Brody handed me. I tried not to sniffle. "I don't know, baby. I'm sure I put the kit in your bag when I packed you up to leave Cleveland, and there was extra stuff in the basement fridge. I don't know what made you sick, either. There was nothing new in the casserole. Did Mrs. Beckwith give you anything to eat in the car when she picked up you and Jenny at school that afternoon?" Something as simple as walnuts, chopped and buried in a brownie where Kikit couldn't see them, would have done it.

"She didn't give us *anything*. *She* doesn't bring snacks like you do. We were *starved*! Daddy was mad when I got sick."

"Not mad. Upset. He knows it wasn't your fault. Are you feeling okay now?"

"Well, I'm not really hungry. Where are you?"

"You have to eat, sweetie. If you're scared, eat pure things, like bananas and eggs. And turkey. I froze packets of it. Tell Daddy to take them out of the freezer."

"Where are you?"

Once, I could ignore. A second time, I couldn't. But I had been Kikit's parent long enough to know that given the slightest push she would fill in the blanks. "Where do you think I am?"

"Daddy said you're in Santa Fe, but we told him you didn't have a store there, so he said you were opening one. You didn't *tell* me about it." I heard Elizabeth's voice in the background, then

Kikit's averted, "But I want to talk to Mommy, can't I talk to her a little more, just a little more?"

"Kikit?" I rushed out before Elizabeth could take her away from me, "Was there itching this time?"

"Yup. I need a gift for Stacey's party, Mommy. When are you coming home?"

"I'm trying to figure that out. Does your chest feel okay?"

"Yeah. Daddy stayed with me the whole day I had to miss school."

That was something, at least. Dennis usually headed in the opposite direction when the children were sick. He claimed he didn't want to get in the way.

"How is school, sweetie?"

"Okay. I didn't get to give my butterfly report yet, because Sammy Hayes took too long giving his one on stars, so I'm giving mine tomorrow. Johnny wants to talk. He got an A on his math test." The voice turned away and yelled, "I do *not* have a big mouth, she knew it anyway, you *always* get As in math—no, I want to talk more, I'm not done—"

"Hi, Mom," Johnny said and my throat knotted up again.

I swallowed hard, pressed the tissue to my eyes. "Hey, congratulations. Another A? That's terrific! When did Ms. Anders hand back the test?"

"Yesterday. I would have called you last night, only Dad said the cell phone wasn't working and he didn't know your hotel. Why didn't you call us?"

I wanted to answer honestly, but didn't know how I could. I hated Dennis for making me lie. "It was too late. There's a time difference."

"What's Santa Fe like?"

I had never been to Santa Fe in my life—but then, neither had Johnny. "Uh, nice," I supposed. "Warm. Dry. Did you finish your book on Paul Revere?"

"Yeah. There's a field trip to Boston to see the one-if-by-sea church. Someone has to sign my permission slip. I have to bring it back tomorrow."

"Daddy'll sign it."

"But I have to bring in six dollars and eighty-five cents for the bus and stuff."

"Daddy'll give you the money."

"I need exact change. He never has exact change."

"Grandma does. She'll give it to you. I'll ask as soon as we get done. Did Grandma cook dinner?"

"No. We went to Bertucci's. Are you okay? You sound like you have a cold."

Tears had a way of doing that. "No cold. I'm just missing you and Kikit."

"When are you coming home?"

"I'm trying to figure that out. I'll let you know as soon as I do."

"Here's Grandma."

"I love you, Johnny," I rushed out to catch him before he passed on the phone.

A chipper Elizabeth came on the line. "Well, hello, Claire. How are you? You missed a good supper. The children had pizza, and Howard and I had pasta. Bertucci's is a national chain, I believe. Have you seen one in Santa Fe? How lucky you are to be there. Everyone I know who goes there loves it. There can't be any better place to open a new store."

"Claire?" came Howard's voice. "I'm in my den, Claire. Elizabeth, hang up the phone."

"I will. Oh dear." There was a ruckus in the background. "Wait, wait, wait."

Kikit came back on. "We were singing last night—'Jeremiah Was a Bullfrog'—and Daddy was so funny when he croaked, only it wasn't the same without you. I miss you, Mommy. When are you coming home?"

My breath went short again. Singing was a Raphael thing. Dennis and I had shared a single year in the same *a capella* group in college, his senior year, my freshman year. We had met singing, had dated singing. Some of the kids' earliest memories were of our singing together. Bedtime, car time, holidays—perfect for harmonizing, for feeling close without saying the words. When the kids were infants, most anything with a soothing lilt worked. The lyrics came to matter more as they grew and joined in. Both loved singing. Both could hold a tune. Johnny was at the stage where he was wanting to deepen his voice—it was priceless to watch him with his chin on his chest and his brow furrowed—so the harmony suffered at times. Still, singing together was special.

We hadn't done it as much lately as we used to. Either Dennis was away, or I was away, or one of the kids was out doing something else. Sometimes, three of us improvised when the fourth wasn't there. But this was different. This time Dennis had sung with the kids, knowing that he was about to boot their mother out of the house.

When was I coming home? I only wished I knew. "As soon as I can, baby, as soon as I can. I'll talk with you soon, okay, sweetie?"

"I love you, Mommy."

The pain was excruciating. Fresh tears flowed. It was all I could do not to let her hear them. "I love you, too, baby."

Brody paused from wiping his neck with a towel to touch my face. He looked as tortured as I felt.

Elizabeth returned. "You have a good trip now, Claire. Yes, Johnny, I do have change. I have all kinds of change. Come, you'll count it out. Take care, Claire."

There was a click, then only the faint rattle of Howard's breathing. He was clearly out of earshot of the kids. "Are you all right?" he asked.

"No, I'm not," I wailed and took a minute to recompose myself. "I'm sick about this. Do you know what's going on?"

"Dennis wants a divorce."

"Did he tell you about the Order to Vacate?"

There was a pause, then a reluctant, "Yes. Look, Claire, I don't care for the method he's chosen, but Dennis is like this when he takes up a cause. He dives into it headfirst."

"I know. I've watched him do it and seen him fail. This time the stakes are higher. I'm worried about the kids." But I was reassured having talked with them. They sounded all right. I was glad I had called. "Kikit sounds all right. Is she clingy?"

"A little, but you know Elizabeth and me. We never mind that."

"Is she sleeping all right?"

"Dennis says they are."

"Do they know any of what he's doing?"

"No."

"Suspect anything?"

"No. He's been good about that, I have to say. He's waiting to tell them until after the hearing on Monday. I'm hoping he'll soften some before then, but his lawyer sounds tough."

"Who is the lawyer?" When Howard didn't answer, I said, "It's a matter of public record. Someone stood there in court with Dennis and convinced a judge to issue this order. My lawyer will be able to find out in a single call. You won't be telling me anything I won't learn anyway."

"Arthur Heuber," he mumbled, then raised his voice. "Dennis will be coming back here soon. I should hang up. He'll be angry if he thinks I'm telling you things."

"But don't you agree that this is insane?"

"Don't put me in the middle. Don't make me take sides."

"Will you talk to him, at least?"

"I did. He says what he's doing is right. He won't budge."

"But how can he want custody of the kids? He's never been a full-time father. There were always too many other things he liked doing. Does he have any idea how full-time parenting will cramp his style? Or is he counting on you and Elizabeth baby-sitting? Where is he now? If he left the house when I did, he should have been with his children two hours ago." Howard didn't answer. More tentatively, I asked, "Did he tell you the charges against me? Did he list my crimes?"

"Claire."

"They aren't true, Howard. You know me. You know I adore my kids."

"It's been hard for you, worrying about your mother and all."

"No. I'm handling it. Dennis is the one who isn't. He should have been with us in Cleveland. He could have come if he'd wanted to. Or was that his last fling at freedom before becoming a full-time father? He had this all planned. He must have been planning it for a while." I took a quick breath, lowered my eyes. "Did he tell you his thoughts about Brody?"

There was a pause, then a quiet, "Yes."

I had to get used to it, I supposed. Such an intimate subject, such a personal accusation. Dennis had told his lawyer, who had told the judge. He had told his parents and God knew who else. I felt betrayed, and angry.

"And you believe it? You *know* Brody," I cried, darting a quick look at the man. He had the small of his back to the sink and his arms folded over his chest. His expression spoke of the same betrayal, the same anger. "He spends holidays with us like he's family. Do you truly think he's capable of carrying on with his partner's wife?"

"He and Dennis ceased being partners five years ago."

"There was never, *never* anything sexual between Brody and me," I swore and lowered my eyes again. I was embarrassed for Brody, embarrassed for me. "Dennis is *wrong*. It's all in his imagination, his own insecurity, jealousy, whatever."

"I have to go, Claire."

"When will the children be back at the house?"

"I can't say."

"Will they be sleeping home over the weekend?"

"Claire."

"I'm just trying to get a handle on this, Howard. I don't know what to do. I don't want them hurt, they're innocent of wrong-doing. I don't want Dennis telling them lies. I don't want him trying to turn them against me. If he has a gripe with me, he should take it up with me and leave the children out of it. They aren't pawns."

"He knows that."

"Once certain words are spoken, that's it. They won't be for-gotten. They can't be taken back. Permanent damage will be done. Take care of my children for me, Howard?" I begged. "Make sure Dennis understands how vulnerable they are. If he says the wrong thing, it's done."

"He loves them, Claire."

Yeah, well, he was supposed to have loved me, too. Hadn't he said the words just last month on my birthday? He had handed me a gift-wrapped package that contained another gift-wrapped package that contained a third. Inside was a pair of ear-rings made by an artist he knew I admired. I had been touched by the thought he put into the gift, touched that he had taken pains in the packaging, drawn, as always, by Dennis's flair for the dra-matic. And yes, he had said, "I love you."

So what had he meant by the words?

I spent the night at Brody's. It seemed the only sensible thing to do; it was late and I was upset. Brody was my dearest friend. He knew how I worried about what the children were thinking and how starkly I felt the separation. With Brody, I was free to rant and rave or sit quietly. I did both. He made me eat his burgundy chicken and take a long, hot bath. He even turned down the bed in Joy's room for me.

In the morning, he insisted on driving me into Boston to see Carmen, and I didn't argue with him there, either. A hole gaped inside me where home and family had always been. I felt washed out and empty, weak, frightened. I'm not sure I could have managed without Brody holding my hand. I was eternally grateful for his presence.

Carmen Niko wasn't.

Four

Carmen's office was on the fourth floor of a building the stone face of which was streaked with city grime. The elevator was quaint, a square lift encased in scrolled iron bars that jangled with the fits and starts of opening, closing, and rising, but the office itself had a newer feel. The reception area was early morning immaculate—neatly fanned magazines beside a telephone on a polished oak table, two chairs and an upholstered loveseat, a receptionist's desk to match the coffee table, scenic prints tastefully framed, vacuum marks on the carpet.

Nothing was glitzy or pompous, overdone or intimidating as Lloyd Usher's lobby had been. This one was attractive and down to earth. The colors were warm—greens, apricots, and tans—clearly meant to be soothing, though that was a tough order. I doubted I would feel better until I was back with my kids, doubted I would breathe freely until I had a grasp of what Dennis was about. Still, there was a gentleness to Carmen Niko's waiting room that gave me hope.

The woman herself was warm and straightforward, not naturally beautiful but put together in a way that belied it. Tall, dark-haired, and olive-skinned, she wore a soft, squash-colored suit and no jewelry save gold hoops at her ears. She greeted me with an open smile and a handshake, greeted Brody with a wry, "Hey, handsome," and a peck on the cheek. Without missing a beat, she gestured him into one of the loveseats, clamped a hand around my arm, and ushered me down a short hall to her office.

Rather than putting the desk between us, as Lloyd Usher had done, she took up a legal pad and settled into the chair kitty-cornered to mine.

I watched her face while she read the court order. No matter what Brody said about the woman, if she turned around and put me on trial the way Usher had done, I was out of there fast. I was too tired, too frightened, too *raw* to withstand another attack.

Yeah. Right. The truth was that I was too tired, too frightened, too raw to go elsewhere if I struck out with Carmen Niko, so my bravado wasn't worth much. I steeled myself for whatever her response might be.

But she simply nodded when she was done, said, "This is a standard order," and set it aside. She uncapped her pen and—softly, sympathetically—asked me to tell her what had happened the day before. She took notes while I talked, asked questions when I skimmed details, returned to the beginning when I had finished, seeming intent on knowing everything there was to know about my homecoming.

"So your husband knew when to expect you."

"Give or take fifteen minutes. He had my flight number and my sworn promise to be on that particular plane." He had been insistent. What had I thought? That he was that eager to see me? Maybe. More likely, that he was tired of baby-sitting the children. Foolish me, I hadn't guessed the truth.

"Between the time when you opened the front door and when he came out of the den, would he have had time to call the constable?"

"Yes. Especially if he saw the car pull up. I still had to sign the voucher and get my bags from the trunk."

"Tell me about the police officer who came. How much did Dennis say on the phone?"

"Not much, I don't think—but I'm not sure." My mind was muddled about the things that had happened when I was most upset and confused. "I was arguing with him. 'Get someone here fast.' That's all I remember him saying."

"But only one officer came. Jack Mulroy. He rang the bell and waited patiently for Dennis to answer. Did he have a gun drawn?"

"Good *God*, no." It was a minute before I saw what she was getting at. My voice jumped an octave. "You think Dennis tipped them off beforehand?"

"It's possible. Probable, actually. They know your family. They know there isn't a history of domestic violence. So the normal reaction to a 'Get someone here fast' would have been that either your daughter was having an attack, or there was a break-in or an assault. But they didn't send an ambulance or a SWAT team. They sent one guy, one peaceful guy, who they figured you knew and would listen to."

Feeling humiliated, I rubbed the spot on my chest that burned. I shot a helpless look at the ceiling. "I left here two weeks ago thinking Dennis loved me. Now I find that he talked with the police? Told them about the court order? *Told* them he thought I would make a scene?" But it did make sense, given the police response. "Why would he *do* that?"

"To make you look bad," Carmen suggested. Her voice was throaty but soft, her manner calm. "We have to find out whether what he really wants is the kids or something else. Most immediately, we need to counter his arguments." Her pen scratched a line across the page. "Okay. Tell me again the examples he gives of how you're a neglectful parent."

I went through the list and gave arguments against each. Finishing, I asked, "How can a judge make a decision after hearing only one side?"

"They do it all the time," Carmen said. "My job is to make sure he hears the other side." She flipped her pad back to an earlier page. "What about the allergy medication?"

I had been racking my brain about that one since Dennis had thrown it at me. "We don't go anywhere without that medication. It's a ritual that goes with having a child with a severe allergy problem—like reading package ingredients, shopping in health food stores, buying baked goods only in certain bakeries. She even wears a small medic-alert bracelet, not always willingly, but I insist. She can't eat shellfish, nuts, or celery. Nuts are the biggest problem. If they're ground up, you can't tell they're there. So we always pack the medicine kit. There's an Epi-pen for injecting epinephrine, and an oral antihistamine. I put them in a carry-on, just in case she eats something on the plane. She always brings her own food with her, but I don't take chances. When she gets sick, it happens quickly. Her throat can be swollen and closing in twenty minutes.

"I spent a whole long time telling the flight attendant what to do. I told her where the medicine was. I'm positive I packed it, Carmen. There's no way I wouldn't have. And, anyway, if I hadn't, my sister, Rona, would have found it. It was in her refrigerator. That was a week and a half ago. I stayed at my mother's apartment on the return trip, but I saw Rona every day, and she didn't mention the medicine. She wouldn't have thrown it out. She knows about Kikit's allergies. She's seen Kikit have an attack. She *adores* Kikit. Besides, I remember packing it in Kikit's bag. I *remember* packing it."

"Who would have done the unpacking?"

"Dennis." But that would mean he had knowingly risked Kikit's life. I couldn't even consider it. "Maybe Kikit unpacked. Maybe she inadvertently tossed it somewhere. I keep spares, but Dennis is a where-do-you-keep-the-milk kind of guy. Then there's the whole issue of what she ate. It wasn't anything in the casserole, that's for sure. But, okay. She got sick. So why didn't he call me when she had the attack? I wasn't incommunicado. He could have reached me. Everyone else who wanted to did."

"Which brings us to Brody," Carmen said. "How often did you talk with him while you were away?"

"Every day. Just like I talked with the children—or tried to, but at the end I couldn't get through. I kept getting the machine."

"Didn't you start to worry?"

I had asked myself the same question and others, had tried to look at different angles during the hours I had spent lying awake in Joy's bed. Had I worried? "Honestly, no. Kikit and Johnny were with their father. I trusted that he would call if there was a problem. It wasn't like a week went by with no word. It was only two days. Besides, once before when I was traveling and couldn't reach them, I called Dennis's parents, and he was livid. Said I'd embarrassed him. Said I'd *insulted* him. Said he was *perfectly capable* of taking care of his own children. So I've trained myself not to worry."

"But you did talk with Brody."

"Brody is business. Besides, I don't have to work through a machine. He answers the phone himself."

"And you talked business." Her insistence might have been accusatory, if it hadn't been for the apology in her voice. "If your husband has phone records, he'll know how long you talked."

"We talked a long time," I said, because it seemed foolish to be evasive, "and it wasn't all business. My mother is getting worse by the day, and it's upsetting. Dennis hates it when I'm upset, hates it when he doesn't have answers. He thinks I deliberately ask him questions that put him on the spot, but I don't. Hell, there isn't any answer to death. There's just airing the fear and the sadness. I need to talk. Brody lets me."

"Do you love him?"

"Brody? Don't we all?"

"But you've never been sexually involved?"

"Never."

"Any close calls?"

"We've never even kissed on the lips. We touch like friends touch. There's never been anything inappropriate. Dennis is jumping to conclusions. He doesn't have a shred of concrete evidence to prove an affair. The problem," my voice rose with the frustration of it, "is that I can't prove he's wrong. All I can do is *say* he's wrong. We've had opportunity, Brody and I. Plenty of it." I had to laugh at the irony of it. "If we had wanted to do it, we could have, and Dennis couldn't have proven that, either. Brody and I are business partners. We travel together a lot. We take separate rooms, sometimes two-bedroom suites—so easy, if we'd wanted to sleep together—but we never did and there never seemed anything wrong with those kinds of accommodations, because Brody is a family friend. Hell, he was Dennis's friend before he was mine."

"So you denied the charges, that one and all the others. What did Dennis say then?"

"He thinks he's right. He thinks the court order proves it."

"And at the time when each thing happened? How did he react, for instance, when you first realized you missed that parent-teacher conference?"

Thinking back, I remembered feeling terrible. What had Dennis said at the time? "He wasn't overly upset. I'd have remembered if he was. He was comfortable with the idea of my setting up another meeting, which I did, which he then didn't even ask about because he was away at the time—fly-fishing in Vermont, I think it was. I can check that out." He kept his calendar on the computer, easily accessible. Two could play the game.

Carmen asked, "Did he ever, then or at any other time before yesterday, accuse you of being a negligent mother?"

"No."

"Did he ever, before yesterday," she flipped back several pages, "suggest that you were in 'a state of personal crisis'?"

"No, and I have to tell you, he didn't think up that term himself. Dennis doesn't go in for pop psychology. Business buzzwords, yes. Psychoanalysis, no. Someone else fed him that. His lawyer is Arthur Heuber. Would he have done it?"

Carmen frowned. "He could have, I guess."

I pointed at the court order that lay on the near edge of Carmen's desk. "Could he be behind this whole thing? It's such a sudden step. Such an *extreme* step. Dennis claims he mentioned separating three times, but he never went beyond the mentioning stage. He does that a lot—says things to upset me, tells me to sell the business or something—but he doesn't mean it, and if he did in this case, he could have pressed the issue, or suggested we see a therapist, or actually moved out. He could have told me he was seeing an attorney. Boy, did I miss that one. They put together a whole case against me without my knowing a thing." A new thought came. I pushed it away, but it slid back with dawning force. "If I wanted to be cynical, I could say he set me up."

I expected her to tell me I was paranoid. Instead, she said, "You could."

"My God."

"What makes you suggest it?" she asked.

"Little things," suddenly making sense. Oh, yes, the evidence was circumstantial. But if circumstantial evidence had been good enough for a judge, it was good enough for me. "Like the smell in the kitchen the morning I left for Cleveland. He made a big deal about it, then produced a rotting half-onion from the wrong cabinet, like he knew where to look. And the mix-up with my ride to Logan. I arranged for it. Someone canceled it," something else struck me then, "and *he* conveniently couldn't take us to the airport, knowing that Brody would, so he could hold that against us, too. And as for the mess-up with Johnny and Kikit's return from Cleveland"—I was on a roll—"Dennis says I gave him the wrong information. Maybe I gave it to him right and he got it wrong. And *then* there's the fact that he wasn't as bad as he usually is when I'm getting ready to leave. Usually he picks fights—about the kids, the house, whatever, and he pushes and pushes until he knows I'm upset. Only he didn't this time. Like maybe he was looking forward to my being away. Like maybe he knew what he had planned and was looking forward to that. Like maybe there was no business meeting in the Berkshires, just a weekend away with some buddy or other. Like maybe he could have come with us to see my mother after all and just didn't *want* to."

I ran out of breath and venom at much the same time. I hated Dennis just then, not because he might have done any of what I was thinking, but because he was making me think it. I had been agreeable for fifteen years. Suddenly he was reducing me to a shrew.

All that, even before I analyzed Kikit's allergy attack.

Carmen's pen scratched across the paper for several more minutes. Then it, too, stopped.

I was close to tears. "I want my kids back. This is a total, *total* nightmare. My life was fine. *Our* lives were fine. Dennis was never a full-time father. He never wanted to be one. So why is he doing this now?"

"Probably for money," Carmen said.

I gawked. "He has *plenty* of money."

"He does, or you do?"

"*We* do. Our savings are in joint accounts. He has access to it all."

"Who earns the most?"

"Me."

"By how much?"

I was about to say twice as much. Then I thought about the figures we had reported to the IRS the April before. I hadn't paid much heed to them then, rarely did when it came to comparisons. Dennis was thin-skinned. If I looked at him the wrong way at tax time, he bristled.

Thinking about those figures now, though, I realized that saying I earned twice what he did was an understatement. "I earned four times what he did last year."

"Will it be the same this year?"

"No. The discrepancy will be greater. He's working less."

"By choice?"

"Partly. He doesn't have to work. WickerWise brings in more than enough for us to live well on."

"What's the other part?"

I hesitated. Dennis was my husband. Bad-mouthing him to a stranger seemed wrong.

Then I realized the absurdity of that, given what he was doing to me. "He isn't very good at what he does," I stated. "He had a few breaks early in his career, but those breaks stopped coming when the economy soured. He tries, now that the market is improving, but he can't make things work the way he used to. The more desperate he gets, the worse his judgment becomes."

"And ego?"

I blew out a breath that said it all.

"So," Carmen said, "I repeat. It could be that he wants money. That's what often happens in cases like this. The father uses custody of the kids as a bargaining chip. He agrees to give his wife custody, if she agrees to lower alimony. In your case, the situation is reversed. Dennis will trade custody for higher alimony."

"He can have it," I cried, because if that was all he wanted, the solution was a snap. I wasn't greedy. Having come from nothing, I prized basics over extras. I didn't give a hoot about things like diamonds and sports cars and the four-hundred-dollar boots that Dennis loved. The joy I took in the success of WickerWise had less to do with money than with personal satisfaction. "He can have all the money he wants, I don't care. Call his lawyer. If this is about money and a phone call will do it, *call*."

"It isn't as simple as that, Claire. Yes, I'll call Art, but if you're thinking something will happen before Monday, it won't. When the judge issued this court order, things were taken out of even Dennis's hands. The issue in court wasn't money. It was your ability to parent."

"I can parent just fine."

"That's what we have to argue. But there are procedures to follow. For us, that means filing counter-affidavits answering Dennis's charges against you. We have to convince the judge to reverse both the temporary custody order and the Order to Vacate."

"But if Dennis drops his objections—"

"He won't. Not before Monday. Not after having gone to court. Art won't let him. It's a matter of his credibility as a lawyer."

"I thought it was a matter of what's best for the children."

"It is, but in time."

"Call him. Tell him Dennis can have however much he wants."

"Whoa. You need something to live on."

"I have plenty."

"What if he asks for a lump sum of ten million?"

My laugh was a reedy sound. "I don't do *that* well."

"He may argue there's that and more in WickerWise."

"Whatever is or is not in WickerWise isn't fluid."

"That won't matter, if you give him *carte blanche*. He'll suggest you borrow against the business, or against the house, or against the investments you've made for the kids' education. Okay, maybe he won't ask for a lump sum. Maybe he'll ask for a monthly check of twenty thousand."

I swallowed. "We don't live on anything *near* that."

"Maybe not in cash. But when you tally the value of the house, the cars, the clothes, when you figure in other living expenses, and entertainment and travel expenses necessary to keep him in the style to which he is accustomed, when you figure out what percentage of your business he's entitled to because he was the one who stood by your side and helped you to build it—"

"He didn't help me build *anything*," I cried. "WickerWise was always a quiet little aside, something I did while Dennis was doing other things. He never helped me with it. He wasn't even aware of it being anything more than a hobby until the profits started to mount, and even then, I kept it in the background. I never made business demands on him, never insisted that he wine and dine or buy Christmas gifts for my people. I did those things for *his* business, but he never did them for mine. WickerWise was my baby from the start, my time, my hard work. It isn't his. He has no claim on it."

"Give him *carte blanche* and that's what he'll take."

I was quiet then. The unfairness of it was too much.

Carmen touched my hand. "I'm sorry for being so blunt, but it's important you know that this won't be simple. Few divorces are."

"Divorce." I swallowed.

"That's where this is headed unless something gives fast. You've suggested marital counseling, and he's refused."

"He says he doesn't need a counselor, that he knows what makes him tick. Maybe he does. I sure don't, not after yesterday."

"Do you want a divorce?"

"He's already filed. I don't have much choice."

"But do you want one?"

Yes, I wanted a divorce. I was furious at Dennis. No, I didn't want a divorce. Dennis was my husband. Besides, if there was a divorce, the children would suffer. But if I was furious at Dennis, the children would suffer anyway.

We had been married for fifteen years and seriously involved for another three before that. There had been rocky times. Oh boy, had there. But good times, too.

"I remember being pregnant," I said with a sad smile. "Dennis was incredible both times. He was attentive. There were bunches of flowers out of the blue. There were pictures of me and my belly that were just beautiful. Dennis was into photography then, and he was good. He made me feel special."

Dennis could be charming. He could be witty. When he was of a mind, he could be a wonderful companion. Yes, indeed, there had been good times. Moreover, I had wanted for myself and my children what I hadn't had myself. I had *so wanted* this marriage to work.

"Think about it," Carmen said. "I'll call Art and find out how serious Dennis is." She rose and turned the datebook around on her desk. "We'll need several hours together to do this affidavit. I'm in court later. How about tomorrow, same time?"

"That's fine," I answered quickly. Tomorrow was Saturday, the weekend. I was grateful she was willing to work. "What about my children? What should I do?"

"Nothing until we go to court."

I had never been in town and missed one of Johnny's games before. "This is hard."

"I know. But Dennis will be watching what you do and reporting it to the judge. Better not to give him anything to use against you. Right now, the children think you're in Santa Fe, so they won't be expecting to see you. Call them on the phone. Tell them you'll see them Monday night. But for now, respect the court."

"Like it respects me?" I asked with feeling. "There's no justice in what it's done."

"At least you have a lawyer. Hundreds of women pass through the probate courts each week representing themselves because they can't afford counsel. *Pro se* litigants, they're called. Believe you me, they get screwed good."

"To hear that, you'd think this was a police state. Why does anyone have to get screwed?"

"Because the courts aren't perfect. I like to think justice prevails in the end, though I've had cases where it hasn't."

I shifted in my seat. "Will it in mine?"

"Eventually," Carmen said, but she was too slow in answering for my peace of mind.

"Why not right away?"

She held up three fingers in succession and ticked off, "Dennis Raphael, Art Heuber, and E. Warren Selwey. I don't know about Dennis, but the other two are tough. Art isn't showy, and he sure isn't talkative, but when he speaks, people listen. As for the judge, well, he's something of a throwback."

"Throwback?"

"He believes in keeping women barefoot and pregnant. As far as he's concerned, the humbler the woman, the better."

Suddenly overwhelmingly uncomfortable, I turned my hips and crossed my legs. "So the fact that I own a successful business was a strike against me even before he heard Dennis's other charges?"

Carmen nodded. "Most likely. Selwey's second wife was a lawyer. She stopped work to have a couple of kids, but when they reached school age, she went back to work. She and E. Warren divorced soon after that. She took him to the cleaners."

"So how can he be in this court? No *way* is he unbiased."

"It was a political appointment. He and our last governor are buddies."

"Hell." I uncrossed my legs. "Hell." I straightened. "Can we get another judge?"

"Not for Monday. Selwey issued the order. He'll be the one to reconsider it. But we have a strong argument—that your husband manipulated events to make you look irresponsible when you aren't. We'll give it our best shot."

I stood. Everything inside me had started to jump—I was used to *doing*, but Carmen was telling me to wait. Hard. So hard. "And if it doesn't work?" I asked.

She must have sensed that I was starting to lose it, because everything about her grew fierce. "If that doesn't work, something else will. We'll follow the rules until Monday, but if we don't get a reversal, there are other things I can do. In any case, you'll be able to see the kids Monday night."

"I don't want to just see them. I want to sleep in the same house as them. I want to sleep in *my* house with them. If Dennis can't stand the sight of me, let *him* leave the house." I made a face. "He's been such a pissy father. I can't believe a judge would grant him custody."

Carmen took me by the shoulders. She was several inches taller than I was and had to duck her head just that littlest bit to level our eyes. "It'll be all right, Claire. If we don't get satisfaction from Selwey, we'll appeal."

"But that takes time!"

"If so, it's to your benefit. Give Dennis enough rope, and chances are he'll hang himself—tire of the kids, tire of parenting. It's hard work. Let's see him stick with it."

"I want my children."

"You'll have them."

"I want them Monday."

"Then spend the weekend working. Meet me here tomorrow, and bring files with you. I'll need financial information about your business and Dennis's. Also, think about Dennis as a father. List the negatives. Be detailed—dates, witnesses. Our argument will be that Dennis set you up and that, in fact, you're the more attentive, more responsible parent."

"In court. In public."

"It has to be done."

"What if Dennis and I reach an agreement before Monday?"

"We still go before Selwey, but it'll be a simpler procedure. I'll call Art and see where we stand. Where can I reach you?"

I was about to give her my home number, then realized that I couldn't go there. So I opened my purse and fumbled around for a business card. "I'll be at the office. After that, at Brody's."

"To sleep?" When I didn't answer, she shook her head. "I don't think so."

"I use Joy's bedroom."

"Doesn't matter. It won't look good."

"But who'll see?"

"Anyone who wants to. Play it safe for the weekend, Claire. Stay at a hotel."

I wanted to argue. I wanted to rant and rave. I wanted to beg Carmen, positively *beg* her to get my kids back for me, in exchange for which I would give her far more than the ten thousand Lloyd Usher had demanded, and I didn't care if she only spent *eight hours* on the case, the money was that irrelevant.

But I think she already knew that. I had said as much, albeit not in as many words. I had also argued, and ranted and raved, and was getting tired of hearing my own voice in that high-pitched tone. The problem was that I wasn't used to putting my fate in someone else's hands. I believed that if you wanted things done right, you did them yourself. Brody was one of the few people I trusted more than I trusted myself.

Did I trust Carmen Niko? She seemed knowledgeable. She seemed experienced. She seemed kind. She seemed to understand my situation.

Did I trust her? I guess I had to for now.

"Hi, Mom. How are you feeling?"

"Claire. Why didn't you call last night? I was worried the plane went down."

"You would have heard if it had," I said in an attempt at brightness. "I was late getting home. Things got hectic."

"I was lying here waiting. That isn't good for my heart."

What could I say? I couldn't have possibly called her last night. It was only now, riding home with Brody after meeting with Carmen, that I felt composed enough to do it. "I'm sorry, Mom."

"Well. It's done. How are the children?"

According to Elizabeth, with whom I had talked three minutes before, "They're fine."

"I take it Dennis made out well enough while you were gone."

Oh yes. "He did. Are you feeling any better?"

"What did . . . say? I can't hear. Something's . . . with the connection."

"I just went through a tunnel." Louder. "I just went through a tunnel. There. Is that better?"

"You're in the car?"

"Yes."

"Where are you going?"

"I had a meeting in Boston. I'm on my way to the office."

"You sound tired."

Tired was one word for it. I wanted to tell her the others, but couldn't. "Getting home is always hard after being gone so long. Things pile up."

"When will you be back to see me?"

"I don't know."

"I feel better when you're here."

"I know. But I've been away from home for two weeks. I need to catch my breath and get things straightened out here before I rush back to the airport. Has Rona been in today?"

Connie's answer was broken by static. I left well enough alone.

"The reception's breaking up, Mom. I'd better go."

"Will you call me later?"

"I'll try. If not later today, then tomorrow."

"What are you doing later today?"

"I have—there are things—" I was desperate to tell her, desperate to have another voice tell me how wrong Dennis was. But I couldn't.

"You're breaking up, Claire. This is a terrible connection."

"I'll call again soon. Okay?"

"Okay. Bye-bye, baby."

Five

At its simplest, the word "wicker" means woven. Common usage makes it a noun, referring to objects made by weaving pliant twigs and willow branches around a frame. Such objects are also called wickerwork. Baskets were the earliest form of wickerwork. According to folklore, the first wicker chair came into being when early Sumerians returning from market grew tired, removed empty baskets from their camels' sides, turned them upside-down, and sat.

The wicker chair that had inspired my love of the medium was quite different from that earlier, primitive one. It was a rocker from my childhood that had sat on the front porch of the house next to ours. The family living in that house was one of the few in the neighborhood that was intact, the rest having lost members either to death, as we had, or to war, marital breakdown, or economic separation. They were as poor as we were, but happier. Laughter came from that porch nearly every summer night. More kisses were thrown from it, more smiles and waves, and in the midst of it all sat the rocker. There was a delicacy, a lightness to it, and a strength. As an adult looking back, I saw that that family had problems of its own. Still, I clung to the image. That old wicker rocker became synonymous with life's joy.

When I studied interior design in college, my appreciation of wicker took on new dimensions. The primitive quality of it intrigued me, the fact that though thousands of years had passed since baby Moses was placed in his basket of bulrushes and set afloat on the Nile, the technique of basket-making remained much the same. I knew that wicker had come to America with the Pilgrims, and that it was wildly popular in the late 1800s and early 1900s. I also knew that it had fallen out of vogue for a while, and I counted my blessings for that. At the time I was starting in the field, there were wonderful finds to be had for a song in old attics, at flea markets and estate sales. I even picked up a piece or two at the town dump. Many a weekend before and after my marriage saw me searching out antiques for my customers.

Refinishing those antiques came naturally to me, particularly when I couldn't find anyone else to do it well. I had the patience, and I learned the skill. In time I could recane a chair, replace broken weavers and spokes, and tighten scrollwork. And paint. Oh, could I paint. That took the greatest patience of all, working the brush back and forth, over and in and around every little thread of the weave for one coat, then a second and often a third. At first I barely charged for the work I did. I might find a matching wicker set—chair, loveseat, footstool—at an auction and earmark it for a customer, then repair it and finish it for the sheer joy of the process.

The joy never dimmed. During the years when I was a furniture buyer for a national chain and no longer advised individual customers, I spent my free time buying and refinishing antiques, then selling them on consignment. My world opened wide when I married Dennis and had access to the storage space in his parents' attic. Suddenly I could collect antiques at will. When Dennis and I finally bought our own home, it was filled with my finds.

Did Dennis like wicker? He never said. What he did say was that he always knew where to find me when I was upset. Working with wicker was therapy for me.

It was still true. WickerWise brought me pleasure, but refinishing antiques brought me joy. So there was a hidden benefit in situating the headquarters of WickerWise in Brody's garage rather than my attic, because that garage was huge, a carriage house actually, large enough for a suite of offices *and* a workroom—and that workroom was a dream. It had exquisite natural light, state-of-the-art air circulation, workbenches, tall stools, storage bins, and plenty of wide-open space. I stole time to work there whenever I could. In recent years, what with WickerWise and the children both growing in leaps and bounds, that wasn't often enough.

Still I squirreled treasures away, because Brody's garage had a storage loft, too. I filled it with the pieces I picked up in my travels and refinished them one by one. Sometimes I did it for a client who needed a particular piece. Other times I did it just for me.

This was one of those times.

Upon my return from Boston, I dropped my bags at a hotel. I did it quickly, pretended I was on business in a strange city. It was blatant denial, but I knew that if I let myself think about what I was doing—checking into a hotel on my own turf—and why, I would fall apart. I felt safer when I arrived at the office.

Angela, our receptionist, who was on the phone when I walked in, waved me a big greeting, pointed to the receiver, and mouthed the name of the sales rep from one of our largest suppliers. I mouthed back a no and hurried into the inner office that Brody and I shared. Within minutes, our secretary, Vicki, poked her head in to say a quick welcome back.

Angela had been with us for three years, Vicki for five. Both women were in their late twenties, and while neither was a close personal friend, both knew Dennis and the kids.

I didn't say a word about what had happened. Eventually, they would learn about the divorce. If they never learned about the custody order, that was fine by me.

Vicki hung on the door frame for several minutes, asking about my trip, before returning to her computer. With Brody gone to meet with the graphic artist who did our ads, I had the office to myself.

Desperate to do something about the mess I was in, I told Angela that I didn't want to be disturbed and dialed Dennis's office. He had a small suite in a luxury building on the far side of town. His secretary answered.

"Hi, Jenny, it's me," I said as I had hundreds of times before. "Is my husband around?"

There was a pause, then a too-fast, "Uh, I'm not sure. Let me see—"

"It's urgent. Please put me through."

Dennis came on. "Yes, Claire."

"We have to talk."

"My lawyer told me not to."

"Mine probably would, too, but this is between you and me. We're adults. We can talk things out. Dennis, I have to see the kids."

"No."

"I'm not a danger to them. You know that."

"I'm not talking with you about this."

"But you've made your point," I begged. "I hear you now. You want a separation. Okay."

"I want more than a separation."

"Okay. We can discuss it. You and me. We don't need lawyers or a judge involved."

"They're already involved."

"But we can *end* it. We can tell them we'll handle it ourselves. We can work this out between us, Dennis. We always have in the past."

"Right."

"I'll listen now. Really I will."

There was a brief silence, then a firm, "I'm hanging up now, Claire. My lawyer is Art Heuber. Have your lawyer call him."

"I'll give you money, if that's what you want. Just don't shut me off from the kids. I love them. They *need* me." I paused for a breath. No sound came from the other end of the line. "Dennis?"

Dead silence. As in disconnected line.

"Dennis?"

Nothing.

Dismayed, I held the phone in my hand for another minute before replacing it in its cradle.

Seconds later, I picked it up again. Knowing that the children weren't home, I left word on the answering machine that I would call them later. Then I called Kikit's allergist. He assured me that she was fine, and that while he was concerned that we didn't know what had caused her attack, he wasn't rushing to order more tests.

"We've done so many," he said, "and they were conclusive about what sets her off and what doesn't. I'm still not convinced she didn't just eat something she shouldn't have."

I agreed. Typically, that was what young children did. To order more tests would only compound the trauma. Better to simply reassure her and watch her more closely.

Not that I could watch her closely from a distance.

Determined to move the process along, I spent a while gathering financial information on WickerWise, but gathering information on Dennis's work was harder. Most everything was in the den at home—our checkbook, bank statements, paid bills. I had the tax forms that we had filed jointly the April before and added those to a large manila envelope marked "CGR Private."

Turning to WickerWise work, I emptied my briefcase of papers from the trip. There was information to be reviewed on our possible franchisee in Atlanta, notes from my interview with her, references and credit ratings to be checked. There was data on the abandoned Buckhead service station where I wanted the store, information from nearby shopkeepers, calls to be made to the demographics expert we consulted before opening each branch. Brody would need the revised figures the contractor in St. Louis had given me after seeing our plans, and we would have to review the decisions we had made and the orders submitted at the show in High Point.

But I couldn't concentrate on any of it now. My mind kept returning to Dennis, and to Johnny and Kikit.

I gathered those papers together, set them aside, emptied my in-box and spread its contents on the desk. From the looks of it, the phone hadn't stopped ringing during the two weeks I had been gone. There were calls from sales reps, many of whom I had seen at the show, calls from advertising people, calls from our own franchisees. There were faxes on fabric deliveries—on the *delay* of fabric deliveries—to our Pennsylvania plant. There were franchisee orders to review and approve, as well as those for the two stores that we owned ourselves. There were decisions to be made on who of our people would be attending the International Gift Show in New York in January.

I studied one paper, then another, and a third, but I didn't know what I was reading. My mind couldn't focus. Doing something with my hands felt right.

So I went into the workroom and changed into the ratty jeans and sweater I kept there. The jeans were worn thin at the knees, but soft as doeskin and familiar. I needed familiarity. I needed softness. I needed the musty, dusty, dried woodsy smell that permeated this space. I needed to do something physical, to see progress, to feel in control.

There were two pieces, actually, a matching rocker and table. Both were in need of repair and new paint. The very first step would be to comb each piece from top to bottom in search of broken weavers and remove every last one.

As I started, I did what I always did when I worked on a piece, in this case imagined the rocker at its turn-of-the-century birth, sitting in a small room with gauzy drapes waving gently in the summer breeze. The rocker might have held a mother and her infant, or a grandmother and her knitting. Beside it, the table was the showcase for a well-loved leather book, miniature portraits with sober sepia faces, or a tall glass of refreshing mint tea. I heard laughter coming from the house, distant echoes of happiness in sync with the creak of the floorboards beneath the rocker's sway.

The image faded.

So Carmen wanted negative things on Dennis? I could give her negative things. There was the time Johnny came home with a B on a report and Dennis read through it to find out why it wasn't an A. Or the time Johnny threw an airball in the last seconds of the basketball game and Dennis went on and on about how close the team had been to winning. Subtle criticism, but hurtful. Like Kikit's lisp, which he imitated until she forced herself past it.

Would the judge consider him a bad father because of things like those?

A psychologist might.

But a judge who was a throwback to the days when men ruled the roost? Not likely.

I removed piece after piece of broken wicker, picking here, pushing there. I unwove with care, cutting the pieces I removed at staggered spots to make for a more blended repair. How had I learned to do this? I had read book after book, had located experts and watched them work. There was an order to wicker repair, a pattern. Aside from the introduction of synthetic materials, the rules never changed.

Clean first. Remove the bad. Soak new lengths. Weave in with the pattern. Cut when firm. Repeat as necessary. Dry. Sand. Paint.

I was an orderly person. I liked having rules and respected them, which wasn't to say I was a follower. To the contrary. I thrived on pushing rules to their limits. That was why, among other novel transformations, I had once ended up with a Victorian bassinet whose wicker was threaded with new wood beads in bright colors and designs that both my client and her baby adored.

It was also why I had ended up with a business that had grossed $20 million last year.

I hadn't broken any rules. I did everything Dennis asked of me as a wife, did everything Johnny and Kikit asked of me as a mother. WickerWise came after that, had always come after that. I had simply pushed my own limits.

Okay, so I was sometimes late, sometimes distracted. All working women were. All working *men* were. My children hadn't suffered for it. They knew they were loved.

So where had I gone wrong?

Carmen wasn't able to reach Art Heuber until the very end of the day, and then the news wasn't good. "They won't settle. Dennis plans to stick to his claim that you aren't of a mind to be mothering. He wants the temporary order extended until a divorce agreement is reached. So we need to advance as strong a countercase as we can. He'll stand by the charges he's already made and introduce any new ones he can find. Are there any?"

I shook out my hands. They were bruised from working, but I didn't feel the pain. They were just cold, circulation gone awry. I was feeling cold all over, numb.

Did Dennis have *new* charges against me? "Good God, I

don't know. The charges he's made so far are crazy. I suppose he could dream up more like them."

"Well, you have an idea of what he's looking for now. Give it some thought. If you're prepared, so much the better. What we need are smooth explanations for anything he cares to suggest. Are you coming up with countercharges?"

"It sounds like war."

"Unfortunately, that's how the game is played. We either do it, or we lose. So. Countercharges against Dennis?"

I sighed my resignation. "Most show insensitivity, not out-and-out neglect."

"You say he's away a lot. How much is for work, how much for play?"

"He works fifteen, maybe twenty hours a week. No more."

"Can you document it?"

I could access his calendar on my computer. That would tell me when he had appointments and with whom. I could separate business from pleasure, could tally the number of lunches at the Ritz and evenings at Fenway Park. I supposed I could call the golf club and ask for the details of our tab there for the past month.

I couldn't believe it had come to this.

"Can you do it, Claire?"

"Yes."

"Then do it. We have no choice. That's the kind of evidence he has against you. We have to throw it right back at him. And Claire? Watch out for Brody."

I glanced at the door. Brody was on the other side, having returned a while back. Since Angela and Vicki had left for the day, he had been the one to tell me that Carmen was on the phone.

Given a choice, I would have had him in here with me while I talked with Carmen. And he would have been, if he had been female. If he had been female, no one would have thought twice about his opening his house to me, or driving me into Boston to meet my attorney, or staying close over the weekend to give comfort and support. Friends did that for friends. Especially best friends. But Brody was male. Dennis had made that a crime. I was being punished for something that hadn't even happened.

"What does that mean, watch out for him?" I asked, angry now. "I've already taken a room at the Royal Sonesta. I've already checked in, changed my clothes there, messed up the bed in case Dennis paid the maid to spy. So now I'm at my office, which just happens to be Brody's too. I can't very well banish him to Siberia for the weekend."

"Maybe you can banish him somewhere else, like to New York or Washington. He called me before. He's angry at Dennis, feels personally betrayed. He wants to call him. Better still, he says, he wants to go see him. He's spoiling for a fight. Don't let him do it, Claire. It'll make things worse. If Brody does anything, it should be going to some big splashy party tomorrow night and getting his picture in Monday's paper on the arm of some hot new babe. Get my drift?"

Thanks to walls of glass, the office space was nearly as open as my workroom. The reception area and Vicki's office were done in wicker, from computer tables to floor lamps to storage cabinets. The larger office, the one Brody and I shared, had a bolder, richer feel—wicker accessories on rattan desks with glass tops and rattan coffee tables, beside rattan chairs with fat cushions. It was a shameless showcasing of our goods, but why not? More than one photo spread of it had been done for magazines profiling successful businesses headed by women, and the advertising was priceless.

More importantly, I loved our goods.

Brody was at his desk, but I doubted he was getting much

work done. He was practically lying down in his chair. All that touched it were his upper back, his butt, and his elbows. His hands were balled together and propped up his chin. His ankles were crossed.

Only his eyes moved when I appeared at the door. They rose within the frame of his glasses to meet mine. He wasn't happy.

"Don't worry," he grumbled. "I won't do anything stupid. I'm furious at the guy. That's all." His fists fell to his lap. "Why didn't he say something to me, for Christ's sake? All he had to do was to open his mouth if he thought I was hanging around too much or doing something I shouldn't have been doing. I could've set him straight. Hell, I'd have backed off, if I'd known he was having nightmares about it." He tossed his glasses on the desk and pinched the bridge of his nose. "But he never let on. Didn't give a hint. He was friendly as ever that morning when I took you and the kids to the airport. Maybe he was pissed that I didn't go visit once the kids got back. Maybe he figured I felt it wasn't worth it if you weren't there—and you wanna know something, he's right. I'd rather talk with you than him any day. I did try calling—actually thought he and the kids would come over for dinner, I'd made steak soup—but I couldn't get through. The machine was on. I didn't leave a message. There didn't seem any point. The kids would only nag him."

I had to smile at that. He was right. "They love your steak soup."

"Yeah, well, he didn't need the nagging. I figured if he was out with them, he had things under control." He put a hand on the top of his head, keeping a lid on, so to speak. "Dennis and I have been through a lot together, lots of years, ups and downs. What's bad is that he couldn't ask me what was going on. What's *worse* is he was thinking it to begin with. Did he really believe I'd make a move on his wife—not that I don't love you, not that there haven't been times when making a move on you sounded just fine—but you're his. I would *never* have done anything to mess up your marriage. So what was it he saw between us?"

"Closeness. Warmth."

"It wasn't like you gave those to me and not to him. You gave him closeness and warmth."

Maybe. Maybe not. Certainly not the same way. My relationship with Brody was free and easy. He was that kind of guy. Dennis wasn't. My relationship with Dennis entailed responsibility. Expectation. "We were married. There's tension in every marriage."

"I made it worse, I guess. Christ, Claire, I'm sorry. I never meant to do that."

"Oh, Brody. You didn't do anything. It was me." I let the door frame take my weight and folded my arms close on my chest. "I didn't listen to him. He was trying to tell me things, and I didn't hear. Those times he talked about moving out, I thought he just wanted to upset me. He knew what buttons to press when he needed extra attention, and that was one. But maybe he meant it. I guess he must have. I should have taken him more seriously." I squeezed my arms. "It's only until Monday. Only until Monday."

There must have been something in my tone, an inkling of doubt that only a person who knew me as well as Brody did could hear, because his feet suddenly hit the floor. He came to me and folded me in his arms. I didn't tell him that Carmen wouldn't approve. I didn't care if she did or not.

"There's a gnawing inside me," I whispered against his shoulder. "I have flashes of something going wrong and Dennis getting everything he wants and my having to see the kids every other weekend, or something else equally gross."

"It won't happen," came his voice. "No judge is that dumb."

"This one hates women who have careers."

"That's his problem."

"It's mine if he rules against me."

"Then we'll appeal." He held me back and looked me in the eye. "Dennis's charges are bogus, every last one. If he wants a divorce, let him have it, but he's nuts. He won't do better than you, Claire. Not in a million years."

Saturday morning, I met with Carmen. Our main focus wasn't divorce, but the immediate issue of regaining custody of the kids. To that end, she asked question after question about my daily life, details like what time I got up in the morning, who made the kids' breakfast, what time I went to work, who did the laundry, shopped for clothes, made doctor appointments. She had to put together a case for my being a responsible and attentive parent.

But custodial details were only part of it. "The judge will want to know about your frame of mind," she said. We were in her conference room this time, seated at a table along with the financial information I had brought and Carmen's ubiquitous yellow pad. "He'll want to know how you're handling your mother's illness, how often you'll be flying out to see her, whether you're so upset that you're upsetting the children."

"Of course, I'm upset. She's my mother, and she's terminally ill. I haven't been the best daughter in the world. I haven't been around as much as I should have been. My sister has borne the brunt of the caretaking, but she and Mom don't get along. Time's running out. I have to be available for her now. If Dennis begrudges that, it says something about *him*, don't you think?"

"What I think doesn't matter. It's what the judge thinks that counts."

"Unless he's a cold-hearted bastard, he'll understand," I said. No matter that he had screwed me once, or that his wife had screwed *him*. He had to have had a mother, had to know what that was like.

"It's not like I'm there every two days. I stop off in Cleveland before or after business, and as for the kids, they did just fine seeing her. They understand how much it means to her when she sees them. It's a lesson for them, you know? You can't run away from illness. When people are weak and sad is when they need you the most. Dennis is the one setting the bad example here."

Carmen held up a hand. "We're not talking about Dennis. We're talking about you."

I straightened. "My mother's condition is heartbreaking, but I don't grieve to the point of obsession. When I'm doing things with the kids, my mind is on them. Same with work. I'm functioning just fine. Maybe I've missed time at home because of time spent in Cleveland, maybe my life is more hectic, but it isn't unmanageable."

"When will you see your mother again?"

"That depends on how she does, and on what traveling I'm doing for work."

"We need specifics," Carmen insisted. "Dennis is arguing that he is the more reliable parent. We're saying you are. The judge will want to know what trips you have planned and how long you'll be gone and who'll be with the kids when you are."

"Dennis will be. At least, that's how we always worked it before. I don't have any problem with that."

"The judge will want to hear that you'll be home for a while."

I wanted that, too. But I couldn't promise it. "My mother is dying."

"Yes," Carmen said.

"Have you ever lost a mother?"

"Not to death. To desertion."

That shut me up. But not for long. "Do you ever see her?"

"Never."

"Did you ever say good-bye?"

"We didn't know she was going until she didn't show for dinner."

"Well, it was like that with my father. He was young and healthy one minute, and dead of a heart attack the next. There wasn't time to say good-bye. With my mother there is. How can I not take advantage of that?"

Small victory. Carmen looked torn. "You can. You *should*." She sighed. "You just have to do it with care."

"I was hoping to get to see her every other week. That won't please the judge, though." No question. I knew the answer.

"Not unless you take the children with you, fly out with them, fly back with them. No more letting them fly alone."

Had I been negligent doing that? But these were the nineties. "It's done all the time."

"Not by mothers who are trying to convince judges that their children come first," Carmen argued. "Look, Claire, I'm not saying the judge is right, just that that's how he thinks. We have to play it his way for now. You ought to keep traveling down to a minimum, period. Obviously, if your mother takes a turn for the worse, go. But the judge will ask about business trips, too. Dennis has already told him that you travel a lot."

"Uh-huh. He counted. According to him, I've been gone thirty-four days out of the last ninety."

"Is he wrong?"

"Probably not. But he never said it was too much. He never complained, other than to say we needed a nanny, but we had one once, an *au pair*, and she was a disaster. He wants to try again, but the kids are older now. We don't need a baby-sitter, as much as a chauffeur. Dennis has visions of getting a cute little Swedish girl. I have visions of getting another hot shot. Besides, I don't mind doing the driving. It lets me talk with my kids. It lets me get to know their friends. It's good quality time. Dennis thinks it's a hassle. Tell *that* to the judge."

Carmen grinned and made a note on her pad. Then she spread a calendar on the table. "What business trips have you planned?"

"Nothing immediately. Brody is making a swing through our West Coast stores the week after next. I was hoping to make a round of our department store boutiques right before Thanksgiving."

"Too soon."

"Right after Thanksgiving?"

Her pen tapped its way through November. She turned the page to December, tapped more, turned again, then back. "Can it wait?"

"Not really. Our boutiques do a huge amount of business at Christmastime. And there are parties, and charity fund-raisers. I like to check out the setup before each one."

"Can't Brody?"

"That isn't really his domain. He's the numbers person. I'm the artist."

"Send him this time. It's important that you be around."

Something didn't feel right, something she wasn't saying. "I understand that, but if we go to court on Monday and get the order against me dismissed, it's done, isn't it? Out of the judge's hands? At least, the issue of child custody?"

Carmen didn't look as optimistic as I wanted her to be. "Only if Dennis cedes, but I doubt he will. He won't give you sole custody, certainly not before a divorce settlement is reached. He may agree to shared custody, but even then the judge will probably want a study done before he makes his final ruling."

"A study?" A new glitch. My gut clenched. "What kind of study?"

"Of you. Of Dennis. Of the children. It's done by someone appointed by the court to be a guardian *ad litum*, someone either in social services or mental health, maybe even in law, a neutral party who interviews you and makes a recommendation to the court."

"How long does that take?"

"The judge allows thirty days. Negotiations for a divorce settlement could take longer. If things get acrimonious between you and Dennis, and you can't agree on the division of property, if we have to go to trial, we could be talking six months, even a year."

I let out a pained breath. "A year in limbo? I won't survive that, not if I don't have my kids. Get me my kids, Carmen. I need my kids."

I had to believe that the judge would reverse his order. I could understand that Dennis and his lawyer might have pulled a fast one when I wasn't there to defend myself, but I would be there on Monday, personally presenting my side of the story. The judge had to see the truth then. Nothing else made sense.

That was the major reason why, when I talked with Johnny and Kikit that night, I told them I would be home Monday afternoon. Okay, so there was willfulness involved. I figured that if the children were expecting to see me—were *counting the hours, Mommy, the minutes, the seconds*, as Kikit had sworn—the court wouldn't dare let them down. We all wanted what was in the children's best interests, didn't we?

Six

I wasn't a big television watcher. By the time I was done with work, the kids, and the house, I was too tired. Sometimes I turned on the set when I climbed into bed at night, but I rarely lasted more than ten minutes before falling asleep. That didn't mean I wasn't aware of what Dennis watched. Often enough, bringing him coffee in the den, I had caught glimpses of "L.A. Law," "Law & Order," or "Murder One." I had a better record with movies, since he and I both loved them. I remembered *The Verdict*, and, of course, *Anatomy of a Murder*, and had loved *To Kill a Mockingbird* enough to rent it when we were having friends over for a Sunday night supper. And then there was the Simpson trial. I would have had to be on another planet not to have seen snippets on CNN and airport monitors, in dentists' waiting rooms, and in the *Globe*.

So I expected something orderly. I pictured a single trial dominating the courtroom, with the judge decorous on his bench, the attorneys and their clients sedate at tables beneath him, the benches behind them lined with respectful observers, and the court officers at attention by the door.

Reality was quite different. Judge Selwey's courtroom wasn't exactly chaotic, but it came close. Oh, yes, the judge was on his bench, but he was a small man who was in and out of his seat, black robe flying as he strode from one end of the bench to the other, grabbing a book here, waving a paper there, as though to make his presence known. Even then, aside from his clerks, the only people watching him were the three standing immediately to his right. The rows of benches that filled the room held small groups, two, three, four to a huddle, whispering, murmuring, rustling papers. Two uniformed court officers were engrossed in their own conversation at the side of the courtroom, and over it all the radiators hissed and knocked.

I didn't see Dennis. I had been looking for him since parking my car—looking covertly, nervously, because I wasn't sure what my reaction to seeing him would be. But he hadn't been on the courthouse steps or in the lobby, and he wasn't in here.

So maybe he had decided not to come. Maybe he had realized the absurdity of his charges and wanted to save himself the embarrassment of having the order against me reversed. That was fine with me. I didn't imagine that we would kiss and make up. I was too angry for that. But we were rational adults. We could talk. There was a way to handle marital problems, and a public forum wasn't it. We didn't belong in a courtroom discussing our problems before strangers.

Carmen scanned the room for a private spot. She ended up guiding me to the jury bench, nudging me along when I thought we wouldn't be allowed to sit there. But it was empty and far enough from the judge to allow us to talk.

No sooner were we seated when she pulled a sheaf of papers from her leather case and leaned close. "Look these over. They're a restatement of everything we discussed Saturday. We've rebutted Dennis's charges point by point and made our own point-by-point argument that you've been the major parenting force all these years, as well as the major responsible force in the marriage."

There were four pages of numerically ordered items. I read through them, found them simple, straightforward, and truthful, took the pen Carmen offered, and signed my name on the designated line.

Carmen took back both pen and papers. Still leaning close and talking low, she said, "As soon as Dennis and Art get here, we'll notify Missy, the blonde over there. She's the judge's administrative clerk—his cousin, I believe, but nice enough."

I kept my voice as low as hers, whispered actually. I didn't want to draw attention, didn't want anyone to know I was there. "Who are all these other people?"

"Lawyers and clients. The judge disposes of anywhere from three to seven or eight cases an hour. Social service workers sometimes show up, plus witnesses if the judge is hearing evidence. The press shows up only if it gets wind of something juicy." Her eyes roamed the room. They were unrushed, unfazed. She seemed perfectly at ease here, and while I certainly wasn't—I would have rather been most *anywhere* else—I took courage from her manner. "I don't see any media here now," she said. "The fellow over there, see, way at the back is just a spectator. He can't possibly hear much from there. Mostly he reads his paper. He's retired, I think."

A raised voice came from beside the bench. Our attention swung forward. After a minute, I whispered, "What was that about?"

Carmen explained. "The man on the right is representing himself. He doesn't know what he's doing—a big problem with *pro se* defendants—so the judge was instructing him in the law. The wife's lawyer, there on the left, objected to the judge's instruction, claiming that it's a conflict of interest for the judge to tell one party what to do, then to rule on the action."

I didn't need Carmen to interpret for me when the judge overruled the lawyer's objection with an impatient wave of his hand.

It was ominous, that wave, a too-hasty dismissal. It belittled the woman and her lawyer, which fit in with the picture Carmen had painted of the judge. Me, I had spent a good part of the weekend denying that picture. I wanted to believe judges were named to the bench for their wisdom and inherent fairness. I had to believe that once this judge saw me in person, once he heard my side and realized how responsible and involved a parent I was, he would reverse his earlier decision.

But there was that impatient wave, directed at a woman who looked decent enough. It seemed to me that if the judge gave legal advice to her husband, it *was* a conflict of interest. That, along with Carmen's reservations about Selwey, along with what I knew about little men with Napoleon complexes and misogynous men with Orestes complexes, made me wonder what I was in for.

"Is every woman who comes before him doomed?" I asked.

Carmen's eyes were on the bench. It was a minute before she said, "Not every one. He has to be careful. There have been complaints against him, even an article or two in the paper. So he walks a thin line. When the argument is compelling, his rulings are fine. He doesn't dare buck the tide. The trouble comes when things are hazy."

I thought my arguments were compelling. I thought they made absolute sense. I was wondering how the judge couldn't possibly see that—when the door at the back of the courtroom opened and Dennis came through. I felt a sharp thump against my ribs, reality hitting hard. He was my husband, now my adversary. I was having trouble making the shift.

With him was a man who was unremarkable in every respect but his carriage. He held himself straight and walked slowly, as though he had all the time and confidence in the world.

"Is that Arthur Heuber?" I asked.

"That's Arthur Heuber," Carmen answered. "Nothing fancy or showy or slick, just solid legal skill. He's been doing divorce work for better than thirty years. Never heard of him, huh? He likes it that way. By keeping a low profile, he takes jurors by surprise, not to mention pleasing judges who don't want to be overshadowed." She pursed her lips, let them go with a smack. "He knew what he was doing when he picked Selwey."

My eyes flew to hers. "'Picked him'? Can he do that?"

"Three judges sit on the probate court. When a motion is filed, it is given a sequential docket number. The last digit of that number determines which judge will hear the case."

"Then it's random."

"In theory. It's possible for a lawyer to manipulate the judicial assignment by picking when to file. Docketing clerks have been known to notify lawyers when the numbers roll around for a particular judge."

"That isn't fair," I said. When Carmen's mouth quirked in agreement, in *frustration*, I felt a flurry of fear. "Can we change judges?"

"Oh, I tried. Believe you me. I was here on another case last Friday afternoon and requested a continuance until tomorrow morning. That would have put us before Judge DeSantis. Not much better, but better. Obviously, since we're here now, my request was denied. It's not that these judges love each other, just that they won't step on each other's toes. Selwey issued the initial order. They'll let him see it through. I'll be right back."

She slipped off the bench, carrying the affidavits I had signed. I watched her cross to the far side of the courtroom and talk briefly with Heuber. Then the two approached the clerk. Heuber had his own papers, though I couldn't imagine what they held. More accusations? But what? I didn't drink. I didn't beat my kids. I didn't put them out on the streets to beg for food.

Nor did I drive to endanger them in the car, or leave my daughter without medicine, though Dennis had accused me of both. Sitting here, watching Art Heuber pass his mysterious papers to Missy, I felt utterly vulnerable. Accusations didn't have to be true to wreak havoc. The last few days had taught me that.

My eyes went to Dennis, drawn there, I swear, by some force of his, because he was waiting, looking straight at me. He held my gaze for a deliberate minute, then calmly looked away. If seeing me had given him a jolt, it didn't show. But I sure felt one. It brought everything back—the hurt and the fear, the anger, the shock, the *disbelief*—everything I had spent the weekend repressing for the sake of survival.

I started to shake.

Carmen slid in beside me. "Take a deep breath. You'll do fine."

"That's his favorite blue suit," I whispered fiercely. "And the tie? That red one? I bought it for him three weeks ago. He was in the process of closing a deal, not the biggest deal he'd ever made, but something. He was getting nervous. I said it was a power tie and that if he wore it, it would bring him luck."

"Did it?"

"Yes. So he's wearing it today. What does that say?"

"The Raphael matter," came the clerk's call.

I was still shaking, which was totally unlike me. I had been in pressure situations before—meeting people I wanted to impress, wading into uncharted business waters, dealing with large sums of money—and had always been collected. Never before, though, had I been in a position where so much to do with me rested on the whim of others.

Calming myself, I followed Carmen to the spot, to the right of the judge's bench, that had been vacated minutes before. We were a foursome this time, Dennis, Art, Carmen, and I, in that order. I didn't look at Dennis again, didn't trust my emotions that far. I kept my eyes on the judge. He was standing against the aged wood bench, reading the papers that the clerk had handed him, the papers our lawyers had handed her. His mouth was pinched at the corners. Every minute or so, he glanced at me over his glasses. I waited for him to glance at Dennis the same way, but he didn't. I was clearly the one on trial, the one causing the trouble, the one endangering my kids.

I stood tall and breathed evenly, proud of my recovery—until I started to think about it. If I was calm with so much at stake, the judge might think me a heartless bitch. But if I gave in to trembling, he would think me emotionally shaky. So I was damned either way.

What to do?

I stayed calm. Calm had worked for me when my father had died so suddenly, though I was only eight at the time and my mother was frantic. It had worked when the money I had counted on for college had to be used when Rona totaled a neighbor's car. It had worked when, after a year of marriage, my husband's past sins came to light.

Had I mentioned those past sins? No. They were ancient history, irrelevant to the present.

The judge began to sway from side to side. He turned page after page, one set of affidavits, then the next. Finally, he tossed both down and, still swaying, looked at Carmen. She took her cue.

In a voice that suggested she and the judge were the only two with an ounce of sense in the room, she said, "Your Honor, as you've just read, my client was stunned by the order issued against her last Thursday. She's led an exemplary life. She is strong, mentally and physically. She is well-known in her community and is respected by her children's teachers, their pastor, their doctors and friends. As the primary caretaker, she has raised two wonderfully happy and well-adjusted children, two children who are confident of the love she feels for them and are missing her terribly right now. Her husband has a history of absenteeism. He never before expressed an interest in full-time parenting, nor did he ever suggest that his wife was an unfit mother. She had no idea he was serious about wanting a divorce, he is that uncommunicative. Behind her back, while she was at her dying mother's bedside in Cleveland, he came to this court and presented evidence purporting to show her in a state of personal crisis. But there is no personal crisis. The evidence to that effect is filled with coincidence, erroneous supposition, even a few outright lies. There are too many unknowns to take it seriously, too many instances where an argument can be made that Mr. Raphael deliberately manipulated the situation to make his wife look bad. To put it bluntly, he set her up."

"We object to that, Your Honor," Art Heuber said in a quiet, but weighty voice. "There is no proof of any set-up."

"And no proof against it," Carmen put in, "but Mr. Raphael's action on this matter has been so furtive that we have to question his motive. His business is failing. He's never wanted to be a full-time parent before. Our guess is that he's after money. My client is prepared to be generous. She would have told him that herself if he'd asked, and the court would have been spared all the time it has spent on this matter. We will be quite happy to negotiate a settlement. We're prepared to discuss that in whatever setting Mr. Raphael wishes, but only after the current situation is resolved. Mrs. Raphael loves her children, and they love her. She needs to be with them. We request that the Order to Vacate be nullified and that the children be returned to her care."

The judge took a paper Missy handed him. He stopped swaying to sign it, and was handing it back when he said, "From what Father says, the children are doing fine without her."

The children didn't know that they *were* without me, I thought on a note of hysteria. They thought I was doing business as usual in Santa Fe and that I would be home tonight.

Carmen picked up where my mind left off. "The children are used to their mother traveling, but as you saw in my client's affidavit, they rely on her being home to do all the things their father doesn't do while she's gone. He doesn't cook. He doesn't buy their clothes. He doesn't help them with homework or meet with their teachers or buy gifts for them to bring to their friends' parties. These children are young. One of them has a medical problem, for which my client is the major caretaker."

"A questionable one," Selwey thumbed the papers, "according to this."

"There was medicine, your honor. Mr. Raphael panicked and didn't know where to find it, though Mrs. Raphael has told him numerous times. In that sense, he displayed the very negligence that he accuses her of. The medicine was there all along, refrigerated, as common sense would dictate."

Selwey stared at her over his glasses. "I wouldn't have thought to refrigerate it. Does that mean I lack common sense?"

"No. I'm saying that for anyone familiar with this problem, common sense points to the refrigerator. Mr. Raphael is familiar with this problem. He should have known to look in the refrigerator. That he didn't suggests something lacking. My client, by contrast, isn't lacking."

"No? She's a busy lady. She has a mother who's sick halfway across the country and a business that keeps her flying around. It seems to me she'd be glad to have someone else look after the children for a while."

I sucked in a breath to object.

Carmen beat me to it. "Not at all. The children have always been her first priority. No matter how busy she is, no matter how big her business has grown, she has always spent more time with the children than her husband has."

Selwey flapped a hand against the papers. "So you claim, but there's the matter of quantity over quality. She may be with them more—not necessarily true in the last few weeks, I understand—but the quality looks doubtful. She's distracted. She's put her children in danger more than once."

"I haven't," I said. I couldn't help it, couldn't just stand there being denigrated by a man who didn't know the first thing about me.

My protest had been a quiet one. Still his eyes shot to mine. "Mrs. Raphael. This is a hearing. Nothing you say has any bearing, since you haven't been put under oath. In this proceeding, your lawyer speaks for you. Do you understand?"

My heart was beating so loudly that I thought for a minute he might scold me for that, too, but I managed to nod.

"Good. Now." He held up the affidavits.

Carmen broke in. "Your Honor?"

With a put-upon sigh, he set down the papers. "Yes?"

"Mrs. Raphael has never knowingly endangered her children. We request that she be put under oath and swear to that. We would also like to bring in witnesses to attest to her diligence as a mother."

He leaned toward the watch that lay farther down the bench. "No time."

No time. *No time?* This was my life, my children, and he had *no time?*

He was moving right on, taking up a fresh piece of paper and writing as he spoke. "Since the parties disagree on who should have custody of the children, I'm naming a guardian *ad litum* to study the case. Requests?" He peered over his glasses at Carmen.

My heart fell. We had discussed GALs, Carmen and I, but I had been hoping we wouldn't need one. GALs studied things for thirty days, but I wanted this over and done *now.*

Carmen's first choice for GAL was a social worker named Nora Spellman. She was divorced, had custody of her own three children, and would have given me a fair hearing, no questions asked. But she was everything Judge Selwey hated. He would have rejected her, and we would have wasted our vote. So, as we had agreed Saturday, Carmen went with her second choice. "Anthony Twomey. He's a lawyer with Cone and Nugent. He's traditional, but fair."

The judge shifted his gaze to Art Heuber. "Do you know Anthony Twomey?"

"I know of him," Heuber said. His disapproval was subtle, the set of his jaw, the tilt of his chin.

"Who would you rather?"

"Peter Hale."

Carmen took in a fast breath, but didn't speak. I could only guess that she didn't want Peter Hale near me, and, if that was so, I didn't either. Not that I was given a choice.

"I'm appointing Dean Jenovitz," the judge said and wrote the name on his sheet. "Psychologist. Ph.D. His office is on Cambridge Street. If you haven't heard from him in a week, give him a call."

A week? Plus thirty days for his study?

"Your honor," Carmen began, "with regard to the order issued last Thursday—"

"I'm leaving the children with their father."

I gasped.

He shot me a warning glance. "There are one too many doubts about your ability to behave rationally at this point in your life."

"What doubts?" Carmen asked.

"She appears to have trouble with the truth."

"Everything in her affidavit is the truth."

"Then what is this?" he asked and unfastened something that had been clipped to what must have been Dennis's affidavit. He passed it to Carmen. Looking on from her elbow, I saw a photograph of Brody and me, taken from outside his kitchen window the Thursday before, if the date in the right-hand corner was correct. We had our arms around each other. Brody's head was bent to mine.

"That was right around the time he called you," I told Carmen in a horrified whisper. "I was distraught. He was comforting me. That's all." I looked across at Dennis in disbelief. Photography had been his thing once. But those pictures had been beautiful. This one wasn't. Not only was it misleading, but it showed the lengths to which Dennis would go to bring me down. All while my mother lay dying.

"Your honor," Carmen said with greater force, "I respectfully submit that if you're allowing for evidence like this photograph, my client should be permitted to testify. Her side hasn't been heard."

"Dean Jenovitz will hear it."

"It'll be a month or more before he files a report. We request that you give custody of the children to my client while the study is being done."

"They'll stay with their father," he said and walked the papers across the bench to his cousin.

Carmen raised her voice to follow him. "Then we request that the Order to Vacate be nullified. There's no reason why both parents can't live in the home during the study."

"The parents don't get along," he said, strolling back.

"They get along just fine. That's one of the reasons why my client is so stunned by her husband's behavior. There was no fighting, no acrimony. Besides, the father is gone far more than the mother. Who will be with the children then?"

"Father's affidavit states that he has no travel plans."

"Mother's states the same. The children are used to both parents. It would be in their best interest to continue that until the issue of permanent custody is decided."

I felt a glimmer of hope when the judge looked at Heuber. "Is that acceptable?"

But the lawyer's face was set. "No. You heard Mrs. Raphael a minute ago. She's angry. Add that to all the other personal pressure she's under, and there's no telling what she might do, either to the children or to her husband."

"I would *never*—" I began until Carmen touched my arm. I turned to the judge, pleading as much as I could without words.

But he was studying something he had pulled from the pocket of his robe. It looked like something Johnny had once had, an earpiece holding a tiny transistor radio. "The order stands pending the guardian's report," he said without an upward glance. "Father and Mother can't be in the same house. Father is already there with the children. Mother travels anyway. She'll just stay elsewhere when she's in town."

"Visitation rights, then," Carmen said quickly. "The children were told that their mother is on a business trip, but they're expecting to see her tonight. They'll be upset if they don't. They're very close to her."

Selwey fiddled with the tiny radio. Then he tossed it on the bench, strode back to Missy, and returned with the papers. "She can see them later today, with Father present, please. For the duration of the study, I'm limiting visits to Wednesdays and Saturdays."

I felt like I'd been hit. "Carmen?"

"That isn't nearly enough," Carmen argued. "The children will be devastated. Their mother has been the primary caretaker all these years. If nothing else, there are custodial things that their father doesn't have the slightest idea how to handle."

"Father can learn," said the judge.

"Two days of visitation a week is too little given how close these children and their mother have been."

"I'm not comfortable allowing more until the guardian assures me she is a reliable influence. On the matter of temporary support, Father will have the same access to funds that he's had all along." He looked over his glasses from me to Dennis and back. "Who pays the bills?"

"My client, your honor," Carmen said with a composure that, just then, I totally lacked. "But we have reservations about leaving things as they are. Mr. Raphael is a binge spender. Cars, clothes, trips—there's no telling what he'll do now that he knows his days of unlimited access to his wife's funds are numbered."

"Your honor," drawled Dennis's lawyer in an old-boy tone, if ever there was one, "that was a spiteful pot shot."

The judge didn't say yea or nay. All he did was to tell Carmen, "Have your client make note of any unusual spending. It will be taken into consideration when a permanent settlement is discussed." He sent the papers down the bench. "Who's next, Missy?"

I made it as far as the courthouse steps before my legs rebelled. Resting my weight against the stone wall there, I braced my hands on its edge and took breath after shallow breath. It was a minute before I was aware that Carmen had caught up. I struggled not to cry, though tears were close. "This is wrong, Carmen. *Unfair.* It is *not* in the best interests of my children."

She put an arm around my waist. More reassuring, though, was her voice. It held a toughness I hadn't heard before. "Damn right, it isn't fair. Selwey was *way* off base. As soon as I get back to my office, I'll put together a Motion for Reconsideration. It'll be filed before court closes this afternoon. Since it has to be heard by the judge who made the initial ruling, I'm not holding my breath for a reversal, but it's only the first step. If Selwey denies that, I'll file a Motion to Recuse, and if he denies that, I'll file an interlocutory appeal. That will be heard by a judge on the Appeals Court."

"What if it's denied, too?" I asked.

"At that point, we'll have other options. One is to get a temporary restraining order against Selwey's rulings by filing a gender discrimination suit against him in federal court. His remarks today suggested that he discriminated against you largely because you work, but the Constitution guarantees you the right to work. So that's one possibility. Another is to sue Dennis."

"For what?"

"Malicious prosecution. Intentional infliction of emotional distress."

I tried to make sense of what he was doing, tried to understand how he could look at me as calmly as he had in the courtroom, knowing what he was doing, after all we had been to each other. "Does he hate me that much?"

Carmen shook her head. "I doubt it's hate. More likely resentment. You've done better than him. Men have trouble with that."

"What's his lawyer's excuse? How can he let Dennis do this? Doesn't he see that it's wrong?"

"His job is to get the best deal for his client."

"But it isn't fair."

"Fairness has little to do with any divorce proceeding."

I rubbed the flat of my hand on my chest. The ache there was immense. It grew even worse when I saw Dennis emerge from between the large granite columns and trot down the steps with his lawyer. He looked to be feeling pretty good, and why not? He'd just pulled off a whopper of a snow job.

So we'd won on the money. He wouldn't be able to wipe out our accounts. Did I care? Not particularly. I'd never been in it for the money.

I saw him smile, presumably at something Art Heuber said. The smile broadened as the two halted. It was only then that I saw the woman who met them at the foot of the steps.

She was small, blond, and young, strikingly attractive in a professional way.

"Aaaahhhhhhh," Carmen murmured. "The missing piece."

"Who is she?"

"Phoebe Lowe. She works with Art Heuber."

"Works with?"

"She's a partner. Doesn't look old enough, does she? She's thirty-two, though people rarely guess it. Looking young and fragile gives her an edge. Her opponents either underestimate her, or feel protective of her. Needless to say, Selwey wouldn't care for her much. That may be why Art is here. He may be the point man, while Phoebe's the brains behind the operation."

"*She*'s Dennis's lawyer, then?"

"Officially, they'll work as a team." Carmen nodded slowly as she studied them. "Art is tough, but he isn't usually underhanded. Phoebe is. She has the flash he doesn't, with none of the moral integrity. She's a manipulator. It'd be just her style to coach Dennis on the best ways of making you look bad. See how they're talking? I smell familiarity. She and Dennis aren't strangers. Yes, I'd guess she's Dennis's original lawyer. She would have listed the kind of evidence that would hold weight in court, and counseled him to be patient until he gathered enough to make a circumstantial case against you. She would have deliberately chosen Selwey for his chauvinism, then sent Art in to front for her."

The threesome seemed pleased with themselves. Their smiles were all the more hurtful, given how devastated I felt. It was something of a relief when they started down the street.

I looked at Carmen. "Do you know Dean Jenovitz?"

"Vaguely."

"Is he bad?"

"Not as bad as Selwey. Not as bad as Peter Hale. I wouldn't have chosen Dean myself. He's only in his early sixties, but old, know what I mean? He's stodgy. Conservative. More annoying than harmful, a stickler for details. He gets hung up on things that have little relevance to the case. Gets past those things, but it takes time. I have breakfast once a month with a group of female family law specialists. We vote one man a month as the man most likely to drive us nuts. Dean's name pops up once in a while."

"Oh no."

"But he's never won. Never come close. Peter Hale, on the other hand, was Mr. February. *And* Mr. July."

I would have been grateful for small favors, had I been in a generous mood. But I was feeling that I'd gotten the short end of the stick, that I was being drawn and quartered and couldn't do much more than lie there and take it. I was feeling violated.

Carmen took my arm and started me down the steps. "I'm sorry, Claire. I wanted this over today, too." Her voice toughened again. "The worst kind of case is when you know you're right and you can't get through to the judge. But we do have options. If anyone knows them, it's me. I cut my teeth on this kind of case. Learned the hard way, actually, but learned good."

Something about the way she said the last made me look at her.

"I raised four little sisters," she said quietly as we walked. "When they were in high school, two of them got in trouble being with the wrong people at the wrong time. We were poor and couldn't afford a lawyer. The public defender assigned to the case was overworked and just wanted the case settled. He negotiated a plea bargain that involved my sisters admitting to something they hadn't done and spending six months in jail. 'Just' six months, he kept saying. I made him go to trial, and then did most of the preparation myself when he said he didn't have time."

She flashed me a dry smile. "I was a bartender then. Served drinks to lots of lawyers. They tipped well. I only had to sleep with two of them to get the information I needed. My sisters got off. I headed for law school." Her smile slanted. "Haven't slept with a lawyer since. Haven't had to. I know the ropes now myself. Right after I file the Motion for Reconsideration, I'll call Jenovitz and get him going. The sooner we start, the sooner we end."

My step faltered when Dennis's car pulled away from a metered spot across the street. It was a white BMW that he had had no business buying, given his own dwindling income. I couldn't see if he was watching me, or if anyone was in the car with him. He idled at a stop sign, then disappeared around the corner.

I breathed a little easier. Seeing him was hard, what with the jumble of emotions he sparked. So I suppose there was a small benefit to living elsewhere. I wouldn't have to see him while I sorted out the jumble.

Carmen and I went down the block in the opposite direction from where Dennis had gone. "Tell me what to expect from Jenovitz," I said, because I felt at a disadvantage, thrown into a situation for which I was ill-prepared.

"Lots of questions. He'll interview you and Dennis and the kids. He'll ask about your marriage and your home life. You'll give him the names of people who have dealings with the kids and he'll check them out, but mostly it'll be talks with the four of you. You and Dennis will go to Dean's office. When the children are involved, Dean will go to your home."

"My home." From which I was now banished. Being away for a weekend was one thing. Same with a business trip. But even with Carmen's motions and appeals, this would go beyond. "I don't have my clothes. Don't have my checkbook. I don't have a place to *sleep* tonight."

"The hotel?"

I gave a sharp shake of my head. I had checked out of the Royal Sonesta after two sleepless nights and would rather die than return.

"No other family here?"

"No." Only in Cleveland, which raised a whole other issue. I had no idea what to tell my mother. I was her bright star. After all she had wanted for me, all she had thought I had achieved, this would destroy her.

Dennis hadn't given her a thought.

Carmen steered me toward the parking lot. "Take a short-term rental."

I didn't want a short-term rental. I didn't want a strange place, with strange sounds and smells. I needed history, needed *roots*. That was what the last fifteen years had been about.

"You know," I said, "I spent months looking for that house. I spent months decorating it. When Dennis's business failed, we took out a second mortgage. I was the one who paid it off so that our monthly bill was workable. The house is mine, far more than Dennis's. So why am I the one kicked out?"

"Because you're the stronger one," Carmen said.

My bark of laughter held a bitter taste. I started shaking again.

Carmen tightened her grip on my arm. "As much of a temptation as it is, Claire, don't stay with Brody. Dennis will be looking for that."

I thought of the picture he had produced and was livid. "He must have followed me to Brody's on Thursday. If he'd been half as clever in business, we'd never be standing here now. This has to do with his ego. He's jealous of WickerWise, jealous of my relationship with the kids, jealous of my friendship with Brody"—I looked at her—"but I swear, nothing is going on between Brody and me. Nothing ever has. He could have been my brother in that picture, it was such an innocent hug."

"I believe you. The judge may have, too, but he'd already made up his mind. He was using the picture to defend his position. And it was legally wrong. He had no right to consider that piece of evidence without allowing us to offer others. That'll be one of the things I'll argue in the Motion for Reconsideration."

"If we don't win on that, these different steps you're talking about—different motions and appeals—they'll take time. What about the kids? Dennis can't cook."

"He'll order in."

"He hasn't ever helped the kids with their homework."

"He'll learn."

"He hates keeping the afternoon activities straight. He hates doing the driving. That's why he harps on hiring a nanny."

Carmen's smile was sly. "If he hires a nanny now, we'll take him back to court and make the argument that the children shouldn't be cared for by a stranger when their mother is ready, willing, and able."

"And if Dennis's parents fill in the gaps? Oh, Carmen," I said with a tired sigh and came to a stop beside my car. The injustice of it was too much.

"I'll keep busy on my end," Carmen said. "Meanwhile, you keep busy on yours. Find a place to stay. Get back to work. Be available for the times when Dennis calls on the phone in a panic because he doesn't know what to do for the kids. Think about the terms of a divorce so that I can approach Art." She held my arm with reassuring strength. "We will win, Claire. It may take longer than you want, but the facts are with us. We will win."

I wanted to believe that so badly. But the facts had been with us today, too, and I had lost. My faith in justice had taken a hike.

Still, I couldn't sit around and do nothing. That wasn't my way. So I would find a place to stay, and I would buy the car that the insurance company had sent a check for, and I would get back to work. I would do anything and everything I could to advance my legal case.

But there was something more immediate, more pressing, more challenging. Thrusting my hands deep into the pockets of my coat, I braced myself for the hard part. "So, what do I tell the kids?"

Seven

I hadn't expected Carmen to answer the question. Without knowing my children, she couldn't know for sure what approach to take. Still she thought for a minute, then made suggestions that reflected her experience with other clients. They might even have reflected her experience with me, because, in our hours together on Saturday, I had shared many a personal thing that she needed to know to represent me well. That, in itself, was interesting. Having grown up thinking of my family as different from others, I was used to guarding my personal life. But I trusted Carmen. She had struck me from the start as being sensible and sensitive. Besides, Brody trusted her, too. So when she gave advice on how to deal with the kids, I listened.

Be honest, she said. Indulge them the inevitable confusion and fear. Admit to sadness, even frustration, but blame the situation rather than Dennis. Leave the children out of your argument with him. You want your options open and your bridges intact.

Monday afternoon, when I put the same question to Dennis shortly before the children came home from school, he looked perplexed.

"We have to tell them *something*," I said and waited for his inspiration. As I saw it, since he had made the mess, he owed me a hand in cleaning it up.

But he was silent.

I rummaged through the front hall closet. Wood hangers clacked against each other as I shoved them aside to remove my trenchcoat, then clacked again when I reached for my wool overcoat. Still waiting for his answer, I grabbed a scarf and a pair of gloves from the overhead shelf.

"Why can't we just say you're traveling?" he finally asked.

I stared at him in amazement. Apparently, the only part of this he had thought through was the one painting me as the villain. "Traveling? For a month on top of what I've just done? With twice-weekly visits and not even one overnight here at home?"

I scooped the coats off the floor and set them on a bench by the door. "They aren't babies. They'll see through that in a minute. Besides, I'm done lying to them. It bothered me having to do it last weekend. I won't do it again." I took off up the stairs.

He came right along. "So what will you tell them?"

"The truth. They'll have to know it sometime."

"You'll tell them you were ordered to leave?"

I rounded the top of the banister and strode down the hall. "I'll tell them we've decided to separate. That may not be the whole truth, but it's the bottom line. If I tell them about the court order, they'll ask why, and if I tell them why"—I shot him a look as I turned into the bedroom—"they'll hate you for it. That wouldn't be in their best interests. I don't want them hating you. You're their father. They have to live with you, for a little while, at least."

"Ahhh, Claire. You're so noble."

I turned on him fast, my anger so strong that it approached rage, which was something new to me, something foreign and frightening. I struggled to keep my tone civil. "I have more to be proud of than you do, Dennis. What's happening here is a travesty of justice. You got the jump on me. You set things up so that I didn't have a chance. But it won't last forever. Reason is on my side. And parenting experience. You're in for an awakening. Full-time parenting is something else. Just wait. You'll see. You *never* wanted to hang around with the kids before."

"That's not true. You were just always there first. I was super-fluous."

"Never," I cried. Good *God*, I had worked so hard to make him feel important. "Whenever you were finally there with us, I made the biggest deal of it with the kids. They loved it when you were around, and I loved seeing them happy. That's all I've ever wanted for them, Dennis. That's all I've worked for. And now you're going to mess it all up." I wanted to be calm. I had spent the time since leaving the courthouse numbing myself against seeing him, being here, doing this. Anger was an analgesic of sorts, but I was losing it anyway. Rage hovered close. "Was it something I did? Something *you* did? Something that happened at work? Something someone else said?" I touched my chest. "I am having *so much trouble* understanding all this. Has our life together been so awful? Have I been such a *terrible wife* that you have to punish me this way? That you have to punish the *kids* this way?"

His handsome face turned bored. "Don't get melodramatic. Marriages fall apart all the time."

"Not mine!" I cried. Those two words said so much. Oh yes, I had seen those marriages fall apart. They were all around us, hard to miss. But I had wanted us to be different. *Needed* us to be different. "You'll just throw it away, good times and all?"

"What good times?"

"Christmases. We always had great Christmases. And vacations. Remember when we took the kids to Arizona? When we hiked through the hills there with them strapped on our backs? I dare you to say that wasn't fun."

"Maybe it was. But those were family times. What about between you and me?"

By way of answer, I glanced at the bedroom wall. It was covered with photographs of me, photographs that Dennis had taken, developed, printed, framed, and hung himself. They captured the ten years between when he and I had become engaged and when his interest in photography had waned. They were beautiful pictures; I had felt beautiful in them. One captured excitement, another pensiveness, another softness, another love—on my face, through Dennis's eye and hand.

Still, he said, "It's over, Claire. I've made up my mind. There's no going back."

"Is there someone else?"

He made a face. "Why do you have to ask that?"

I held my ground. "Because I'm trying to make sense out of this. There was someone else once."

"Way before you."

"You were with her, knowing she was married to someone else. That's not much different from your cheating on me."

"Look who's pointing a finger."

"Brody and I aren't involved that way."

"Sure."

"It's true. You know it, Dennis. You know it's true."

"Uh-huh."

"Our marriage wasn't perfect, but it wasn't awful, either."

He settled in against the wall.

I stared at him for a minute, then pulled a suitcase from the closet, opened it on the bed, and went to the dresser.

"It's done," he said. "I'm not changing my mind."

I filled my arms with underthings, dropped them in the suitcase, and went back for more.

"You talked me out of it one too many times," he said. "I want my freedom."

That stopped me. I choked out an incredulous laugh. "You want your freedom, with sole custody of two young children? That shows how much you know, Dennis. You haven't the *faintest* idea what it means to be a full-time caretaker. Fault me all you will for having a career, but at the same time that I worked, I've been doing things for the kids that you can't begin to count, let alone know about. Telling Kikit what not to eat is one thing, making sure she doesn't eat it is something else. I don't know about you, but it terrifies me to think she had an attack and we don't know its cause. She'll have to be watched closer than ever. And Johnny is intense anyway. Think of the extra care *he'll* need, dealing with a divorce. Freedom? Good Lord, if that weren't so pathetic, it would be funny."

He had the gall to grin. "So why are you sore? The judge was right. You should be pleased to have a little time off."

The grin did it, made everything roiling inside me roil harder and faster. I felt a powerful, primitive urge to hit him, and though I had the good sense not to do it, I hated him for reducing me to that.

With a conscious effort, I relaxed my jaw. I returned to the dresser for sweaters this time. "I'm sore," I said carefully, "because neither that judge nor you have the foggiest notion what parental love is about." I dropped the sweaters into the suitcase, pushing them to fit. "I love my kids. I've done well by them. You two say I haven't. Well, let me tell you"—I straightened and faced him head-on—"this is just the beginning. You want a divorce, I'll give you a divorce, but if you're thinking to use the kids as a bargaining chip to get more money, think again. Drop all this now, before the kids know the worst, before the *world* knows the worst, and we can reach a comfortable agreement. Keep it up and I'll fight. My lawyer knows what I want. We'll go from court to court, if need be. You can't win, Dennis. Not in the long run. I've been too good a mother, damn it."

"You overrate yourself," he said and turned toward the door. "Johnny has practice at five, Be gone by four."

"What?"

"I want him settled down and ready to play."

"Right after we tell him his *world's* coming apart? He won't be able to play."

"His world isn't coming apart. It's just changing some. Going to practice will be the best thing for him. The most normal thing."

"Then I'll drop him off."

"No. I will."

"Let me talk with him a little more."

"Do your talking by four. If there's a problem after that, I'll call Mulroy." With a last, long, warning look, he left the room.

It was a miracle that my body held together, my inner turmoil was so great. But I had lots to do in a very short time. So I went on automatic.

Not wanting the children to suspect anything amiss before I could explain, I put the suitcases I had lived out of for the past two weeks in the backseat of the car. They would know what those were. I filled the trunk with everything I didn't want them to see—older suitcases holding the rest of my clothes, dress bags, and coats. I took the CD player from the bedroom and a box of CDs, because I couldn't be without music. I took as many pictures of the children as I could without leaving gaping holes on dressers and bookshelves. I took a box containing our checkbook, bank records, and the financial information that I hadn't been able to access on the computer.

With fifteen minutes to spare before the school bus passed through, I headed for the kitchen. Within seconds the oven was on, and cookie-makings covered the counter. The children loved hot, fresh-from-the-oven cookies, and I loved making them. It was such a mommy thing to do, such a little way of saying I love you in a day and age when gourmet cookies could be bought at every stop. Totally aside from making Kikit-friendly food, I baked whenever I could, particularly before and after trips, when I was feeling guilty about being away.

Yes, guilty. I never left home without qualms.

I wasn't feeling guilty now, but desolate. I wanted the closeness that came with sitting at the table mixing mouthfuls of hot cookie and cold milk. We had been doing that forever, Johnny and I alone in the days before Kikit, then the three of us together. I had been doing it even longer, though those very, very first times seemed so far away. I hadn't thought of them in ages—and didn't know what brought them to mind now. They weren't really the same at all. I had been a child then. Couldn't have been more than ten or eleven. My mother was out working all day and didn't have time to bake, but I knew mothers who did. I had been in their houses. Those houses had been warmer and more inviting than mine. So as soon as the Girl Scout leader showed us how, I made cookies myself. Rona grabbed them and ran, often returning for seconds with friends. By the time my mother came home from work, the cookies were usually gone. I didn't do it often. But I do remember, so clearly, sitting alone in that kitchen, mixing the melty warmth of those things with a glass of cold milk and pretending our lives were safe and secure.

I had the first batch in the oven now, had the second on sheets at the ready, and was scrubbing out the mixing bowl when I heard the kids charge through the garage. It was panic time. I pressed the back of my hand to my upper lip, wondering how I was going to keep from crying when I saw them, knowing what had happened in court.

Then the door to the mudroom swung back, and I didn't have time to think about tears or court or the future. I barely had time to wipe my hands and open my arms when Kikit launched herself into them. Exuberant at seeing her, I swooped her up and around. She smelled of little-girl warmth, dried leaves, and chalk.

"Mommeeee! I knew you'd be here when we got home." She squeezed my neck hard enough to pinch nerves, but I didn't care one bit. When Johnny followed her in, I opened an arm and hugged him, too.

"Hi, Mom." The voice was pushed deep, no doubt to compensate for the way he hugged me back. "When'd ya land?"

"A little while ago," I said. It was only a little white lie. I wasn't ready to tell them what I had to yet, wanted to enjoy them a bit, and it was easy, so easy, like this was just another excited homecoming.

I held them both back, Kikit with her bottom on the counter and her legs around me, Johnny still within the circle of my arm. "You guys look great." I focused on Kikit. She was the image of health. "Feeling okay?"

"Yup."

"Eating okay?"

"Yup." She opened her mouth wide. "Ook ahhee I ost a oot."

"Another tooth?" I admired the spot her tongue was touching. "My goodness, that's a beautiful hole. I take it you do have the tooth?" She would have been in tears otherwise. That was what had happened the last time.

But she was bobbing her head up and down, digging into her pocket, and producing a tiny enamel nugget from a fistful of lint, then telling me everything that she planned to write the tooth fairy in her letter, which had been the solution last time and had so pleased her—*how else can the tooth fairy know how special I am*—that she had vowed to do it even when she *did* have the tooth. She was still talking about her letter when Johnny said, "Mikey Rubin broke his arm in the playground today."

"I'm not done," Kikit cried, taking my chin and guiding it back.

"This is more important. It was so gross, Mom."

"Mommy, he's interrupting."

"This is *important*. There was a bone sticking out from the skin and blood all over. They took him away in an ambulance."

"He was crying," Kikit reported with sudden authority, taking over Johnny's conversation when she couldn't sustain her own. "We could hear it all the way in second grade, but I didn't cry when my tooth came out." She crinkled up her nose and gave a sniff. Her eyes lit up. "Somethin's in the oven," she sang.

"Chocolate chocolate chip," Johnny said to her, then to me, "Mikey wasn't even doing much when it happened. We were playing bombardment against the wall, and he was trying to get away from the ball when he tripped and did this kind of jump and turn and then—*wham*—there was this awful scream. I mean, the bone was right there, coming out of the skin—"

I muzzled him by dragging him close and said against a thicket of raven-dark hair, "Say that one more time and I'll be sick in the sink. You're making me feel woozy."

"Yeah, I kind of felt like that when I was looking at it," he said when I let him up for air.

"I'll bet lots of your friends did. It's a pretty normal way to feel."

"I want a cookie, Mommy," Kikit said. "Are they almost done?"

Two more minutes, and they were, then another two to cool. While we waited, Kikit told me about the turkey that had visited her classroom, the Barbie doll that she had decided she wanted for Christmas, and the note that her teacher had sent home—she had dropped it on the playground, she thought, or maybe on the bus—that said something about white bugs in some kid's hair.

Lice. Swell. I did a quick check, saw nothing, but vowed to tell Dennis to look. See how he liked *that*.

Johnny wasn't as chatty as Kikit. He didn't hold my hand, or touch my hair or my face, as she did, but he stayed close to my side until I gave the word, then wielded the spatula himself. We were incorrigible—always rushing this part, peeling off the first of the cookies when they were too hot to hold their shape so that they curled around our fingers instead, but we laughed. We licked melted chocolate from our fingers. We drank milk in a way that left the kind of mustache we saw in the ads, bubbly white smears over toothy grins.

Then Kikit said to the doorway, "Hurry up, Daddy. They're nearly gone."

I wanted to chase him away, wanted to cherish these final moments of innocence. It felt so good, so safe, so *normal* to laugh over cookies and milk.

But the look he gave me was sobering, expectant, in a sharp-focused way.

Johnny jumped up from the table and retrieved his backpack from the mudroom. He was passing back through the kitchen en route to the hall when he asked, "What's for supper?"

I wasn't making supper. I was supposed to pack up my things, visit with the children, and leave by four. If I didn't, Dennis would have the cops usher me out. In front of the children.

Unless he realized how much the kids had missed me and was having second thoughts. Unless he was wondering if there wasn't a better way to do this. Unless he was thinking that he didn't know what in the hell was for dinner and that it would be easier to simply let me stay a while.

Answering Johnny, I said, "You'll have to ask your dad what's for supper."

Johnny was frowning at me from the door. "You always make something special when you've been gone. I want lasagna."

"Fried chicken," Kikit chirped. She was doing a little hip-hop, with her elbows on the table and her knees on the chair.

"We had fried chicken last time Mom came home. It's my turn. Lasagna."

"How about pizza," Dennis said.

Kikit crinkled her nose, in distaste this time. "We had that last night with Grandma and Grandpa. Besides, Mommy's making supper."

"No," Dennis said. "She's not."

It was a minute before that registered. Kikit stopped dancing. Her eyes grew round. She looked from Dennis to me and back, then sucked in a breath and her elbows, and said with hushed excitement, "Are we celebrating something?"

I waited for Dennis to answer her, but all he did, the yellow-bellied coward, was to hitch his chin my way. The children's eyes followed.

I let out a breath. "No celebration. Just talk. Come sit, Johnny."

He didn't move. "Is it Grandma?"

I gave him a sad smile—such a sweet, sober, intuitive child—and shook my head. "Not Grandma. Us." There wasn't an easy way to say it. I had tested dozens of words in the time between last Thursday and now. No combination was good. Simpler seemed better. "Your dad and I are separating."

"What does that mean?" Kikit asked.

I gave Dennis a look that asked him to explain, but he stood with his hands on his hips and seemed as curious to hear what I was going to say as Kikit. Apparently he wasn't there to help. He was supervising. He didn't want to do the dirty work himself, but he wanted it done his way. He must have felt that the court had given him that right.

Well, it hadn't. If I wanted to tell the children that their father was an insecure SOB who was lacking in loyalty, compassion, and common sense, I would. Neither the court nor Dennis dictated my words. Love did. Worry did. Self-respect did.

"Separating means that we'll be living apart from each other," I said.

Kikit took that in stride. "In separate houses?"

"Yes."

"But you can't," she stated. "You're our parents. You have to be with us."

"We will be. Just in different places."

"But *I* can't be two places at once."

"You won't. You'll be with Daddy some of the time and me the rest."

"Isn't that what we do already?"

Well, it was. She was absolutely right. But only to a point. "What we've been doing is having overlapping lives. Sometimes all four of us are here, other times just three. From now on it'll be three—either you and Johnny and me, or you and Johnny and Daddy. Daddy and I won't be here with you guys at the same time."

"Why not?" she demanded.

I turned to Dennis again, hoping he would take a stab at that one, but he was looking blank—no help in the answer department. Not that I blamed him this time. Saying the right thing was crucial. The wrong words could cause permanent damage.

Only I didn't know the right words. So I fell back on the age-old, "Because we think it's best."

"Well, I don't," Kikit insisted. "Who'll live where, and where'll *we* live?"

"You'll live here. I'll have another place."

"*Where?*"

"I don't know yet. But you can be with me there or be with me here."

"I want you *here* all the time. Why can't you live in the den upstairs? I'll clear all my babies out. You like the sofa bed, you told me you did."

It was Johnny, plastered to the wall just inside the kitchen, who said, "They don't want to live in the same house with each other. They don't like each other anymore."

I left the table and went to him. His body was stiff, his eyes sunken. It was like he was trying his best not to collapse inward but was losing the battle. I slipped my arm around his shoulders, no easy feat given that outer rigidity, and said, "There's more to it than that. I'm not sure even I understand it myself. It's pretty complicated."

"Tell *me*. I wanna know!" Kikit cried, but I continued talking to Johnny, jiggling his shoulders in an attempt to loosen him up.

"The one thing you have to remember—the only really important thing—is that we both love you and Kikit."

"But you don't love each other," he said.

Four days before, I would have argued. Now? "I don't know. This is kind of a trial period. We'll be doing lots of thinking and talking." I didn't want to mention Dean Jenovitz or, worse, the court order against me. In time, the children would know about Jenovitz, since he had to meet with them. I hoped they would never have to know about the court order.

"You won't really notice much of a change," I said, trying to be comfortable and upbeat for me as much as for them. I was feeling hollowed out. "Things'll be pretty much the same as they've always been."

He didn't believe me for a minute. I could see it in his eyes. But he didn't say a word.

"Are you gonna cook, Daddy?" Kikit asked.

"Sometimes."

"And bake cookies with us?"

"I may leave that to your mother."

"What about my medicine?"

"What about it?" he asked.

"Who'll make sure it's here?"

"I will."

Her little face crumpled then. Tears welled and spilled. She rocked on her knees, back and forth, and raised a fist to her eye. "I didn't mean to get thick I didn't mean to really I didn't."

"Oh God," I whispered and dragged Johnny with me to the table so that I could hold Kikit, too. "You didn't do anything, baby. Shhh. This isn't your fault."

"I got thick—*sick*—and didn't have my medicine—so he got mad at you—"

"No, baby, no, it wasn't that, don't ever think it was that." I had picked up on her rocking, and while Johnny wasn't exactly rocking with us, he wasn't fighting my hold. "This *thing* between Daddy and me is just between Daddy and me. It's been building for a long time, maybe even longer than you've been alive. We aren't working well together, Daddy and I. We aren't making each other happy. You guys make us happy. But we should be doing more for each other, me and Daddy, and we're not."

"I want you to live here," Kikit said. Her voice was muffled against my breast, her face warm and wet and nuzzling.

"I can't do that now. But you'll see, I'll find someplace to live that you'll just love."

"In Santa Fe?" asked my son, clearly grappling with the puzzle, trying to get the pieces to fit.

"No, sweetie, not in Santa Fe, that's much too far away. I was thinking about something five, maybe ten minutes from here. How does that sound?" It sounded good to me. "And I won't even be traveling so much. Wait'll you see, I'll be with you more than I was before." Especially once we appealed Selwey's decision and got the court order reversed.

"What about Thanksgiving?" he asked.

"Hmm. I haven't given that much thought." It came out sounding like we were off on a new adventure, which wasn't all that bad. The children could relate to adventures. "We could go to Cleveland to be with Grandma. Or—what do you think we should do?"

"Have it here like we always do."

"We could do *two*," Kikit said, hopeful eyes rising from the chenille of my sweater.

"We could," I conceded. Not that I would be at two. There would be Dennis and his parents and the children at one, and me and the children and Brody and Jill and all the family-less friends I usually invited to ours, at the other. Of course, I had no idea where ours would be, or how it would feel to be in a strange place without Dennis, without my mother. And when I thought of having to tell all those friends I would invite that we were separated, I felt a major ache.

The court session had been real. Telling Kikit and Johnny was real. Now friends? And Connie—*how am I going to tell Connie?*

Thanksgiving. Christmas. Johnny's birthday, then Kikit's. They were all family occasions, but it struck me—shook me to think—that they would no longer be the same.

"Mommy," Kikit whined, her head free of my sweater now, "tomorrow is look-see at ballet. Will you bring cupcakes for afterward?"

Tomorrow was Tuesday. Not Wednesday, like the judge had said. If Dennis was willing, we could change days for this week, and the judge wouldn't be any the wiser.

But Kikit wasn't done. She was hanging on me now. "And Wednesday is parents' day at the library. I told Lily we would take her, 'cause her mom has to work."

So much for switching days. But I could do both.

No, I couldn't. Dennis told me that in the next instant with the subtlest shake of his head. It was accompanied by the kind of look that warned what would happen if I argued, the same kind of thing that would happen if I wasn't gone by four.

No, I didn't want him calling Jack Mulroy. No, I *didn't* want to be charged with contempt of court. What I wanted was a reversal of the ruling against me. Carmen was working on that. The best I could do to help was to be a model of obedience.

It was now three-thirty-five.

"I'll do Wednesday at the library," I said. "Daddy will do look-see at ballet tomorrow."

"But I want *you* to. The mother sets it all up, you know, on the table in the back room?"

"Tell you what. I'll buy the cupcakes and Daddy can bring them."

"It's not the *same*," she cried, then went all round-eyed. "And Thursday, what about Thursday? Thursday's Halloween. You'll be here for Halloween, won't you? You always take me out, I don't want to go out alone."

"Johnny's going alone this year," Dennis said. "He'll take you with him."

"Da-ad," Johnny protested, and I agreed. Kikit had to be watched every minute to make sure she didn't pop something into her mouth that would make her sick. It was unfair to ask Johnny to do that.

"I don't want to go with Johnny," Kikit declared. "I want *Mommy*."

"*I'll* take you," Dennis said.

That gave her pause. There was a tentative, "You will?" Then, still tentative, "So Mommy'll stay home and give out candy?"

"Either Mommy or Grandma."

"I want Mommy to. You'll do it, Mommy, won't you?"

Of course, I would. I always loved Halloween, bought candy weeks in advance, made special costumes. This year's were done— Kikit's a mouse, Johnny's a pirate. Of *course*, I would be part of the ritual.

"She may not be able to," Dennis said.

Kikit turned on him. "Why *not*?"

He hitched his chin my way. Kikit looked up at me. I was trying to decide whether to argue with Dennis, or to tell the children the truth or lie, when she pulled back. "Is it because you
don't want to live here anymore?"

"I do—"

"You don't *love* us anymore," she wailed.

When I reached for her, she skittered away. Her mouth was
turned down, her chin quivering. Releasing Johnny, I came out of
my seat, caught her, and pulled her into my arms. I held her there,
tightly, tightly, even when she squirmed to escape.

It was a minute before I cleared the emotion that clogged my
throat. Then my voice was hoarse, fierce as I bent over the top of her
head. "I love you dearly. Never, never think that I don't. You and
your brother mean more to me than anything else in the world."

"So why can't you be here?" came the high-pitched wail from my
middle.

"Because the judge says I can't. He says you'll be with Daddy
for most of the week and with me for Wednesdays and Saturdays, just until we get all this worked out."

"But *why*?"

"I don't know, baby," I crooned against the warmth of her hair, "I
don't know, but that's what he said, so that's what we have to do."

It was nearing three-forty-five. Time was running out.

"But I'll miss you."

"Bah," I teased. "You'll be too busy to miss me, and whenever
you do, you'll call me. You'll call me whenever you want, night or
day, *both* of you." I looked around to include Johnny, only he
wasn't there.

My eyes flew to Dennis. He shot a thumb toward the hall.
Furious that he had just let the child go, I scooped Kikit up and
deposited her in her father's arms. "Hold tight, baby," I told her in
a tone far gentler than the look I gave Dennis.

Johnny was in his room, sitting with his back to the head-

board of the bed. The way he stared at me as I crossed to him
nearly broke my heart. I sat and took his hand. He took it back
and made a fist against the comforter. I had to settle for holding
his wrist.

"This isn't what I want, Johnny. If I had my druthers, things
would be different. But I don't have my druthers. Things are out
of my hands."

"Moms stay with kids."

"Usually. Not always. Especially now that so many mothers
work."

"So it's easier for you to let Dad stay here? So you can work?"

"No. You kids come before my work. You always have. Dad is
staying because the judge said so."

"Since when do judges tell parents what to do?"

He was right. "It's a long story, sweetie. Complicated."

He crossed his arms on his chest and wore a look that I suspected I had worn myself more than once, when I wanted an explanation for something I felt was wrong. Another cliché wouldn't do.

"The judge thought," I tried, "that, with Grandma being so
sick, Daddy would be able to give you and Kikit more attention.
It's just for now."

"For how long?"

"Not long."

"*How* long?"

"I don't know. It could be a few days, or a week, or a month."

"Then what?"

"Then, whatever we decide is best for you and Kikit."

I heard a noise and looked back to see Dennis in the doorway.
He was still holding Kikit. "Everything okay here?" he asked.

Johnny didn't say a word.

"Everything is fine," I said. But it wasn't. Kikit's face was
streaked with tears. Johnny looked like he was crying inside. And
I was bleeding, positively bleeding from the soul.

It was three-fifty.

Johnny's arms were no longer folded, but he continued to stare. I took his hand again, relieved when he allowed it, and tried to mold it to my grasp. "The important thing to remember is what I told Kikit. We'll talk on the phone all the time. I'll go to the library with Kikit on Wednesday and pick you up after practice, and then we'll do something together for dinner. Hey. There's a big game Saturday, isn't there?"

He didn't say anything at first. Then he shrugged.

"Can I come?"

There was another pause, another shrug. His hand lay limp in mine. I gave it an encouraging squeeze.

"When can we see where you're gonna live?" Kikit asked.

"As soon as I find a place."

"So we'll have two homes?"

"Two homes."

Her eyes lit. "Can we build one in the tree, you know, the one I always climb?"

"No, we cannot."

"Then at Brody's." She came alive then. "That's the *best* idea, Mommy. You can live at Brody's."

I didn't look at Dennis. "Uh, sorry, baby, but that's out."

"Why not?"

"Because Brody's house belongs to Brody. I need something for me."

"He wouldn't mind it if you stayed with him. He loves it when we come." She gasped, put her hand to Dennis's cheek and said, "*I* know what to do for dinner. Let's get Brody to make us steak soup!"

I refused to look at Dennis, but concentrated solely on my children during those last few minutes that I had with them. Kikit found a dozen different ways to ask the same questions, most of which had to do with how she could reach me if she needed me. I tried to be reassuring, directing my answers as much to Johnny as to her, but I felt as though my insides were being pulled, pulled, pulled slowly away from my body. The feeling increased when Dennis started looking at his watch. When he set Kikit down and came toward me—I think he would have taken my arm if I hadn't risen on my own—I felt a tearing.

"Say good-bye to your mother now," he told the children.

Fighting tears, I reached for Johnny. He didn't budge.

"Please, John," I whispered. "I need your help."

He let me draw him into a hug. I swallowed against his head and managed a wobbly, "I'll talk with you later, okay?"

"Hold me, Mommy," Kikit cried. "Hold *me*."

Drawing back, I kissed Johnny's forehead, whispered, "I love you, sweetie," and turned to Kikit. She was in my arms in an instant, holding me so tightly she trembled. Or was the trembling mine? No matter. We sat there together on Johnny's bed, holding each other, not saying a word.

"Claire," Dennis said.

I kissed her and whispered, "Gotta go, baby."

Her arms tightened. "No, Mommy, don't."

Dennis scooped her up from behind, breaking her hold of me. The sight of her reaching for me, arms and legs, even while Dennis drew her away broke my heart.

"Wednesday," was all I could manage, and that, brokenly. I didn't look back again, didn't think I could survive a greater level of loss than that which was already shredding me to bits. I ran down the stairs, grabbed my purse and keys, and ran out the front door to the car.

Kikit must have escaped Dennis, because no sooner had I backed out of the driveway, then she bolted from the front door and began running toward the car. Dennis caught her when she was halfway across the yard, swept her up in his arms, and turned back to the house.

I nearly stopped. That I didn't was only partly because of Dennis's threat. The rest had to do with knowing that prolonging the parting would only make it worse.

It was bad enough without that. Nothing that had come before had prepared me for the pain of walking out of that house and leaving my children behind. As symbolic moments went, it was brutal. As pearls went, it was black.

My last view of the house that day, burned indelibly in my mind, was of Dennis's rigid back, Kikit's furious feet kicking over his arm, and, off to the side and alone, my first-born, John, staring off down the street after me as I drove away.

I went to the office straight from there, because I was too upset to go anywhere else. Carmen had said I couldn't live with Brody, so I wouldn't, but this was where I worked. What with avoiding unnecessary travel for a while, I would be spending more time than ever here. Neither the court, nor Dennis, nor Carmen could deny me that.

Anyway, Brody wasn't around. He was on the Vineyard negotiating with contractors to work on our store there. A fierce tropical storm had blown through in early October. We needed a new roof and siding. He had wanted to postpone the trip after learning the results of the hearing, but I had insisted he go.

I was half sorry now. I kept reliving those final moments, seeing that final scene over and over and over again. I could have used his company.

The place was deserted. I left the car and wandered through the lowering dusk to the seaward ledge. The tide was in. Below me, beyond rocks and sand, it rushed forward, fell back, rushed forward, fell back. Had the wind been up, there would have been explosions of spume, but it was as calm a night as the ocean saw, breezy was all.

I held myself there on the high rocks and listened to the rhythm of the surf. But the hollowness that I'd felt at the house had started to swell, and the sight of Kikit's flailing legs and Johnny's aloneness haunted me. Though I wore a sweater, jeans, and a long gabardine coat that should have protected me from the breeze, I felt chilled. Staring out at the endless sea, I felt pitifully small.

Back at the office, soft night lights burned, the glimmer of sconces by the door, the pale glow of others inside. I let myself in and dropped my coat on the divan by the reception desk. Then I stood in the dimness and looked around.

How many other times I had done the same, feeling pride at what WickerWise had become. I felt none of that now. Wicker-Wise seemed a liability, a reason for Dennis to rebel, an excuse for the judge to take away my kids.

Knowing that the office held no lure for me, I headed for the workroom. The rocker that I had been working on was there, neat holes where I had removed broken pieces of wicker. There were more to be removed before I began the reweaving, but I didn't feel like doing that either. I had gone one too many nights with too little sleep, one too many hours with too little hope. I felt drained of life, beaten down and weak.

Without turning on a light, I made my way up the open staircase that hugged the wall. The storage loft extended over half of the workroom and the entirety of the office space, and was festooned with skylights that, at their lowest, offered night glitters from boats, houses ashore, even the lighthouse several miles up the coast. The moon was half shrouded in clouds, silver scallops around billows of slate. Whitecaps on the ocean came and went.

I stepped carefully over and around stacked pieces until I reached a long wicker sofa. I had found it several years before at a yard sale that my Kansas City franchisee had taken me to. Its cushions were long lost; without them, its enveloping quality was even more marked.

That enveloping quality drew me to it now. Its seat was deep, its arms broad, its back tall to the shoulders, angled behind that for neck support.

It creaked when I sat, the soft, easy creak of time and heart. There was more creaking when I wedged myself in a corner and kicked off my flats, more creaking when I snagged a bedraggled afghan from the perambulator that stood nearby. Knees bent, heels touching my bottom, I covered myself and closed my eyes.

The smell of old was there in the loft, worn wicker that life had touched with sun, flowers, dust and rain. I tried to put a story to the sofa—imagined it in a Southern parlor under ladies in lovely lawn dresses, or on a wide verandah overlooking a rolling acre of newly cut grass. I tried to hear gentle voices, soft laughter, sweet promises, but all I heard were Kikit's screams as Dennis carried her into the house and Johnny's silence. My imagination was shot, my heart fractured, all of me dead tired.

I must have fallen asleep, because the view from the skylights was different when next I looked. More lights had gone on up the coast in pin-pointed clusters, and a half-baked moon had cleared the clouds. I heard the *shoooo-sha-shoooo-sha* of the ocean and something else—a car, probably what had woken me. Since Brody wasn't due back until the next day, I guessed it was Dennis checking to see where I'd gone.

A flare of anger held me where I was. If he wanted to think I was in Brody's bed, let him. He wouldn't get a picture this time. Besides, the judge had already ruled against me. I had nothing to lose.

I heard the door open in the reception area, heard footsteps, a pause, then, "Claire?"

Not Dennis at all. Brody.

My anger held. He was supposed to be on the Vineyard seeing to things that I couldn't.

"Claire?" Closer now, at the door of the workroom, then inside. *"Claire?"*

"Yes," I said and tightened the tattered afghan around me.

I heard him cross the workroom floor and start up the stairs. "What are you doing up here?"

"What are you doing *back* here?"

He materialized at the top, shadowed but large. "I got to Woods Hole. There was a problem with the ferry, so I turned around and came back. I didn't want to be there anyway."

So much for relying on my right-hand man. "You had meetings planned."

"They'll hold."

"That work needs to be done."

"It'll hold, Claire," he repeated and began picking his way through the rubble of treasures to my sofa. The closer he came, the more detailed he was in the thin blue of the moon. "Why are you up here?"

"Where else should I be? I'm homeless."

"Not homeless. You have my house."

"*Mi casa es su casa?* Yeah, well, that's what got me into this mess. No"—I took a quick breath—"it's *men* who got me into this mess. My mother had it right. She used to talk about a defective gene, what with my father dying and leaving a mess and Rona's two husbands—and I always argued against it, but, damn it, here I am, in a *major* mess, thanks to men. Dennis, the judge, even Johnny—Johnny'll be a problem, you mark my words, he won't take this as easily as Kikit—so *what is it* about the male of the species? Power? Ego? Innate weakness?"

"Hey. I came back here because I was worried about you."

"God *save* me from chivalrous men. No, don't sit there," I cried when he lowered himself to my sofa. He raised himself fast. "This is my space."

He moved away, bumped into something.

"Be *careful*, Brody. You're kicking things that are worth millions."

He had the good grace not to contradict me, though we both

knew "millions" was an exaggeration. Instead, with caution, he asked, "Has something else happened?"

"No. Just the same old shit, the same *new* shit." I could have told him about that moment when I had driven away from my children, and he would have bled for me. But, damn it, I didn't want sympathy just then. I wanted *justice*.

I hugged my knees while he drew up a ladder-back chair that awaited recaning. He slouched into it, crossed his arms and his ankles.

"Do you know how bad that is for the chair?" I asked.

I got no response at first. Then I heard a chuckle. Granted, it was gentle. Still.

"You think it's funny? This is my *livelihood*, Brody. Clearly, I can't rely on my husband anymore, though God knows I haven't been able to do that in years, but at least there was an illusion of it. Well, that's gone. For all I know, he'll sock me so hard for alimony that I'll be forced to drain every reserve I have, and then, and *then*," my imagination was back in force, "if the market turns bad and we have to declare bankruptcy, I'll have *nothing*, so it could be that refinishing this stuff will be the only thing standing between me and the local soup kitchen."

Brody snickered.

"And you sit there and laugh," I groused. "Well, what should I have expected? Compassion? Understanding? *Respect?* That's it. The problem is respect. Men choke when it comes to giving it to a woman, because maybe, just maybe, it means she's stronger than he is, and that is *so threatening* he can't bear it, but it's the truth. Women *are* stronger. We create and construct and accommodate, and look at the world with wider eyes than men do. We keep trying harder, because it isn't an ego thing for us. It's survival. And necessity. And good common sense. Good *God*, it's amazing, men have always let me down."

"Not me."

"Yes, you," I shouted, because it felt good to shout.

Brody sat up and leaned forward, all innocence. "What did *I* do?"

"You *hugged* me. Right there at the window, in full view of anyone who was outside. Didn't it occur to you someone might be watching?"

"Frankly, no."

"Well, it should have."

"If *you* knew, why didn't you warn me?"

"Because I was upset. And besides, I'm a woman. Women trust people. Women give people the benefit of the doubt, rather than assuming the worst. It didn't occur to me that someone was out there. But you're a man. You should have *known* what Dennis was capable of."

I heard the creak of Brody's chair.

"Don't come near me," I said against my knees. "I want to be alone."

"I don't believe you. I think you want to let off steam, and you have every right, but I'd rather be sitting beside you, than opposite you when you do it."

"Don't *sit* here," I warned as he lowered himself to the sofa. I straightened my legs and pressed the soles of my feet against his thighs to keep him at that distance at least, but with an easy scoop he had my feet in his lap. "Brody," I protested.

"I've never heard you like this. A new Claire."

"I'm human," I grumbled. "I have fears and vulnerabilities, just like the rest of the world. I bleed when I'm slashed, and I hurt when I'm kicked. If I want to spit and yell, I will. Damn it, if anyone has a right, I do. I've been royally *fucked over*."

It wasn't until he began rubbing my feet that I realized how cold they were, and then something about the warmth of his hands, something about his presence, even his amusement, because it held such affection, got to me. Absurdly, I started to cry.

When he pulled on my legs to draw me closer, I kicked out against him, but with that small movement went the last of my anger. I didn't fight when he pulled a second time, first my legs, then my arms, until he had me turned and drawn to his chest.

I cried for a long time, belly-deep sobs that gradually shallowed and slowed, lulled by the motion of his hand on my shoulder, my back, beneath my hair. In time the tears stopped, but I didn't move away. I was too tired, and he felt too good against my battered psyche.

"Oh Brody," I sniffled a whisper at one point, "I don't know what to do. I have never felt so helpless in my entire life."

If he answered, I didn't hear, because within seconds, the strain I'd been under and sheer exhaustion combined with the security he offered and his warmth put me to sleep.

When I awoke, we were sprawled on the sofa with our arms and legs entwined, my head on his chest, and his heart beating too fast by my ear. I knew right away that something was different, and it wasn't just that runaway heartbeat. It might have been the way my hand was splayed over his ribs, or the way his arm held me to him. More likely it was our lower bodies. My thigh lay over his, high up, over an erection that was as impressive as it was startling.

I drew my leg back, pushed myself up, and looked down at him. His eyes were wide open, clear as day, though the moon was lower and dimmer. He didn't speak, nor did I. Nor did either of us move. Shock, I told myself. Embarrassment, I told myself. But there was intrigue, too, because I liked the way he felt and wanted to feel more.

That was when I knew I was in trouble.

Eight

Early Tuesday morning, I called the house. Dennis picked up the phone after a single ring, said that he was in the middle of making breakfast, didn't I have any maple syrup in the house, and I'd have to call the kids later. When I asked if they were still upset, he said they weren't and hung up the phone. I thought of calling back, then thought better of it. I was furious that he had hung up on me, and feared I would say something I would regret. Better, I decided, to have Carmen take up the issue of phone calls with Art Heuber.

Next, I called my mother. She sounded frail and discouraged. No, she wasn't hungry for breakfast. No, she didn't want to watch the *Today* show. No, she wasn't interested in having someone wheel her to the solarium. When I suggested that we talk more when she was feeling better, she perked up and asked me about work. I gave her a preview of the sales meeting I was leading that morning in our Essex store, told her about the line I was introducing to our staff, and the sales rep I was bringing along to speak. I kept an eye on the clock, not for the sake of the meeting, as much as for the sake of the third call I wanted to make.

It was to the school, and my timing was right. I caught both of the children's teachers while they were still in the teachers' lounge. These women saw my children every day, and I trusted them. I felt they should know of the change at home. I didn't go into detail, shared only as much as I needed to to ensure that sensitive adults would keep an eye on my kids.

Finally, I called Carmen's office and left word where I would be at roughly what time. She had filed the Motion for Reconsideration the afternoon before and was expecting Selwey's clerk to notify her about a hearing. That hearing would be no earlier than Friday, to allow time for Dennis and his lawyer to be notified and prepare.

I was off the phone, dressed for work, and at the store with ten minutes to spare. Sales meetings were a weekly ritual in all our stores. Lasting anywhere from thirty to forty-five minutes, they gave each manager an opportunity to pass on product information, push new designs, and discuss new groupings to her entire staff in one fell swoop. I led the meetings in Essex whenever I could. I liked being with my staff, liked sharing the excitement that came with healthy forward movement. If that excitement was forced this morning, few knew it. I talked for ten minutes about a new line that would be arriving after the first of the year, showed samples of the various finishes and fabrics offered with it, then passed off to the sales rep who had come to pitch a second line that we were also introducing. By the time he was done, it was time to open the store.

Ducking out as only the president of the company could do without a twinge of guilt, I drove across town to meet with Cynthia Harris. Cynthia was the real-estate broker who had originally helped us buy our house. Working with her was time-effective; she quickly grasped what her client wanted and showed only houses that fit the bill. Ten years ago, I had been pregnant with Johnny, spending six hours a day at my first WickerWise and hours more seeing to Dennis's needs. I couldn't possibly house hunt full-time then.

Time was scarce now in a different way, but scarce nonetheless, and my order was a big one. I wanted a short-term rental that was equidistant to the kids, the office, and the store. It didn't have to be large, but it had to have charm. It had to lend itself to wicker furniture. It had to have appealing outdoor space.

I watched Cynthia browse through her listings. She rejected one after another with a grimace here, a headshake there. "Too far away," she would say, or, "No land." She kept returning to study one, frown, move on, then return again a short time later. Finally I asked what it was.

"Not a rental," she said, but she didn't turn away from it this time, simply left the listing on her desk and grew pensive. At one point she swiveled her chair and leaned toward the file cabinet, caught herself and sat back again.

"Strictly for sale?" I asked.

"Uh-huh."

"Are the owners living there now?"

Cynthia shook her head. "They moved south. The place has been on the market for a while. It's a special kind of place and needs a special kind of buyer. There haven't been many nibbles."

But something interested her. I could see it. "Tell me about it. Just for kicks."

She did go for the file cabinet then. Seconds later, when she opened a folder and I caught sight of the color photograph inside, I knew what it was that kept drawing her back.

Reaper Head was a small, egg-shaped island connected to the mainland by a causeway. A newly automated lighthouse stood at its wide end, private homes were strewn among pines through its middle. At its narrow end stood a second lighthouse. This one had been built in the mid-1800s and relieved of service a century later, at which time it had been bought by the adventuresome young couple that, no longer young, had just moved south.

Made of fieldstone, it stood three stories high and was broader than most lighthouses, more a thimble than a needle. Its entrance was through the keeper's cottage, a single-story structure also of fieldstone, that housed an eat-in kitchen, an open living area, and a bathroom. Through an archway, the ground floor of the tower offered a den in the round with a spiral staircase at its heart. Up the staircase, the second floor was divided into three arced rooms and a second bathroom. The top floor, originally the lantern room, was narrower than the lower floors but bounded all the way around by windows and, outside, through a door as well-insulated as the windows if the muted sound of the sea was any judge, a railed walk.

There wasn't a stick of furniture in the place. The stuccoed walls needed painting, the wood floors needed sanding, the windows needed washing. I guessed that the Franklin stove in the keeper's cottage might need replacing. But the kitchen was state-of-the-art and polished, as were the bathrooms. There was no mildew smell, just that of stone and, faintly, from beyond, wisps of pine and the sea. The place felt warm, no hint of a draft when I put my hand to the window. And the lantern room—what could I say?

"Bingo." A helpless smile, a flicker of hope.

Cynthia smiled back. "Uh-huh."

"Not a rental?"

"That's what the owners say. I could give them a call and make an outrageous bid for the use of the place for a month, but I don't think they'll bite. Aside from redecorating needs, it's in good shape. They wouldn't trust what a renter might do."

"I'm not any old renter."

"Maybe not, but they love this place. They'd be here still, if it weren't for his arthritis. They want to sell to someone who'll love it too, and they're prepared to wait. Money isn't an issue. They're not hurting."

That was clear. The asking price was reasonable. I could afford it.

I walked through the place again, picturing wicker, wood, and rattan, some new, some antiques that I would take from the big house, picturing art on the walls and fabric above the windows and nothing, absolutely nothing blocking that all-around view from the top. Johnny and Kikit would love that room, though I wouldn't give it to them. Their bedrooms would be on the second floor and seafaring in decor. The lantern room would be mine.

Even if the order against me was reversed that very day. It wouldn't be, of course, though it might be by week's end. Still, I wanted the lantern room.

"I must be crazy," I said when I rejoined Cynthia in the kitchen, but somehow this seemed the most sane thing that had happened since I had returned from Cleveland five days before. Everything about the lighthouse was right—from the fact that it was a short ten minutes from the children, the office, and the store, to the fact that it was the perfect size, to the fact that it was unoccupied, unfurnished, and in need of little more than cosmetics to aid its charm. But there was more. It was a challenge at a time when I desperately needed a diversion.

"And at the end of the month?" Cynthia cautioned. "Will it be right back on the market? I do feel an obligation to the owners. They want a permanent resident here. What'll you do with the place once things are settled at home?"

"I'll keep it," I answered, perhaps impractically, but I didn't care. I had spent my life being practical, being rational and responsible, and look what had happened, thank you very much. If I was back in the big house by the end of the week, I could use this as my own private hideaway. I could use it as an office or a workshop. I could use it as a beach house. It was an investment. If worst came to worst, I could always rent it out.

My gut said I wouldn't regret the purchase. That was good enough for me.

The only condition I put on buying the old Reaper Head lighthouse was that I had to have immediate access. I wanted to start sanding and painting and cleaning, wanted to actually sleep there that night. As fate had it, the attorney for the owners was a local man familiar with my business. He readily vouched for my character—what a balm *that* was, after the battering I'd taken, another something telling me that buying the lighthouse was right—and the owners, contacted on the phone, agreed. I spent the rest of the day finalizing the sale, dashing between Cynthia's office, my own, and the bank, making phone call after phone call, setting things in motion.

More than one of those phone calls was to Carmen, because no matter how diverting buying the lighthouse was, I couldn't forget why I was doing it. No matter how caught up I was at any given moment, waiting in the wings were thoughts of what the children were doing right then. Carmen hadn't heard from Selwey's clerk by noon, or by two. She promised to talk with Art about giving me unlimited phone access to the children. She had already talked with Dean Jenovitz and directed me to give him a call. At the advice of his voice mail, I left my name, the number of my cell phone, and an offer to meet with him wherever and whenever suited him best.

I called the phone company to have a line connected at the lighthouse. I called a floor man, a painter, and a window washer.

I called Dennis to remind him to bring cupcakes to Kikit's ballet look-see, and kept the conversation brief and to the point. I was angry still, didn't really care to be talking with him at all.

I didn't tell him about my new home. Nor did I offer to buy the cupcakes. If I was on my own, so was he.

I would have liked to share my news with Brody, but he was off to the Vineyard again. There had been a faint tension between us that morning, so we had kept our breakfast talk light and business-related. I sensed he was as unsettled by what had happened on the sofa in the loft as I was, and as ill-prepared to deal with it just then. That was why I planned to sleep in the lighthouse that night.

Carmen called shortly after four to say that Selwey had denied the Motion for Reconsideration without a hearing.

"Can he do that?" I asked, appalled. It was one thing to argue and lose, another to be denied the opportunity to argue, period.

"He can. I'm not surprised. It's in character. So I'm preparing a Motion to Recuse. We'll ask that he disqualify himself from this case because of bias. It'll take more time to put this one together. I'll need to go over everything he said during yesterday's hearing and even go back to earlier cases over which he presided. But I'm aiming to get it filed by Thursday."

"Is there anything I can do to help?"

"Keep your spirits up. That's all."

The lighthouse did it. Moving in enough so that I could sleep there that night kept me busy until well past sunset. Then, perched on a stool, eating pad thai from a takeout container, I called the kids. Kikit answered the phone.

"I've been waiting for you to call, Mommy. Where are you?"

The sweet sound of her voice was an instant balm, a far cry from the screams that had reverberated in my ears since the afternoon before. She wasn't crying now. She wasn't whining or angry. She had bounced back, resilient as children were. I never failed to be amazed. And relieved.

"I'm in my new place," I said.

"What new place? Where is it? Is it near us? Come get me now, Mommy. I want to see."

"You can't see now. It's too late. You'll see it tomorrow."

"Where *is* it? What's it like? Will I have my own room?"

"Yes," I said, dipping my chopsticks into the container, "and I'll tell you the rest as soon as you get your brother to pick up so he can hear it too. Where is he?"

"Upstairs. Want to hear the coolest thing? Know what kind of cupcakes Daddy brought to ballet? *Hostess* ones."

The chopsticks had noodles halfway to my mouth. I returned them to the container. "Yuk!"

"I was thinking that, too, when he took them out of the bag, but they were really soft and squooshy, and everyone *loved* 'em. I'm glad for Daddy. He was feeling funny, I think, because it was him and all the moms at the look-see. Mommy, I want to hear about your *place*."

"Tell your brother to pick up upstairs, so I can tell you both." Hostess cupcakes? Had Dennis actually stood there tearing open two-pack after two-pack? I was intrigued.

"Johnny," Kikit screamed, nearly popping my eardrum. I held the phone away while she yelled, *"Pick up, it's Mommy,"* which was followed quickly by, *"You* have *to, she wants to* talk *to you!"* then, to me, "He says he's busy. What a grouch. He wouldn't talk to Daddy, either. So *tell* me, Mommy. I'm here and I *want* to talk."

My heart ached for Johnny, standing alone watching me drive away, sitting alone in his bedroom.

But denying Kikit would only compound the wrong. So I told her about the lighthouse, about the room that would be hers, about the view from the lantern room. Her excitement was precious. I was sure Johnny would feel it, too, but when I had her call him again, he still refused to talk.

What to do? Short of making a big deal about it to Dennis, which would likely make things worse, I was helpless, which brought back the whole of my predicament in ways that preoccupation with the lighthouse had freed me from earlier. Again I felt the anger, the sorrow, the fear, all made worse by the distance at which I was being kept. After working so hard to make a secure and happy home for my kids, I felt thwarted.

Minutes later, Dennis called. Without so much as a hello, he said, "You bought a lighthouse? Lighthouses are cold and damp. If they're not surrounded by water, they're damn close to it."

I hadn't expected that he would love the place, but the force of his censure took me by surprise. It was in stark contrast to the excitement we had shared buying the colonial. On the day we passed papers, he had given me a huge hug in the lawyer's office, followed by a fancy lunch, and on the day we moved in, he had actually carried me over the threshold. Such a romantic gesture. I had loved it.

Now his displeasure flowed, rivers of cold water dousing the memory. "What is this, a cockamamie scheme to win over the kids? Give them something that's fun and irresponsible and *dangerous*? Right on the water, with winter nearly here," he sputtered. "That's brilliant, Claire. Wait till the judge hears about this."

I was in the kitchen still, trying to finish my first dinner in my new home and resentful of his intrusion. I told myself to be pleasant. Carmen had warned against acrimony. *Leave the tough stuff to me,* she had said. *You need to stay on peaceful terms with the man who has custody of your children.* But I couldn't not respond to his charge.

"I'll bring pictures for the judge myself this time," I said. "This is a great place." I slid the last of a spring roll into my mouth and talked right through it. Dennis wasn't spoiling *my* dinner. "It's warm and bright. It's farther from the water than my office is. You've never complained about the kids spending time there."

"What possessed you to rent a lighthouse?"

"I'm not renting," I said, delighted to feel in control again, "I'm buying."

"*Buying.* Talk about binge spending—"

"Whoa," I cut in, all nonchalance gone. "I need a place to live because, thanks to you, I've been kicked out of the first place I bought. So I found a place that I like, and that, yes, the children will like. That was a priority, because I want to please them, want to cheer them up, because, thanks to you again, they're facing a major adjustment in their lives. I'll do anything I can to make it easier for them. If finding a home that diverts them will do it, fine."

"I'm sure that's just the beginning. Kikit said you're going to let her decorate. I can see it now—expensive little dolls, expensive little furnishings, anything and everything her little heart desires— you're trying to buy her love, it's common when parents separate."

I nearly laughed, the charge was so absurd. "I don't need to buy her love."

"Talk about *me* harming the kids. I'd be careful what you do, Claire. They'll ask for the world if you give them a chance. They'll be spoiled rotten in a flash. You bought them a lighthouse? Incredible."

My anger flared. "I bought *me* a lighthouse. I bought it because *I* love it. Me, just me. No one else."

"Not Brody?"

I took a steadying breath. "Brody is out of town. Brody doesn't know I looked at it, doesn't know I bought it. Brody is not an issue here. He never was." I was trying to contain myself, but I had spent too many long hours since last Thursday asking questions I couldn't answer. Pulling a foot up on the stool and cinching my knee close, I asked, "Just out of curiosity, how long do you allege this affair has been going on?"

"For all I know, it's been years. For all I know, it started when the two of you paired up for work. For all *I* know, my partnership with Brody fell apart *because* he took up with you."

"Don't flatter yourself, Dennis. That partnership fell apart because your investments were lousy. Brody was the marketing half. He busted his butt trying to keep clients from jumping ship, but there was only so much he could do when your deal-making failed. He stuck with that partnership longer than another man would have."

"It was guilt. He knew where he was going when he quit."

"Sure he did." I released my leg and stood. "Because he'd been working with me to support himself, working two jobs, practically."

"And dying to get out of mine for months before he finally did."

"He knew a sinking ship when he saw one," I said from the window now. The view was lovely, open ocean with its muted roar, a little wild like I felt. "He spent those months trying to convince you of that, but you wouldn't let go, wouldn't let go."

"Because that firm was my baby. I was the rainmaker."

"*Please*, Dennis," I cried. Fine and dandy for Carmen to advise restraint, but she wasn't the one hearing absurdities. She wasn't the one whose anger bordered on rage. "Brody was the one who set the whole thing up. He got the office, the name, the logo. He was the one who gathered the capital for your ventures, but when those ventures failed, what could he do? If he'd been ego-driven, he'd have demanded his fair share of the assets and then some, and if he'd done that, you'd never have been able to go out on your own."

"So I went out on my own, and he stole my wife."

"Why do you keep *saying* that? If you honestly believed it, how could you have lived with me so long?"

"Because *I didn't know*."

"So how'd you find out?"

He paused, then muttered, "It just became obvious."

"Lipstick on his collar? Love notes in my purse? Romantic messages on our answering machine? Or was it your lawyer, Dennis? Not Art Heuber. Phoebe Lowe. Did she put a bug in your ear about Brody and me?"

"She's handled cases like ours before," he said, but a mite defensively. "She's seen everything."

So. I had hit the nail on the head. The satisfaction of it goaded me on—that, and the fact that I was in my very own place. "In, what, seven years of practice? She's quite a veteran. But you didn't answer my question. Was she the one who thought up the idea of Brody and me as a couple? How did you meet her, anyway? And when? Last summer? Last spring? Or has it been going on for a while? A year? Maybe two? And what *is* it between you, anyway? A professional relationship, or something more?"

"That's none of your business. We're separated. I can do what I want."

"She's attractive, Dennis. You make a dynamite couple. Is that what this is all about, you having a mid-life itch that Phoebe Lowe wants to scratch?"

"You're a shrew," he said and hung up the phone.

When the phone rang again five minutes later, I figured it was Dennis with a second wind and nearly didn't answer it. Then I thought of the other people it might be—most importantly, one of the kids—and I couldn't let it ring.

"Hello?"

"Hey."

Brody. I let out a breath, habit telling me I could relax, then drew it in again, because relaxation wasn't all I felt. Somewhere way deep inside was an illicit little hum. I wondered if he felt it, too. A single *hey* didn't tell me a lot. "Where are you?"

"Home. The Vineyard's taken care of. Where are *you*?" He

sounded easy, casual. Either he wasn't feeling that hum or had decided to ignore it.

I followed his lead and took a deep breath. "I'm at the old Reaper Head lighthouse."

There was silence, then a warm chuckle. "Care to elaborate on that?"

I did care to elaborate, went on for a good ten minutes describing my surroundings—walked through them as I spoke—because I think I'd been wanting to tell him all day, maybe even more than I'd wanted to tell the kids. His reaction was adult. His approval came from a different source.

I knew he would love the sound of the place, and he did. I knew he would understand why I'd bought it, would see the challenge in it, the artistic possibilities. I knew he would appreciate my need to thumb my nose at conventionality. Maybe he would even understand my need to be by the sea.

By the time I was done with my description, I was in the lantern room, standing in the dark, looking out. The view at night was spectacular, a little frightening, a little awe-inspiring, a little lonely. I was glad he was on the phone.

Then again, maybe I was lonely *because* he was on the phone.

I hoped not.

But when I pictured him, I felt that same little hum.

Brody? Brody and *me*?

It was an intriguing thought. A little odd after all these years. A little funny. A little *embarrassing*. Still, intriguing.

"Okay," I summed up my thoughts on buying the lighthouse, "so it could be I'll be free to move back to the house by sometime next week, but maybe, just maybe I won't want to. That house was where I lived with Dennis. It's part of a life that he ended. Let *him* live there and pay for the upkeep. It's tainted."

"Is that anger I still hear?"

Oh, it was. Surprising, since I wasn't a chronic brooder or

complainer. A new side of me was emerging. I wasn't sure I liked it, though it was probably healthy enough, given the circumstances. "It's like the anger of years has been packed away and is just now pouring out. Makes me wonder if I loved him at all."

"You did. Otherwise you wouldn't have stayed with him all those years."

But I wasn't sure. I could reminisce all I wanted about one happy time after another that Dennis and I had shared, but the fact was that they had been fewer and farther between in recent years. That first year we met, when our *a capella* group had spent spring break singing for our keep at luxury resorts in Bermuda, Dennis and I had done a duet, backed up by the rest of the group. It was "For All We Know," a song of hope and promise, and we had been the perfect couple to do it, attractive, attracted to each other.

It had been a long time since we had sung together, just the two of us.

I had been raised to believe that marriage was the root of stability, success, happiness. So had I loved Dennis? Or had I loved the institution of marriage and simply accepted him as the price I had to pay to maintain it? I did things like that, made the most of situations that weren't ideal. Buying the Reaper Head lighthouse was a perfect example, a new house as the price for sanity, a *lighthouse* as the price of a smile.

"I think something's wrong with me, Brody. My life is a nightmare. I've been evicted and slandered, my mother is dying and I'm afraid to call her because she won't like what I say unless I lie through my teeth. My sister would jump at the chance to tell me how awful I am, my son won't talk to me, my husband is just waiting for me to trip up—and in spite of it all I had fun this afternoon. I went up and down the aisles of our warehouse, pointing at what I wanted, Bill and Tommy loaded the truck up there and unloaded it here. Granted, I'm talking basics—bedroom stuff, kitchen stuff, a sofa, a couple of chairs—and even that was probably dumb, what with the floor guys sanding tomorrow and the painters coming after that, but I did it anyway."

"Nothing's wrong with you," Brody said. "You needed a break from the mess in your life. You needed to make that place yours. Is it livable?"

"Very. Warm, dry. Marginally empty still, but yes, mine. The view is—how to describe it? I'm up at the top, in a circular space maybe twenty-five feet in diameter, with glass all around. I'm looking in your direction. I think. Wave. No. Come see me?"

It was the most natural thing to say. But the words were no sooner out then I felt another twinge of that illicit little hum. With utter clarity—a memory, but so real—I felt his chest beneath my hand and his arousal beneath my thigh. I felt his warmth and smelled his smell, and liked both, wanted both.

Definitely wrong.

No, not wrong. Forbidden.

"Claire. About last night."

"Don't mention it. Nothing happened."

"Something did."

Oooh, yes, I thought, and the memories sharpened. "I think maybe we should forget that it did, though. Things like that can ruin good friendships. Not to mention the whole custody situation."

Brody was silent for too long.

"Brody?"

"I don't want to forget it happened."

I wrapped an arm around my middle and held on tight.

"And it doesn't have to ruin our friendship," he said. "Not if it's what we both want."

The question was there, begging my denial. But how could I deny the humming inside? It was picking up strength, tingling in my belly in ways Dennis had never quite caused.

"What about Ellen McKenzie?"

"What about her?"

"What's between you two?"

"We're friends. Never lovers."

"I find that hard to believe."

"She's in love with a woman in Paris."

For a minute I couldn't think of a single thing to say. Then I swore softly. "The timing of this stinks."

"Yup. But it's there."

"Why *now*?"

Brody was silent again. Finally he said, "Because you need it now."

"I don't need sex."

"You need holding. Holding is foreplay when the chemistry's right."

I felt a shimmery ache. "Don't say things like that."

"It's true. And if it hadn't happened last night, it would have happened tonight, or tomorrow night. It's there, Claire. Has been for a while."

"It has not."

"Oh, yes, it has."

"I have never felt what I felt last night."

He sputtered out a laugh. "Well, you're right, there. But you've never slept with me before."

"I didn't sleep with you last night," I insisted and had an awful thought. "What if this line is bugged?"

"It's not bugged."

"People hear things on cellular lines. Listen in, sometimes. Be careful. Anything you say may be held against me."

"It already has been," he charged, all humor gone. "You're being punished for doing it anyway, so what's left to lose?"

"My kids!"

"You won't lose your kids. Not once your side of the story comes out. Not once the kids have been interviewed."

Reality returned with a shattering crash, like surf on the rocks below me, and the day's euphoria faded. I looked around my glass room, at the large bed with its wicker frame, the two huge sink-in-able wicker chairs, a wicker dressing table, two wicker dressers, all in a caramel shade to match the cedar holding the thick windows in place. My suitcases were on the floor, which would be carpeted in plum come morning to match the deep green and plum of the billowy down quilt I had bought for the bed. Everything here was mine. Everything was pretty and new and charming.

Still I wondered whether Kikit was in bed and what babies were sleeping with her and if she was singing them to sleep in her child-sweet soprano—my little Annie, singing her favorite, "Tomorrow," pretending that I was listening and beaming with pride. I wondered whether Johnny was lying in his bed looking at the night-glow stars we had put on his ceiling and wanting either to tear them off or ride one to find me and ask for a hug. I felt an awesome emptiness.

Needing to share my worry, I told Brody, "The judge shot us down on the Motion for Reconsideration, so Carmen's filing a Motion to Recuse, but that may not work, either. For each extra step we have to take, the process takes longer. I want something to happen, but nothing is. I called to make an appointment with the psychologist doing the study, and he hasn't called back."

"He will," Brody said.

"When? The sooner we start, the sooner we're done."

"He's probably still seeing clients. He'll call later, or tomorrow."

"What if he hates me?"

"How could he?"

"Selwey did."

"Selwey's a jerk."

"How do we know Jenovitz won't be?"

Brody didn't have an answer for that one, and didn't try making one up, which was another of the things I loved about him. It made what he did say that much more credible.

"Oh, Brody," I whispered and nearly invited him over again. I wanted him to repeat everything he had said about things working out with the kids, and I wanted him to hug me while he did it. I could control that little hum. I didn't have to act on it. Brody was my best friend, and I needed his support. It wasn't fair that I should be deprived of this, too.

Quietly, with a gentle understanding that made me want to cry, he said, "I'll come over in the morning, in daylight. Okay?"

Since Dean Jenovitz was fresh in my mind, I was sure he was the one calling when the phone rang again, but it was Rona. I braced myself at the sound of her voice.

"Why haven't you called, Claire? Mom keeps asking, asking, asking. She only wants you, and I'm the one who has to make the excuses. Would it be so terrible to pick up the phone?"

"I talked with her this morning."

"That isn't what she says. She's been imagining all sorts of awful things have happened. She isn't good, Claire. I don't know how much longer it'll be."

Looking out at the night ocean, I felt an enveloping darkness. "What do the doctors say?"

Rona snorted. "I spend half the day running around trying to *find* them. I think they're avoiding me, and you want to know why? Because they don't have any answers. When I finally pin them down, they frown, tap their pens on the chart, and look deep in thought, like they're considering new treatments. Only there aren't any. Mom knows that. She's gotten so morbid that being with her is impossible. She told me what she wants in her obituary. Get this. She wants to be remembered as a homemaker."

I had to smile. "I can understand that."

"She was *never* a homemaker. She was a bookkeeper. She rarely cleaned and never cooked. If anyone was the homemaker when we were kids, it was you."

"But she wanted to be one. Isn't that what counts?"

"See? You see eye to eye with her. That's why you should be here, not me."

"I want to be," I countered. "Believe me, I'd rather be there than here."

"No, you wouldn't. You have no *idea* what it's like here, day in day out. When I sit with her, she accuses me of keeping a death watch, and when I'm not there, she accuses me of desertion. Never accuses you of it, mind you, even though you're more a deserter than me. Why haven't you called?"

"I *did* call. But things aren't easy here either."

"Why not?"

I slid down against the glass, back to the ocean, face to all the new things that meant absolutely nothing in the face of death. I wasn't sure which weighed me down more, guilt or grief. I wanted to tell Rona everything. But I couldn't.

"I've been preoccupied," I said, realizing only after the fact that that would invite more questions.

Perhaps from someone less self-centered. All Rona said was, "I need you here. I need you here. When can you come?"

"I don't know."

"Well, I don't know how much more I can take. I wasn't cut out to do this, Claire. You know that."

"You're doing a great job."

"I'm not. I don't comfort her. I try, but nothing works. She doesn't want me, she wants you. I really need you here."

"I know, Rona, I know, but I have my hands full. I have to tell you—"

"Uh-oh. There's my call waiting. Listen, I'm expecting an

important call. I'll talk with you tomorrow. See what you can do about flights for the weekend. I'll even pick you up at the airport. And call Mom? Please?"

"Hi, Mom," I sang. "How are you?"

"Dying," came her feeble response.

It shook me. If she was giving up, I would be furious. She had no right to give up, not after all this time. "We're all dying, right from the day we're born. How are you feeling otherwise?"

"Why haven't you called? The pain is bad, and your sister is useless."

"Have you asked the doctors about the pain?"

"What can they say? They've given up."

"Doctors don't give up."

"There's nothing in it for them. I'm poor. No chance of money from me when I go."

"You're in the majority. It's the rare patient who makes a big bequest."

"You could promise them something. Maybe that would help. Will you promise them something, Claire?"

"Of course. That's a nice idea, actually."

"Is something wrong?"

"No. Why do you ask?"

"You don't sound right."

Connie had known about most other ups and downs in my life. I wanted her to know about this one. I wanted her to tell me that going along with the court ruling even though it was wrong was the right thing to do. I wanted her to tell me I was the best mother in the world.

But she would be sick with disappointment. And she was already so sick. I couldn't risk letting her take this kind of heartache to her grave, or, worse, having it send her there.

"There's a problem with work," I finally said. "Nothing that time and attention won't solve."

"When will I see you again?"

"Soon, Mom. I'll get back as soon as I can."

"The doctors listen to you. I feel better when you're here."

"I'll try. But it may be a few weeks."

"I miss you."

"Let me see what I can do. I'll call again soon. You rest until then. I want you strong for Thanksgiving. Okay?"

I almost didn't answer the phone when it rang next. It was nine-thirty. I was exhausted, felt as though I had lived three lifetimes in a day, and I still had to unpack my last bag and hang up my clothes if I had any hope of wearing them without major repair work. But if it was Johnny, I wanted to talk. Or Kikit. Or Dean Jenovitz.

It was the last. I was immediately alert.

"I understand we have to meet, Mrs. Raphael." I heard the shuffle of pages at his end. "Is next Monday at two doable?"

"It is, but I was hoping for something sooner." I sounded a little desperate, but that was fine. I figured he was used to squeezing desperate people in.

There was more shuffling, and the slow, deliberating tick of his tongue. "I have a possible Friday at ten, though I don't know as that's much of an improvement."

"If I took the Friday slot, my husband could take the Monday slot. Have you heard from him yet?"

"No."

"Have you heard from his lawyer?"

"No. Since the Monday slot is a definite, I'll put you down for that one. I'll make separate arrangements with your husband when he calls."

"When do you want to talk with the children?"

"After I've spent sufficient time with their parents."

"How much is 'sufficient time'?"

"That depends."

"Ah."

"Custody studies take time, Mrs. Raphael."

"I understand," I said and bit my tongue, but only for the space of a breath. "It's just that being separated from my children is an unnatural state, for them as much as for me."

"They're with their father. They'll be fine."

How did he know that? How did he know that Dennis wasn't an abusive parent? How did *he* know what emotional harm my children were suffering with their parents splitting up out of the blue? How did he know they would be fine *at all*? I didn't care if he had *ten* degrees. That didn't make him an expert on my kids!

"Monday at two?" he asked.

"Yes. Dr. Jenovitz, I really am worried about my children."

"So was the court, which was why they were placed with their father. Why don't we talk about this on Monday. Do you know where my office is?"

"Yes."

"Good. I'll see you then."

I hadn't gone through life second-guessing myself. I had simply done what had to be done and moved on to the next task. I might have done what had to be done and moved on this time, too, had I been back home with the kids. They kept me busy. With them around, I didn't have time to brood.

But they weren't around now. I didn't have chores to do for them, or for Dennis. I had plenty to do for WickerWise, but not here, not now. Here and now was the new home that was mine in name and deed and things, but still not mine. It was different at night, dark, silent, and in that dark silence, I second-guessed my talk with Jenovitz. I wondered if I had sounded too pushy or controlling, wondered if I had been humble enough, reasonable enough. First impressions were important. I agonized over the one I had made.

I second-guessed my handling of the children—had I said too much or too little to Kikit, had I accepted Johnny's refusal too easily? I assumed they were both asleep, wondered if they were dreaming and whether they would wake in the night. I had always been the one who handled nightmares, who got up and held little bodies, who climbed into little beds and sang sweet little songs. I wondered if Dennis would—and I second-guessed my handling of him, too. It was fine to stand up to him, but if he turned around and took it out on the kids, the effort had backfired.

As I unpacked the last of my clothes, I tried to boost my morale by thinking back through the evening, but my talk with Connie held no solace. Nor did my talk with Rona. They saw me as their rock. It had always been that way, and I had never minded, but things were different now. I needed a rock of my own.

There was only one person who understood that, and I wasn't supposed to be with him.

Desperate for a little pampering, I took a hot bath in the tub of my new home, dried myself with an oversized bath towel, wrapped myself in another, and uncorked the bottle of Chardonnay that Cynthia had left on the kitchen counter for me. I had no wine glasses, but I wasn't fussy. A plastic cup did just fine.

Wine in hand, I climbed the spiral stairs to the top of my tower, piled my pillows against my brand-new wicker headboard, and climbed into my brand-new bed.

Then I began to hum. I didn't pick any one song deliberately, just went with whatever came, but what came were things that Dennis and I had never sung, sad songs, soulful songs. On to the next I went, eyes closed, a sip of wine, a deeper snuggle. Hum became voice, soft and wispy, always with a beat, I loved a good beat, and the words were my heart's cries.

I sang a little Carole King, "You've Got a Friend," "So Far Away," and James Taylor's "Fire and Rain." I sang to soothe myself, to lift my spirits, because music had always done that for me.

This time was different. I didn't finish the wine, didn't even finish the song I was singing last, because emotion and my startling state of aloneness choked me up. First I cried, then I sniffled. Then, in the wee hours of the night, the beat of the ocean did what exhaustion couldn't and rocked me to sleep.

Nine

I'm not sure that anyone who hasn't ever been granted "visitation rights" to his or her children can possibly understand what they mean. Visiting is the least of it, and there are precious few rights. I had to tell Dennis what time I was picking the children up, where we were going, and what time I would have them home, but that wasn't the worst. The worst was being with them, loving them to pieces and prizing every second of my time with them but feeling an awkwardness, trying to pretend things were the same when we all knew they weren't. The worst was feeling like a second-rate mother because the court said I was, and wondering if the children thought it. The worst was having to entrust their daily well-being to someone else. The *very* worst was having to drop them back with Dennis and return alone to my own place, which was deadly empty once the kids had been and gone.

Predictably, they liked the lighthouse. Even Johnny was fascinated with it, though he started glancing anxiously at his watch as our time together neared an end. When I tried to get him to talk about what he was feeling, he gave me one-word answers and shrugs, and then Kikit was tugging at me with talk of her own. I needed time alone with him, but she wouldn't leave my side. Given the paucity of our time together, I couldn't ask her to.

Dropping the children back at the house, I begged Dennis to let me pick Johnny up from school the next day and take him out alone for an hour to talk. He said we had to stick to the schedule.

Carmen filed the Motion to Recuse late Thursday. So began another wait for a call from Selwey's clerk.

The lighthouse was shaping up well. The floors were done and, by week's end, the walls were painted and the windows washed. The children had already picked their furniture from my warehouse—Kikit a pretty wicker set, Johnny one of the wood sets that we stocked—along with the bedding they wanted, but I did the rest. Carpets, lamps, window coverings, framed posters—their rooms looked precious when I was done.

"So when can I *sleep* there?" Kikit asked when I updated her on the phone.

"Soon," I said. I was hoping for a reversal of the court order by the end of the following week, and if not then, during the week after that. Worst case scenario, if we had to wait until the GAL's study was done, it would be Thanksgiving. I refused to think that I wouldn't win at that point.

In any case, I wanted the children to see the lighthouse as home. To that end, I felt justified in neglecting other things to finish the decorating.

WickerWise was sturdy enough to bear the neglect without suffering much damage. I answered only the most urgent phone calls, dealt with only the most urgent problems. When the manufacturer of one of the major fabrics we used for cushions in our factory declared bankruptcy, I chose another company's fabric and submitted the order. When the line we had been most successful with in our western stores was discontinued, I chose a replacement. I kept *Furniture Today* close at hand and read it when I could. The rest of the work I left for Brody.

I saw him each day when I checked in at the office, talked with him about what had to be done, then left. He was leaving the following Monday for the West Coast, at which point I would be back in the office working. It was better this way, I told myself. Less tempting.

But I missed him. I was going through the worst time of my life, and he was the one person who might have helped. He knew about visitation rights. He knew about being alone. He knew *me* and what made me tick.

The court said we were having an affair. We weren't. But something had changed between us. Whether it was the power of suggestion or the fact that I was now separated and theoretically available, or whether there had been an attraction all long, I didn't know. All I knew was that our friendship wasn't as innocent as it had once been. I definitely felt it—little looks, quick thoughts, an absent, innocent touch that brought a shock of awareness.

He was right. Something did exist. But I couldn't pursue it.

That wasn't to say I didn't think of him often. I wanted to call him Thursday night to tell him how dismal Halloween had been. Dennis had opted for having his mother give out candy at the house while he took Kikit around the neighborhood, and though I trusted that he would go through every last bit of the candy she received and throw out anything with nuts, I would have rather been there than sitting alone in my lighthouse with a bag of candy and not one child ringing the bell.

I wanted to call Brody Friday night after discouraging talks with my mother and sister. They wanted me in Cleveland, and while I couldn't go, I couldn't tell them why. I was frustrated when they pushed, then angry, then—again and always—riddled with guilt.

I wanted to call him Saturday night, when I was feeling blue as blue could be, cold turkey after a day with the kids. After

Johnny's game, I had taken them to lunch and a movie, then brought them to the lighthouse and sat with them in my tower overlooking the waves. Kikit had hogged my lap—not that I didn't want her there, but I wanted Johnny to feel a little warmth, too. When I reached out to him, he eluded my grasp. "Talk to me," I begged him, and he talked, but never about what needed to be said. When I broached the subject of the separation directly, he answered with headshakes and shrugs. The closest he came to making a statement was when Kikit asked me to sing and he suggested "No Man Is an Island."

"No Man Is an Island" had been the theme song of the group Dennis and I sang with. It had been the closer for our shows, sung at that point where the audience was dewy-eyed and mellow, caught up in the sense of community that characterized the times, swaying and singing along. The melody was strong and anthemlike, the harmony rich. Dennis and I had always sung it with a sense of nostalgia, and had had it played at our wedding. It was, in its way, the theme song of our marriage.

It stood for much more though, I realized as I thought about it Saturday night after the children were gone. I had grown up in a joyless home. Singing had been my escape. I felt no oppression when I was singing, felt nothing pulling me down when I tapped my toe to the beat and heard the harmony click. I had met Dennis singing and had transferred to him those feelings of pleasure.

It occurred to me, looking back, that Dennis had lost interest in singing, just as he had lost interest in taking pictures. Two sources of shared pleasure, both dried up. I should have seen it sooner. I surely saw it now.

I wanted to tell Brody that and more. But I didn't dare call. I didn't trust myself that far.

Sunday morning, he took things out of my hands. I had been up at dawn feeling lost, so I had driven to the office and set myself up in the workshop removing the rest of the broken weavers from the rocker I had started on the week before. I found the growing number of holes jarring, so I worked quickly. I wasn't more than an hour into it when Brody showed up with brunch.

I gave him a short hi, said something about having parked out of sight of the house where he wasn't supposed to have seen the car, and went on with my work. I tried to pretend he was there on his own business, even tried to drum up anger or indifference, but neither came, and then he had warm bagels and veggie cheese and lox arranged on paper plates on the empty end of the work-table, and it was too much. I told myself I was hungry.

Was I ever.

How could I resist warm bagels—they were whole grain, my favorite, smart, smart Brody—and hot black coffee, chicory blend, my favorite, too. When my best friend said, "It's been a shitty week for you, and you haven't told me a thing, so, come on, I want to hear," how could I not answer?

It spilled out, all the frustration and the heartache, and, yes, the excitement of seeing the children, but that was a given. It was the other that was new, that I needed help with, the business of visitation rights. "Was it as hard for you with Joy?"

We were on stools at the worktable with a token corner be-tween us. I had my thighs crossed. Brody's legs were sprawled. He was on his third bagel, though for the life of me I couldn't see where the first two had gone.

"Hard, yes," he answered, "but in a different way. When it happened to me, I'd only been married for four years and a father for two, nothing like the length of your marriage or how long you've been a parent. Marriage and parenthood is a way of life for you, so changing it hurts more." He paused to frown, then went on without pride. "Me, I was never into it that way. My marriage was shaky from the get-go. Joy was supposed to help." He snorted. "Brilliant, huh? Boy, were we dumb."

"Young."

"That, too. I took all the away assignments, because Mary Anne and I got along best when we weren't breathing down each other's necks. So when it came to a split, it wasn't like I was used to seeing Joy every day."

I had met Mary Anne when she and Brody were dating, when she was studying law and he business. Dennis and I had been at their wedding and seen them several times a year during their marriage. We guessed early on that things weren't right, and had been neither surprised nor terribly disappointed when they split. Mary Anne prided herself on being an intellectual. She had been drawn to esoteric thinking and had surrounded herself with others of that mind. They had an air of superiority, off-putting for those of us not quite as gifted. I had always found her—them— boring. She went into teaching soon after Joy was born, and was still there. I hadn't talked with her in years.

Nor had I talked about her. It had seemed an invasion of Brody's privacy during those early years, and later had been irrelevant. I had always assumed Brody felt the same way, either that, or that his loyalty to Mary Anne kept him quiet. Suddenly I wondered.

"Go on," I urged.

He took a long drink of coffee—mostly cream and sugar, I didn't know where those calories went, either—then smacked his lips, set down the cup, and said, "I was a lousy father."

"You're a *great* father."

"Now, maybe. Not then. The divorce agreement gave me certain times with Joy, so I saw her then. I'm not sure I would have otherwise. She scared the hell out of me."

I smiled in disbelief. "Joy?"

"She was *two*," he said, embarrassed. "Diapers, bibs, braids—I didn't know what to do with her. I'd never done *any* of it until Mary Anne and I split. Then it was like instant parenthood. I was nervous with her, which she sensed, so she clung to Mary

Anne when I came for her and ran back to Mary Anne when I brought her back, which made me feel about as welcome as BO. She didn't want to come near me. So I said, that's okay, that's great, I'll spare her the pain. I canceled a visit here, a visit there, more than I care to recall."

I was trying to fit the Brody he was describing with the one I knew. "When did it change?"

He didn't answer, just sat there chewing on the second half of that third bagel.

"Brody?"

"When Johnny was born."

I didn't make the connection. "Yes?"

He finished the bagel, wiped his hand on his jeans, looked me in the eye, and said, "I was jealous. You guys were so happy to have this little thing. I sulked for a while—"

"You didn't."

"I did. I'd go home after holding Johnny and feel sorry for myself that I didn't have something like that. Then I realized I did."

"Joy would have been seven by then."

"Yup. Past diapers and bibs. She could take herself to the bathroom and braid her own hair. She didn't scare me so much."

It occurred to me then. "That was when you took her to Disney World."

"Had to do something super to win her over. She barely knew me. Remember what I did? First came Disney World, then Hershey Park, then the Grand Canyon and Yellowstone. It was easier being together if we were busy. She was nine, Johnny's age now, before I had the guts to have her here with me for more than a day or two at a stretch."

"Who'd've guessed it," I said. "You were great with my kids right from the start. I recall your changing a diaper or two, even giving a few baths."

"It was different with your kids. No one expected me to do anything. No one even asked me to do anything. There was nothing of the power play that there always was between Mary Anne and me. With your kids, it was the kind of thing that if I didn't just jump in, I'd miss out." His voice lowered, eyes glinted. "I was tired of missing out. Having your kids was the next best thing to having you."

I choked on my coffee. It was a minute before I could catch my breath, another minute before I had my chin properly wiped. Then I wailed, "You aren't supposed to say things like that."

He shrugged, but the light in his eyes didn't dim.

I lowered my own to my coffee, took one sip, then another. I brushed bagel crumbs into a pile with the side of my pinkie. I looked at the container of veggie cheese, the plastic spreader, the discarded coffee cup lids—anywhere but at Brody.

"Think Dennis knew?" he asked.

"You never did anything improper."

"I keep thinking I caused this."

My eyes flew up. "You didn't. Dennis has been dissatisfied with our marriage for a while."

"Have you?"

I didn't answer as quickly. I had only begun to soul-search on that score. Thinking aloud, I said, "Not consciously. I wanted my marriage to work, so I clung to the positives and glossed over the negatives. I should have been more honest, I guess. More realistic. But no marriage is perfect. So where's the cut-off point? At what point is there more bad than good? At what point do you say 'enough'? Dennis clearly reached it before me."

"Clearly," Brody said. He shifted on the stool, reached into a back pocket, pulled out a piece of newsprint, and handed it over. It was folded in half, then again.

I unfolded it and read the short caption beneath the picture. "Dennis Raphael and Phoebe Lowe, dancing at Friday night's

Bar Association Gala," and having a wonderful time of it, to judge from their smiles.

Dennis had a great smile. It made a woman feel like she was the light of his life. There had been a time when he had smiled at me just the way he was smiling at Phoebe.

I studied the clipping a little longer. "Why am I not surprised?" Not surprised, but hurt. Very hurt.

"That's from Hillary's column. It could mean anything."

I refolded the paper. The pain was muted that way. "I think they're involved. I mean, seriously involved. When I threw it at him—I was being facetious—he didn't deny it."

"And he accuses *you*?"

"He says the rules change once you separate."

"He's right, there," Brody said in a pointed way that put us right back where we started.

Looking at him then, I searched my conscience for germs of infidelity. His features were so very familiar—warm brown eyes behind those wire-rimmed glasses of his, the ghost of freckles across his nose that were visible only at skylit times like these, a jawline that was faintly squared and shadowed, full lower lip. I had never touched those features as a lover would, neither with my fingers nor my mouth. But there were different ways to love.

I had loved Dennis because he was my husband. I loved Brody because he was my friend. I had loved Dennis because of what he was, loved Brody because of *who* he was.

I respected Brody, craved his company, relied on his opinion. Was my love for him deeper than my love for Dennis? Was I more attracted to him than I was to Dennis?

Why hadn't I *seen* it before?

"I need time, Brody. If I do something that even *hints* of wrongdoing, I'll lose my kids."

"There's a double standard here, you know that, don't you?"

I threw a hand in the air. "What else is new? Every woman

knows there's a double standard." I left the end of the worktable where we had eaten and went to stand at the end with my rocker. I studied the folded paper, the picture of my husband with his paramour—his *alleged* paramour. I wasn't ready to say it was fact, wasn't ready to think that Dennis had cast me off so fast, much less for someone younger, for someone *blond*. It was just a picture. Like Brody and me hugging was just a picture.

Double standard. Not fair.

"When a woman competes in a man's world under a man's standards," I said, "she has to be twice as smart, twice as good. Oh, sure, there's affirmative action. That may get her in the door, but once she's in, she hits a walkway of glue. I offer franchises to women. I *favor* female franchisees. So they're in the door, but to get a loan to make it happen? You've seen the grief they get sometimes. They can't get the loan because they have no track record, and they can't get a track record without a loan. Are you going to get pregnant and default the bank officer asks. Or leave town with your husband and default? Or decide after six months that you don't like owning a franchise after all, and default? Men would never be asked those things."

I pushed the picture of Dennis and Phoebe into my pocket. Out of sight, it was less hurtful. "So what do we do? If we want to succeed within the system, we have to work within it. I'm trying to do that, Brody. I'm trying."

He rose and came toward me. "Maybe more than you have to."

I wasn't sure I knew what he meant, I only knew that my insides stirred the closer he came.

He stopped within an arm's length, and hooked his fingers in the back of his jeans. "Don't sacrifice our friendship. Don't give Dennis the satisfaction of that. Okay, so we don't need to be together, to *be* together, but we can still spend time together, can't we? I don't like feeling guilty when I look at you or call you on the phone. I don't like having to think twice before I give you a hug. I don't like having to measure every word I say."

"You? Measure every word?" I tried to laugh, but it came out sounding choked.

He touched my cheek then, hand warm from the heat of his body. His thumb traced my jaw, fingers outlined my cheekbone and slid into my hair, all light and tempting, almost make-believe. When I couldn't stand it anymore, I tipped my head into his palm, though whether to stop him or make it real, I didn't know.

"Did you ever wonder what it'd be like if we kissed?" he asked in a voice that was hoarse.

"No."

"Or slept together? Made love?"

"No. I can't, Brody. I can't now."

"Someday?"

"Maybe. I don't know. Up until two weeks ago I assumed Dennis would be the only man I'd ever sleep with."

"You were gone for two weeks before that, which makes a month. How much longer than that since you made love?"

I pressed my lips together and shook my head to warn him off. I wasn't ready to tell him that.

"Okay," he said as though he'd heard, "but will you start thinking about me that way?"

I tried another laugh. This one was slightly hysterical. "How can I help it?"

He grinned, then wrapped his arms around me and drew me close before I could protest. Once there, I didn't want to. Being held by Brody was being in the safest place that I had ever been in in my life. I just might have stayed there forever, if he hadn't kissed me on the forehead and released me first.

He was grinning as he backed away, one step after another,

holding a hand up as though to slow me down, like *I* was the one rushing things. Then, as quietly as he had come, he was gone.

I cursed him as I cleaned up the remains of our brunch, but halfheartedly. It had been a long time since I'd felt sexy, but Brody made me feel that way. As distractions from reality went, it wasn't bad.

Carmen had it right. Dean Jenovitz was definitely stodgy. I guessed that he had spent the last thirty-five years in the same office, behind the same desk. Once settled in the chair there, he blended right in with the rest of the decor—a little old, a little musty, a little ingrown.

He reached for a pipe, rapped it against an ashtray, filled it with tobacco, tamped it down. It wasn't until he had a match lit and poised mid-air that he paused. "You aren't allergic, are you?"

"No, no. Go ahead." Pipe smoke—any kind of smoke— bothered me. But I could live with it more easily than I could live without my kids. I wasn't about to risk getting on Dean Jenovitz's bad side, not with so much at stake.

He lit the pipe, took a long drag, blew out a thick white stream of smoke, and sat back in his chair. "So. How are you?"

Not quite knowing what or how much to say, I dared a quiet, "I'm all right. A little shaky, I guess. This all has taken me by surprise."

"Court orders can be upsetting. But you must have had some inkling of a problem beforehand."

"No. My husband sent me off on a trip without giving me a clue."

"Sent you off? It's my understanding that you were the one who instigated this trip. Wasn't it for your business?"

"What I meant," I said with an apologetic smile, "was that he was there all the time I was getting ready to leave, kissed the children, kissed me, stood on the porch and waved good-bye. He was totally pleasant. I had no idea what he was planning."

"It's my understanding that he wasn't planning anything. Not then. He gave you slack, what with your mother sick. Then came the mix-ups with the children's flight and your daughter's medicine. What with things that had happened before, he saw a pattern emerging and felt compelled to act."

So he had read Dennis's affidavit. I wondered if he had read mine as well.

"I think he had this planned earlier," I said quietly.

"Do you have evidence of it?"

"Phone bills. Dennis has been calling his lawyer since last January."

Jenovitz frowned, stuck the pipe in his mouth, and pushed some papers around. "There's nothing about that in your affidavit."

"No. I only went through the bills last night. It's been bothering me how Dennis has been so calm through everything that's happened. I had no idea a separation was coming, but he took it completely in stride. The only thing that made sense was that he had time to get used to the idea. I guess he has."

"It's my understanding that he's been mentioning divorce to you for months."

"Not divorce. Separation, and we always decided against it."

"You decided, says your husband. He raised it, you argued against it, he went along."

That was one way of putting it, I supposed.

Jenovitz asked, "Why did you argue against it if he seemed so unhappy?"

"He didn't. At least, not with our marriage. He was unhappy with work. That spilled over into other things. He would say that I didn't understand him, or that he didn't have enough *freedom*. He never once said that he didn't love me, or that he loved someone else, or that he was going to file for divorce whether I liked it or not."

"So you were taken by surprise. Are you acclimated now to divorce?"

"I guess so. Yes."

He studied me for a minute, before saying, "That's a fast turn-around. How long has it been since the court order was issued?"

The discussion wasn't going the way I wanted it to. Quiet and humble, in an attempt to appease, I said, "Ten days, and I didn't want to accept it. I did everything I could to get it reversed, but Dennis wouldn't budge. I suggested we talk. I suggested we stay in the house, both of us, and try to work things out. Dennis wouldn't hear of it, and the court went along. The judge wouldn't even give us a hearing on the Motion for Reconsideration. Now you're involved in the case." I frowned. "I'm confused. Are you suggesting we should reconcile?"

"No. My job is to make a recommendation with regard to custody. The assumption is that this case will end up in divorce."

"Whose assumption?"

"The court's. Certainly your husband's, since he initiated the suit."

"That's right." I made my point. "He did, not me, and the court is standing behind him. Divorce isn't my choice, but every other door has been shut to me. I don't see any option. My husband doesn't want me. He's made that clear. So what am I supposed to do?"

"Most women would be mourning."

"I am. I lie in bed at night and feel empty. I wake up in the morning and feel hurt. I think of what was good in my marriage. It had potential. That doesn't seem true anymore. I feel sadness. And regret." I didn't know what else to say, so I didn't say a thing. But neither did he, just sat there studying me, and I couldn't take it after a while. So, with a tight laugh and a hand through my hair, I said, "I'm sorry, Dr. Jenovitz. I think I'm flunking this test. I'm trying to be up front, but clearly you aren't impressed. I don't know what it is that you want to hear."

Still he didn't speak.

So I said, "Maybe I should be falling apart. Some women would be, I guess. I *know.*"

His brows went up. He didn't ask how I knew, but the question was there, along with that painful silence.

I ended it by explaining, "My mother fell apart. My father died suddenly, no warning at all, not a day of ill health before that. I was eight, my sister was six. Mom panicked. Didn't know what to. Didn't do anything. For weeks."

"That must have been hard on you."

"I did what I could."

"You were only eight. What could you do?"

"Help with my sister. Keep her busy. Help around the house."

"What kept you from panicking yourself?"

"Ignorance, probably." I smiled ruefully, recalling the extent of it. "I didn't understand what it meant to have him gone. Oh, I missed him. But I was too young to see the broad picture."

"Do you see the broad picture now?"

"Of his death?"

"Of divorce. Isn't that what we're dealing with here?"

He didn't like me. I had known he wouldn't, and he didn't. Did I see the broad picture? Oh, God, more and more by the second, and it was scaring me to death. "Yes, we're dealing with divorce. And yes, I see the broad picture."

"Describe it to me."

I touched my mouth, wanting to protest. He was asking me to voice thoughts and fears that were still so new as to be raw. Either he wanted to see how insightful I was, or he was, plain and simple, a sadist. I hated him a little just then, but didn't dare refuse.

"The broad picture of divorce?" I asked, placing my hand in

my lap with care. "It means that the intact family I always wanted is no more. That one of us will miss some of the children's special times. Holidays and family celebrations will be split up. Birthdays. Graduations. The kids will be torn. Pulled in two directions at once."

"That didn't happen on Halloween."

"No. They did okay on Halloween, but maybe that's just because this is still so new. Like when my father died. My ignorance. Maybe they're experiencing the same thing right now. What'll happen when they're older and they understand more?"

"They may do just fine."

"I hope so."

"Do you?" he asked.

For an instant I couldn't respond. Then, sharply, I asked, "Why wouldn't I?"

"Well, you are the one who is against this divorce. Some mothers in your situation would make everyone involved miserable."

"I love my children," I protested. "No one, not even my husband, can deny that. Hurting them has been my single greatest fear. I'd have done most anything to have spared them the confusion, the upset, the *pain* of divorce, but now that it seems inevitable, I'll do most anything I can to ease them through it."

"The question," Jenovitz said before I had taken another breath, "is whether you're of a sound mind to do that. That's what I'm trying to find out, Mrs. Raphael. You may not like my questions, but the court expects me to ask them. I'm doing my job as best I can."

I held my tongue, didn't say a thing, let *him* wallow in the silence this time.

But he didn't seem to mind it as much as I did. Barely a minute had passed before I said, albeit calmly, even agreeably, "I'm sorry. Ask whatever you want. I promise to answer as best I can."

He drew on his pipe, exhaled a thick stream of smoke. "You do fly off the handle."

"Not normally. Really, I don't. I've always been the calm one in the house. I've had to be to counter Dennis's moods."

I was hoping he would pick up on that and ask more, but he didn't. "Your husband says you're under a great deal of strain."

"Only because of the divorce. I wasn't before. I was handling things just fine."

"Your mother's condition has to be stressful."

"Well, it's another thing to think about. To worry about. The stress I'm feeling comes from wanting to fly out to see her but fearing that it'll be held against me, that someone will think that because I'm absent, I'm negligent. The thing is, it's normal for a husband or wife to leave the children with the other to spend time with a dying parent."

Jenovitz shrugged. "You're free to go."

"Last time someone said that to me, I came home to chaos."

"But was the chaos of your own doing? You've taken on a great deal, Mrs. Raphael. The question is whether you're up to it. Your husband says no."

"The chaos had nothing to do with my visiting my mother." I pointed at his file. "Those examples my husband uses to show I'm not in control are the kinds of things that happen to people all the time. Good Lord, *I* could have been the one going to court to show that my husband messed up the kids' arrival times and lost my daughter's medicine, or, worse, let her eat something she shouldn't have eaten. Would the court have taken the kids away from him for that?"

Jenovitz gave a smoky sigh. "You know that's simplifying the situation. There were additional elements in the complaint. Besides, your husband's life is simpler. You're the one running every which way trying to do everything."

My stomach was starting to twist. The office wasn't large, and the air was thick. I was feeling more discouraged by the minute.

He regarded me speculatively.

Quietly, I said, "I'm not running every which way. I have my sister to help with my mother, my husband to help with the children, and my CEO to help with the business."

He nodded. His eyes moved down the paper before him and stopped. His tongue ticked around the stem of his pipe. "Tell me about the CEO."

"His name is Brody Parth," I said. "He was my husband's business partner before he became mine. He is godfather to both of our children."

"Are you sexually involved with him?"

"No."

The pipe left his mouth. "That's an unequivocal no?"

"An unequivocal no."

The pipe went back in. "Why does your husband say you are?"

"You'd have to ask him that."

"I did. He showed me pictures."

"That picture was taken from outside Brody's kitchen window the night Dennis had me evicted. I was upset. Brody hugged me. He was a friend offering comfort. That's it."

"There are telephone records. There are hotel records. They're pretty suggestive."

"So are the ones between Dennis and his lawyer. He works with Phoebe Lowe far more than with Art Heuber."

"Are you changing the subject?"

"No. I'm making a point."

"Making a point, or trying to justify your relationship with Brody Parth?"

"Making a point. There's no more proof that I'm having an

affair with Brody than there is that Dennis is having an affair with Phoebe. I don't see why I'm being accused, and he isn't."

Jenovitz sat like a rock, staring at me.

"Look," I said, frustrated, "Brody is my CEO. That explains telephone and hotel records. He's also a long-time friend, which explains the hug he gave me, *and* the amount of time he always spent at our house. Brody was like a member of the family. Having an affair with him would have been like committing incest." But Jenovitz claimed to have seen pictures, plural. To my knowledge, only one had been presented in court. "Have you already met with Dennis?"

"I saw him last Friday."

Ahhh. In the slot I might have had myself. I wondered how that had happened, wondered when *I* would get first dibs for a change.

"Does that bother you?" the psychologist asked.

"No." I looked at the bright side. "I'm glad he came in. I was worried he'd try to hold things up. Thanksgiving is less than a month away. I'm hoping this will be resolved by then."

Jenovitz sat back in his chair, sucked in on his pipe, and studied the ceiling.

"Will it?" I asked nervously. I had to believe there was a limit to what the court was making me endure. Totally aside from the motions that Carmen swore she would file until we won, she said the GAL had thirty days. I was counting.

"Is there anything I can do to make it happen faster?" I asked when he didn't speak. Then, with an anxious laugh, "This is very painful for me."

"Understandable. It's a situation that you can't control."

That was quite a statement. It was direct and judgmental. I didn't know whether it came from his own observation, or from Dennis. In either case, I disagreed. "It isn't about control. It's about being without my children. It's about having my every move watched. It's about not knowing what the future holds."

"It's about control."

I gave him the benefit of the doubt. "Maybe," I conceded, "but not in a negative way. It's not about controlling people. It's about controlling me, about determining what I do, about deciding on a course of action and seeing it through. It's about being in control of, yes, okay, the situation. I've been doing that since I was eight. I did it then, because no one else was doing it, and someone had to. I did it during my marriage, because Dennis wasn't doing it, and someone had to. Is that wrong?"

"Not unless it holds other people back."

"It hasn't. At least, I don't think it has. No, how could it? I'm a booster. I boost Dennis's ego, boost the kids' egos. I've taught them they can take control and be anything they want to be. How can that possibly hold them back?"

"It can backfire. If you tell the children they can be anything they want, and then your son doesn't make a team or your daughter doesn't get the part she wants in a play, they can feel they've let you down."

I was shaking my head well before he was done. "They wouldn't feel that. I wouldn't let them. We talk, my kids and I. We talk about feelings." I was vehement about that. It was one of the things I had missed as a child and had vowed my own children would have, an open ear, unconditional support. I didn't want either of them suffering the way Rona did.

"Your son isn't talking."

"Not yet. Mainly because I'm not there. He's used to talking with me, but it's hard to push a button and suddenly get into deep emotional talks with a child when the court limits you to two visits a week. Dennis is with him more than I am. He'd have more opportunity to talk with Johnny. I don't know if he has. Heart-to-heart talks were never his long suit."

"He says the boy is tense and won't open up."

"The boy is angry." I was angry myself. In my wildest nightmares, this wasn't what I wanted for Johnny. "He thinks I've abandoned him. That's what the court has done to us."

Jenovitz set the pipe in his ashtray. "A word of caution, Mrs. Raphael. That kind of attitude can be harmful to a child. He'll pick up on your resentment in a flash."

"Not if I don't let it show. I haven't said a word to him against the court, or against my husband. I'm very careful."

"But you do resent the court's judgment?"

"What kind of parent would I be if I didn't? My place is with my children, not exiled from my home."

"According to your husband, you're quite happy in your new home."

"Happy? There are moments when I like where I am. But, *happy*? No. I'm making the best of a bad situation. That's what I'm trying to say. That's what I do in life."

He nodded. "It's one way of feeling in control."

Okay, so I liked feeling in control. "Is that so awful? Excuse me, Dr. Jenovitz, but I'm getting mixed signals here. Isn't it my alleged lack of control that got me into trouble in the first place?"

A bell rang. The psychologist's next client was announcing his arrival, just as I had mine an hour before. I had been hoping for more time—the longer we talked, the sooner the study would be done.

But Jenovitz was emptying his pipe of ash with one hand and flipping through his datebook with the other. "How's your schedule?"

"Wide open."

"Same time next week?"

"I'll come in again this week, if you'd like."

"No. This is a good slot for me." He made a notation.

I moved forward in my chair, but didn't rise. "How many times will we meet, do you think?"

"Three, four, depending on how things progress." He stood. "Next time, bring me a list of the children's teachers, coaches, doctors, any other adults who know them well. Names and phone numbers, please."

"Do you meet with them?"

"A phone call will usually do." He moved toward the door. "I may want a written report from the school. I'll see."

"When will you talk with Kikit and Johnny?"

"When I know more about you and your husband." He opened the door and waited beside it.

Gathering my coat, I approached him. The door wasn't the one I had used before, but led directly to the stairwell, apparently to save the current client the awkwardness of seeing the coming client. So there was no one to hear what I said. Still, I lowered my voice.

"They don't know about you. What should I say?"

"Nothing for now."

"They don't know there's a contest here."

"That's fine."

"I don't want them fearing they have to take sides."

"And you think I'll make them choose, one parent or another? No, Mrs. Raphael. I won't do that. Credit me with a little sensitivity. Please?"

I wanted to do that, truly I did, but driving home from Boston, I struggled with it. If Dean Jenovitz was sensitive, I hadn't seen evidence of it. He hadn't been warm or understanding, hadn't been encouraging or solicitous. He must have known I was nervous, yet he hadn't tried to put me at ease. He certainly hadn't tried to hide his opinion of me.

"Take heart," Carmen told me when I called from the car. "If he heard the worst from Dennis, that's fine. He'll get great reports from the people he calls. They know you far more than they know Dennis, and they like you. It's uphill from here."

"He didn't seem particularly upset by what's been done to me. He didn't seem overly committed to justice."

"His focus will be the children."

"Can I trust him with them?"

"Yes. He's better with kids than adults. The grandfather in him comes out. Good thinking to ask how to tell John and Kikit about him. He'll give you advice, and give you points for asking."

I hadn't done it for the sake of points, and was feeling vaguely sick, though how much of that was still from Jenovitz's pipe I didn't know. "I can't tell you how distasteful this is to me, Carmen. It's like a game—timing, strategy, calculated moves—only the ante is *my life*."

"I know. And I apologize if I make it sound petty. It's not." She paused. "So Jenovitz didn't pick up on Dennis and Phoebe?"

"No. He turned it around and said I was accusing Dennis of something to justify my affair with Brody. I need proof. How do I get it?"

"We get it. We hire Morgan Houser. He's a private investigator, and he's good. He'll find out if they're currently having an affair. That's easy. It may be harder to prove that they were involved before the separation, though proof of that will help us the most."

It would definitely boost our case. I wasn't sure it would boost my morale. I cringed thinking of Dennis in bed with another woman. Now or before, it didn't matter.

My silence must have tipped Carmen off. More quietly, she said, "If proof is there, we need it. Selwey agreed to hear the Motion to Recuse, but his clerk says he isn't happy about it. No judge likes being accused of bias. My guess is that the hearing will be a token one."

Still, it was a hearing. My spirits rose. "When?"

"Thursday morning at ten."

"I'll be there."

"I have a meeting scheduled with Art Heuber later that day to talk about what Dennis wants by way of a settlement. We could use a bargaining chip. Proof of Dennis's infidelity would give us that."

Proof like that smacked of blackmail. Yes, Dennis had used much the same against me, but I resented having to stoop to his level. It would be another instance where I was being forced to be someone I didn't like at all.

Such irony. I was a peace-loving soul newly prone to fist-clenching rage, a level-headed person newly prone to the shakes, an optimist newly prone to dread. They had accused me of being someone I wasn't, and in so doing *made* me into someone I wasn't. It wasn't any more fair than the whole custody situation was fair.

Ahh. The custody situation. The bottom line. I might resist using blackmail to strike a better alimony deal, but when it came to the children, I would use it in a heartbeat.

"Call Morgan," I told Carmen. "See what he can find."

I would do most anything in a heartbeat, when it came to the children.

That was a prophetic thought, if ever there was one. I had barely bathed and settled into bed that night, worn down by alternating calls to Rona and Connie, who were bickering with each other, when the phone rang. It was Dennis saying that Johnny was sick, that he didn't want to disturb Elizabeth so late but that he didn't know what to do.

I knew what to do. I slipped into a sweatsuit and drove right over.

Ten

My key still worked. I let myself in, dropped my coat on the stairs over scattered tiers of school books, sneakers, and laundry, and ran right up. Dennis was coming out of Johnny's room when I reached it.

"He threw up after dinner. Can't seem to keep anything down."

I could smell that the minute I entered the room. Johnny was huddled under a blanket on the bare mattress. Mattress pad, sheets, and comforter were wadded up on the floor.

"Hi, sweetie," I said. My throat knotted as I sat down on the bed by his side. He had been my firstborn, as easy a baby as could be, my one and only for two years. Ours had been a mutual admiration society, a symbiotic craving. Time and circumstance had muted the craving—Dennis's wants, Kikit's arrival, Johnny's own need for independence and growth—but it flooded back now.

Praying that he wouldn't turn away from me as he had done the last time I was at the house, I stroked his face. His cheeks were flushed, fever-hot. "Not feeling so good?"

He shook his head and scrunched up tighter. "I couldn't get to the bathroom in time."

"It's okay, it's okay, sweetie." I fished one of his hands from under the blanket. He was wearing undershorts and nothing more. I assumed his pajamas were in the pile on the floor. "Does anything hurt?"

"I didn't know I was gonna do it," he cried, "just woke up and felt awful and then it just came up. I tried to hold it in."

His hair was damp. I stroked it back. "Shhh, I'm not angry."

"But you had to come all the way over here." There was nothing of the would-be man in his voice. He was little-boy sick, little-boy frightened.

I was sick and frightened just then, too, thinking that my nine-year-old son imagined I begrudged taking care of him, because I knew what it was to feel like a burden. Year after year during my childhood, my mother had come home from work wanting solitude and silence. I remembered having things to ask her but not daring, having things to show her but not daring, the fear of rejection was so great. I had sworn my children would never experience that, had gone out of my way to let them know they came first. And they did. Still. Always.

I held Johnny's hand tighter, pressed his mouth closed with my thumb. "I didn't *have* to come over here. I *wanted* to. Didn't have to, Johnny, *wanted* to. I came the minute Daddy called." I moved my thumb to let him speak. "Tell me what hurts."

"Everything."

"Nothing special, just aches all over?"

"Mm."

"Flu going around school?"

"Mm."

"Still nauseated?"

"Mm."

Dennis stood at the door. His hair was mussed and his shirt untucked in a way that might have suggested concern for his child, had it not been for the hands on his hips and the peeved look on his face. I wasn't sure what annoyed him more, Johnny's flu or my being there, but I wasn't brooding on it. It was the least of my worries just then.

"Did you give him anything—aspirin, water?" I asked.

"No. I got out the aspirin, but he wouldn't take it."

"Is there anything left in his stomach?"

"There can't be. Not with all that came up."

"I didn't mean to," Johnny protested.

I rubbed the back of his neck. "Daddy knows that. He's not angry, just upset that you're sick. Maybe even scared. He's new at this. We have to be patient with him. Know what I think would be good? A nice bath. While you're in it, I can put on fresh sheets. How does that sound?"

"Okay."

While Dennis ran the bath, I sat with Johnny, wiping his face with a damp cloth, humming a soothing song. When the tub was ready I helped him into the bathroom, then left Dennis with him so that I could see to the rest.

First, though, because I couldn't wait a second longer, I looked in on Kikit. The sight of her sleeping with her babies, the crowd of them profiled by the pale glow of her Pocahontas nightlight, brought a swift tightening to my chest. The picture was definitely a pearl in my life's strand, taken for granted for so long, but no more. It was all I could do not to go in and touch her, but I didn't want to wake her, lest she be upset.

Lest I be upset. More than I already was. Because it was odd, moving around the house, so like I had never been gone that I could almost forget the circumstances. Things were just the same, organized the way I had left them, fresh sheets piled neatly in the linen closet and laundry detergent at the ready beside the washer in the basement. Granted, the washer held clothes I hadn't washed, the dryer held others waiting to be folded, and the detergent bottle was covered with blue drips. Granted, coming back through the kitchen, I found the refrigerator filled with food I hadn't bought, mostly cartons of orange juice and milk, loaves of bread, wedges of cheese, more of each than I expected the children would eat or drink in a month. Still, the bulletin board held the very notes I had left there, the wide cranberry candles still stood on the table on either side of the apple bowl, and the answering machine was blinking red to indicate a message waiting to be heard.

Dennis never erased his messages, just left them for me to erase. I pressed the play button.

"Hi," came a clipped female voice. "Selwey gave them a hearing on a Motion to Recuse. It's for show. He'll never grant it. But we have to be there for the hearing, Thursday at ten. Be at my office early, and we'll get breakfast. For the settlement meeting that afternoon, I revised our demands. There's no reason we can't shoot for more, since we're in the driver's seat. I'll give my list to Art. He'll do the talking. Anything else? No. *Ciao.*"

I stabbed at the erase button, then further vented my fury by chipping ice into small pieces in a bowl. Returning to the bedroom, I closed the window I'd opened. By the time I had the bed freshly made, Johnny was walking bleary-eyed from the bathroom wearing the clean pajamas I had passed in to Dennis.

I helped him into bed and gave him the ice chips to suck. He was still ghostly pale, but cooler. I rubbed his back and sang softly. He loved "Let It Be," so I started with it and moved on to others that I knew he liked. He started to doze, caught himself, started to doze again, caught himself again.

He was so obviously fighting it, that I coaxed, "You can sleep."

"What if I get sick again?"

"Do you feel like you will?"

"No, but what if I do?"

"There's a pail right here." I pointed to it. "And me. I'll help."

"Are you staying?" he asked so directly that it hit me, with a gnawing twist inside, that that was why he was fighting sleep. He didn't want to sleep and find me gone when he awoke.

"I'll stay for a while. I like watching you." He seemed pleased enough by that to let himself go. Only when he was sleeping deeply did I slip away.

I was in the laundry room, shifting sheets from washer to dryer, when Dennis came to the door and said, "That was messy."

My first impulse, sheer habit, was to offer sympathy—*poor Dennis, swamped in vomit during his watch, I'm so sorry*—but it was followed by a swift anger. "It wasn't deliberate."

"I know. But I couldn't ask my mother to come. She's seventy-five."

My hands went still for the space of several stunned breaths, before tugging another sheet from the washer. "You could have done it yourself. It doesn't take an advanced degree to clean up after a sick child." I stuffed the sheet into the dryer.

"Well, this worked out fine."

I didn't say anything to that, couldn't think of a comeback that wouldn't be snide. Sad, but not so long ago, snideness wouldn't have arisen. I would have given Dennis the easier chore without a second thought, would have done the harder simply because it was there to be done and I knew how. I was a mother. Dirty work was part of the job.

The job belonged to Dennis now. So why was I doing the laundry?

I consciously set down the box of fabric softener sheets. "What would you have done if I hadn't been home?"

"Called Brody's house," he said.

I didn't dignify the remark with a denial. "And if I wasn't there?"

"I'd have done this myself. I'm not helpless. You may find it hard to believe, but we're doing okay without you."

I slid a pointed look at the laundry that I had personally folded and piled high.

Dennis said, "No one asked you to do that. No one asked you to do any of this. You made such a big deal when I didn't call you about Kikit's attack that I figured I'd be a good guy and call you about Johnny."

My jaw dropped. "You figured you'd be a *good guy*? Come *off* it, Dennis. You didn't know what to do! You *panicked*."

"You'd have a hard time proving that. What's more, if you try, people will think you resented being bothered tonight, which wouldn't reflect well on you as a mother. You can't win."

"I'll win," I said, but I felt suddenly worn. Leaning back against the washer, I braced my fingers on the edge and studied Dennis. He was the same man I married—same looks, same quick tongue, same ego—but different. A stranger. I had thought it before. Now I wondered when it had happened. For the life of me, I didn't know. "Where *did* we lose it, Dennis?"

"Lose what?"

"Whatever it was we had. Whatever it was that made our marriage work."

"Our marriage never really worked."

"It did. At the beginning, at least."

"It was a novelty. We were young."

"We were twenty-five and twenty-eight," I argued. "That's not terribly young, and we dated exclusively for three years before to make sure. You were happy. Unless you put on such a good show that I never suspected," which, come to think of it, he would have been capable of doing. "But if you weren't happy back then, why did you want to get married? Were those romantic gestures just big fat lies?"

"No."

"So what did you see in me then that you don't see now?" I

was still slim and attractive. Judging from Brody's response, I was sexually appealing.

"Humility," Dennis said. "You were approachable back then."

"I'm approachable now."

"You're up on a high horse now. You weren't back then."

Arrogant? I wasn't arrogant. "I have more confidence now, but that's different from arrogance. What else did you see in me then?"

"You were there for me. You were willing to do what had to be done. Things changed when the kids were born and later on when you started the business. You were there for other people more than you were there for me. Your loyalties changed."

"They didn't change. They broadened. I just had more people to be loyal to."

"They changed."

"*You're* the one whose loyalties changed," I argued. I was tired, so tired of being unjustly accused. "You turned on me, Dennis. You went to a lawyer, then a judge, with stories that weren't true. Good *God*, the story I could have told about you. If character is the issue, messing around with your boss's wife says something, don't you think? But I *do* value loyalty. I have never told anyone about that."

"Brody knows."

"Because you *told* him. For what it's worth, he's been as close-mouthed as I have."

"Two peas in a pod," Dennis said with just enough flippancy to set me off.

"Damn right, two peas in a pod. We never even discussed it. If he thought there was more to the story than you let on, he never said a thing. Maybe he didn't want to know. Maybe *I* didn't want to know. So who's loyal? Think about it, Dennis." Disgusted, I slammed the dryer door and stabbed at the start button.

"Have you told your lawyer?"

"About Adrienne? No." I headed out. "I chose to think you'd changed, in which case it was irrelevant." I stopped. "Unless there is more to the story. Is there?"

"I can't believe you're asking that, after all we've been through together."

Incredulous, I stared at him. With a bark of exasperation, I started up the basement stairs, then, in a moment's boldness, turned back and said, "Is it Phoebe?"

He stared up at me from the laundry room door. "Is what Phoebe?"

"What went wrong with us."

"What are you talking about?"

"She's young and attractive."

"Beautiful. She's beautiful."

Talk about arrogant. There was more than a touch of it in his tone. It dug into me just where he wanted it to. So I was hurting already. What was a little more? "Are you in love with her?"

"She's my lawyer."

"Anyone walking into this house would know that. Do me a favor? Erase messages once you've listened. And tell her to watch what she says. The kids listen to those messages."

"Her messages are harmless."

"They're telling. It sounds like she's running the show. Does she tell you what to do and how to do it?"

"For *Christ's* sake, give me credit for something. I don't have to be told what to do. I've been running my own business for years."

I could have pointed out the sad state of that business. But I had suddenly had enough of the argument, had enough of vituperative spit. So I turned and went on up the stairs.

"What about the rest of this stuff?" he called.

"Since you're so capable of doing things yourself," I called back, "I'll let you do it."

"Where are you going?"

"To check on my son."

"He's fine now. You can leave."

I wasn't leaving until I knew for sure that Johnny was all right. Let Dennis call the cops. Let Jack Mulroy smell the lingering sickness in Johnny's room and make me go. Let Phoebe Lowe or Art Heuber or whoever the hell was his real lawyer explain to the judge why Dennis had asked me to come in the first place.

Defiance carried me back up to Johnny's room, but was replaced by something softer the instant I stepped inside. His cheeks were flushed again, but he hadn't moved since I'd left. His breathing was even. If experience was any indication, he would sleep through the night.

I sat with him for a while, mostly because I wasn't ready to go. Then I reached the point where his sleep was so sound that I knew he was fine, and the dread of leaving ruined the pleasure of staying. So I wrote a note and left it propped by his pillow. Then I went looking for Dennis. It was nearly two in the morning. Since I hadn't heard him, I guessed he had fallen asleep. He had a history of doing that when the going got rough.

Indeed, he did. And I had allowed it—worse, encouraged it. So I was as much at fault as he was.

Funny thing, a woman's guilt. We blame ourselves when things go wrong, far more than we praise ourselves when things go right, and when we do the latter, someone calls us arrogant, which discourages further praise and encourages further blame, which suits men just fine.

It wasn't fair at all.

Determined to right that particular wrong by waking Dennis now, I started for the bedroom. Halfway there, I stopped. The door was ajar. I found myself staring at it, unable to move.

Militancy was fine. Women standing up for women was fine. But that was generic, and this was specific.

Specifically, I didn't want to go inside. I didn't want to see the bed, didn't want to see Dennis in it. I didn't want to remember our lying there together, much less playing there with the children, singing, laughing. I didn't want to think of another woman lying there.

Mercifully, I was spared the pain. A quick search found Dennis asleep, all right, but stretched out on the sofa in the den. I called his name from the door, once, then more sharply. When he raised his head, I told him I was leaving. Then I slipped out into the cold November night.

Odd. I should have been more upset. Oh, I wasn't pleased at having to leave the children behind, especially not with Johnny sick. But I wasn't sad to be leaving the house itself. Dennis was there, and the tension that went with him. I felt it start to drain away the instant I started my car.

Had it always been there? Possibly. Had I been aware of it? No.

My lighthouse, on the other hand, was tension-free. No one could make demands on me there—not Dennis, not the kids, not my mother or Rona. It was a first for me, not having to please someone else, a first being able to choose what I wanted to do, just me, when, where, and how.

What I chose to do was to call Brody. It was midnight in Seattle, where he was, and he was asleep. But his groggy hello warmed me up, and when he heard my voice and smiled out a greeting, I was glad I had called. We had talked earlier in the evening. I had heard about his meeting with our Seattle franchisee and had told him about my meeting with Jenovitz. Now I told him about Johnny, but only the barest outline. I didn't tell him about my encounter with Dennis in the laundry room, didn't want Dennis intruding on our conversation. I just wanted to touch base with Brody.

I hung up the phone picturing him stretched out on his stomach in bed, wearing precious little under a sheet that barely, just barely, skimmed his hips. I fell asleep wondering if I had ever seen him that way, or if I was simply dreaming it all up.

The phone woke me less than four hours later. "You were here, Mommy, and you didn't even *tell* me!" She was as irate as irate got. "Why didn't you *wake me up*?"

I fell back to the pillow and pulled up the puff. "Kikit, honey, you were sound asleep."

"But I wanted to *see* you. I could have shown you the spelling paper I did. Daddy and me spent a whole long time on it before dinner. Johnny says Daddy says he can stay home from school. Can he?"

"He should. He was pretty sick last night. How is he now?"

"Hogging the remote. Shouldn't I get to hold it now, since I have to leave soon? It isn't fair. He gets to do *everything* good." She whimpered, "I wanted to *see* you, Mommy."

"Didn't you?" I asked, cajoling now. I was fast learning to improvise in this new landscape of my life. "I stood there at your door for the longest time and talked with you in my thoughts. I'm sure you heard. You may have even seen me, but what happens is that when you're asleep like that, you forget. Think hard. Did you hear me talking my thoughts to you last night?"

There was a small silence, then a sweet, "Were you talking about taking me skiing? I think I heard that. You were saying I could go on the lift with you and Daddy this year. I don't want to be stuck in the ski school again."

"That wasn't what I was saying at all," I scolded, but in a playful way that ignored the fact that there might not be any ski trip this year, period, certainly not one with Dennis and me both. "What I was *saying*," I drawled, thinking fast for something that would please her, "was that you looked like a little angel lying there, but that something was missing."

"A halo?"

"Nail polish." If I had promised her a new jacket, doll, or Walkman, Dennis would have accused me of trying to buy her love. I wasn't. I just wanted to make her happy.

"Angels don't wear nail polish," was her cautious response.

"Beautiful ones do. Want me to put some on for you tomorrow?"

She drew in a breath. "Will you?" It wasn't often that I painted her nails, just once in a while, as a special treat. "I want Mellow Mellow."

The color was Mellow Melon, but I got the point. "I can arrange that, but only if you pamper Johnny a little. He's sick."

"He can keep the remote. I gotta go to school anyway. Talk with you later, Mommy. Bye."

I called Johnny several times during the day to see how he was feeling. One of those times he was alone, and while he didn't seem to mind, I did. Dennis was at the supermarket, he said. I said, albeit silently, that if Dennis needed a break from the house—what mother didn't understand the feeling of being cooped up with a sick child?—he should have found someone to stay with Johnny. His parents would have done it. I would have done it.

Not that Dennis had been cooped up with a sick child for long. What had it been? Fifteen hours?

There were six people whose names and phone numbers I planned to give Dean Jenovitz as sources of information on the children's well-being—one teacher for each child, their pediatric nurse-practitioner, Johnny's two-time basketball coach, Kikit's allergy doctor, and our minister. Since I was more often with the children than Dennis, these six people knew me better than they knew him. I felt relatively confident that they liked me, but a reminder wouldn't hurt.

So I spent the better part of Tuesday calling each on the phone, dropping by in person in the case of the nurse-practitioner, the allergy doctor, and our minister, to explain the situation and ask if I might give the GAL their names. They agreed, of course. Asking was a formality. But it gave me an opportunity to thank them ahead of time, to express my apprehension in some cases, and ask for their help. It also gave me an opportunity to follow up on past discussions. People loved talking about themselves. I was a good listener.

And if I played on my relationship with each? If our discussions touched on favors I had done for each in the past?

I had never, would never attach strings to things I did. But I was helpless with regard to so much else of the legal quagmire. Hard as it was to ask for help, it was a relief to finally be able to do something on my own behalf.

Kikit called at dinnertime to say that her stomach hurt. I was quickly alert, what with her allergy problems. There was still that last unsolved attack. But the symptoms now were different. She wasn't having trouble breathing, wasn't swelling up. I was thinking that she probably had Johnny's flu—until she broke away from telling me she just might throw up, to accuse Johnny of squirting more whipped cream on his Jell-O than he had squirted on hers.

I asked to speak with Dennis.

"He's on the phone in the den. It's business. Are you coming over, Mommy?"

How could I not? Kikit didn't sound sick, but I wanted to make sure. I also wanted to see for myself that Johnny was better.

Ten minutes later, I was reassured on both counts. Johnny still had a vaguely washed-out look, but his skin was cool and he was eating again. As for Kikit, she was so engrossed in an animated retelling of the story her teacher had read them in school that day, that she forgot she was supposed to be sick.

Dennis was still on the phone when I arrived. Incredibly, he didn't even know I had come—what if I'd been a stranger with mayhem in mind?—until he walked into the kitchen fifteen minutes later.

At least he was tactful. He had the children give me hugs and sent them upstairs to do their homework before asking why I had come. Clearly he thought I had initiated the visit.

"Kikit called," I set him straight, pulling on my coat. "She must have figured that if being sick had worked for Johnny, it would work for her."

"Work how?" he asked. "What did she want?"

"Me," I said on my way to the door.

"But she's seeing you tomorrow."

I sighed, turned. "You don't get it, do you? They're used to living with me. They're used to seeing me every day, not just on Wednesdays and Saturdays. You may have convinced a judge that I was too scattered to be with my kids, but you'd have a hard time convincing them of it. I'm their mother. No court order can change that. They miss me. They feel the loss."

"Don't try to tell me that Johnny deliberately got sick to get you here."

"Of course he didn't. We both know he was sick. That isn't to say that he wasn't relieved that I'd come, relieved to know that I'll come in the future when he needs me." I sighed, held up a hand in surrender. "Let's not argue. I just think we have to be aware of the things kids do in situations like these."

"They'll get used to your living somewhere else."

"That's not the point. The point is that they're too young to understand some of what they feel and do."

"I have things under control here."

"I'm not saying you don't. Who was the business call to, by the way?" I wondered if it had been business at all.

"No one you know."

No one I knew. For a minute, I didn't speak. Then, because the court order had broken the tie between us, and that broken tie had loosened my tongue, I charged, "I've heard that a million times. 'No one you know.' You shut me out, Dennis. For *years*, you shut me out. And you say *I* wasn't approachable. You knew *much* more about my business than I ever knew about yours."

He looked bored. There was nothing new in that, either. It was his pet response when he knew I was right.

Then, as though looking bored wasn't enough, he said, "You won't win on the Motion to Recuse. Judges never grant them. My lawyer is meeting with yours on Thursday. We need the third quarter figures on WickerWise."

"We need the third quarter figures on DGR." Dennis's initials. Short for the DGR Group, the formal name of his company. No matter that it wasn't a group at all, strictly a one-man operation, but it sounded good, group. Chic and successful.

"If you're thinking," he warned, "that the profits of one will cancel out the profits of the other, don't. I'm going for blood, Claire."

If it was money he wanted, he could have it. I had made that clear to Carmen from the start. Me, I defined "blood" differently.

Wondering if we would ever see eye to eye, or if it even mattered now that we were splitting, I said a quiet, "You already have," and let myself out.

Dennis was right about the Motion to Recuse. Selwey made a show of listening to Carmen argue that he should remove himself from the case, then denied the motion.

Forewarned wasn't forearmed. I was frustrated beyond belief. "There you have one more reason why he should bow out of this case," I cried. "He dug in his heels on principle alone. That decision had nothing to do with anything you argued."

"It rarely does at this stage, but it's part of the process," Carmen remarked as she directed me through the clusters of lawyers gathered on the courthouse steps. "Now we go for an interlocutory appeal."

"How does that work?"

"I write up a petition setting forth the facts of the case and requesting relief from Selwey's ruling. I file it with the Appeals Court. A clerk there screens it to make sure that I've filed it on time and that it limits itself to what's been done in Selwey's court and nothing more. He'll write a synopsis of my petition for the judge, who will read that, then be interested enough to read the whole thing and grant us a hearing."

"When?" I asked.

"I'll have our petition filed by Monday and send a copy to Heuber. We should hear something later that week."

"About my getting the kids back?"

"No, about whether a judge will hear the case."

So many steps. Agonizingly slow. "If he hears it, when will that be?"

"A few days after that. Unless he gives Heuber time to write an opposing argument, in which case the hearing will be a few days after he receives that."

We had stopped at the curb. Shivering, I buttoned the collar of my coat and buried my hands in its pockets. "Will I get the kids then?"

"I hope so. Interlocutory appeals are hard to win, but at least we'll be dealing with a different judge. Anyone is more reasonable than Selwey."

I hugged my arms to my sides and studied the road. The wind

was plucking leaves from the gutter, sending them tumbling every which way off down the street. I hurt on their behalf.

"Meanwhile," Carmen said, "I'm meeting with Heuber this afternoon at three."

"What if his demands are easy? What if we have an agreement signed within the week?"

"If we do, we'll notify Selwey. He's just stubborn enough to insist that the divorce agreement has nothing to do with the custody issue, and that he wants to let Jenovitz finish his study."

"As things stand, that might be the quickest thing," I said with a discouraged sigh.

From the courthouse, I drove to the Essex store and spent a few hours working the floor. I did it often, both for the sake of staying in touch with the mood of the clientele and for the sheer pleasure of the work. It was particularly meaningful now. Our St. Louis franchisee was there, doing the two weeks of on-site training we required. If anything could distract me from my personal woes, this was it.

Back at the office, I sorted through the latest orders submitted to our Pennsylvania plant. Brody had been the moving force behind the plant, which had opened three years before as a means of controlling product and price. He had found a small factory in the Philippines that worked with only the finest quality rattan from Indonesia and was willing to build frames to our specifications. I sent the specifications and approved the prototypes; they produced the product in the quantities we ordered. Once the frames arrived by the container in California and were shipped east, our refinishers and upholsterers in Pennsylvania completed the work.

Initially, we had concentrated on turning out high-quality reproductions. In no time, we were producing original designs, and what a challenge they were. The most basic details could make or break an item—the pitch of the back, the height and depth of the seat, the width of the arm, the density of the cushions. I had to keep tabs on what was selling. What wasn't was discontinued and, once an analysis had been done as to the why of it lest we make the same mistake twice, was replaced by something fresh.

Brody called from our boutique in Palm Springs. The franchise had just changed owners, and while we knew the new one—she had trained here, too—this was our first on-site visit. I had already seen the first sales figures. Understandably, given the number of retirees there, the most successful pieces had higher, firmer seats. Now Brody told me about an eye-catching reconfiguration of the showroom, about the new sales help, about the owner's community contacts. The word was good.

I took as much solace from the sound of Brody's voice as from what he said. I loved his enthusiasm, loved his optimism. I loved the way I could sit back and let him talk, loved the way I could sit back and let him work. I didn't have to watch everything he did. I trusted him to do things right.

He was easy. So easy. And sexy. That voice. I kept him on the line as long as I could. He was the best distraction of all.

Three o'clock arrived. Doubting I would be able to concentrate while Carmen's meeting was in progress, I took refuge in my workroom. I removed the last of the broken weavers from the antique rocker and considered just going right on to the cleaning and reweaving. I was eager to put in, rather than take out, eager to rebuild. But I didn't want to have to backtrack when that was done, so I put the matching table where the rocker had been and set about removing its bad weavers, too.

There were fewer broken pieces here. I had most of them

picked out and discarded, when Angela poked her head in to say that she and Vicki were leaving for the day.

That was my sign. I was meeting Carmen in her office at six. I cleaned up, changed back into my suit, and drove to Boston.

I hadn't been in her reception area long enough to do more than blindly skim the table of contents of *Forbes,* when Carmen strode down the hall. I searched her face for a hint, any hint, of what had gone on in that meeting, but saw none.

"What's the word?" I asked.

She hitched her chin toward her office and waited until we were in it. Then she sat on the edge of the desk and sighed. "He isn't making it easy."

"Tell me."

"He wants half of all assets."

"He can have half."

"Including the business."

"Give him *all* of the business. It's his. I don't want it."

"Half of yours."

"Half of mine? My business? You mean, half of its worth?"

"No. He wants part ownership of WickerWise."

"You're kidding." But I could see she wasn't. "What for?" I asked, then realized it didn't matter. I shook my head. "No. The answer is no."

"That's what I told Art."

"First my children, then my business." Another headshake. "WickerWise is mine. He played no role in creating it. He played no role in making it grow. He has no claim to it." But once too often of late things had happened that I had thought impossible. Less surely, I asked, "Does he?"

"That depends on how strong an argument he can make."

"He has *no* argument."

"He does," Carmen cautioned. "He has the same argument

that women traditionally made in divorce negotiations. He was there. He was married to you the whole time you were building the business. As the principal breadwinner in those early years, he was the one who made it possible for you to spend time on the business. You didn't have to worry about providing living expenses." She broke from the litany to ask, "Did he contribute any money to WickerWise?"

"No. None. Zero. I saved money from the other work I did and took out a loan for the rest. He didn't offer to help. Not with money. Not with time. He thought WickerWise was an indulgence that wouldn't amount to much. So now he wants a piece of it? No *way*." I was furious. "And there's *more*. That other work I did? The stuff that gave me the money to start WickerWise? I did that on my own time, in between being the pretty little hostess, the efficient little homemaker, and the competent little mommy. Another woman might have been having lunch with a friend or getting a manicure. Not me. Any free time I had I spent restoring antique wicker."

Furious? That didn't begin to describe what I was feeling. "Dennis wants to be a partner in WickerWise? What a *joke*! He doesn't know the first thing *about* WickerWise. He never wanted anything to do with it—never asked questions or made suggestions other than that I should put it on the market and get what I could. He thought it was a losing proposition. Thought wicker was a passing fancy. He sneered at the thought of my tying myself up with it. Trust me. If he wants WickerWise, it's only because it's mine. Like the kids, I swear, more mine than his. He's a little boy playing his sour grapes game. What in the *devil* would he ever do as part of WickerWise? And working with Brody and me? After all he's accused us of doing? No, Carmen. It has to be the money he wants."

"He says it isn't. He says he wants the job. Apparently he's dissolving his own business. It isn't doing well."

"No surprise there," I scoffed, but the joke was on me if I didn't turn things around. "Is he dissolving DGR for the sake of these negotiations? What about the money he'll take from it?"

The look on Carmen's face should have warned me. She turned, took a paper from her file, and handed it over.

I studied it. The figures were astonishing. "It's worth nothing! What about his other holdings? When he puts together an investment package, he often takes a small piece for himself. Those small pieces must amount to something."

Carmen handed me another sheet. There wasn't much to see.

"This is it?" I was appalled. "The sum total of his business worth? What about life insurance? A retirement account? Stocks. He owns stocks."

"Sold. And as for the others, he borrowed against them. They aren't worth much."

I was stunned. "He kept talking about a nest egg. Every time he made one of his little investments, he said it was for our future. I felt safe all those years, thinking there was something." The fury returned. "Not even for his children, the bastard." I shook the paper I held. "Some of these were supposed to provide for the kids' education. Now anything that was there is gone. And this is the man who wants to run *my* company? I don't want him *touching* it. He'll run it right into the ground!" I sat back in my chair. In the next breath, dawning realization brought me forward again. "I know what he's up to. He wants a foothold in Wicker-Wise so that he can find a buyer and make me sell. That *sleaze*. He's been tossing out that possibility for years, kept telling me to sell and cut my losses. He wasn't thinking about my losses, because there aren't a hell of a lot. He was thinking about his gains!" I grew cautious. "Can he do this, Carmen? Do I have to take him in?"

"We're negotiating a settlement. We don't have to agree to a thing. Will the court make you do it, if it comes down to that?"

She didn't answer right away, seemed to be thinking, weighing and balancing. "If the court decides that everything built during the course of the marriage should be considered joint property and split, Dennis has a shot. If we can make a case for his lack of accountability—if we can argue that he shirked his financial responsibility during the marriage—the advantage is ours. Unfortunately, either way involves a trial. A trial could be six months or more down the road."

"I don't care. I can wait. He's the one in the rush, not me. As long as the issue of child custody is decided sooner." I was counting on it. I wanted my kids. "The custody issue is decided separately, isn't it?"

"Theoretically. Heuber didn't mention it today. I assume he'll try to use it for leverage when we balk at the offer they made today. As far as court activity goes, everything we're doing there at this point relates to the custody issue only. Jenovitz's study certainly does. But if we disagree with his finding, we have the right to appeal. In that case, we would go to trial on the custody issue concurrent with the divorce."

"Six months down the road?" I started to rise, sat back down. Panic was beating its wings right around the corner. "Jenovitz can't go against me. I'll die living apart from the kids for six months. Something else has to give. So, what's our next step? How do we answer Dennis?"

"For starters, we stall. Let Dennis think that we're considering his demands. If he asks you about it, don't answer. Say that you aren't sure, or that you don't know what your lawyer's latest thought is. Give him a sense of security, and he'll speak about you more gently when he talks with the GAL. In the meantime, Morgan is working on documenting a romantic link between Dennis and Phoebe. That could give us leverage of our own."

"A little character assassination."

"Uh-huh. He did it to you. What's sauce for the goose."

I hated Dennis a little more just then for making me stoop so low.

Some said that love and hate were two extremes of the same emotion. I didn't know about that. I did know that what I felt for Dennis in my anger was stronger than most anything I had felt for him before. If that meant what I thought it did, the overall shape of my marriage had been pretty sad, and if *that* was true, what was sad was my blind adherence to it.

I might have spent hours brooding on that, if Rona hadn't called soon after I returned to the lighthouse to say that Connie had had a heart attack.

Eleven

Rona's panic came over loud and clear—Connie's heart had given out, she was in intensive care, the next few hours were critical. I phoned Carmen, phoned Dennis, phoned Brody. Then I took the first plane to Cleveland.

The trip was excruciatingly slow. I had bought into Rona's fright hook, line, and sinker, and imagined finding Mom unconscious, kept alive by machines alone. I imagined the doctors shaking their heads in despair, imagined us having to make unimaginable decisions. I imagined utter stillness in that hospital room, imagined utter stillness in Mom's apartment. I imagined the final farewell of a funeral.

In fact, Mom wasn't quite that far gone. As heart attacks went, hers had been mild, caught quickly, and treated effectively. Yes, the next few days were crucial, the doctor told me when I arrived, and yes, she was definitely weak enough to be at greater risk than the average mild-heart-attack sufferer, but she was conscious and alert, sleeping lightly as we spoke.

"Don't ever, *ever* do that to me again," I begged Rona in a hushed whisper as we stood in the ICU corridor a short distance from where Connie lay. "I thought she was *gone*."

"So did *I*," Rona argued, sounding thoroughly aggrieved. "It's scary seeing her hooked up to a million monitors. The way the doctors were racing around, you'd have thought they had brought her back from the dead once and were expecting to do it again. Don't get mad at *me*, Claire. I'm the one who's here with her, trying to hold things together."

I took a deep breath, my first in too many hours. "I know. It's just that I suffered during that flight."

"I was suffering *here*. It's one thing, now that she's stabilized, to look back and say she was never that sick. It's another thing when you're going through it. I'm sorry if I dragged you all the way out here under false pretenses, but she's your mother, too. I thought you'd want to know what was happening. Was I wrong?"

"No." I sighed. "You weren't wrong." I pushed a weary hand through my hair, put a shoulder to the wall. "Of course I wanted to know. I'd have come anyway. A heart attack is a heart attack, and even without it, she's sick enough. Believe me, Rona, I wish I could be here more. But things are tense at home."

"Tense how?" she asked, but it might as well have been, "What's the excuse this time?" for the doubt on her face.

I supposed it was time. Given all that she was doing for me here, she had a right to know. "Dennis and I have separated."

She was utterly still for a minute. Then came an elongated, "No." Her voice might have held disbelief, even upset, but her face told a different story. She was clearly intrigued. "When?"

"Two weeks ago. Right after my last time here."

"You and Dennis? *You and Dennis?*"

I gave her a look, couldn't help it. Feeling beholden to my sister was one thing, protecting my own wounds was something else. "Yes, Rona. Me and Dennis."

She moved in on my swath of wall, clearly eager for details. "What *happened*?"

"Long story. I can't go into it now. The bottom line is that I've bought a smaller place."

"*You* moved out? Ah, so that's what the new phone number was about. But why did you move out? You're the woman. You're the one with the kids. He's the one who's supposed to move out."

I rubbed the back of my neck. "Yes, well, that's how things usually happen, but this isn't the usual situation."

"Why not?" she asked, indignant now.

"Because I'm the one with the money, and he's the one with the kids."

"*Dennis* has the kids? *Claire*." She made my name a three-note protest.

"Look, this isn't how I wanted things, but I didn't have much choice. I travel for work, my career is more demanding than his, and then there's Mom," so Dennis's argument went, then my rationalization. "I wouldn't have been able to get away as easily as I did tonight if I'd had to start arranging for the kids. I know you think I should be here more, and I want to be, but I want to be with my kids, too, and the weekends are the best time for that. So where am I supposed to be, there or here? You tell me."

It wasn't the whole story, for which I felt guilt and more guilt. But I wasn't ready to tell the whole story. I was feeling too vulnerable to open myself to Rona's gloating.

"Does Mom know about this?" she asked.

"No. I can't tell her yet." I imagined Rona waiting for a wakeful moment and slyly inserting my separation into the conversation. "Don't do it, please? She'll be too upset."

"Disillusioned, you mean. She thought you were the perfect one."

"She knew I wasn't perfect. She knew my marriage wasn't perfect."

"Funny, she never told me. All she did was tell me that I couldn't manage to stay married to either of *two* husbands, while you and Dennis were solid as a rock. Like I had something to do with Harold's dying. Ah, but her problem with him was his age. 'Old enough to be *my* husband,' she said so many times I could die myself. Lucky for Harold he wasn't her husband. He'd have croaked that much earlier just to escape her."

"Rona."

"She's a tough nut. You don't see it, because you two have a special something going. You're the only one who comes close to being good enough for her. Do you think she did Daddy in, too?"

"*Rona.* That's *crazy.* Mom wasn't tough when Daddy was alive. Just the opposite. She took security for granted. Then he died, and she had to fight to survive. Call that tough if you will, but it's only because she wanted us to have and be and do everything she couldn't have and be and do herself. She wanted us to have an easier time than she did."

"Well, we have, in some ways. We have money, at least." She was looking at me strangely, speculatively. "So you see the kids on the weekends. Incredible. I'd never have thought it of you, Claire. To hear Mom tell it, your kids are your life. To hear her tell it, it's a good thing I never had kids because I'd *never* have been as good at it as you. Only on weekends, huh?"

"More than that," I said to make things sound casual. I didn't want her knowing about the court order, didn't want her knowing that a judge had thought me inadequate. Okay. So I had my pride, too. "I see the kids whenever anything comes up. I was with them on Monday, then again yesterday. We talk several times a day."

"Still, Dennis with custody? Whew. That's quite a blow to the old image."

"The old image," I said with a level look, "was a figment of your imagination."

"A figment of *Mom's* imagination."

"Maybe. Okay. Probably. And she was wrong if she held you to a cooked-up standard, but maybe she held me to it, too, you know?" It hadn't occurred to me before, but it made sense. "Maybe I felt pressure, too."

Rona didn't respond to that, simply stood there looking gorgeous—more gorgeous than I ever could, though Mother had picked on her for that, too—leaning against the wall within arm's reach of me. Sad, we didn't touch. At a time in our lives when physical contact might have offered solace, we couldn't give it. Our relationship wasn't defined that way. I wasn't sure why.

But, boy, was I sorry. The need to hold and be held was great just then, because no matter that Connie wasn't as sick as I'd feared, the prognosis was poor.

Brody came to mind for holding. Not Dennis. Brody. I wouldn't have minded being held by him just then.

"Is this a trial separation?" Rona asked.

I reined in my fantasy life.

A trial separation? I tried to think of reconciling with Dennis but couldn't.

Again Brody came to mind.

It struck me then that my marriage had been a break-up waiting to happen. How else to explain the feelings that had burst into existence—no, not into existence, into *awareness*—in two short weeks? Feelings against Dennis. Feelings for Brody. Had he been an *affair* waiting to happen all this time?

"No," I told Rona. "No trial separation. This is the real thing."

"That bad, huh?" She smiled. "I'm amazed."

I pushed away from the wall. "For the record, it's been a painful experience. I would have thought you'd understand, having gone through it yourself." I might have said more, might have shared thoughts and fears, had Rona and I been able to communicate. But we couldn't. I had always blamed that on Rona's competitiveness. It struck me now that maybe I was competitive, too. I was embarrassed to confess that my marriage had failed. I had wanted to be better than that.

So now I was humbled, as Rona had been all those times. Again I thought to reach out to her. Again something held me back.

Not wanting to argue, and unable to do anything else, I started down the hall. "I'll go sit with Mom for a while."

She looked old, more like eighty than sixty-three. It was as though illness had compressed the passage of time, taking the twenty more years she should have had and, with each week that passed, shrinking them to ten, five, two. I tried to recall the face with the warm smile, smooth skin, and healthy glow, but this other one was overpowering. Nor could I look away. That would have been desertion. This was still my mother, needing love in the last days of her life.

Though she slept most of the weekend, she knew I was there. From time to time, she opened her eyes and focused on me, squeezed my hand, whispered my name. Unlike the last time, I didn't ramble on and on. For one thing, my throat was tight much of the time. For another, what could I talk about? Not the situation at home. Not my relationship with Rona. I might have liked to tell her about Brody. But what?

So we were quiet together, Mom and I, and it was surprisingly peaceful. She seemed comforted enough by my presence that I didn't feel the need to perform. Her heart behaved. There were neither cardiac aftershocks nor new traumas. By Saturday afternoon, she left the ICU and returned to her room.

Rona brought fresh flowers. She brought Mom's favorite cologne, brought a cassette recorder and more audio books than Mom would be able to listen to in a month. She brought a matching nightgown and robe that were just as beautiful as the matching nightgown and robe she had given Mom last time I was there. She brought crème caramel from Mom's favorite restaurant.

Was Mom grateful? Hard to tell. There were smiles, nods, and the same sad look I knew well. Even in her dimming view of the world, she thought Rona was hopelessly ditzy.

Did I? No. But I didn't know how to tell Rona that without confirming that Mom felt it, which would have done even more harm. So I praised her for the presents she brought, and thanked her for being there for Mom, and the part of me that hated being competitive and took my humbling as just punishment, didn't mind at all that she knew about the demise of my marriage. I suspected she found satisfaction in precious little else.

I've always had trouble with partings. Having lost a parent, I knew about mortality. Having lost a parent young and with no warning at all, I knew about untimely loss. As optimistic as I was in other regards, I was no innocent when it came to matters of life and death. Back then, Connie could have been healthy as a horse. Still I felt a twinge of fear each time I left her, fearing she wouldn't be there when I returned.

I got a handle on those emotions after I married Dennis, probably because there was such a to-do at the time of the parting, especially once the children were born, that I didn't have time for morbid thoughts. Leaving a sick mother brought them all back. The sicker Mom got, the worse they were. This time was truly the pits. I promised to call her that night and be back to see her in another week or two, but I saw that look in her eyes again, that sad, knowing, sweetly chiding look. We both knew that my words could well prove empty if by the time I returned she was gone.

Walking out of that hospital room on Sunday morning was so

hard, that had things been different, I would have said *to hell with this, the children will understand* and stayed. But Dennis wouldn't understand. Nor would his lawyer, or the judge, or the GAL, with whom I had a Monday appointment. If I had chosen my mother over my children, I would have been called a lousy mother. So I was a lousy daughter instead.

Life was a shopping list of compromises, Connie had once bemoaned. I only wished I could have explained to her why I made this particular compromise. It would have helped to know she agreed.

Once airborne, my thoughts turned to all that I had put on hold that now needed addressing. The first was the children. Having missed my Saturday with them, I had asked Dennis if I might pick them up on my way home from the airport. He hadn't been eager to accommodate me at first. Then he had given in with surprising speed.

I wanted to think that he sympathized with my mother's condition and saw the reasonableness of my request. The cynic in me—something new, barely two weeks old—wondered if he had simply come up with a good alternative for Sunday. And that was fine, too, I decided. He had been doing his own thing on weekends for years, working us in where and when we fit. This way was more honest—and a damned sight easier than having to make excuses to the kids for his absence.

Besides, part of me didn't care if he was planning to make love to Phoebe Lowe on the balcony at City Hall Plaza for all the world to see, as long as I had that time with Johnny and Kikit. I needed to see that they were being well-cared for. Given what I had come from, with Mom so ill and Rona and I unable to connect, I needed their warmth and vibrancy.

I needed someone else's warmth and vibrancy, not to mention

business advice, but he had stopped on his way back from the West Coast to visit with his daughter in New York and wasn't due back until that night—and he was a fantasy, anyway, a bug put in my ear by my husband, irony of ironies. Only a fantasy. Dream stuff when I needed it. No more.

The plane landed right on time. Gathering my carry-ons, I went through the jetport into the terminal, then down the concourse, past the security point to the spot where my driver usually met me. In his place, standing apart from whoever else waited for passengers, not in New York at all and impossible to miss, was the fantasy himself.

I came to a stop and stood there, unable to move for a minute. In the next, I looked around, half-expecting everyone else in the area to be staring at him too, he stood out so. Deep bespectacled eyes, long denim legs, T-shirt, unbuttoned flannel shirt, fleece vest—the sight of him made me warm all over, and when he smiled, a small, skewed smile that was a little helpless, even shy, I felt it deep inside.

He was leaning against a wall, his fingers flat in the pockets of his jeans, one knee bent, the sole of his boot flat to the wall. I had the feeling he didn't know if he should have come, what with Carmen's warnings and all, but that he hadn't been able to resist. Then again, that might have been my own wishful thinking.

But he was there, right or wrong. And, right or wrong, I was thrilled to see him.

My feet moved, taking me right up to where he lounged with such nonchalant grace. His eyes didn't leave me for a second, and his smile stayed. Eyes and smile, mine matched his. I might have known Brody would be there for me.

I sighed in relief, nodded in pleasure. Then my chest grew tight. I pressed my lips together tightly against a sudden urge to cry. He must have sensed it, because his smile faltered. He took my bags from me and set them down, then, before I could worry about who might be watching, wrapped me up in his arms.

I sighed again, more a moan this time, high and shaky. Fleeting thoughts—why he was here instead of in New York, how he had known which flight I was on—came and went, unimportant in the overall scheme of things, certainly irrelevant to the moment. The shakiness hit me all over, the aftershock of an emotional weekend, and while I didn't cry, I slipped my arms under his flannel shirt and held on tight. He was solid at a time when everything around me was changing. Frightening, how much I needed him.

His hands moved, stealthy but sure, on my back. Likewise, his lips against my hair, then my forehead. And it was safe, as safe as his presence. What I had come from made it so, as did where we were, because airports were unique. They were places of transience, the crossroads of a modern age. They were a hothouse of emotional extremes, one minute witness to the indifference of the seasoned traveler, another to the joy of reunion or the sorrow of parting. People kissed in airports all the time, not only lovers, but friends, family, even colleagues.

So I didn't protest when Brody kissed me. Didn't protest? Raised my head for it, if the truth were told, because I felt it coming, felt his mouth touch my right eye, my cheekbone, the hollow beneath. Suddenly it seemed the most natural, most urgent thing in the world that we kiss, and as for having a cover, the airport was it. No one had to know this was a real kiss, that those initial tentative touches were breaching a threshold. No one had to know when our lips grew more sure, then opened, or when the hunger grew and our tongues met.

I knew all those things. I knew Brody knew them too, could feel it in the thrum of his body and the shortness of his breath. Not that I was any better. I was shaking badly by the time he tore his mouth from mine and, with a large hand cradling my head, pressed my face to his throat.

Did he ever smell good. Clean and soapy over just a hint of musk.

"Let's move it," he said in a hoarse voice, and at first I thought he was angry. That lasted until he bent to pick up my bags and I got a look at him. It wasn't anger that put that burnt color on his cheeks, or anger that had him carrying one of my bags against his fly.

Ah, the pleasure I took in that, the sense of power I felt. Pleasure, power—nearly as heady as his smell.

Illicit? True. We weren't supposed to do anything to validate Dennis's charge. But the charge was already made and believed, Dennis and I were separated now, and Lord *knew* what he was doing with Phoebe or some other young thing. Besides, I had spent my life calculating my risks, carefully weighing one side against the other before making decisions, and look where it had gotten me. On the other hand, I had bought my lighthouse on impulse, and I loved it. So if I kissed Brody and loved that too, what was the harm?

"Live dangerously, Claire," I urged without realizing that I'd spoken aloud until I heard Brody snicker beside me. My eyes flew to his, surprised, then defiant.

He shot me a whoa-there expression that said he wasn't disagreeing, and his actions followed suit. No sooner had he guided me to the Range Rover and tossed my bags in the back, then he took my face in both hands and kissed me again.

There were no tentative touches this time, just a full, wide-open, no-holds-barred kiss right off the bat. Yes, I had imagined what kissing Brody would be like, but this was something else. It was the kind of thing that cleared my head of any other thought that might have been there. I didn't mourn Connie, didn't pine for the kids or simmer over Dennis or worry about WickerWise. I didn't think about anyone's disapproval, not Carmen's or the court's or Dennis's. Nor did I worry about whether someone would see us and tell. What Brody was doing to me with his hands, his mouth, his body, right there, pressed tight to the Range Rover's side, was worth the risk. He smelled good, tasted good, felt good. He had me coiling my arms around his neck and kissing him back, teasing his tongue, nipping his lips, sharing my breath with him and wanting more still.

I hadn't known I was so hungry. I hadn't known this kind of hunger even existed.

Where it would have ended, had it been up to me, I didn't know. I was out of control and entranced. Brody was the one who had to draw back, though he did it slowly and with reluctance, if the way his lips clung after his body had left and even then kept coming back for one-last-times.

He dragged in a long, ragged breath and dropped his head back for a minute. When it came forward, he looked naughty.

"There," he said. "Was that so bad?"

It was my turn to snicker, which I did loudly. I put my forehead to his chest. It picked up the beat of his heart. Hard not to, it was so loud and fast.

"Just think what it would be like to neck," he said.

"What did we just do?"

"Kiss. Period."

"It felt like more."

"Soon, baby. Soon."

I thought to say that he shouldn't be so smug, or assume certain things, or call a nineties woman baby, for heaven's sake. But, so help me, his smugness was earned after a kiss like that, his assumption had a fifty-fifty chance of being right, and as for the baby part, nineties woman or no, it had felt pretty good.

Dennis had never called me baby. He had sung to me and taken pictures of me, and I had felt special each time, but he had never coddled me or treated me like I needed protection, and maybe I didn't. But, boy, was it nice to lean on someone for a change. Boy, was it *nice* to be taken care of. Even competent women needed that, every once in a while.

Soon after the start of our meeting, Dean Jenovitz outlined a game. I couldn't very well refuse to play.

"Consistent," he said.

I considered his scale. If I rated myself low for the sake of modesty, he might buy into that rating. Modesty had a limited role when it came to salesmanship, and salesmanship, it seemed, was what this study was about. Not justice. Salesmanship.

I gave myself a nine.

"Resourceful."

"Nine."

"Competent."

"Eight."

"Why not a nine again?"

"Because competence is relative. What I do, I do well, but there are other things that I don't do well at all. I farm those things out. I know how to delegate. That's half of why I'm good at what I do."

Jenovitz sat staring at me. I thought to say more. But I didn't *want* to say more. I had said what I felt. So I just sat there staring back.

Finally he said, "Are you angry?"

I blinked. "No. Why do you ask?"

"When you were here last time, you were nervous. You're different today."

Nervous last time? Hell, yes. My future pivoted on this man's opinion. Different today? After the past twenty-four hours? After the past *ninety-six*?

"Maybe," I said.

"Maybe what?"

"Different." I looked down, frowned, studied the black beads on the tail of my belt and said more quietly, "Angry."

"Care to say why?"

My head came up. "Because I'm in the middle of a situation that I didn't want and don't like. I spent the afternoon with my children yesterday. Every other word out of the little one's mouth has to do with when I'm coming home, and the big one is subdued, and they both get edgy—hell, I do, too—when the end of our time together nears. I don't know what they're feeling after I drop them back with their father, but I know what I am, and it isn't warm and fuzzy. It's lonely. It's afraid. It's worried. I keep thinking that it didn't have to be like this, that it could have been gentler, but thanks to my husband and the court, it isn't. This is very, very hard for me, Dr. Jenovitz. I'm a mother. I love my kids. Every ounce of maternal instinct I possess is telling me they'll be hurt. So, yes, I'm angry. I have a right to be, don't I?"

"Not if the charges against you are true."

"They aren't," I insisted and sank into the chair. There were times when the bid to prove my innocence seemed futile. Okay. I had only had a single hour with Jenovitz so far. But, God, it felt like more.

"That's what I'm trying to determine," he said. "Anger gets in the way."

"Last time you said I should be mourning. Isn't anger just like it, kind of a natural step in the process?"

"Yes. Though not as productive."

"It vents feelings. I do have lots of those, even though the judge would like to think I'm a coldhearted businesswoman."

"Speaking of which," he said and paused to lean sideways, open a drawer, and fish inside. I heard the rustle of plastic wrap. When he straightened, he was fumbling a sourball from its wrapper. Seconds later, he pushed it into his mouth. "Speaking of which," he talked around the candy, "we were discussing competence. And delegating. Would you say that delegating is necessary for a working mother?"

"No," I answered more calmly. The venting had helped. "I'd say it's necessary for any successful executive."

"But a working mother can't do without it?"

I often discussed that with the women I worked with—my office assistant, the manager of my local store, franchisees around the country. Most were mothers. We shared war stories all the time. "A working mother needs help. We're holding down one too many jobs to do everything ourselves."

"Lining up that help can be a job in and of itself. It takes being organized. Rate yourself there."

"Organized?" Not hard to choose. "Nine."

He shifted the sourball, then said, "Imaginative?"

What the hell. If he wanted to call me conceited, he would anyway. "Nine."

"Compulsive."

"Three."

He looked surprised, sitting there with his bushy brows raised and the candy bulging against his cheek. "You don't see yourself as compulsive?"

"No. Does my husband?"

He bit down on the candy. I had to wait for my answer until the crunching was done. Then his words poured out as if to make up for the delay. "He mentioned it. He feels you're compulsive with regard to achievement. He fears you're too rigid when it comes to the schedules your children keep. He fears you're too demanding of them."

"I'd have said he was the demanding one. He's the one who gets upset when Johnny's grades aren't good enough, or when Kikit lapses back into a lisp. I'm not demanding. The kids' schedules aren't rigid. I make them go to school, that's a must, but they've always been the ones to ask for the after-school things. They have musical ability, but neither has wanted lessons either in voice or an instrument, and I haven't pushed. So Kikit does ballet and gymnastics and library, and Johnny plays sports. The only thing I ask of them is that if they take something on, they give it their best shot."

"Your husband says they're busy nearly every day after school. Does it worry you they don't have down time?"

"They have down time—suppertime, evenings, days when they don't have plans, weekends. I schedule my own work around those times."

"Must be a challenge."

"Not usually. Since I'm the boss, I can work when I want. It gets back to the issue of help. I have good support staff. That's one of the things I decided on as soon as WickerWise started to grow. My kids come first. My staff knows that."

"Sounds pat." What he meant, what his tone inferred, was that I was being glib.

"Ask the people I work with," I suggested. "Please. Their names are on my list." In addition to the six who knew Kikit and Johnny best, I had included the managers of both the Essex and the Vineyard stores, plus, of course, Brody.

"Did you ever want to be anything else?"

"Career-wise?" When he nodded, I thought back. "I wanted to be a doctor, had that childhood dream, you know, of saving lives. That was before I took biology. I wasn't very good at it."

"Was that why you didn't pursue it?"

"Partly. The other part had to do with money. I didn't have it.

Then I met Dennis, who had a little, but by that time I was involved in interior design and had forgotten about being a doctor. Good thing. Dennis wanted a full-time wife."

"So how did the interior designing fit in?" Jenovitz asked and opened the drawer again.

"I had been working as a furniture buyer for a national chain of home stores. I resigned my job when I got married and started doing freelance design work instead."

He was listing toward the drawer, looking at me while rummaging inside. "How did Dennis take to that?"

"Just fine. He hardly knew I was working. He was stunned when tax time came and he saw how much I was earning. Not that it was that much. But it was more than he expected. It was like that for a long time, my work being unobtrusive."

"Not now," Jenovitz said. He came up with another sourball, pulled the wrapper off, popped it in.

"Maybe not, but back then we didn't depend on my income to live. Now we do."

"You certainly do." Sucking hard, he leaned forward and shuffled through papers. "Your house is worth"—his brows rose when he saw the figure—"quite a bit."

"Dennis fell in love with the house."

"You didn't?"

"Not that house. My first choice was another one. It was older and had more unusual lines. It was less expensive, but it needed work."

"Didn't Dennis see the same potential?"

"No. He loved the colonial. So we bought it."

"But you do like fine things."

"Don't we all?"

"We're talking about you, Mrs. Raphael. Materialistic. Rating, please?"

"Five," I said without pause. "I spend money on things I can afford, and enjoy them, but I can live without them. I did for a long time."

"Ah, yes. Growing up. You had less than your children do now. Do you think that they're spoiled?"

"Maybe a little. Parents enjoy giving their children things they didn't have themselves. I'm no exception."

He pushed the sourball into one cheek. "Would you say that your children are happy?"

"Right now, no. They're confused about what's happening between Dennis and me. In general, yes, they're happy."

"How can you tell?"

"They smile. They relate well to people. They don't act out. They do well in school."

"They've been in a two-parent home," he remarked. "How important do you think that is?"

Of all the things he had asked me, this was one of more relevance to my children's future. Uneasy, I said, "It's something I always wanted for my children. Something I assumed they would have. That's one of the reasons I didn't want Dennis to talk about separating."

"You haven't answered my question."

No, I hadn't, because it upset me. Dealing with the everyday details of my life kept me buffered from the overall reality, which was that my kids wouldn't be living with both of their parents, together, ever again. And they shouldn't, under the circumstances. It wouldn't be healthy. Dennis resented me, and, increasingly, the feeling was mutual. Not a good atmosphere for adults, much less kids.

"Mrs. Raphael?"

"A two-parent home is nice," I said, "but it isn't the be-all and end-all. It isn't a guarantee that the child will be happy. Many a happy, well-adjusted child has come from a single-parent home."

"You, for example."

I had been well-adjusted. Happy was another matter.

For simplicity's sake, I said, "Yes. Me. It depends on how that single parent handles the situation. It depends on the child, too, and on the dynamics between parent and child. My mother and I were alike. We helped each other."

He sat back, sucking his candy, waiting.

I filled the silence by saying, "My sister, Rona, was something else. She and my mother had a different relationship."

"In what way?"

"I wish I knew," I said with a diffident laugh. "Actually, I know how it was different. I just don't know why."

He frowned, set his elbow on the arm of his chair, put his chin on his fist.

"They rubbed each other the wrong way," I started in with the how. "What one wanted, the other couldn't give. What one had, the other belittled."

"Which of you is older?"

"Me."

"You must have been a hard act to follow."

"It wasn't that. Mom and I were close. Rona felt left out. So she tried harder. But the harder she tried, the more she bombed."

Jenovitz looked intrigued. It occurred to me that, being an experienced psychologist, he might suggest how I could deal with Rona better.

"Mom had a thing for security. She never wanted us to feel helpless like she had. I took the message in a general sense and grew to be self-sufficient. Rona took it in a specific sense and married the richest guy she could find. That marriage failed, so she married again, and *that* marriage failed. She has money now, trust funds and all, and she doesn't understand why Mom isn't thrilled."

"Why isn't Mom thrilled?"

"Because Rona doesn't have any ties—no children, no reliable friends. She isn't trained to do anything and doesn't want to be anything, just flits around. Mom thinks she's shallow."

"Do you?"

"No. I think—" I tried to decide. "I think she's stalled. She's spent so long trying to please Mom that she doesn't know what she wants, so she can't move in any direction. I also think she's terrified. Since she can't do things right for Mom, she feels she can't do things right, period."

"Poor girl sounds demoralized. She must think Mom doesn't love her. Does Mom worry about that?"

"I'm sure she does." I frowned. "I guess. That generation was never good at expressing some things."

"That generation is my generation. I express what I want to express."

"Well, my mother doesn't, or can't, or won't."

"Which is it?"

"I don't know. But I know she loves me. She may not be big on saying the words or holding my hand or hugging me, but I know she loves me. It's right there in her face."

"Is that where Johnny and Kikit see it?"

"They do, but they don't need to. I also say the words, and I use my body. I hold them *a lot*. I've *never* wanted them to doubt what I felt. I'm very different from my mother that way, if that's what you're getting at. My children know I love them. Ask them. They'll tell you." Had I been too vehement? No. It was impossible to be too vehement about something like that.

"So. Your mother worked long hours. Did you resent that?"

"I understood the need. I knew she had no choice."

"But did you resent it?"

I didn't want to resent it. Connie had tried so hard to make a life for us that criticizing her seemed ungrateful. Still, there were times when I was frightened by something I had experienced—girlfriend squabbles, money worries, menstruation—and had wanted to curl up in a ball against her, only she hadn't been around. "Sometimes. I was lonely."

"Don't you worry that your children feel the same?"

"No. The situation is different. For one thing, my mother was the only parent I had. When she was at work, my sister and I were alone. For another, we didn't have things to keep us busy after school. For a third, we couldn't call her."

"Couldn't?"

"Her boss didn't like her getting calls. My kids call me all the time. I encourage them to. They love coming to work with me during school vacations."

"Don't they get in the way?"

"No."

He looked skeptical. With a slight, almost teasing smile, he asked, "There weren't ever times, even when they were little, when you wanted to give them back?"

"Give them back?"

His smile lingered. "A figure of speech. You know what I mean. Had it up to the eyebrows with spills and squabbles."

"Of course there were, but—"

"Patience. How would you rate yourself?"

"With regard to my children? Nine-point-five."

"Amazing you never thought of teaching, with a patience level like that."

I returned his teasing smile. "Just because I'm patient with my own kids doesn't mean I'm patient with other people's kids."

"Did you always know you wanted only two?"

"Yes."

"Why?"

"Two seemed right. Few enough for individual attention. For individual love. Besides, children cost money. We had no idea back then that we would have what we have now."

"Is that why you put it off?" When I frowned, he said, "You weren't young, having your first."

"I was thirty-one. That isn't old."

"But you were married at twenty-five. You told me you resigned your job at that point and freelanced. Plenty of flexibility there, so why the hold on kids?"

I didn't know what he was driving at, but it didn't feel right. Cautiously, I said, "I felt we needed time alone, Dennis and I."

"Did he agree?"

"He certainly didn't argue. He was busy trying to build his own business."

"If he was busy doing that, you couldn't have gotten the time alone that you wanted."

"We had what we needed. Is there a point to this, Dr. Jenovitz? I don't see what it has to do with how I mother my kids."

"It has to do with your attitude toward being a mother."

"In what way?" I asked.

"Some women want children, but resent their presence."

"I'm not one of those women."

"Then explain the abortion."

Abortion, I echoed silently. *What abortion?* I wanted to ask.

But I knew what abortion he meant. It might have been buried away under the layers of family we had built subsequent to it, but a woman never forgot an abortion. She might try to pretend it hadn't happened, might keep it a secret from her mother, her sister, even her closest friends, but it was always there.

I understood that. What I didn't understand was why, after years of silence, my husband had mentioned it now.

Twelve

My silence had nothing to do with defiance. I was initially too startled to speak, then, when my thoughts started darting every which way, too confused.

Finally, Dean Jenovitz asked, "Did I hit a sore spot?"

"Sore spot? Whew. I guess you'd call it that. Who told you about it?"

"About the abortion?" He seemed to stress the word, though I might have imagined it. A sore spot, indeed—the word, the memory. "It doesn't matter," he said. "I want you to tell me about it."

"How did you find out?" I asked again.

"It doesn't matter," he repeated and sat back, waiting for me to explain.

But I wasn't doing any explaining until he did some himself, because emerging from the confusion were anger and suspicion. "That abortion happened a long time ago. Dennis knows how painful it was for me. We haven't talked about it, haven't *mentioned* it in years. By unspoken agreement. I'm stunned that he chose to raise it now."

"He didn't raise it. It was right there in the file I received when I got this case."

"Then the *judge* knew?" Not likely. Had Selwey known I'd had an abortion, he would have delighted in bringing it up.

"I don't know what the judge knew," Jenovitz said. "That isn't my business. All I know is that these medical records came with the file."

Medical records. "Medical records?"

"They do exist, you know," Jenovitz said.

"Actually, I didn't. I mean, I assumed there would have been a record of it in some old file, but wouldn't confidentiality laws prevent its release? I wasn't aware that anyone had gone looking for it, much less made copies and given them to the judge or to you."

"I take it you'd rather they hadn't?"

I laughed at the absurdity of the question. "Of course, I'd rather they hadn't. I didn't enjoy that abortion. I didn't enjoy it physically or mentally. It wasn't something I would have chosen to do—"

"Excuse me, Mrs. Raphael, but you did choose to do it." He put a hand on the file. "According to this, the abortion wasn't a medical necessity. You simply decided to terminate your pregnancy."

"'Simply'?" My voice rose. I let it. "There was no 'simply' about it. It was an agonizing decision."

"Which you made nonetheless."

"Which *my husband and I* made nonetheless."

"That isn't what he says."

"Excuse me?"

"He says that he wanted the baby, but that you were vehement about postponing parenthood."

I was dumbfounded, hurt, *livid*. Sitting erect, I said, "Let's set something straight. It wasn't that I didn't want the baby. That's rarely the issue when a woman has an abortion. She wants the baby, but the circumstances of her life are such that having a baby will be a hardship."

"What was the hardship in your case? Your husband was earning a decent living."

"It wasn't the money. We were having personal differences. I wasn't sure the marriage would last. I envisioned having to raise the child alone."

"And that would have been the hardship?"

"Emotionally, yes. I was desperate to have my children raised differently from me."

"In a two-parent family."

"In a secure setting."

"Your marriage was that shaky?"

"It seemed to be at the time. We hadn't been married very long, and there were problems. My energies were going into saving the relationship. It wasn't the right time for us to have a child. Dennis agreed with me on that."

"Then the abortion was your idea?"

"Actually, it was Dennis's idea."

"That isn't what he said."

"No, it wouldn't be, would it. He would have dug up those records to show what a lousy mother I am. He would have painted himself as an innocent, but that wasn't how it happened. Dennis is no innocent. The problems we were having stemmed from something very wrong that he did. Did he tell you about that?"

"No."

I hesitated for only a second longer. Dennis had raised the abortion, I could raise this. Fair was fair. I wanted my kids.

"Several years before we were married, Dennis had an affair with a married woman. She was the wife of his boss. When it ended, she blackmailed him with threats of telling what they'd done and having him booted out of the firm and black-balled in the field if he didn't pay up. So he sent her a monthly check. We were married a year when I found out about it. It mightn't have been so bad if he'd been up-front about it, but even when I had the canceled checks in my hand, he gave me a story or two before the truth. Adultery and blackmail. It was hard for me to accept."

Jenovitz regarded me patiently.

"Up until then, I had thought he was just about perfect."

Jenovitz nodded.

"So, suddenly, I was disillusioned. I kept thinking there were other things I didn't know about him. Dennis denied it, but I had learned the hard way that he could put on a good show when he wanted to."

Jenovitz shrugged with an eyebrow.

"So things were tense between us. I was seeing a side of him that I hadn't known existed. We were arguing a lot—and that included the night he came home from work and I told him I was pregnant." Now that the door had been opened, I recalled the scene well. "The first thing he did was to blame me for *getting* pregnant, like I'd done it alone. The next thing he did was to say that there wasn't anything wrong with our relationship, other than problems I'd seen fit to magnify. Then, *he* suggested that if I didn't want the baby, I should get an abortion. So if you want to be technical, he was the one who said it first, not me."

"But you made the arrangements."

"Yes. After a month's anguish, nights and nights of debating it, and finally agreeing that it was the sensible thing to do. I made the arrangements, because I was the one with the ob-gyn man, but Dennis came with me when I had the procedure." I was fast organizing my thoughts. "So if you think that an abortion thirteen-plus years ago says something about the kind of mother I am today, I have to point out that Dennis was as much a party to it as I was. If having an abortion says something about me, it says the same thing about Dennis. More. After Kikit was born, he had a vasectomy. What does that say about a desire to parent?"

"A vasectomy and an abortion are two very different things. A vasectomy prevents conception, an abortion kills what has already been conceived."

I was sorry I'd mentioned it, and held up a hand. "Don't let's argue that. The issue here is parenting. Neither thing—abortion or vasectomy—has any bearing on what kind of parents Dennis and I are."

"Then why did you mention the vasectomy?"

"Because you mentioned the abortion! *And*," I added, "because it was something Dennis did all on his own. I found out about it two days before he had it done, after he'd seen the doctor, made the appointment, committed himself to it emotionally. What does *that* say about Dennis? And what about that affair he had? If it was so serious as to warrant blackmail, it must have really been something. What does *that* say about Dennis?"

"Good grief, you're belligerent."

"You people have *made* me belligerent. I wouldn't have mentioned that affair on my own. It was over and done years ago, just like the abortion. I wouldn't have thought that abortion had any relevance to what's happening today, but you apparently do, since you raised it. So am I supposed to sit here without speaking? There are two sides to every story. Am I supposed to hold mine in? Am I supposed to say nothing while you draw conclusions that aren't true? Am I supposed to do nothing when my husband comes in here and lies? I didn't ask for this. I didn't ask for *any* of it. Belligerent? Hell, yes. I'm fighting for my kids, Dr. Jenovitz. How else should I be?"

It took me three tries before I reached Dennis, and then he wasn't at the house or the office, but in his car. I was too angry to bother with a hello, but launched straight into, "I just came from meeting with Jenovitz. What possessed you to dig up those medical records?"

"What medical records?" Dennis asked, but his question was barely out when Kikit was yelling toward the phone from the back seat.

"Mommy? Is that you? Hi, Mommy. Guess what? I'm singing a solo at the Thanksgiving assembly. You're coming, aren't you? It's the Tuesday before Thanksgiving, or maybe the Monday, I don't know, but you have to be there."

I heard a click, then Dennis's voice more clearly as he took the phone in his hand. "What medical records?"

"The ones that had to do with the abortion—"

"Sit *still*, Clara Kate," Dennis said away from the phone. "You'll talk with her when I'm done."

"I had that abortion years ago," I said. I was in my car, still in the parking lot by Jenovitz's building. "It has nothing to do with what kind of mother I am today, or what kind of father *you* are. That abortion was a joint decision. Okay, you didn't want it at first, but neither did I."

"Keep *quiet*, Kikit!" Dennis yelled. "I can't hear a word she's saying!"

"I didn't want it *at all*, but our marriage was iffy, and if we'd gotten divorced, that child would have suffered. You knew that as well as I did. Not to mention the *gall* of raising that whole thing, without telling Jenovitz the cause of the problems between us. Fine to paint me the villain and you the saint. Well, I told him, Dennis. I told him about Adrienne."

"You said that was irrelevant."

"So was the abortion! If that says something about me, your affair with Adrienne says something about you. You don't seem to get it, Dennis. I want the kids. I'll do things I would never otherwise do to get them back."

"For the record," Dennis said in a surprisingly quiet voice, "I didn't get those files."

"Then who did? Art Heuber? Or was it Phoebe? How would either of them have known to go after medical records, if not because you told them? Did you tell them about Adrienne, too?"

"That was a long time ago."

"So was the abortion!"

"*Kikit!* Here, Claire. I can't take this. Talk to your daughter."

"Mommy, are we going to the circus on Saturday? You said you had to make sure it was okay with Daddy." There was a pause, then, "Why *not*, Daddy? No, I won't eat something I'm not supposed to. No, I *haven't* been sick every night this week. I just say that sometimes. Everyone else in my whole class is going. Same with Johnny's. Can we? But we have to decide *now*, not later." To me, defiantly, "I'm going, Mommy. I don't care what Daddy says." A quick breath. "Mommy, when am I gonna see you? I have stuff to *show* you."

I had seen her the afternoon before, but it seemed like an age to me, too. I needed this separation over and done—which was a sobering thought if ever there was one, because I couldn't help but fear that by arguing with the GAL, I had only prolonged it.

I didn't have an appointment with Carmen, but I was upset enough to go to her office without one. I was shown into a conference room to wait. By the time she joined me, I was as angry with myself as I was with Dennis.

"I blew it," I said after I told her what had happened. "I should have been humble, should have been apologetic, should have talked of regrets. But I was furious—still am, at Jenovitz for wanting to judge me as a mother now by something that happened so long ago, at Dennis for lying. I'm sorry, Carmen. I've made things worse. But I couldn't just sit there without defending myself. So," I held my middle, "is it over? Will I lose the kids?"

"No," Carmen said. "We have other irons in the fire. This morning I filed for the interlocutory appeal. We should get a hearing scheduled by week's end." But she looked worried.

"I know. Interlocutory appeals are rarely granted. But then there's hope with the federal suit, isn't there?"

"Yes, but it'll take more time. Jenovitz may still be our fastest bet." She was frowning. "You're right. An abortion so long ago has nothing to do with what kind of mother you are now. I don't know why Jenovitz brought it up."

"He doesn't like me. We got off on the wrong foot, and it's gone downhill." My fears broke free. "He's going to recommend against me. I can feel it. *When* he finally makes his recommendation. Every time I ask when he's planning to talk with the children, he says he isn't ready. I thought maybe he was done with me after today, but he says he wants another meeting, so he set it up for two weeks from today because he'll be away all next week. Two weeks from today is three days before Thanksgiving. If he hasn't even set up a meeting with the kids, but wants more meetings with Dennis and me, how can he talk with them and file a report with the court by the end of the month? One way or another, I've been counting on this all being done by then." I could feel hysteria rising. What Carmen said next didn't help.

"It may take longer. The court will give Jenovitz extra time if he needs it."

"How much extra time?"

"Two more *months*?" Brody echoed when I told him what Carmen had said. He was just as disbelieving as I had been, just as incensed. "*Ninety* days to decide whether you're fit to take care of your kids? That's the craziest thing I've ever heard. Anyone with any common sense wouldn't need *nine* days. What in the hell is the man doing?"

We were in my workroom. I had come here after returning from Boston. Since Brody had been out running, I had thought to work on the wicker rocker and table, but, in the end, had been too upset to do a thing. Neither the scent of warm wood and age, nor the texture of the weave beneath my hand, offered solace. Before me stood the two pieces, both chock-full of holes where I had removed broken reeds.

I went to the window and stared out at the night. Feeling very small just then, I said, "I don't understand. The first court order was dead wrong, but we can't seem to change it. Carmen's doing what she can, I'm doing what I can, but nothing's working. Two more months—I don't know if I can make it. Even aside from not seeing the kids and not seeing Mom, there's this feeling of sense-lessness, and injustice, and *anger.* It eats at me."

Brody approached. He didn't touch me, but I felt him. His warmth was a lifeline.

"Ironic, how things come full circle," I remarked. "At the time of that abortion, I was terrified of having a child. I kept thinking that Dennis and I would divorce, and that I'd end up like my mother with a baby and nothing else. So the divorce part's finally coming true. Wouldn't it be something if I lose my kids now, be-cause I didn't want kids then?"

His hand was a whisper against my ear as he tucked back a wisp of hair. "You won't lose the kids. Not in the end."

My fingertips gripped the mullion. "I want to believe that. But these *things* keep happening to set me back, and my hands are tied. I need to *do* something." I thought of an earlier talk with Jenovitz. "So maybe I am controlling." I looked up at Brody. "Am I controlling?"

"You've never controlled me, not in any negative way."

"You're strong. You wouldn't allow it. But Dennis isn't strong. Maybe I did control him. I keep thinking back to those times he suggested we separate. Keep remembering those discussions. I argued that we had too many good things going for us, that I loved him, and that there were the kids to consider. He would always say things like, 'The good things aren't there anymore,' and I would say, 'But they can be,' and they were, for a little while after each talk. Things were better. We both tried. Maybe me more than him, because I was the one who really didn't want a divorce. So, am I a controlling person?"

"No. Dennis could have argued more. He could have stuck to his guns. He could have moved out. You didn't chain him to the house."

"Well," I sighed into the quiet night, "when he finally acted, he finally acted."

"In more ways than one," Brody said.

My eyes flew to his.

His voice was low, possibly to soften the blow, possibly in anger. "The thing about Dennis wanting into WickerWise? You were right. He wants in, so that he can turn around and sell it. He's already negotiated to buy into another business."

My jaw dropped.

"Pittney Communications. It is a telecommunications company in Springfield, small but growing. One of its major players died last July. The widow is looking to sell his share. If we want to make the argument that Dennis launched this divorce when he did for the sake of the money, the timing is right. He met with the surviving partners for the first time late in August."

"We were visiting Mom late in August. He flew back early to fish."

"He was fishing, all right, but not for trout."

I had thought myself past the point of being hurt, but I was wrong.

Brody must have sensed it. "Look," he hedged, "maybe he didn't go with the idea of buying into it himself, but was thinking of putting a group together. Telecommunications companies are hot. The market has mushroomed."

But we both knew the truth. I wanted it out in the open, wanted to deal with it, hurt or no hurt. Too often in the past I had looked at my life through a narrow tunnel of my own making. I had left myself a sitting duck for Dennis's backroom machinations. But no more.

"Pittney's for him," I said. "The timing says so. He had been talking to his lawyers for months by then. He was probably biding his time, waiting for the right business to open. If it hadn't been August, it would have been later, if not Springfield, another place." Dennis had been scheming, and I hadn't sensed a thing. *Where had I been?*

But agonizing over my shortcomings wouldn't help now. "He's barking up the wrong tree," I vowed. "WickerWise isn't his to sell."

"What if he offers a swap, half-ownership for custody of the kids?"

Kikit and Johnny were my heart and soul. WickerWise meant a lot to me, but not *that* much. I could live without WickerWise. I couldn't live without the kids.

"If it's just the money he wants," I said, "I'll give it to him."

"Half the net worth of WickerWise? That's how much he needs to buy a piece of Pittney. You'd have to take out huge loans to come up with that amount."

"I can do it."

"Besides," Brody added in a way that definitely suggested anger, "it could be that the money alone isn't it. It's the satisfaction he'll have forcing you to sell WickerWise."

"I'm not *selling*." I was starting to feel cornered. "Carmen will negotiate. What Heuber suggested is only a starting point." But I didn't have much room for maneuvering where the children were concerned. Dennis had me over a barrel.

I had to do something.

Brody touched my hair lightly again, then moved away. I turned and watched him. He went to the loft stairs, sat on a rung, and stretched out his legs.

"Talk to me, Brody," I begged.

"You had doubts. Way back when. You were never completely sure that Adrienne's blackmail stopped at infidelity. You always suspected something more."

"Did you?"

He shrugged. "I used to hear things. Not often. Never first-hand or factual. People wondered, that's all. Dennis hit the big time real quick. His performance since then has been mediocre. There's been nothing to validate that early brilliance."

Old thoughts. Long-buried fears. Suspicions set aside for the sake of the marriage.

I drew in a deep, shuddering breath.

"Maybe I'm wrong to bring it up," Brody said, "but he's screwing you over, Claire. I don't think I'll ever forgive him for that."

"What if it's Phoebe who's calling the shots?" I asked. In spite of everything, there was still a part of me that wanted a fall guy other than Dennis. "What if he isn't solely to blame?"

"He's a big boy. If he's letting Phoebe call the shots, he should be doubly ashamed. You were his wife for fifteen years. Where's his respect? Where's his loyalty? If Phoebe is suggesting these things, he should be vetoing them. Since he isn't, he shares the responsibility."

I knew in my gut Brody was right. I also knew that if Dennis was simply going along with what Phoebe said, it wasn't out of character. He had gone along with what I said for years, hadn't spoken up, hadn't taken the lead. He was a follower.

Funny, that was what I had said way back when. Adrienne Hadley had led, he had followed; she was the spider, he the fly. I had hoped he had developed more backbone since then. Either I was wrong and he was still following, or the ill will toward me was his and his alone.

The problem was that things were different now from how they were way back when. Now I had the children to consider.

Playing dirty wasn't my first choice. But what other leverage did I have?

I approached Brody. Sitting on the loft stairs, he was on eye level with me. I came between his legs and looped my arms around his neck.

He didn't speak, just looked at me. I couldn't even see the question in his eyes. If he wanted to know what I'd decided, it didn't show. All that showed was concern.

I came in even closer.

"Give me a hug," I whispered. "I need fortification." When his arms went around me, I kissed him once, then again. I closed my eyes for the third kiss, and concentrated on the feel of his mouth and his taste. It was probably the most unconditionally pleasant thing I had done since that kiss at the airport the day before. So I indulged myself. It struck me that unconditionally pleasant things had been few and far between in my life.

Not that I was deprived. Far from it. I had had plenty of pleasure, but nothing like this. This was smooth and soft. It was sweet. Secret. Special.

Dennis said I was a lousy lover. Brody said I was the best. No words. Just response. The way he breathed. The way he touched me, the way everything about him begged for more. Yet he was so unrushed in his hunger that I knew he took the same pleasure in the moment that I did.

So I let it linger, dragged it out until I was the one ready to beg for more. A storm raged inside, a great tempest in my womb. The need was so strong it was frightening.

But the ramifications were, too.

I took several breaths and waited for the shakes to ease. Then I rested my chin on his shoulder and just let myself be held, because there was unconditional pleasure in that, too. No rules. No strings. Just the feel of Brody's body and the knowledge of his love.

It amazed me that I had been so close to him all these years, without having this. "I must have been blind," I whispered.

"No," he whispered back, on my wavelength as always. "Just married."

And still was, which brought me full circle, back to the dilemma I faced. I indulged myself in Brody for another minute, then drew back. "Gotta run. Gotta think."

"Gotta eat, too. How about dinner?"

I smiled, but I was backing away. "I'll munch at home."

"On what?"

"Frosted Flakes."

"Come on over to the house. I'll make you a real dinner."

"What a line."

"I mean it."

"I know. That's the trouble." Dennis hadn't made me *any* kind of dinner in all the time I'd known him. Pampering me wasn't on his agenda.

But did it ever sound good.

I ran back across the floor to where Brody sat, gave him a last, light kiss, then fled before I forgot what I had to do.

Back at the lighthouse, sitting cross-legged on the carpeted floor of my dark bedroom with my face to the sea, I thought back to that first major trauma of our marriage. How I had agonized! I hadn't wanted to trust Dennis again—kept fearing there was more to the story—but he had fought for our marriage. He had been its advocate then, as I had been in more recent years. He had sworn he loved me. He had sworn I knew *everything*.

Maybe I did.

Then again, maybe I didn't.

Going downstairs, I dragged a carton from the small storage bin off the living room, opened it, and thumbed through the files.

They were ones I had taken on that day when the court had up-held the Order to Vacate, mostly records of my earliest Wicker-Wise days.

But the folder I wanted had nothing to do with WickerWise. It contained canceled checks, a letter, and an obituary notice. I singled it out and tugged it up. The minute it cleared the others, I knew something was wrong. It was way too thin. Opening it was a formality. I already knew it was empty.

If I had any qualms about looking for dirt, they were put to rest the following morning. Even before I could call her myself, Car-men called me to say that Morgan had hit gold.

"Dennis's calendar says that he attended an investment semi-nar in Vermont last July. Morgan cross-checked those days with hotel records and credit card receipts. Dennis was in Vermont last July, all right, but there wasn't any investment seminar within a hundred-mile radius of where he stayed, and he stayed, literally stayed, didn't leave his room for more than an hour here or there the entire time. It wasn't a hotel, it was a motel, a *small* motel. The owner and the desk clerk, both male, identified photos of Dennis and Phoebe. It didn't take much prodding. Seems they coveted Phoebe *and* Dennis's car."

It was certainly good news for my case, though I couldn't deny the hurt. July. The thought of it made me sick. And angry.

I had already told Carmen about Adrienne. Now I shared my deeper doubts.

Two days later, she and I met Morgan Houser in a no-name cof-fee shop in Charlestown that was, apparently, as close to an office as Morgan had. We had our own private corner and a steady sup-ply of hot coffee and sweet rolls. Morgan, a tall, fair-haired, fair-skinned Swede, was neat, clean, observant. For the most part, he listened and took notes while I talked.

"When Dennis graduated from business school, he took a job with an investment firm in Greenwich. It was a mid-level position, with room to move ahead if he proved himself. He was determined to do that. He wanted to be a millionaire by the time he was forty. He hadn't been with the firm long when he met the wife of one of the senior partners. She was much older than he was, but sexy and smart.

"Was her marriage on the rocks?" Carmen asked.

"She told Dennis that, but he found out it wasn't. She lived with her husband and had no plans to divorce him. She just liked playing around. Dennis, being young and slightly egocentric, was flattered. He couldn't believe that this gorgeous woman—this gorgeous *worldly* woman—had singled him out. The way he told it to me, he knew that what they were doing was wrong, but figured that if she was going into it with her eyes wide open, and if *he* was going into it with his eyes wide open, it was okay."

"Were you and Dennis dating at the time?" It was Carmen again. Morgan just listened.

"Long distance. I was a senior in college. We talked a lot but didn't see each other more than once a month. We hadn't made a commitment yet."

"Not sexual?" she asked quietly.

I pushed my coffee mug around on the yellow Formica. "Yes, sexual. Innocent me. I had no idea what was going on during those work weeks between visits."

"When did you find out?"

"A year into my marriage."

"He married you, all the while he was having an affair with her?"

"Oh, no. The affair ended before we got to the altar. Funny, but we waited. We could have gotten married sooner, but something held us back. I always thought it was just Dennis needing time to get settled and me needing that extra security. In hindsight, I realized it was Adrienne."

"Adrienne who?" Morgan asked.

"Hadley." I watched him write down the name. "I learned about her by accident—or so I thought at the time. Only after did I realize it wasn't an accident. Dennis wanted me to know. Otherwise he never would have left a letter from her right there with the rest of the bills. It seems he'd been paying her hush money to the tune of a thousand a month. She wanted more. That was probably why he wanted me to know. He was feeling squeezed."

"Hush money for what?" Carmen asked.

"He said it was to keep their affair a secret. Apparently, her husband let her play around as long as it wasn't with anyone in the firm. Her husband was Lee," I told Morgan. "They lived in Greenwich. If Lee found out about Dennis, he would have kicked him out. She threatened to tell him everything, if Dennis didn't pay up."

"A thousand a month," Morgan said. "That had to have cut some into his take. He couldn't have been making a whole lot starting out. Why didn't he just quit and go work somewhere else?"

"I asked him that. More than once. To me it seemed the better thing to do than bowing to blackmail, but he said that she could hurt his career, no matter where he worked, and that at the time the payments began, he was doing too well at Hadley and Gray— that was the firm—to rock the boat. And he *was* doing well. He knew exactly where to point his clients. They made money. So did he. He moved up fast. The firm thought he was brilliant. Then things quieted. By the time I found out about the payments, after we were married, his career had leveled off. Oh, he was still doing well, but he wasn't the *wunderkind* anymore. I told him that I didn't see why he had to keep paying Adrienne. If Hadley and Gray wasn't magic for him anymore, he could tell Adrienne to go to hell and open his own firm, couldn't he?"

"Couldn't he?" Carmen asked.

I paused while the waitress topped off our coffees, then said, "I'd have thought so. He did it a few years later, anyway. At the time, though, he argued that Adrienne was threatening to spread a rumor that he was involved in illegal trading. I actually read that in the letter she sent. She said—and this is pretty nearly a quote, I read that letter so many times—that he would be hard put to find clients if they thought he was on the verge of indictment. She said she needed more money, that she was desperate. She hadn't seen her husband in a year, and she was sick. MS, she said. It was right there in the letter. She actually died four months later, but not of MS. Of lung cancer. I read that in the obituary that was supposed to be in my file along with the letter and a handful of canceled checks."

Morgan asked for dates—when Dennis had signed on with Hadley and Gray, when the affair had taken place with Adrienne, when she had died. Then he asked, "Why did you keep the file?"

"I've asked myself that dozens of times. I'm not sure. I guess I thought that having it was like having insurance, like as long as I had proof of what Dennis had done, he wouldn't do it again. That affair shook me up. I was young and naive. I thought he was pretty perfect, then he went and had an affair with his boss's wife, all while he and I were dating. The trust I'd felt," I waved a hand, "gone. I considered divorce. Dennis talked me out of it. He was able to reestablish that trust, but it took a while."

I turned to Carmen. "That first pregnancy? I conceived right before I found Adrienne's letter. By the time I learned about the baby, I was a mess. I would never have had an abortion had I felt more secure."

Carmen turned to Morgan. "The medical files pertaining to that abortion somehow fell into Jenovitz's hands. Claire's husband claims he wasn't responsible. Can we find out who was?"

Morgan's skewed smile left no doubt that he could.

When he asked, I had no trouble remembering those particular names and dates. They were etched for eternity in my brain.

Carmen directed me back to the Hadley file. "Does Dennis have access to the lighthouse?"

"No. I'm the only one with a key. That file must have been emptied before I took it from the house. I didn't check it at the time. It was tucked in with the rest. I just swept the whole bunch up and put them in a box."

"Did he know the file existed?"

"I never thought so, but he must have. No one else had either the opportunity or the cause to clean it out."

"Any idea when it was done?"

"None. I haven't opened that folder in years. For all I know, it's been empty that long. Maybe he found it one day, was disgusted that I'd kept it, and just threw everything out. Or maybe he did it last month, as a precaution."

"A precaution against what?" Carmen asked.

"Precisely," I answered with a pointed look at Morgan. "I have to know if there's more."

I left that coffee shop in Charlestown knowing I was justified in what I was doing, but feeling guilty nonetheless. Old habits died hard. Part of me still saw Dennis as my husband. That part felt I was betraying him.

Back in the office, my guilt feelings multiplied.

First, Kikit called to say that her stomach hurt. I had barely finished asking her what she had eaten, when Dennis took the phone from her and said she was fine. She came back on the line in tears, said I didn't love her anymore, and hung up. When I called back, she was the one to snatch up the phone. She listened to my protestations of love, but she was still crying, small hiccoughing sobs that wrenched me when Dennis took the phone again. Though I could hear him comforting her—he was actually surprisingly gentle—I felt awful.

Then Rona called, painting a dreadful picture of Connie's condition and begging me to come. Having talked with Mom that morning, I didn't think things were as bad as Rona made them sound. Since she didn't know the details of my situation here, she didn't understand when I said I couldn't leave.

So I felt guilty betraying Dennis, guilty deserting Kikit, guilty telling Rona half-truths, guilty abandoning Mom.

And then there was Brody. What was I guilty of with him? Staring.

At the hand splayed on the spreadsheet before him. At the arm that corded up when he reached for the phone and the chest that broadened when he stretched. At the long legs that wore jeans, but that I had seen enough times without to know the color of the hair thereupon.

I looked up to find his eyes on me and a knowing half-smile on his face, and I looked away fast.

On Friday afternoon, a clerk from the appeals court called Carmen to say that the judge was giving Arthur Heuber until the following Wednesday to file a written opposition to our petition.

I knew that it was a victory of sorts, that the judge might have summarily refused to review Selwey's decision and ended it there. But his action meant that nothing would happen for another five days.

One delay after another. When would it end?

Thirteen

How are you, Mom?"

"I'm okay."

"How was your night?"

"Pretty good."

"Did you sleep?"

"More important, I woke up. I wonder sometimes, though."

"Wonder what?"

"Why I'm still here. Is there a purpose?"

"Yes. Us. You give us a focus. Just knowing you're there means a lot."

"Are you happy, Claire?" Out of the blue.

"Happy?" I asked, thinking fast.

"In life. I need to know. I miss seeing you smile."

"I'm smiling now. We're off in another hour to the circus. The kids are excited."

"Well, that's good. Memories, you know. Me, I couldn't bear the animal smell."

I laughed. It was an old line, the standard excuse.

"I should have taken you," she said sadly. "I blamed the money, but I had enough. I was just frightened to spend. So there's another regret."

"No regret. Rona and I did fine without the circus."

"Well, I didn't. I lie here thinking maybe I wouldn't have minded the animal smell at all. But I'll never know."

"I'll just have to bring you a whole bunch of souvenirs, then."

"When? I miss you."

"Same here, Mom. I'm hoping to get there next week."

"Monday? Tuesday?"

"Thursday. As early as the planes fly. Shall I bring breakfast?"

"Oh, I'd like that," she said with the first sound of a smile. "And the latest catalogue? The one with winter cruisewear? Has it come?"

She had said the one thing that could boost my spirits. The day when my mother no longer cared to dream over lacy lingerie would be the day the end was truly near.

"I'll bring it if it has," I assured her. "Mom, it may be too late for me to call when we get back tonight. Can I talk with you in the morning?"

"If I'm here."

"You'll be there. Who else will appreciate how awful the elephants smell?"

I pulled into the driveway at ten and let the car idle while I waited for Kikit and Johnny to join me. They were usually out the front door before I shifted the car into park. This day I sat for five minutes, then, concerned, climbed out.

"Oh, it's *you*, Claire!" Malcolm Addis called from his yard, which abutted ours. "I didn't recognize the car. Is it your new one?"

I waved and called back, "It is," but I continued on up the walk.

"Not red this time?"

"Nope."

I wondered, as I had more than once picking up the children, what the neighbors thought was going on. Even in spite of the times when I worked late or traveled, they usually saw me around more. They must have known something was up.

Determined not to look as though I had anything to be ashamed of, I held my head a bit higher. When I reached the front door, I made a show of fishing through my keys while I unobtrusively rapped on the wood.

Dennis opened the door looking harried. The way he motioned me in suggested I was the latest in a line of annoyances.

"Not a good morning," he muttered and turned to yell up the stairs, *"Get a move on, you guys!"* He scowled back at me, thrust a hand through his hair, went to the stairs. *"Clara Kate! John! Your mother's here!"*

Kikit was the first to appear. She looked nearly as disgruntled as Dennis. Her chin wobbled as she ran down the stairs. "I wanted to wear my green overalls. Daddy said they'd be clean, but they aren't."

"You only wore them Thursday," Dennis argued.

"I didn't. I wore them *Tuesday*. And that isn't all that isn't clean," she told me. "My *best T-shirts* are still in the wash."

"What's wrong with the one you have on?" Dennis asked.

She grimaced down at it. "It's all *wrinkled*!"

"Am I supposed to iron T-shirts?" Dennis asked me.

"No. You're supposed to smooth them and fold them while they're warm from the dryer."

"Okay," he said agreeably enough, "I can do that." To Kikit, he said, "Where *is* your brother? *John? Get down here!*"

"I look awful, Mommy."

"You look beautiful."

"I wanted to look nice for Joy. Is she in the car?"

"She's back at Brody's. We'll swing by on the way." I took her jacket from the hall closet. "Go wait outside, sweetheart. I'll be out with Johnny in a minute."

"No, you won't." She slid her arms into the jacket on her way out the door. "He isn't coming."

Dennis started up the stairs. "*John! Where in the*—there you are." He stopped midway up when Johnny appeared at the top.

I joined Dennis on the stairs. "What's wrong?"

Johnny shrugged. "Nothing. I just don't want to go."

"But you love the circus."

"I've been lots of times. I kinda wanna stay here with Dad."

The sting of rejection was swift and sharp. I was trying to parry it, telling myself not to take it personally, that Johnny simply felt caught between us, when Dennis sighed. "I wasn't planning to stay here, John. As soon as you leave, I'm going to Boston."

"Can I come?"

"No."

Johnny's shoulders drooped. "Can I wait here till you get home?"

"No," Dennis said again, but gently. "I have business there. It'll take me most of the day. You'd be bored to death. Go to the circus with Mommy and Kikit, and another day you and I will go into Boston."

Johnny looked doubtful.

Dennis climbed several more steps until he and Johnny were on eye level. Taking Johnny's shoulders, he said softly, "I promise. Just us two. Now go on. Get your sneaks."

Either he was more sensitive a father than I'd given him credit for, or he was so desperate to get to his business in Boston that he would promise his son the world. I didn't care the cause. I just prayed he would follow through.

Johnny disappeared down the hall.

At first, Dennis and I just stood there, side by side, waiting for him in silence.

Then I asked, "Did you know that was coming?"

"I didn't put him up to it, if that's what you mean."

"Did you know he didn't want to go?"

"No. He didn't tell me. He doesn't say a hell of a lot."

"Do you ask? In general. If you see him brooding, do you ask what's wrong?"

"Yes. That doesn't mean he answers."

"Do you think he's disturbed?"

"God, no."

"Upset. Maybe we should sit down with him, both of us, and get him to talk."

"He's doing fine, Claire. So's Kikit. I may still be a novice with some things around here, but the kids aren't suffering."

I had to admit that the house didn't look bad. Presumably he had kept the cleaning service coming once a week. "I'd have thought you would want to hire someone to cook and do laundry. And drive. That nanny you always talked about?"

"I can handle the driving. I can do the laundry, too. The kids should know that, shouldn't they?"

"Definitely," I said and meant it. "Has Jenovitz talked to you about meeting with them?"

"He wants to see them when he gets back."

"The week of Thanksgiving?" I didn't want the children upset for the holiday, didn't yet know what we were *doing* for the holiday. I kept hoping I would regain custody by then, but since I could neither assume it nor bear to rule it out, I was ignoring the whole thing.

It didn't help when Dennis said, "Thanksgiving, or the week after."

The week after was worse. I was praying the interlocutory appeal would go our way, but if it didn't, we would be stuck waiting for Jenovitz. "I want this decided, already," I said. "Isn't it getting to you?"

"Isn't what getting to me?"

"The limbo we're in."

"It's only been three weeks."

"It's been an eternity." I took a new tack. "Aren't you afraid that if this thing drags out too long, someone else will buy the piece of Pittney you want?"

He grew wary. "How did you know about Pittney?"

A small movement caught my eye. When I looked up, Johnny started down the hall. "All set?" I smiled and held out his jacket.

He took it and went out the door.

I followed him. "Johnny?"

He stopped. I caught up and wrapped an arm around his shoulders. "Are you okay?"

He shrugged.

"Any special reason you wanted to stay here?"

He shook his head, broke away, and ran to the car. By the time I reached it, he was inside with Kikit and the moment alone was lost.

Joy Parth was special. In hindsight, I did remember a time when she had been shy around us, though I had attributed that more to her age than awkwardness with her father. In any event, by the time she was ten, she had overcome it. She spent her visits either shadowing Brody or coddling my babies like they were her dolls. It was when she became a teenager that she and I became really close. I was the one she complained to when she had a gripe against her parents or her friends or the world in general. We loved going off by ourselves for lunch. I found her thoughtful, soft-spoken, and remarkably grown-up.

So many of the same things that I loved about Brody, I loved about Joy, but it was never more true than that Saturday. I wasn't sure what Brody had told her about the situation between Dennis and me, but she handled herself like a pro. Having lived with her own parents' split, and being intelligent and sensitive on top of the rest, she answered Kikit's questions with aplomb.

Not that I was supposed to hear those questions. Kikit usually squished herself close to Joy, sometimes even spoke into a hand held to Joy's ear. But her eyes touched me more often than not, and her voice was just loud enough to carry.

"What's the difference between being separated and being divorced?" she asked at one point, and at another, "Who decides when you see Brody and when you don't?" Many of the questions had a fearful edge, like, "If parents stop loving each other, can they stop loving their kids?" or, "Do Johnny and I get split up if Mommy and Daddy do?" or, "What if one of them marries somebody else?"

Johnny listened intently, sitting on the other side of Joy, which was where he stayed for most of the day. I tried to coax him out so that I could talk with him more, tried talking about innocuous things like how he felt about the football season starting to wind down, and occasionally he responded, though not for long and never comfortably. Inevitably he gravitated back to Joy.

Each time it happened, I died a little inside. Each time that happened, Brody sent me a look that said, *He's navigating strange waters, give it time.*

I didn't have much choice. No amount of kicking and screaming on my part was going to make either of the kids suddenly comfortable with the fact that their parents had split. Nor, though, would I let it ruin our day. The truth was that Dennis had rarely come to the circus, so it being five of us rather than six wasn't a first. I just pretended this was like one of those earlier times.

It got easier as the day went on. By the time the circus ended, even Johnny seemed to have forgotten anything was amiss. It came back to him when we unwittingly stopped for dinner at a steakhouse that Dennis had taken the children to shortly after our separation. Kikit was the one who pointed it out, but only after we were settled inside, well after Johnny had withdrawn.

We made the best of it, but I was beginning to feel the strain.

There was some relief when we drove back to the lighthouse. Since Joy had never seen it, Kikit and Johnny showed her around. The instant their footsteps had faded from the second floor, saying that they had gone up another flight, Brody looked at me.

"Hangin' in there?" he asked.

I choked out a laugh. "I'm hangin', all right, swinging back and forth, neither here nor there. I need this settled, Brody. Everything about my life—the kids, Dennis, my mother, WickerWise—it's all up in the air."

He came close. "What about me?"

"You, too."

He gave me a short, sweet kiss. It was still new, still that little bit shocking, but hot. Before I could melt, he took me in his arms and held me, just held me, standing there, swaying as if in a dance.

"What's the song?" I asked against the musky warmth of his neck. He smelled so much better than the elephants had. I would have liked to tell Connie that.

"No song."

"There has to be one. You're moving in time to it."

"Nope. I'm tone deaf. Can't hear the tune *or* the beat."

I drew back and stared at him. "No. *No.* Really?"

"You knew that."

"I didn't. I swear it. If I'd known, I never would have kissed you. I don't mess with men who can't sing." I caught myself. "Of course, look where I got messing with a man who could. You might not be such a bad risk after all."

He started swaying again, this time with his hands linked on the small of my back and our lower bodies fitted neatly together. The look on his face was precious, a naughty blend of amusement and defiance that I had no intention of calling him on, since my own face must have worn much the same expression. I laced my fingers together at the nape of his neck, occasionally moved my thumb against his skin or his hair, and all the while our eyes clung.

Before I knew what I was doing, I started to hum, the lightest possible sound that would carry recognition. I timed the tune to the movement he set, so that even if he couldn't hear, the beat matched. After one wordless run-through, I began to sing softly.

Brody was up to the challenge. He recognized "Anticipation" and laughed. I felt the vibration down low, where out bodies met and pressed, and didn't back off this time. His being aroused didn't startle me, other than in how much I liked it. Returning to a hum, I moved ever so subtly against him. His arousal grew.

"Are you teasing me?" he asked.

"I guess I am."

"Feel safe, do you?"

"Uh-huh." Nothing could possibly happen with the children upstairs. Indeed, I felt so safe that I asked, "If there was nothing with Ellen MacKenzie, what did you do for sex?"

His cheeks colored adorably. "I managed."

"With whom?"

He started to roll his eyes, stopped, grunted. "You want a history?"

"You know mine." As we swayed, his fingers inched lower, pressed harder. I breathed my pleasure in a sigh, then said, "I'm curious, that's all. I figured the sex with Ellen was great. Now you say it didn't exist. It had to be great with someone else."

After a long moment that looked to be deliberative, he blurted, "Gail Jensen."

"For two weeks, three years ago. That was as long as you saw Gail."

"No. That was as long as Hillary Howard thought I saw Gail. It was more like two years."

"No kidding?"

"No kidding."

Gail had been a local anchorwoman before taking a job in New York. Not only was she stereotypically gorgeous, but she was ten years younger than me. I was sorry I'd raised the subject. But the damage was done. "How was she?" I made myself ask, lest I always wonder.

Brody was starting to look amused. "Uh, imaginative."

"What does that mean?"

"She liked to push the envelope."

I stopped swaying. "I don't know if I can do that. I'm forty."

He laughed. "Age has nothing to do with it."

"But I've only been with Dennis. I'm one step removed from a virgin."

"Are you feeling like a virgin right now?"

"In a way." The words were barely out of my mouth when he spread his hands over my bottom and moved me against him. "No," I corrected, suddenly short of breath. "Not like a virgin."

"Like what, then?"

"I don't know." I tucked my chin in and put the top of my head to his chest. "Like something else. Curious, maybe."

"Achy?"

"Uh-huh."

"Where?"

"You know where."

"Say it."

"I can't."

He put his mouth to my ear, whispered, "You will," and slowly eased me back. When I raised my eyes, I saw promise in his—and mischief, and need.

Then his eyes went to the ceiling and I heard what he had. We had barely separated when Joy bent over the top rung of the spiral staircase.

"I need help, Dad. We're sitting up there in the dark and I'm trying to tell a pirate story, only mine stinks. Yours are the best. Will you come up?"

Intrigued, I looked up at Brody. "A pirate story?"

"I used to tell them to Joy when she was younger."

"We'd be sitting on the cliff by the house," Joy filled in, "in the pitch black, sometimes with a storm coming in. Your room up here is even better. It's like we're right in the middle of the ocean."

We sat in the dark of my bedroom. Kikit was tucked in the nest of my legs. Joy was leaning against Brody's far side. Johnny was between Brody and me, with his elbows on his knees and his nose to the glass, such that he didn't touch either of us.

Brody pointed to the right. "See that inky blotch down there? On the coast. See it?"

"I see it!" Kikit said.

"Do you, Johnny?"

"The one past those circles of light?" Johnny asked with reluctant interest.

"That's it," Brody said. "You're looking at rocks, but not just any old rocks. They're the rocks where the good ship *Mariana* finally hit and broke up. Ah, but I'm getting ahead of myself. Ever hear of Captain Roy Stiggens?"

"No," said Kikit.

"Pirates don't come this far north," Johnny announced.

"Not usually," Brody conceded, "but since no one expected

them here, it was one of the safest places for them to be. Okay, so there weren't any palm trees or coconuts, and the natives were buttoned up to their chins, and the winters were so cold that a pirate who made the mistake of being caught here when the snows came didn't usually get out until spring. Still, there were pubs and good lodging and the best cappuccino—"

I cleared my throat. Cappuccino was a more modern invention, I believed.

"Right," Brody said. "Anyway, Captain Roy Stiggens was one of the most notorious men ever to be put in command of a vessel. His home port was Plymouth, England, where he'd been a little waif of a pickpocket for the earliest years of his life. From the time he was not much bigger than you, Johnny boy, he was out on the bounding main on one mission or another. If it wasn't carrying sugar cane from the Indies, it was fetching flour from Havana or wine and rum from Bermuda. He apprenticed aboard the schooner *Marley* under Captain Malcolm Drewhurst, and was barely eighteen when he was given the helm of his own ship. She was the *Mariana,* launched in the year 1710, and a good sloop she was. Still, crossing the mighty Atlantic was never easy. No matter what the season, there were high winds and rains and choppy seas like we rarely see here. If anyone could handle 'em, though, Roy Stiggens could. He was a challenging man. There was nothing he liked more than to stand up at the bowsprit and dare the seas to sweep him up. Mind you, once he reached his maturity, he was fierce looking—tall and broad, with long black hair that blew free and a bellowing voice that could carry stem to stern in all but the meanest of winds—so my guess is the seas weren't so keen on taking him. The long and short of *that* being that by the time he was twenty-five he had crossed the Atlantic so many times he was looking for new adventure." His voice took a dramatic turn. "He was also looking to avenge the long-ago death of his parents at the hands of the Earl of Walthrop."

"So he became a pirate?" Kikit asked.

"So he became a pirate," Brody answered and snapped his fingers. "Took to it like that, got a real kick out of sailing right up to another boat and boarding her, easy as pie. The *Mariana* was such an innocent-looking craft that no one suspected its captain and crew were anything but hard-working sailors until they ran up that old Jolly Roger, and by then it was too late for escape. Ships that surrendered right off suffered little more than fright. Those that fought had greater losses. But for vessels from the fleet of the Earl of Walthrop, the crew of the *Mariana* showed no mercy. They burned and looted. They marooned whole crews on deserted islands. They took silks and fine china, medicines and guns. And gold bullion. They took gold bullion. See, Captain Roy had a dream. He'd been to the Colonies many a time. He figured, quite correctly, that there would be fine living to be had there once the Revolution was done."

I figured that if Captain Roy Stiggens started sailing the *Mariana* in 1710, he would have been dead and buried before the Revolution, but I wasn't about to say so. The children were entranced, and, frankly, so was I. Primed by what had happened downstairs, I was looking to be lost in fantasy, which was what Brody so skillfully engineered. The soothing lilt to his voice—deeper when he spoke as the captain, soft and enticing in the narrative—held the kind of charm our lives hadn't known of late. Even Johnny succumbed. By the time Brody had established the existence of one Prudence Cooper, and been through the part about this innocent young girl taking the captain's heart and then dying of scarlet fever, after which the ruthless pirate couldn't bear the thought of living where she had lived, so he returned to retrieve the treasure he had hidden in the caves beneath the rocks that were the inky blotch down the coast to the right out my bedroom window, Johnny had an elbow braced on Brody's knee and was listening as closely as Kikit.

Brody answered their questions—yes, the captain had left the treasure for the innocent young girl, no, the hidden caves were never found, yes, the innocent young girl was purported to be walking the cliffs that night, no, Captain Roy hadn't listened to the weather report.

By that time we were late. I had told Dennis we would be back at nine, and it was after ten.

What I wanted was to call Dennis and see if the children could stay overnight. Then I saw how nervous Johnny suddenly was, and I decided simply to get them home as quickly as possible.

Dennis greeted us at the door with a thunderous look. I held up a quelling hand and hurried the children past him, but when I went to take them upstairs, he blocked my way.

"Go on up," I told them. "I'll come kiss you goodnight in a minute."

The instant they were out of sight, Dennis said, "You were supposed to be back at nine. That was the agreement. You violated it."

"I'm sorry. We lost track of the time."

He blew out an exasperated breath. "Y'know, that's why this all has happened. You lost track of the time. You lost track of the children. You lost track of Kikit's medicine. Damn it, I had plans."

"What kind of plans?"

"Things to do with the kids."

"At nine at night? You were taking them *out*?"

"We were doing stuff in."

"What stuff?" I asked, only then noticing the smell. With a curious look at Dennis, I went down the hall and into the kitchen. It was a mess. Dennis had apparently been trying to bake. The cookies on the cookie sheet were more than a little burned around the edges, but they were definitely chocolate chip. Farther down the counter was the video cassette of a movie that Dennis had promised for so long to take the kids to, that it had left the theaters without their having seen it.

I was startled, begrudgingly impressed. "I'm sorry. If I'd known you were doing this, I'd have kept a closer eye on the clock. You should have told me."

"I don't have to tell you anything. I'm the one with custody. You're the one who's walking on thin ice. Getting back here an hour and a half late is a perfect example of irresponsibility."

Any positive feelings I might have had faded. I headed back to the front hall. "It's Saturday night. The kids can stay up later. Do your thing with them now."

He was close behind me. "You're missing the point."

"No, you're missing the point," I shot back. "The children were with me. They were fine and safe and happy. If you were worried, you should have called us." I braced a hand on the newel post and faced him. "I was late. I've already apologized for that. But this is very difficult, Dennis. I need more time with them. These limited visits aren't fair, and you know it. Do you really, honestly, truly think that I'm an irresponsible mother? Do you really, honestly, truly think that I ever, ever harmed the kids?"

"How did you know about Pittney?"

"You're changing the subject."

"No, I'm not. That information is confidential. If you found out, it had to have been through sleazy means. That says something."

My jaw dropped. I snapped it back up. "Sleazy? What about stacking the deck against me with lies? What about confidential medical records showing up in Dean Jenovitz's file? What about *Adrienne*, for God's sake?"

He took my arm and tried to steer me to the door.

I snatched it free and held my ground. "If there's more to that story, it'll come out. In court, if it comes to that. I'll raise Adrienne and more, Dennis. I'll do whatever I have to get my kids back."

"You're a vindictive bitch."

The way he said it stole my breath. Fast as I could, I stole it back. "It's called self-defense. I wasn't the instigator here. I wasn't the one who brought up the past. You did those things, Dennis, and for the life of me I still don't know *why*. What was *so horrible* about our marriage that you had to end it this way?"

I heard a sound from above. My eyes flew up the staircase and down the hall just as Johnny disappeared.

I started up the stairs. Dennis called my name, but I ignored him. When I heard his footsteps behind me, I started to run. I turned into Johnny's room in time to see him looking frantically around for a place to hide.

I caught him, wrapping him tightly in my arms. My heart was in my mouth. I pushed it aside enough to urge a soft, "Talk to me, John. Tell me what's bothering you most."

He fought to get free, but I wasn't letting him go.

I weathered his struggles with my cheek to his hair. "I know this is hard for you," I said. "It's hard for me, too."

"Let me go," was his muffled reply.

"Not until we've talked. We haven't been able to do that, you and me. Either someone else is around, or you have homework to do, but I want to talk with you, Johnny, I need to talk with you. We used to talk all the time."

"You lived here then," he said, still muffled, now angry, too.

"Lots of things were different then. There are times when I'd give anything to be able to turn back the clock."

"Why don't you?"

"Because I can't."

"Why can't you?"

"Because there are legal issues involved. That's part of what makes this so hard."

I instinctively tightened my arms around him when he yelled, *"If it's so hard, why is it happening?"*

Good question, I wanted to say. Then I caught myself. I could throw my hands in the air all I wanted, but the truth was that I had made some very basic mistakes. I had decided what my family needed without giving Dennis equal say. I had been wrong to do that.

"This is happening," I said, "because Daddy needs some things that I can't give him."

"He needs us. Don't you?"

"Yes," I breathed against his hair, "*God*, yes. That's the *biggest* part of what's so hard. It bothers me not to be here when you get home from school. It bothers me not to have dinner with you, and breakfast with you. I want to be with you all the time, just like Daddy does."

He had stopped struggling enough so that I could gentle my arms and let them soothe without fearing he would escape.

"You tell me that if I want something, I should go for it," he said. The anger had given way to confusion. "Why don't you?"

"I am. You just don't see me doing it. I spend a good deal of the time when I'm not with you thinking about the best way to resolve this."

"Why doesn't the judge want you with us? Did you do something wrong?"

My hand went still on his back for an instant, before resuming its gentle kneading. "No. Nothing illegal or immoral."

"Did Dad?"

I glanced back. Dennis was at the door. But even if he hadn't been listening, I wouldn't have slandered him in front of Johnny. "Daddy loves you as much as I do. What we're trying to work out here, is how best the two of us can love the two of you without the two of us living in the same house."

"But we're a family. Families work things out. Why can't you and Dad?"

Again I glanced at Dennis. He looked tired and, to his credit, upset, but I didn't feel the need to soothe him that I once had. I was distanced. It struck me that it was by choice. My choice. Because there were two sides to every coin. Just as I had failed to satisfy Dennis's needs, he had failed to satisfy mine.

Could we work out our differences? "I just don't think we can."

"Then we're not a family anymore?"

"We are. Just a different kind. Two, actually. Two families."

"Are you and Daddy always gonna fight?"

"No. The fighting will be over pretty soon."

"Then what?"

"Then we settle in and get used to a new order of things."

"I want things the way they were."

"I know," I said and kissed his crown. There had been times in my childhood when I was desperate to make things the way they had been before my father had died. I remembered that pain.

"Don't you?" he asked, bringing me back to the present. I must have waited a few seconds too long to answer, because his voice rose in pitch. "Won't all of us *ever* live in the same house again?"

Gently, sadly, I said, "Probably not."

"This *sucks!*" he cried and started to struggle again. I held him, tightening my arms when he tried to pull away, wrestling to keep a hold when he squirmed. Finally, he abandoned the fight and started to sob.

Though my heart was breaking, I kept as tight a hold on him as before. I moved with him as I had when he'd been a baby, though then the cause had been more simple, either hunger, discomfort, or fright. Not only had life grown more complex, but

Johnny had grown more controlled. Who had taught him not to cry? Had I? Or Dennis? Or his peers?

"Let it out, Johnny," I whispered. "You can cry with me all you want. I'll love you just the same."

I actually think he would have cried even if I hadn't given him permission. The emotion had built too high. The dike had been bound to burst.

When I saw the first easing of the flow, I said, "It's okay to be unhappy sometimes. It's okay to be angry and confused and scared. Those are normal things to be feeling."

"Dad'll be mad," he said in a broken little voice.

"Dad won't be mad. He's feeling lots of those things, too. He may not talk about it, but he is. But things will get better, Johnny."

"How do you know?"

"I just know."

"How?"

Johnny had been appeased with a second, firmer, "Because I know," and so had I, but only until I got him into bed and kissed him goodnight, kissed Kikit goodnight, then got into my car and drove off. By the time I was back at the lighthouse, I was thinking of all the things that could go wrong and needing a little reassurance myself. When I picked up the phone to call Brody, though, I didn't get a dial tone. I pressed the disconnect button. "Hello?" Pressed it again. "Hello?"

"Claire?"

I thought I had heard my sister's voice in every possible emotional state, but this one was new.

"You have to come, Claire. She's comatose. They don't know how long she'll last."

Fourteen

Rona hadn't exaggerated this time. I flew out on Sunday morning to find that the doctors shared her pessimism. No dramatic medical twist had brought on the coma. Connie had simply slipped into it. Just as simply, she didn't have the strength to pull herself out.

Rona looked devastated. She had taken the call in bed the night before, had thrown on a warm-up suit, pulled her hair into a ponytail, and raced to the hospital, where she had spent the night. When I arrived, she was standing beside Connie, clutching the bed rail.

"Thank God," she breathed. "I thought for sure she'd die on my watch, just to make me feel guilty the rest of my life. Bad enough that she won't say a thing. Do you think she knew I was here all night?"

I stood at the door trying to find the wherewithal to enter. Loss was heavy in the air. In normal times I might have borne the weight of it more easily, but I was already depleted by what had happened back home. I was feeling weak and frightened. I wasn't sure I wanted to see my mother this way.

She was nearly invisible in the bed. Her skin blended in with the sheet, both inert, both lifeless. She was leaving us, I knew, and felt the same tiny panic in my belly that I had felt as a child when she left us each morning, not to return until night. That was where the similarity ended. I wasn't a child anymore, and she was leaving for good.

"Claire?"

With an effort, I tore my eyes from Connie and focused on Rona.

"Are you all right?" she asked, sounding frightened.

I paused, swallowed, nodded. "Just shaky." Then I forced myself past the door, went to the bed, and leaned down. "Hi, Mom. I'm here. See, even sooner than I said." My voice broke on the last word. Her face was pale and waxy. No matter that I knew she was close to death, no matter that she hadn't looked like herself for weeks, I wanted the old face back. "Mom?" I called softly. My hand hovered over hers, awkward in a second's doubt, then lowered. I felt skin and bones, cool, smooth, surreal. I gave a little shake. "Mom?" She didn't respond. I tried another shake. "Mom?"

"The doctors say we should talk to her," Rona said in little more than a whisper inches from my ear. She had crowded in beside me, which would have felt awkward, too, if I hadn't been feeling the need to lean on someone. True, I had never thought to lean on Rona. But I had never felt so light and weak.

"They say she might be able to hear," Rona went on in that whisper, "so I've been telling her all the things I've done in my life to please her, but she won't nod; or smile, or even open her eyes and stare at me. She used to be great at staring. It was a sure sign that she didn't like whatever it was I'd done." She gave body to her voice, pleading, "Come on, Mom. Stare at me now. I dare you to."

I squeezed Rona's wrist. Then my hand found the railing and

held tight. "I talked with her yesterday morning. She sounded stronger at the end of the conversation. How was she during the day?"

"I didn't come in the morning. Maybe that upset her, but I was here for a while in the afternoon. I read her half of *Vanity Fair.* I'm really not a terrible daughter."

"No one said you were."

"Maybe not in as many words."

We fell silent. I couldn't take my eyes from Connie's face. It was hollowed out, deathly quiet. The only sound I could hear was the faint beep of the machine that said she was still alive.

The nurse came and went twice. We didn't move.

"She looks so pale," I finally whispered. "I wish I knew if she could hear."

"What would you say if you knew she could?"

"I'd tell her about the circus."

I paused, then did just that. I told her about the lions, the horses, and the elephants. I told her about being terrified by the trapeze artists and delighted by the clowns. I told her about Hoodsies, and cotton candy, and the purple alligator that Kikit had bought. At the end, I told Rona, "It was a good circus. She would have liked it."

"She hated the smells."

"She never smelled the smells."

"What?"

"She never went to the circus."

"Never?" When I shook my head, Rona said, "Funny. I thought she had."

* * *

We continued on for a while in silence, then I kept the vigil alone when Rona left to get coffee. I talked softly, calling Connie's name, touching her hand. I had expected that Rona would take her time, what with me there, but she was back in under ten minutes with coffee for us both.

We drank it without speaking, threw the cups in the trash, kept standing close. Awkwardness had given way to the need for human warmth. We were family, all that was left of the core unit now that Connie was edging away.

"How's everything at home?" Rona whispered.

"Lousy," I whispered back.

"Want to tell her?"

"Want to, but won't."

"Maybe that would bring her around. Shock her out of it, y'know?" She gave me a moment's fright when she raised her voice. "Mom? Can you hear me, Mom? Claire's here. She came all the way to see you. Wake up and talk with her. It's all right with me, really it is."

Connie showed no sign of waking.

Rona sank back beside me. "She's fighting me even now, keeping her eyes closed just to spite me."

"Maybe we're taking the wrong tactic," I said. "The doctor said we can tell her it's okay to let go."

Rona looked appalled. "He told me that, too, but I can't tell her to die."

"We wouldn't be doing that. We'd be saying she doesn't have to hang on if she's too tired. It may be the merciful thing."

"But I need her. I need her to wake up. I need to tell her things."

I put my arm around Rona's shoulder. She and I hadn't seen eye to eye on many things in life, but I could relate to this pain. There was desperation in it, fear that the buzzer would ring and leave her knowing that she hadn't tried her hardest.

The best you can be is the best you can be, Mom had always said, the last time not two weeks before. So the lesson hadn't been lost on Rona, either.

"She thinks I'm shallow, but I really loved Jerry, and I really loved Harold, and they really loved *me* for a little while, and it felt so good. For that little while with each of them it was like I was the only other person in the world. I felt so good. So safe. Okay, so I didn't work like she did and like you do, but does that make me a bad person?"

Safe. I needed that, too. I had married Dennis for it. But Brody provided it. Did that make me a bad person? "No."

"Then why did she make me feel that way?"

I had to work to keep my thoughts on Rona. "Maybe she was jealous."

"Jealous?"

"You had luxuries she wanted but couldn't have. Either couldn't have, or didn't take. She felt like a coward. You had guts. She envied that."

"She did?"

I imagined so.

Sunday morning became Sunday afternoon. Doctors and nurses stopped by, but other than make a show of fiddling with charts, machines, or drips, they did little. Connie's minister dropped in for several minutes. Connie didn't so much as blink.

Rona curled up in the chair and slept for a while, then woke up and returned to her post at the bed rail. I kept expecting her to go home to shower and do herself up in her usual done-up way, but she wasn't budging from the room other than to go for coffee or food. Once or twice she rinsed her face in the sink and brushed her hair, but otherwise she remained more unadorned than I had seen her in years. I found her more approachable this way, though that might have been my own need for company. I also thought she was even prettier this way and told her so.

She sighed. "Mom always said that, too." She closed her eyes, rolled her head around on her neck, sighed again. "So here I am at this late date, trying to please her still." She opened her eyes and looked my way. "Do you ever think of dying?"

"I try not to."

"No wonder. Your life is pretty full. But I think about it. I think about things I won't have done that I will wish I had."

I felt a fast flare of anger. Connie had said nearly the same thing—but damn, it hadn't had to be that way. She could have done more. She could have enjoyed life, instead of playing the martyr. She could have enjoyed *us* more than she had.

I took a deep breath. The anger broke and scattered. "What do you wish you'd done?" I asked Rona.

"Had kids." She shot me a look that dared me to laugh.

"That doesn't surprise me. You're great with mine. It isn't too late. Mom would love it."

Rona leaned over, propping her forearms on the rail. "She thinks I'm too flighty."

I leaned over and propped my forearms beside hers. "Do you?"

She shrugged. "When you hear it enough, you come to think it, too, though, for the life of me, I don't know why I listen."

"It's not just you. I listen, too. Connie's my rock."

Rona looked at me in surprise. "You're *her* rock. You were always the strong one in the family, Claire. Argue all you want, but there it is."

"I could always count on her for unconditional support."

"Right. For support. But you were the answer person. The voice of reason. The doer. Much more than Mom or me."

* * *

I didn't feel like the answer person, the voice of reason, the doer. I felt totally helpless, standing, sitting, waiting there for Connie to make her move. Life or death—it was her choice. Then again, maybe it wasn't, which was as scary a thought as anything. It only confirmed my own helplessness. I wanted to think I had more control over life.

So, *was* I a control freak?

Rona and I might argue forever about who was the rock, but the fact remained that the foundation of my world was shifting. Here, back home—I felt the shaking and was left weak in the knees.

More than once I wished Brody was with me. *He* was an answer person, a voice of reason, a doer. I would have leaned on him with relish.

But this wasn't a time for Brody. It was a time for Connie, Rona, and me. As the hours passed, as afternoon gave way to night and still Connie stayed with us, her face grew more polished, almost opalescent. I thought about the story of Grandmother Kate's pearls, and couldn't help but imagine that Connie was becoming one herself. It struck me that that was what death watches were about, a chance for family to pull together for a few last hours of peaceful communion, the creation of a final memory, a last pearl to add to the strand. In that sense, I was grateful Connie lingered.

I made Rona go home that Sunday night for a few hours' sleep while I dozed by Connie's bed, but she was back well before Monday's dawn. She had showered and changed into jeans and a sweater, still the ponytail and the naked face remained. She looked about eighteen.

We curled in side-by-side armchairs by the bed, pulled at

fresh croissants, sipped coffee, and talked—hushed and intimate—as we hadn't done since we had been pubescent teen-agers intrigued with boys. Now, instead of boys we talked about men—Rona of her husbands, me of Dennis. Whether we felt drawn to confessions because of the quasi-religious nature of the occasion, I didn't know. But, there in the purple-blue light of dawn, with the hospital world barely launching its day, Rona con-fessed to having a nonexistent sex life with Harold, and I con-fessed to being evicted by Dennis.

"Do you miss him?" she asked when I was done with my tale.

I had asked myself that more than once. By rights, what with the suddenness of the separation, I should miss him, well beyond the mourning period Dean Jenovitz had presumed. When a per-son was part of your everyday life for fifteen years, the place he had taken up should feel empty, shouldn't it?

"Those first few days were so filled with fury that there wasn't room for missing much besides the kids," I said. "Now? I miss knowing I'm married. There's security in being married. I miss having my life settled. There's security in that, too. I miss the anonymity I used to have walking around town. People have questions now. Sometimes they just look at me and I know they're wondering. Obviously, I miss the kids. That never stops. Do I miss Dennis? The man himself?" I thought for another minute, just to be sure I wasn't being rash. But, of all the emotions I had felt in the last few weeks, missing Dennis wasn't one. Those good parts of my marriage were memories now. Pearls. I would never lose them. But there wouldn't be any more that included Dennis.

"No. I don't miss him. We had grown apart emotionally." It was so very clear to me now. "We aren't the same people we were when we got married. We shaped each other in ways that made us less compatible. Ironic, isn't it? And pathetic that it took such drastic action on Dennis's part for me to see it. Boy, was I blind. I kept thinking that every marriage had its rocky spots, that no marriage was perfect."

"Did Dennis cheat on you?"

"No." I thought of Phoebe. "Well, not until the end." At least, I assumed that. Was I off base there, too?

"Did you cheat on him?"

"No."

"Nothing with Brody?"

"Not yet."

She didn't say a thing, just gave me a sly smile.

Quickly I said, "I don't know what I'd do without Brody. He's been just about running the business single-handedly since all this began. It's a big load off my mind."

"Does Dennis know you're here?"

"I called him yesterday." My eyes drifted back to Connie. My voice was low, one step up from a thought. "I felt he needed to know. To be prepared. He said he would fly out with the kids . . . if necessary."

Connie remained comatose through Monday. Exhausted by evening, Rona and I left the hospital, picked up pizza on the way to Rona's house, scarfed it down in her kitchen, and slept until early morning. Then we returned to the hospital.

That Tuesday we talked about our childhood, tossing memories back and forth across Connie's bed. Sometimes we included Connie in the discussion. Other times we talked above her. On occasion we laughed, and laughed hard. Our own emotional survival demanded it.

Besides, we didn't think Connie would mind. She would have liked the idea that Rona and I were communicating after being emotionally distant for so long. She had asked me to look after

Rona. I rather thought we were going one better, looking after each other, at least for this short time.

During those hours, I grew complacent. Enclosed in that small hospital room, with the machine beside Connie beeping rhythmically and my sister and I getting along, I felt oddly relaxed. I was with my mother. I was with my sister. For that little while, I had nowhere else to go, nothing else to do. Work, the children, the custody battle—all seemed distant. I was living through an intermission in the drama of my life, actually enjoying it, in an odd kind of way.

Tuesday night, the bubble of tranquility burst with the rattle of Connie's breathing. The doctor diagnosed pneumonia and started an antibiotic drip. Rona and I took to looking at each other across that bed in alarm with each new sound that Connie made.

The noise ended in abrupt silence just shy of midnight. The doctor came and made the pronouncement, followed by the nurses, who turned off the machines. Rona and I stood holding each other while they did what they needed to do, but when they would have taken Connie from the room we protested.

"A few more minutes?" I begged. Rona was crying softly by my side.

They backed out and closed the door, leaving the three of us alone a final time.

I drew Rona with me toward the bed. On initial view, Connie looked much the same as she had looked before. The differences were subtle.

"How smooth her skin is," Rona whispered. "Every last wrinkle is gone."

"They left with her tension," I said. It had been gradual, of course, the slow releasing of life. The waxiness I had noticed earlier had been a movement toward this. "She looks peaceful. I hope she is."

"So do I. She wasn't such a bad mother." She drew in a shaky breath and said a wry, "Something has to explain why I stayed around so long."

"You loved her. And she loved you. Why else would *she* have stayed around so long?"

"Guilt? A misguided sense of responsibility?"

"No. Mothers are simply, always *there*. They never give up on their kids. They can't. It isn't in their constitution."

"So now she's gone," Rona whispered and started to cry again.

My own eyes filled. I reached down and touched Connie's hair, ran my fingers over her forehead, then her cheek. I couldn't remember having ever done that before. It struck me that there was something else we had missed—and suddenly I wanted to grab her up and breathe the life back into her, and do all those missed things, so that there wouldn't be this awful regret.

Of course, I couldn't.

We buried Connie Thursday morning in a brief graveside ceremony beneath a cold and somber sky. It did my heart good to see that not only the minister, but more friends than I had known Connie had, were touched by her death.

I hugged Kikit through the service, passing her to Rona from time to time, while Dennis held Johnny close.

Brody had flown out, too, though his presence was as much torment as comfort. I loved having him close. But I wanted him to hold me, and I had to show restraint.

Brody flew home Friday morning, Dennis and the children later that day. I stayed on until Saturday evening to be with Rona.

Our goal was to spend the day at Mom's apartment deciding what to do with its contents, and for a time we did try. First memory distracted us, though, then grief. By the time Rona drove me to the airport, the only decision we made was that I would take the cat. I boarded the plane with my overnighter on one shoulder and Valentino in his bag on the other.

Brody met me in Boston. We had planned it this time. He took my bag and Valentino, threw an arm around me, and guided me to the car. I remember driving over the bridge, but I slept right through a stop at the market for cat food and litter. He woke me when we reached the lighthouse, carried everything inside, and got Valentino set up while I stared out at the sea. Then he poured me a glass of wine and held me close in the huge wicker chair-and-a-half in the dark of my den.

He had been my haven through the worst of my ordeal with Dennis, and this was similar. He made me feel safe enough to give up control and let go. So I cried. I cried for Mom and for Rona, cried for unfulfilled dreams and regrets that didn't have to be. By the time I ran out of tears, I was sleepy again, but I wouldn't let Brody leave. We fell asleep there in the chair, my body burrowing into Brody, his molding me close. I was so overloaded with feelings that the only thing making sense was how much I loved him.

I don't know how long I slept, an hour, maybe two. I awoke restless, and moved against him. By the time I realized that he was awake, aiding and abetting, I was needing him so badly that, short of the lighthouse falling into the sea, nothing was pulling us apart.

We kissed, and kissed deeply, but no amount of tongue play could ease the hunger. We touched—my hands under Brody's sweatshirt sifting through the hair on his chest, his hands under my sweater kneading my breasts. We rubbed and arched and shifted, pushing clothing aside to feel flesh, and if there was anything unwise in what we did, I couldn't think of it. I loved Brody. He filled my empty places, gave me a sense of peace even in the midst of the storm we stirred. I needed to be closer, then closer and closer. If I could have buried myself in him, I would have.

I don't think I'll ever forget what I felt when Brody entered me that very first time. We had joked about my being virginal, but, so help me, I had never known the kind of fullness I did then. It wasn't only his penis, though that was so engorged inside me that I felt its every quiver and thrust. It was the rest of him—broad chest expanding as the feeling built, tight belly clenching with the bowing of his back, lean hips undulating under my hands. It was his heat and the scent it released. It was his heart and soul filling me until I cried out in wonder.

I cried out more than once, in near-fear at the end because the sensation was so high and my body so out of control that the goal it reached for was a puzzle. That goal came with explosive force, no puzzle at all, simply the most exquisite and divine pleasure.

Brody felt it, too. I heard it in the hoarse sounds he made, felt it in the trembling of his arms, savored it in the long, hard pulsing inside that signaled his release. I might have actually come again, the pleasure of his pleasure was so strong and prolonged, but I wasn't of a mind to make such fine judgments as where the body stopped and the mind began. It was enough to know that the pleasure was there and was right.

We curled against each other and slept. When I awoke, Valentino was sitting inches from my face, staring at me with large obsidian eyes. He might have been named for a lover but not the lover I wanted.

"Brody?" I called and listened for a response. Frightened, I sat up and hugged my knees to my chest. *"Brody?"*

He didn't answer. But I heard water start to run through the pipes.

I ran to the second floor bathroom, slipped inside, and leaned back against the door. His body was fogged by steam on the glass of the shower stall, but I could see his arms stretched to the wall and his head hanging low beneath the spray.

My own head was suddenly clear. I removed the few of my

clothes that remained, slipped into the stall, and leaned back against that door, too.

Brody looked at me over his shoulder. The small shift in his body was enough to redirect the spray. I yelped.

"It's *freezing cold*!"

"That's the point."

"Warm it up, Brody!"

"Not a good idea."

Taking shelter in his body, I wrapped my arms around him from behind, locked my fists over his chest, and said a fast, "I know how your mind works, Brody Parth. It's saying you took advantage of me at a time when I was weak, and if not that, it's saying you've single-handedly blown my chances of getting the kids back, but it isn't so. I don't regret what we did for a minute. Not for *one minute*!" I emphasized the last with squeezes to his rib cage and waited for his response.

It was a sputtering laugh and the shake of his head.

"What?" I challenged, shivering against him.

He unfurled my fists and pushed my hands down his body until they collided with an impressive erection. I barely had time to possess it when he turned, barely had time to take a breath—or realize that the water had warmed—when he took my mouth with a hunger that would have given me plenty to think about had I been able to think. But it was like before. Thought left. Fear left. There was only a need to be part of him, and he me.

Foreplay was unnecessary. I was ready for him when he hiked me against the shower wall and drove into me. My arms were around his neck, his were under my bottom. I linked my heels at the small of his back and went with his thrusts, wanting to feel him, taste him. The pleasure rose and rose. It crested with a shimmer and a series of gasps, then, incredibly, rose again. I reached my second climax at the same time that Brody reached his first. I loved that his lasted longer. Not for anything would I have missed that pulsing sensation, or the satisfied sounds he made as awareness slowly returned.

He kept me against the tile for a while, half-holding me, half-sagging against me. From time to time he pushed his hips forward and made sounds that said he was savoring a sweet little afterspasm. Finally, shifting me higher, he turned so that we shared the direct force of the spray, and still he held me. He didn't speak. Our eyes said all that was needed—*that was wonderful, even better than my dreams, I've wanted you for years, I love you.*

Eventually, he lowered me, soaped me, rinsed me. Odd, but I felt shy. After all those years of being close in every respect but this, it was the first time he had seen me naked in the light, and he looked his fill, *touched* his fill of those parts previously hidden. Not that I kept my own eyes shut. Brody was beautifully endowed. I couldn't seem to look away—which embarrassed me even more. I blushed when he caught me at it.

"I can't help it," I muttered, annoyed with myself for being so naive.

Grinning, he resumed his ministrations.

I put on a long robe, Brody his jeans. He made us cappuccino with the machine he had given me as a house-warming gift—no *pffffft-shhhhhhhh* sounds and instant powder for us, only the real thing would do. We drank it sitting on stools at the breakfast bar, smiling inanely at one another between sips. He took my hand to his mouth, kissed it, pressed my palm to his chest.

"I have no regrets," he said. "Not a one."

"Good."

"I've wanted you for a long time. A loonnng time."

"You never let on."

"How could I? You were married to my best friend."

I moved my hand on his chest, smoothing the hair there. "Did you ever think the marriage would fall apart?"

"No."

"Did you think it should have?"

"Hard to separate what I thought should be from what I wanted to be. There were things that bothered me. I didn't think Dennis was doing his share. I didn't think he was giving you emotional support, or financial support. I didn't know what to think about the sex."

I ran my hand down the center of his chest and hooked my fingertips into his jeans. "It was okay. Nothing like—" I hitched my chin toward the den with its just-christened chair-and-a-half, glanced up in the direction of the shower, shrugged, winced, grinned. "Dennis thought I was pretty lousy."

"I think you're pretty incredible."

"You weren't disappointed, not even the tiniest bit, after all that waiting?"

"Did I feel disappointed to you, up there in the shower?"

No. He hadn't felt disappointed to me. He had felt hard and huge, and, afterward, satisfied. Still, I had had to ask. Too clearly I recalled what Dennis had said that day at the house. I hadn't satisfied him, that was for sure. "Did Dennis cheat on me? Before Phoebe?"

"I don't know."

"You never suspected anything, not even once?"

"No. Did you?"

"No. But the wife is the last to know. And there was that thing with Adrienne."

"He wasn't married then."

"She was. And he knew she was. That bothered me for a long time. I finally put it aside because it wasn't something I could live with. This thing with Phoebe brings it all back."

"From what I hear about Phoebe, it won't last. She flits from client to client. I'm amazed there haven't been any complaints filed with the Bar Association. There would have been, if it had been the other way around, but a man isn't about to complain that he was seduced and then jilted. It'd kill his pride. You watch. Dennis will say he dumped her."

I was thinking about what he'd said. "Maybe I can file a complaint against her with the Bar Association." When Brody shook his head, I asked, "Why not? If she stacked the case against me—"

"She isn't his lawyer of record. Heuber is, and he's a powerhouse himself. We'd be hard-pressed to prove she's calling the shots. And there's nothing unethical in Dennis screwing his lawyer's partner."

"Maybe not unethical, but certainly immoral." I was starting to feel differently about certain things. "I'm going to win this case," I said with conviction, and tugged at Brody's jeans for emphasis. "I'll do whatever it takes, Brody. I'm not going to find myself five or ten years from now wishing that I'd done more. My mother died thinking of all she didn't do. I don't want to be like that."

I was silent then, thinking of Connie.

Brody gave me that time, a silent meditation. Then he put the pad of his thumb to my mouth. "Is that what our making love was about?"

I slipped from my stool to his lap, took his face in my hands, and said in a whisper-soft voice, "Our making love was the most positive thing to happen to me in days. It was the most honest. The most real. I've been sitting around feeling helpless for nearly a month now, but, God, I'm tired of it. I need to be proactive, not reactive." I tipped his glasses up with my thumbs, pressed kisses on his eyes and the bridge of his nose, and let the glasses return. "What time is it?"

He glanced at the clock behind me. "Two."

"Sleep with me?"

His mouth twitched. "Didn't I just?"

"No. *Sleep* with me. In my bed. Until morning. I need to roll over and feel you there. I need to wake up and see you there. It's been one hell of a week."

I could see he was pleased. Still, he said, "What if there's someone out there on a boat with an infrared telephoto lens?"

"I'm a separated woman," I said, for the first time feeling the full freedom of that. "I can do what I want."

That thought held when Dennis rang my bell the next morning at the ungodly hour of eight. I might have lied when he mentioned Brody's car outside. I might have said Brody had come over for an early breakfast, but there were two problems with that. One, with my hair disheveled, my eyes flecked with sleep, and no nightgown visible at the neck of my robe, I had clearly just rolled out of bed, and two, I was done with being made out to be the guilty party.

There was actually a third reason. I was proud to be Brody's lover. Brody was infinitely more virile than Dennis—something I might have seen earlier, had I not been so concerned with being a good wife. And I had been, damn it. I had been a good wife to Dennis right up until the day he booted me out.

So when he asked if Brody was still in bed, I said, "Yes. We didn't fall asleep until late."

He seemed almost sad, then curious. "No more denials?"

Valentino came from nowhere to curl around my leg. Scooping him up, I said, "I never denied what was true. Brody and I weren't romantically involved until you and I separated. You planted the bug in our ear. Ironic, isn't it?"

"Aren't you worried it'll hurt your chances for custody?"

"No. We weren't sexually involved until this weekend. You and Phoebe were doing it last July. I have records from your stay in that motel in Vermont." When he blinked, I rubbed it in. "Didn't it occur to you that I'd find out?" But, of course, it hadn't.

I had been an optimistic wife, a dumb wife, in hindsight, but no more. "I'll raise it in court, Dennis. I'll raise that, plus anything else, if there is anything else, about Adrienne."

"What else could there be?"

"You tell me. She threatened to implicate you in illegal trading. At least, that's what you said at the time, or was that just a stab at painting you as the victim?"

He didn't respond, other than to say, "You won't find proof of anything."

"Do I need it? All you had against me was innuendo, and the courts went for it. You really shouldn't have emptied that file. That's what made me suspicious."

Dennis looked sober. "Innuendo can't hurt me. That business with Adrienne was a long time ago. Even if there was something more, the statute of limitations has expired. The law can't touch me."

"Maybe not. But Pittney wouldn't be pleased to hear about it."

That shook him. "You'd go to Pittney?"

"If I have to, I will. I want my kids back."

"Christ, you've gotten tough."

"You've *made* me tough. You were the one who took me to court, and took away my kids and my home. You were the one who brought up the abortion business."

"I told you. I didn't pass those records to Jenovitz. And I didn't tell my lawyers to get them."

"Did you tell them you didn't want the abortion? That's what you told Jenovitz. That was a lie, Dennis. *Another* lie." I was thinking clearly, feeling stronger than I had in days. "For the past month you've been playing dirty. Well, I can play dirty, too. I don't want to, but if I have no choice, I will. I'll also take you to court on the divorce settlement. You've pissed away all the money you ever made. You're not pissing away mine. So, back off," I warned and was about to slam the door in his face, when I frowned. "We agreed that I would come for the kids at noon. Why are you here now?"

"They spent the night with my parents," he said, still sober. "I'm on my way to pick them up. I wanted to talk with you first. But it's a bad time."

If I'd had to describe him just then, I'd have said he looked deflated. I had never seen him that way before. More quietly, I said, "It's never a bad time when it comes to the kids. What's wrong?"

"We have to tell them about Jenovitz. I thought we should coordinate our stories."

"Did you ask Jenovitz what to say?" Of course he hadn't. Just like he would drive for miles on the wrong road without stopping for directions, lest someone think he didn't know his way.

"I wanted to ask you first."

I stared at him in a moment's amazement, wondering what was behind his solicitousness and when it would jump out to hit me on the head. But he looked perfectly serious, even humble. Still I waited, thought, puzzled. When I couldn't see the slightest hint of either arrogance or deceit, I let out a long breath and stood back. "Come in. I'll make coffee and we'll talk."

So Dennis intruded on my first morning after with Brody. But it was necessary, a precedent-setting of sorts. Dennis and I had to learn to deal civilly with each other where the children were concerned. Dennis also had to learn to see me with Brody.

That didn't mean I lost my resolve. As soon as he left, I called Carmen at home. She reported that Art Heuber had filed his opposition to our petition on Wednesday, that the judge was studying it and would be in touch on Monday. Morgan had learned that Phoebe was the one to obtain my medical records, but, as for the rest, he was still searching.

I told Carmen to keep him at it. I was sorry that my marriage had come to this, but it had. My sole concern now was for the right to raise my kids.

I may not have had the courage to tell Connie about the demise of my marriage. I would live with the guilt of that for years. But I wasn't living with the regret of letting resources go untapped. In that sense, she had given me sound advice.

Fifteen

Carmen called first thing that Monday before Thanksgiving with good news and bad news.

The good news was that a justice of the appeals court had agreed to a hearing on our petition.

The bad news was that the holiday would hold things up. The hearing wouldn't be held until the Monday after.

Discouraged, I spent the morning in my workroom. Having removed every last broken weaver from both the rocker and its table, I set to cleaning and sanding the areas needing repair. It was busy work, neither here nor there in terms of construction or destruction, and, in that sense, the least exciting part of the job, but important. Working first and last with a damp cloth, and in between with a metal file, sandpaper, and a hand vacuum, I had to smooth down all the rough spots to make way for new lengths of reed.

The goal was to make a seamless repair. Skimping at this stage, tempting as it was, would have jeopardized that. So I threw myself into the work.

* * *

That afternoon, I had my third meeting with Dean Jenovitz. He was back to the pipe this time, though he only lit it once. He held it cold in his mouth for the first thirty minutes of the session, busied himself through the next fifteen by filling it with tobacco and tamping it down, scrutinizing the bowl, tasting the stem, studying the bowl again, retamping the tobacco, and so on, before he finally caved in and set it burning. At the time I wondered if he was more interested in the pipe than in me.

I continued to wonder that, well after the meeting ended. No matter how many times I replayed the discussion, either alone or in retellings to Carmen and Brody, I couldn't find a point to it. Jenovitz expressed his condolences on the death of my mother and asked how I was doing, though he wasn't interested in pursuing my response with more than a nod. He asked how my visits with the children were going, but didn't pick up on it when I mentioned Brody being at those visits. Nor did he show any reaction when I said that I was going to Johnny's basketball practice that afternoon and Kikit's concert Tuesday morning. He asked how work was going, and whether I had any travel plans in mind, and, if I wasn't making the rounds of the Christmas boutiques this year, who was? When I said I was hoping Brody would, he let that go, too.

There was ample opportunity for discussion on the subject of my parenting ability. He might have asked how my mother's death would free me up for the children, or what I had done, if anything, with Dennis to help prepare the children for her funeral, or, if nothing else, whether I worried that Kikit would be allergic to Valentino.

I had the impression that he was bored.

Worse, I had the impression that he had already made his decision and was simply marking time.

"He doesn't react to things he should," I told Carmen on the phone when the meeting was done. "When I told him about

Dennis and Phoebe being at a motel in Vermont last July, he grunted, then nodded, then asked me why I was fixated on their relationship. He didn't get it. Not even when I spelled it out. What's going on?"

"I'm wondering," Carmen said, "if he has a sweet deal with Selwey."

"Sweet deal?"

"I brought up his name to my gal group last week. Word is he's tired, that managed health care has left him behind, and he's thinking of retiring, but that money is an issue. By way of compromise, he's starting to ease back on his private practice and let court cases like yours support him. He's paid by the hour. More than half of his billable hours are court-related. It's easy money."

"Easy money?" It was *my* money, my *problems.* Easy? "Gee, thanks."

"You know what I mean. There isn't any therapy involved. He just listens and makes a written recommendation. Some cases are cut-and-dried. If one of the parents is abusive or unstable, the children are placed with the other parent. For the other cases, he usually recommends shared custody. That could either be the right choice, or simply expedient."

"He hasn't mentioned shared custody to me." I wondered why not, and found no comfort in the answer.

"How would you feel about it?"

"Annoyed. I don't want to share my children." The thought of it brought back all the anger. "Dennis had no right doing what he did. I don't want a man like that being a major influence on my kids."

"He *is* their father."

"So?"

"He's doing an okay job of it, isn't he?"

No, I wanted to say. *He's doing a lousy job. He's messing them up.* But the truth was that he wasn't. The children were clean, well-fed, well-supervised. Between what I had seen and what they had told me, Dennis was trying. I hated to admit it, but there it was.

"But I like knowing what my kids are doing," I burst out, then paused, sighed, admitted a self-incriminating, "I do. All the time. So maybe that's wrong. Maybe it's another reason I was never willing to consider divorce. I didn't want to have to share them."

"You may have to let go a little."

"Brody said that, too."

Carmen cleared her throat. "Speaking of Brody."

I could hear it coming and said a fast, "Brody is my lifeline. If he weren't here, I'd have gone under weeks ago."

"Flaunting Brody in front of Dennis wasn't the best idea."

"But it sure felt good," I said. "Besides we have him cold on Phoebe. Now, we need to know more about Adrienne. What's with Morgan?"

"He's getting inklings of things."

"Illegal things?" I asked. I wasn't sure whether to feel jubilant or dismayed.

"He won't elaborate until he has proof, and that's hard to come by with something that happened so long ago. Finding witnesses is tough. Some have died, like Adrienne. Others have moved, forwarding order expired. Dennis was right about the statute of limitations, though. He isn't at risk."

"Maybe not legally," I said, "but Heuber will be wanting a counter-offer on the settlement soon, and we need a lever. I meant what I told Dennis. I'll call people at Pittney. If I have to, I'll slip gossip to Hillary Howard. Gossip can turn off future clients. It's not that I want to ruin Dennis, I just want custody of the kids." That raised what was still, always, more than ever my fear. "Carmen?"

"Yesss?" came her deep voice.

"What do you think? Will I get them? Or is Jenovitz Selwey's puppet?"

"I'm looking into that possibility. One of my associates is tabulating the number of cases Selwey assigned Jenovitz in the last year, and whether the recommendation was in keeping with or different from the initial decree."

"Can we come right out and ask Jenovitz if he's reached a finding?"

"We can. I doubt he'll tell us."

"Won't that tell us something?"

"That he's ruling against us? No. It's the power thing, Claire. He'll keep his secret like he's the president of Price Waterhouse protecting the Oscar winners. He's not giving away a thing until he gets his moment on stage."

Dennis had initially put in to have the children on Thanksgiving Day. When there was early snow in the southern New Hampshire mountains, he suggested I take them on Thursday so that he could take them for a weekend of skiing.

I could have been difficult and insisted we stick to the original plan. After the fuss Dennis made each time I was early picking up the kids or late getting them back, he deserved to be stymied.

But Rona was flying in on Wednesday, and I liked the idea of celebrating the holiday on the holiday.

And Dennis sweetened the pot by offering to let Johnny and Kikit sleep over at the lighthouse Thursday night. I had been repeatedly asking for sleepovers, to no avail. Whether the kids' pleas had finally gotten to him, or he wanted to spend Thanksgiving night with someone else, or his heart was truly softening, I didn't know. But I wasn't looking a gift horse in the mouth.

Besides, I wanted points for flexibility.

How quickly I had joined the game. It was a side of me I despised—a cynical side that I hadn't possessed before all this had begun—but cynicism was armor and we were at war. If I wanted to win, I had to wear it.

The words we used were something else. I hated them—*have* the children, *take* the children—like they were things to be shifted here or there, albeit the most precious possessions to emerge from our marriage. These words weren't part of the war. They were part of the new vocabulary I was learning, the vocabulary of the divorced parent. Oh, I fought it. I tried to dress up the concept by using more humanizing substitutes—I was *spending* Saturday with the kids, or I was going to *be with* the kids on Saturday, or I was *seeing* the kids on Saturday—but these were sometimes so self-conscious that they drew more attention to the mess. In time, I succumbed to *have* and *take* as the lesser of the evils.

Thanksgiving was an eye-opener. It was my first major holiday separated from Dennis, my first major holiday without Connie. Technically, little was different. I was still the one cooking the turkey, still the one laying the table out with the fine linen and polished silver that I had retrieved from the house, still the one seeing to little details like fresh flowers, tapered candlesticks, gourmet chocolates.

What was different was Brody, who was either freed by Dennis's absence, so used to doing for himself, or so much in love with me that he did more than his share of the work.

What else was different was the lighthouse, which dressed up so beautifully, with its view of the ocean, that we might have been at an idyllic Plymouth Rock.

What *else* was different was Rona. She was more agreeable than I had ever found her.

And then there were the children. I hadn't been sure what they would be feeling about spending the day without Dennis, and hadn't been able to discuss it with them beforehand, given the last-minute change in plans. I was worried that the holiday would be like salt on the wound of their parents' divorce, and, yes, I'm sure there were moments that stung. But they were pleased to be spending the night here—*can we sleep in your bed, Mommy, and turn out all the lights and pretend we're in the middle of the ocean for the whole night, and watch the sun come up, can we, pleeease?* asked Kikit—and they loved being with Joy, and with Rona, and with Brody.

Yes, even Johnny. It took him a while to warm up, perhaps to forget that Dennis wasn't there, but once it happened he was more his normal self than he had been since the split. He responded in detail when I asked about his basketball team, even said he couldn't wait for me to watch his games, which was the closest he had come to restating his love. For all the times I had worried that I wasn't doing enough, I felt justified now. Children adapted, give or take. The key was in understanding the give or take, so that trauma was neither created when it didn't exist nor ignored when it did.

I think I did an okay job. When they left with Dennis on Friday morning, they were happy. I wasn't sure how happy *he* was after an hour in the car with Kikit retelling every detail of their night—not the least of which would have been a blow-by-blow of Brody's tale of the ill-fated whaler, *Godsend* and the first mate's wife, whose will alone was reputed to have brought its surviving crew safely home—but at least I felt I had done my part.

My own moments of thought—of regret, if you will—in the aftermath of that Thanksgiving had to do with Mom. I missed her. It wasn't that she had a history of coming east for the holiday loaded down with cakes and cookies and the makings from old family recipes. It wasn't even that she did much after she arrived. Coming to visit me was her vacation, she said. Knowing how hard she had worked to support Rona and me, I was pleased to indulge her.

I missed the pleasure she took in my house and my kids. I missed the look on her face when I called everyone in to dinner.

Even more than the children, who took prosperity for granted, Connie delighted in seeing the table filled to overflowing with goodies. I chose to think she would have loved this year's table even in spite of Dennis's absence.

Rona disagreed. "There's good reason why you didn't tell her you were getting divorced. She would have been so hung up on the concept that she wouldn't have seen the reality. I can see the reality, and it isn't so bad."

It was Friday morning. The children had left, Brody had taken Joy to Boston, and Rona and I were braving the winds, bundled up on the rocks not far from the base of my light. We had our feet tucked beneath us, and were watching the swirl of the water a mere ten feet away. The air was so heavy with fog that it might have been a sauna, had the temperature been fifty degrees higher. Even cold, there was something of a balm to it.

"The reality," Rona went on, "is that there isn't the tension there used to be when Dennis was here. When he was here, you needed to make things perfect."

"Did I?"

"Definitely."

"Why?"

"You tell me."

I thought about it. "Maybe I wanted to make him proud. Certainly, satisfied."

"Maybe you knew his eye was wandering and wanted to make yourself indispensable."

"That does sound controlling. Then again, maybe I did it for Mom. To please her. Y'know?"

Rona laughed. "Nu-uh. Mom was so enthralled by everything you did that she wouldn't have noticed the difference between perfection and a hair less so."

"She wouldn't have been enthralled by my divorce." That thought did haunt me still.

"But you're adapting to it."

"What choice do I have?" I swiveled on my bottom to face Rona. "How do the kids seem to you? I'm worried they'll be screwed up. Do they seem different?"

"Johnny, maybe. More introspective. That may be his age, though. I wouldn't worry about them, Claire. They're well-grounded kids."

"Tell that to the GAL," I muttered.

"Sure. Point me in his direction."

My muttering had been rhetoric. I hadn't expected Rona to take it as an offer. But she was serious. More than serious, if her look meant anything. It was purposeful. She was testing me, *daring* me to trust her with a part of my life that was so important to me.

Jenovitz would have a field day with Rona. A question here, a bit of silence there, and he would have her spilling her guts. With the best of intentions, she might say something all the wrong way.

"I think he has a problem with women," I hedged.

Rona's look didn't change.

"He dislikes me," I tried again. "You're my sister. He's apt to dislike you on that fact alone, so where will that get us?"

"I can still tell him you've been a great mother." Her mouth thinned. "Look, Claire, I may resent you for a lot of things, but I'd never take that away from you. You have been a great mother. Besides," her voice went hard, "Dennis is a prick. He cheated on you for years."

"I don't know that."

"He did. Trust me. Where there's smoke, et cetera." She tipped up her chin and looked out to sea. "Dennis made a pass at me once."

"What?"

"Touched me in a totally inappropriate way. I mean, *totally* inappropriate way. Nothing innocent intended, nothing innocent taken."

"When?"

"Between Jerry and Harold."

"Why didn't you tell me?"

She gave me an are-you-*nuts* look. "Because you were *married* to the guy. Besides, Mom would have killed me. She would have blamed me for wearing a tight dress and accused me of making a pass at Dennis and asked *what did I think I was doing trying to ruin your marriage.*" She put her chin on her knees, but not before I saw that her look had turned stricken.

I patted her arm. When I realized she couldn't feel it through her jacket, I increased the pressure of my hand. It was a small gesture. We had pretty much reverted to our touch-me-not style of old. I knew that the habit of years couldn't be changed in a single week, but I wanted to make the effort. I was comfortable touching the children, Brody, even friends. Not so Connie. Or Dennis. I wanted things to be different now with Rona.

"How are you doing, without Mom?" I asked gently.

"Fine."

"Really?"

"Really. There's plenty to keep me busy—big sale at Neiman Marcus, huuuuge gala at the country club, incrrrrredible special on sculpted nails at the Ten-in-a-Row Emporium."

"I'm serious, Rona."

"So am I."

"I'll rephrase the question, then. How are you during the time when you aren't busy?"

"Lost," she said without pause, then straightened her back and took a breath. "I was thinking of moving. I'm tired of Cleveland."

"You've lived there all your life."

"Yup, and everyone there thinks I'm as much of a ditz as Mom did. I need a new start."

"What did you have in mind?"

"Australia. I read *Mutant Message*. I could shed my worldly possessions and spend five months walking the outback in a search for the meaning of life. Or, I could go to Harvard Square, browse the coffee shops wearing my John Lennon glasses, and look for an intellectual who's smart enough to see the woman inside."

Laugh or cry—I could have gone either way. It struck me that even without Dennis, my life was filled with people, while Rona was alone.

"But I won't," she said. Taking a visible breath, she relaxed her stance. "Actually," she turned her head and met my eye, "I'm feeling more responsible than I used to. Like since I don't have a mother anymore, I'm not a child anymore. Know what I mean?"

I hadn't had that particular feeling, and shook my head to let her know.

"No," she said, "you wouldn't. You grew up when Daddy died. Me, I just kind of bided my time until I could live my life without Connie watching and judging my every move." She gave a small sigh and sought the horizon. "But you wouldn't know about that, either, would you?"

She was wrong. I did know. I had learned what it was to be judged—and judged unfairly, though it hadn't occurred to me to make the connection between Rona's experience and mine. I did now, and the connection was there—in the anger I had felt, the sense of helplessness and injustice, the nights of sleep I had lost and the tears I had shed.

So, had I been as blind about Connie as I had been about Dennis? Had I seen what I wanted to see? Worse, had I bought into Connie's criticisms of Rona because they had made me look good by comparison?

One thing I did know. I had put Connie on a pedestal, because she was my mother and I wanted her there. But she had abused Rona. My silence had condoned it. That made me partly responsible.

No amount of apologizing on my part could change what Rona had experienced, but I could help her in other ways. The first of those came to me late that afternoon. We were at the office—Rona, reading *USA Today*, and I, reviewing the monthly reports from our franchises in Milwaukee, Kansas City, and Charleston. We were waiting for Brody, who was dropping Joy at the airport and coming back to take us to dinner.

When he finally arrived, he looked distracted. He went to his desk and turned papers around to study them from the front so that he wouldn't have to unseat Rona. Then he straightened and put a hand on the top of his head.

I knew that gesture, all right.

"Brody?"

He looked my way, held up his hand, and smiled. "No sweat. I'm cool." He bent over the desk again, turned his day-at-a-glance calendar around, and flipped several pages over and back. Then he straightened again and blew out a breath. "I'll handle it."

I had a feeling I knew what the problem was. "The Christmas boutiques?" Not only the boutiques, but three charity events begging for our attendance.

"I can handle it. Being at the airport and thinking about flying out Monday must have gotten me a little crazy, is all."

We had been wrestling with the problem for days. Technically, the boutiques would survive without us. We had already received detailed reports on the Christmas displays, had given our approval or disapproval where it fit. The visits were more for employee morale.

But we were big on morale. It set our operation apart from

many another, and was a powerful incentive for hard work and loyalty. We hadn't yet had a franchisee sell out and open a competing business. Granted, Brody had put a clause in our contracts to prevent that, but there were ways to get around clauses, such as opening beyond the ninety-mile limit we had set out. No one had done that to us. We chose to think it was because we made our people feel important. Personal visits did that.

Since I couldn't make them this year, Brody had agreed to. But he was also doing double the work at home, what with my distractions. He had worked late most nights this week and was planning more of the same for the weekend.

I glanced at Rona. She held the newspaper in front of her, but her eyes were raised above it, focused on nothing in particular. She looked half asleep.

"*Rona,*" I called sharply.

Her eyes snapped to mine.

"How would you like an all-expense-paid trip across the country?"

Her brows rose.

"We need someone to check out our Christmas boutiques," I said. "There are twelve of them. Brody was going to hit two a day. You could spread it out more. What do you say?"

She looked confused.

"We'd give you a checklist of things to look for. You'd report back at the end of each stop. It'd actually be kind of fun. You'd take our people out to breakfast or dinner, whichever works out best, be a goodwill ambassador of sorts. Same with three charity events—literacy, cancer, and AIDS."

Rona looked from me to Brody and back. Eyebrows still raised, she pointed a questioning finger at herself, and for a minute, just a minute, I shared her doubt.

Then I realized that it wasn't me sharing the doubt. It was Connie's voice in my head, warning that Rona could as easily ignore the WickerWise boutiques for the sake of shopping in other departments, spending money she shouldn't spend on clothing she didn't need, forgetting about the plane she had to catch until it was so late she flat-out missed it.

"Yes, you," Brody told Rona, and Connie's voice went still. "You'd be the perfect one to do it. The way you looked when you got here on Wednesday—" He smiled in a way that said the solution to our problem was simple and right.

The way she had looked when she got here on Wednesday was subdued, which for Rona meant a suit that was navy instead of hot pink, jewelry that was mid-sized instead of over-sized, and hair that was brushed to a shine, without an ounce of tease.

Rona looked guarded, but definitely interested. "I'd be like the cosmetic specialist visiting Bendel's from Yves St. Laurent?"

"Without the smock," I said, leaving my chair, "and without the work. You wouldn't have to do any selling yourself, or stand around waiting for customers to come. You'd be there strictly in a supervisory capacity."

"Part of the managerial team," Brody added. "The only catch is that you'd have to head out this Sunday. We can route you through Cleveland so that you can pick up more clothes, and you can take up to two weeks, but everything has to be visited by mid-December."

I came up beside him and said to Rona, "You weren't planning on going anywhere else. What do you say?"

Rona scowled. "Are you sure this isn't just a makeshift dummy's mission to give me something to do with Mom gone?"

Brody's expression was nearly as priceless as his voice. "'Makeshift dummy's mission'? Christ, Rona, I've been pulling overtime all week trying to get ready for this, it's that important. If you don't do it, it's right back in my lap. You'd be doing me a huge favor."

"Twelve cities?" she asked.

"Well, if that's too many—"

Brody cut me off. "Twelve cities."

"Could I fly first class?"

"No," he said.

I would have bargained with her, which was why Brody was the money person.

Rona sat back. "What about a salary?"

I wasn't touching that subject.

Brody didn't blink. "Two hundred a day."

She made a face. "That's less than ten bucks an hour. I'd make more as a janitor at Cleveland Heights High. Three hundred a day."

"Two-fifty. You wouldn't want to be a janitor. Besides, you don't need the money. Two-fifty, plus expenses. Take it or leave it."

"You drive a hard bargain, Brody Parth," she said, but there was a smile on her face that made me feel nice.

Three days later, on the first Monday in December, Carmen and Art faced off before Justice David Wheeler of the Massachusetts Court of Appeals. Wheeler's courtroom was far quieter than Selwey's had been. The floor was carpeted, for one thing. For another, there were no spectators, no hum from the rows of empty wood benches.

The room itself was large. Before those wood benches was the bar, beyond which were tables for each of the lawyers flanking a podium, then, raised, a longer bench for the justices. Three high-backed leather chairs sat behind it. Justice Wheeler occupied the central one.

There was no sense of crisis, no frenzy here. Aside from the creak of Wheeler's chair when he alternately leaned far back to listen and came forward to question, the only sounds were his voice and those of Carmen and Arthur.

Each lawyer argued his or her case from the central podium. Since the justice already knew the facts, the purpose of the hearing was to allow him to ask questions, but only as they pertained to the earlier hearings with Selwey. This hearing was simply a review of that court action. No new evidence would be put forward. Carmen's argument, dictated by the nature of the appeal, was that Selwey had abused judicial discretion by making a decision that was beyond the bounds of reason. Heuber argued to the contrary. Neither Dennis nor I were asked to testify, but remained seated at the tables below.

The hearing lasted for just under an hour. We had been hoping that Justice Wheeler would announce his decision from the bench at the end of that time. In fact, he took the matter under advisement, promising a written opinion within several days.

So we waited. Again. Still.

Dean Jenovitz knew how disappointed I was when the court granted him an extension on the original thirty days allowed for the study, but I didn't think for a minute that my impatience spurred him on. More likely it was the ten-day trip to Florida he had planned for the end of December. Whatever the reason, I was relieved when I got the first of the calls telling me he had started down my reference list.

I was actually relieved in more ways than one. Whether my calls to each of those people had helped or they simply thought well of me, I didn't know, but they gave positive reports.

The children's pediatric nurse-practitioner, with whom I had developed a close enough friendship over the years to have her daughter spend one summer working in our Vineyard store, called to say, "He was pleasant enough, Claire. He asked if I thought the children were well-adjusted, happy, well-cared for, that kind of thing. Naturally, I said they were. I laughed and said a big no when he asked if I had ever seen signs of abuse. He didn't ask anything specific about you or Dennis. So I took it upon myself to tell him. I mean, I didn't say anything against Dennis. He would have thought you'd prepped me, and really, you haven't, but you've been the one I've dealt with all these years. I told him that. I just slipped it right into the conversation in the middle of praising you as a mother. I said that there was no way those children wouldn't be well-adjusted and happy and well-cared for with a mother like you."

Kikit's teacher, who had been Johnny's two years before, at which time I had been a room mother, called to say, "He was asking about Kikit, since she's in my class now, but I made it clear right at the start that I knew both children well. He asked how they did in school. I told him the apple didn't fall far from the tree. He asked how they got along with other kids, how they handled new problems, how they reacted to disappointments. Then he asked to see Kikit's report card. I explained that we don't grade the children this young, but that if he'd like a preview of the written report I'll be sending home on Kikit in January, I'd do hers early and send it along." When I started to protest the extra work, she said, "I'm thrilled to do it, Claire. I don't know your husband well at all, so I can't say much about him either way, but you've always been generous with your time with us, and you're clearly devoted to your children."

Our minister called to ask how I was doing and say that he was still hoping Dennis and I would reconcile, which was what he had told the GAL. "I said that the children seemed fine to me, but that I only see them for a few hours each week, so it would be hard for me to see how they were adjusting to the separation unless there were a marked change in their behavior, which there hasn't been. I suspect you're working hard to keep this as painless for them as possible. I told him that. I did invite him to join us this weekend, but he declined."

Encouraged, I called Johnny's basketball coach on the pretense of saying that, separation or no separation, Dennis and I would like to hold the team's holiday banquet at the house again this year. I knew that Dennis wouldn't dare object. Lasagna, Italian bread, a huge tossed salad—as banquets went it was easy enough. I could do it spending little more than the afternoon and evening of the event at the house, even less if Dennis helped. The coach was grateful for the offer.

"I've had lots of people come forward and say they'd chip in to help at someone else's house," he said, "but you're one of the few with the courage to take on twelve nine-year-olds plus their parents for dinner at your own. I told that to the fellow who called. He wanted to know how long I'd known Johnny and whether I'd seen a change in him since you two separated. I told him that Johnny's always been one of my hardest-working players, which is a tribute to you and Dennis. You've always been there on the sidelines, and now Dennis is jumping right in. He's helped me coach these last few weeks. Knows some pretty good drills. Think he's after my job?"

I was more hesitant calling Kikit's allergy doctor. I feared that he would align himself with a fellow health professional and take confidentiality to heart. So I called him on the pretense of asking if there was any chance that Kikit might have a slow-building reaction to Valentino's dander. I had already checked it out with his nurse, and would never have taken Valentino if there had been the slightest chance of a problem. The doctor confirmed that and was pleased when I said that Kikit hadn't so much as sniffled in Valentino's company. Then he told me about his GAL call.

"We talked for a while about whether Kikit's anaphylaxis could be affected by emotional upset. I told him you had called and asked me that yourself right after Kikit's last attack. I told him what I told you, that an extremely upset child could bring on psychosomatic symptoms, or that an extremely disturbed child could deliberately eat something he or she shouldn't for the sake of getting the parents' attention, but I don't put Kikit into either of those categories. I told him that she's a strong little girl who doesn't seem afraid to tell her parents much of anything, even when they're wrong. Actually, your husband called to ask about the cat, too. I could hear Kikit in the background. She wasn't very happy with him. But he handled her fine. And I handled him fine. So the cat's okay, Claire. Anything else?"

Rona, too, talked with Jenovitz, long distance from I-wasn't-sure-where. She said that she had raved about me, that Jenovitz had been receptive, and that—*get this*, she said—he went to high school with *Harold*.

When Jenovitz called to arrange a visit with the children for the following week, he advised us to simply say that his coming to the house was an ordinary part of the divorce process. I wasn't sure the children would buy it. Johnny kept comparing his situation with a friend whose parents had just gone through a smoother, quieter, more conventional divorce, and as for Kikit, she questioned everything.

Jenovitz assured me that he had done this many times before and that the less said, the better. I went along with him, though I was apprehensive. I didn't want the children worrying about what they were or were not supposed to say. I didn't want them feeling the pull of conflicting loyalties. If Jenovitz upset the children, I would be furious. I would be *doubly* furious if he upset them and I wasn't allowed near to patch them up.

I didn't have to worry about Jenovitz upsetting Brody, with whom he arranged a meeting for the day after he met with the kids. Brody was tough. He could give as good as he got. What I did worry about was why, given my relationship with Brody and his importance to the kids, Jenovitz hadn't wanted to see him sooner. A meeting at this late date seemed more an afterthought, which was in keeping with what I had felt during my own last meeting with Jenovitz. I couldn't shake my fear that the study was perfunctory, that he wasn't really into it, that the outcome was preordained.

Common sense dictated that I would get my children back. But I hadn't seen much evidence of common sense lately. My single best hope rested on Justice Wheeler.

I waited for his decision. Tuesday came and went without, then Wednesday. I tried to apply myself to WickerWise, but working was easier said than done. Two hours at a time was as much as I got before restlessness set in. When Brody was around, the restlessness was easy to cure—a walk on the bluff, a drive to the store, kisses here, a little loving there. When he wasn't around, I retreated to my workroom.

The dirty work was done on both the antique rocker and its side table. I had cleaned and smoothed every area where broken wickers had come out. Now I cut new reeds to the approximate lengths that would allow for comfortable overlap, soaked them to make them pliable, and started to weave them in, one by one.

Following the pattern was the most obvious requisite, a more subtle one being the tension used. A reed woven too loose or too tight would stand out forever, which was pretty much how I felt about my life just then. If my split with Dennis didn't soften up and start blending with the rest of my life, it would indelibly mark everything to come.

The GAL could help by reinstating me as a parent of worth.

Justice Wheeler could help by countermanding Selwey's orders.

By late Thursday, I was vacillating between hope and despair. Then Carmen called.

Sixteen

My heart began to hammer at the sound of her voice. "What?" I asked.

She hesitated a second too long.

"Oh, no," I said.

"I'm sorry, Claire. I just got the call. A written opinion will follow, but the gist of it is that since Dennis appears to be a capable father, Wheeler didn't think Selwey's decision was irrational."

I let out a heartsick breath and sank into a chair. I had been counting on this, so sure we were in the right that this turn left me stunned. "What about *me*?" I cried. "Does he think I'm an incapable mother?"

"No. Simply that leaving the children with their father pending the guardian's study was a reasonable move. Not necessarily the one he would make. But reasonable. That's all the appeal was about."

I closed my eyes and pressed a fist to my heart. What was *wrong*? I had admitted to making mistakes. Had they been *that* bad that the punishment should go on and on and on?

"Are you there?" Carmen asked cautiously.

"I'm here." I sighed. "Then everything rests on Jenovitz?"

"For now. He'll be our fastest source of relief."

My heart dropped. "Assuming he rules in my favor."

"Well, we're working on that, too. If we can get figures to show that his findings are inordinately supportive of Selwey's rulings, we'll have a shot at another Motion for Reconsideration. It'd help if we could reach an agreement with Dennis on custody. Unfortunately," another hesitation, one I liked even less, "there's a problem. Heuber called right after the judge's clerk did."

I braced myself. "What?"

"Dennis has a buyer for WickerWise."

"WickerWise isn't for sale."

"Heuber says," Carmen mocked, "that Dennis had been weighing the Pittney option all along and now feels he wants that instead, so from you, by way of a settlement, he wants half the market value of WickerWise. Since you don't have that kind of money lying around, he suggests selling WickerWise and paying him off. Your instincts were right."

That was small solace. "I'm not selling. I'll take this to trial before I do that."

"Well, they're ready."

"To go to trial? Will they? Carmen, I can't *last* that long."

"No, no, sweetie. It won't come to that. We have Dennis on Phoebe and Adrienne and whatever else Morgan is getting. Call this Heuber's last stand. They're posturing. Calling our bluff."

Playing with me was what they were doing, and I was getting tired of it. "Hold out," I ordered. My breath was coming from the place inside that had been messed with once too often. It was the same place that still heard my mother speak of regrets. I refused, absolutely refused to fall into that trap.

Brody had another solution. "Let Dennis find *ten* buyers for WickerWise. You don't have to sell to any one of them. You can sell to me. That'll give you the money to pay Dennis off, and you'll still have WickerWise."

Carefully, I said, "No, *you'll* have WickerWise."

"Same difference."

"No. If you buy WickerWise, it's yours."

"What's mine is yours."

"You're missing the point," I insisted. "WickerWise isn't for sale. I don't want to sell to *anyone*."

We were in the workroom. I had been working frantically since Carmen's call, but my hands weren't steady. The new reeds weren't going in evenly. It was just as well that I stop.

"This is coming out wrong," I tried. "It's sounding like I don't want you owning WickerWise, and that isn't it." I went to him, put my hands on his shoulders, and pleaded, "I'll give Wicker-Wise to you free and clear—but only if it's of my own free will. I won't have Dennis dictating something like this. He has a right to a say in what we do with the kids. I accept that. But Wicker-Wise is mine."

It sounded good. It sounded tough. Still, I knew I could lose it.

There was nothing I could do but wait. That was the worst. I waited for Carmen's associates to find dirt on Jenovitz, waited for Morgan Houser to find dirt on Dennis, waited for Dennis to tire of fathering, waited for Jenovitz to reach his decision.

Seven weeks to the day after my children were removed from my care, Jenovitz spent an hour with them. One hour. Since neither Dennis nor I were allowed to listen, we didn't know what was said. We waited in the kitchen, while they took the den.

Carmen had been right. Jenovitz was good with kids. Kikit liked him better than Johnny, who was naturally wary, but even he emerged from the meeting unscathed.

It was rather comical, those moments after, with Dennis and I hovering close, dying to ask what had been said in that room and not daring to. I don't know how Jenovitz did it, whether he had sworn them to secrecy or what, but not even Kikit revealed much. She was more concerned with showing me the nest she had built for the purple alligator she had bought at the circus.

My heart nearly broke when Johnny asked, with unmasked hope, if I was staying for dinner.

Of course, Jenovitz didn't see that. He was long gone by then.

Brody's meeting with Jenovitz was more upsetting.

It was held at six on the Thursday evening of that second week in December. I had taken refuge after hours in our Essex store and was sitting on the floor, in the light of a single lamp, surrounded by sketches of spring displays when Brody came in. Beyond my pool of light the store was dark, so I didn't immediately see his expression, but his footfall on the carpet was emphatic.

My hands lay still on the pad. I held my breath.

He strode to the edge of the light. He had worn a dark suit for the meeting, but what with the knot of his tie loosened, his shirt collar undone, his hair spiked on his forehead, and my light flashing against his glasses, he looked stormy.

"Something stinks," he said.

I didn't have the breath to ask what.

"You're right, Claire. He has his mind made up. He knew how he felt about me from the get-go. Talk about a stiff handshake. When he wasn't being antagonistic, he was totally disinterested. He had a list of questions in front of him, but once he asked them, the answers might have been irrelevant for all the attention he paid them. What the fuck's going on?"

"I wish I knew. It's like someone has a personal vendetta

against me. Either that, or I'm being made an example of." I put my pencil aside. "What did he say?"

" 'Tell me about yourself,' was what he said, and then he just sat there staring at me. I told him when and where I was born, where I grew up, how many siblings I had, where I went to school. I was just getting to the part about Dennis, when he started fiddling with the pipe." He dragged his lapel to his nose, sniffed, tossed it away. "Let me tell you, if he'd asked *me* whether I minded, I'd have said yes. But he didn't ask me that. He asked about my divorce. Didn't want to know about my friendship with Dennis. Didn't ask any of the pertinent questions, like what did I feel for the kids. Only wanted to know what had happened to my marriage. Assumed it broke up because of me. Assumed my wife got custody of Joy. Assumed I was the bad guy there." He hissed out a breath and turned his head to the side. "Okay, so I was." He faced me again. "But whenever I tried to jump ahead a few years and tell him the kind of father I've become, he asked some other insulting question. Like whether I ever had 'my women' in the house while Joy was visiting. Like whether I didn't feel like a turncoat working first for Dennis and then for you. Like wasn't I worried Dennis would name me in an alienation of affection suit. Like didn't I feel like an impostor when I spent time with Kikit and Johnny." He spat out a bark. "Boy, did I answer him quick when he hit me with *that* one."

His indignance made me smile. He was such a laid-back, easygoing sort on the average, that explosions of passion were all the more meaningful. When those explosions were on my behalf, I loved him even more. Not only was he championing my cause, but he was validating every one of the feelings I'd been getting from Jenovitz myself.

"Then he asked what my intentions were," Brody said.

I waited to hear his response, but he wandered off to the shadowed front of the store. His large frame bent when he set his fists on the sales desk.

"Brody?"

His voice was less distinct coming back to me. "So I told him. Maybe it was defiance, after the impostor crack, but it seemed to make sense. He knows your marriage is ending. He knows how close you and I are. I figured he'd be thrilled to know I wanted to marry you. I figured he'd be thrilled to know we'd be able to offer the kids a stable two-parent home."

I rose and went to him. My hand found its way to the highest, broadest part of his back. It was stretched tight by his pose. "He wasn't?"

"Nope. Said I had gall, wanting your business *and* you. Said I was complicating the custody issue. Said I was confusing the kids. Said I was distracting you at a time when you couldn't afford it." He turned his head, almost looking at me but not quite. "Said I'd be doing you more of a favor by leaving town."

"No."

He didn't move his head. His eyes found mine past the inner rim of his glasses. "Maybe he's right."

"No."

He pushed up from the desk, drew himself to his full height, and looked at me directly, and for the briefest moment I imagined what it would be like if he left. The sense of loss was devastating.

"No," I said a third time. I grabbed his tie, high, and held on.

"I'd do it, Claire. I've loved you for years—"

Pulling on the tie, I raised up and silenced him with my mouth. The kiss was hard and willful. When it was done, I covered his mouth with my hand.

But Brody could be willful, too. Taking my wrist, he lifted the hand and said, "I lived most of those years thinking I'd never have you, and I could have survived that way. I was acclimated to it. It was better than nothing. But I know you, Claire. I know what your kids mean to you. If the choice comes down to me or them, I'll give it all up and vanish."

"Without asking me what I want?" I cried in a burst of anger. "Without giving me a say in the choice? You're starting to sound like *them*!"

He hooked an elbow around my neck and dragged me close.

"In the first place," I reasoned from that sheltered spot, "if it's true that Jenovitz has already made up his mind, it won't make one bit of difference whether you're in the picture or not. In the second place, I'm not living without you." My palms were under his jacket, moving over his shirt from waist to armpits. I knew just what was beneath that shirt, had nuzzled every inch.

It was mine. I wasn't giving it up.

"They'll make you pay."

I drew my head back fast. "Who? Dennis? The judge? The GAL? Who in the hell are *they* to tell me how to live my life? Like they're paragons of virtue," I muttered, feeling a great swell of contempt. "Well, I'm *tired* of being put on the defensive. I'm *tired* of having to second-guess everything I do for the sake of meeting some standard that isn't anywhere near as good as the standard I've always set for myself. I'm done doing it, Brody," I warned. "If Jenovitz doesn't give me my kids, I'll take Dennis to trial, and I'll go from one court to another, if I have to. I'm fighting. I'm fighting for the kids, and I'm fighting for you. I'll even fight *you* for you if I have to."

I stopped talking. There was only one person who could tell me if I would have to do that. I awaited his decision.

It came in slow increments—a movement at the corner of his mouth, a sibilant catch in his breath, a quiver in his biceps, the quickening of his pulse—until finally I saw it there in the dark, felt it in marrow and memory. We had discovered each other,

Brody and I, making love anywhere and everywhere as though we had been abstinent for years. We had, in a sense. At least I had. I had never had sex like that, *conscious* sex, the kind that made you aware of each of its intricate elements. I had never known the pleasure of the process. With Brody, it could be slow and sweet, or hungry and hard. It could be dark or light, verbal or silent. He might not have been able to clap to a song, but the rhythm of his tongue was compelling and the beat of his hips was strong. He knew what to do when for the utmost sensation. In that, his timing was perfect.

In Brody's arms, I rediscovered each of my body parts. Beneath his hands and his mouth, they became things of beauty, and the appreciation wasn't one-sided. I had never before explored a man's body, had never before had the desire. What I had with Brody went beyond desire to insatiable curiosity. I knew how soft the hair under his arms was after a shower, and how vulnerable the skin was at his groin. I knew how tight his nipples could get, and how the ridge on the underside of his penis curved ever so slightly when he was fully aroused. I knew how his hair varied in texture from one part of his body to another. I knew how the pattern of scars on his knee felt against my lips, and the way his crooked pinkie fit the curve of my breast. I knew the taste of his earlobe, his navel, his semen.

"Christ, Claire," he managed to rasp before he brought his open mouth down on mine. His hands were fierce holding my head, flexing here, shifting there to better angle me. He ate at my lips, used his teeth on my tongue, pulled the breath from me again and again.

We had made love in lots of places. After those first times in my chair-and-a-half and shower, there had been our beds, our kitchens, Brody's laundry room, my workroom, even under a thermal blanket on the rocks outside my lighthouse. I'm sure there were lots of reasons for it—defiance, daring, curiosity, novelty—but the bottom line on each occasion was need. We needed each other, right then, right there, needed to make the ultimate connection that said we were something more than we had been before, that we weren't alone, that we loved in the most intimate sense of the word.

So now we made love in the store. It was a challenge, what with Brody wearing a suit and the store so pristine, but accomplished with surprising ease—what wonderful things aren't?—the freeing of one of my legs, Brody's unzipping. There was added excitement to being fully clothed on top, to feeling the abrasion of fabric against breasts and nipples, so discreet there, so bare and naughty below.

We didn't move much at first, and that, too, was exciting. I liked holding still with Brody rock-hard inside me, liked the feel of his slightest shift, liked the hoarse, whispered words that told me how tightly I sheathed him and how splendid it felt.

In time, we did move, of course. After a slow slide down the leg of the desk, we sprawled on the carpet and gave in to the need that had built. Brody had the ultimate control, coming close time and again, time and again holding back. Only when I reached my climax did he let go.

When it was over and we lay in a decadent heap, he said, still short of breath but in a verbal eruption not unlike the physical one he'd just had, "We can't go back, Claire. Can't be just friends again. I can't be with you without wanting this. So if I stay in the picture, we're hooked up. It's out of my hands. Christ, it all is. Here, this. In that bastard's office. I want to do something, baby. Want to make things right for you, only I don't know what in the hell will help."

"This," I whispered. "You. Incredible help."

"But the kids—"

I pressed his mouth. "Help keep this part of my life on track, and I'll take care of the kids. I'll get them. So help me God, I will."

*   *   *

Often in the darkest hours of the night I awoke feeling empty inside. When Brody was there, the emptiness was little more than a shadow in a corner of the room. When he wasn't, the shadow closed in. Part of it had to do with Connie, with the number of times in the course of a day that I reached for the phone, wanting to tell her something I had seen or thought or felt. The rest had to do with the kids, with the fact that they were surviving without me and the fear that I would never get them back.

During one of those night awakenings, I imagined squirreling them away on one of the days when they were in my care. I imagined hiding out with them in Argentina, changing their names, and raising them without the interference of Dennis or the court.

Would I do it? Seriously?

So help me, I wasn't sure. I was a law-abiding citizen. But the law hadn't treated me well. In that sense, what had started for me as a simple case of regaining custody of my children had become something more. I needed to right the wrong of the court. It was a matter of principle.

"What are our options?" I asked Carmen. I had driven into Boston, as much to feel I was doing something as to brainstorm.

"Legally? We can file another Motion for Reconsideration, but without new evidence, it'll be turned right down. Same with another Motion to Recuse. There's the federal angle, a gender discrimination suit, but that'll take time. You want custody back before that."

"What about suing Dennis? You mentioned that once."

"It's definitely an option. We could sue for malicious prosecution, and for intentional infliction of emotional stress."

"That sounds about right," I said, nodding. "I've been on the up-and-up through all this, trying to be honest and agreeable. I've tried to be positive. Tried to talk about my strengths. Tried to tell Jenovitz what I've done for my children in the past and what I can do for them in the future, and all the while Dennis is out there on the hustings slinging mud. So Jenovitz listens to the mudslinger. The good guys lose. I think I've had it with that. Let's threaten a suit."

"It'll take time."

"What if the threat does the job? What if that's my lever in negotiating a settlement?"

"Dennis may rethink his position. Then again, he may decide to hold out. Make you squirm. Count on Selwey saving his neck."

"If we went to trial, when would it be?"

"Late spring."

"If we lost that round and appealed, when would that happen?"

"Anywhere from six to eighteen months after the first."

I couldn't begin to imagine waiting that long to regain custody of Johnny and Kikit, and cursed—for the hundredth time—the system that had worked so well against me. I rose from my chair and went to the window. Behind me, Carmen's phone buzzed. I heard her pick it up and deliberately tuned out to give her privacy, concentrating instead on the narrow alleyway lined with shops. People came and went, pulling scarves tighter and overcoats closer. For an instant, I imagined I saw Dennis. Then whoever it was was gone.

Dennis. I had to hand it to him. I had expected he would have thrown in the towel on full-time parenthood by now, but he was hanging in there. For the children's sake, I wanted to think it was love. Selfishly, I wanted to think it was stubbornness. Stubbornness would wear itself out. Love wasn't about to.

An arm circled my shoulder. Something in its tension spoke of a change. I looked at Carmen. Her face held bridled excitement, her voice the same.

"Morgan's on his way over."

"He found something?"

She grinned and nodded.

"What?" I asked. I told myself not to hope. Too many of my recent hopes had been quashed. Still, that look on her face wasn't going away. "Carmen?"

"He's on his way over. Come on. Let's get coffee while we wait."

The wait was worth it this time.

"There was meat behind Adrienne's threat," Morgan said. "The deal between them wasn't just for sex. It was sex in exchange for inside stock tips. Dennis wanted the stock tips, Adrienne wanted the sex. She knew her husband would be furious—that part of the story was right—but she liked that, daring the devil. And she had the tips. She got them eavesdropping on conversations her husband had. Easy enough to pass them to Dennis."

I was torn between wanting to believe and wanting to argue. "Who told you this?"

"Three people, so it's corroborated. That's what took the time. One was an old friend of Adrienne's, another a colleague of Dennis's, the third a cellmate of Adrienne's husband."

I swallowed. "Cellmate?"

"Soon after Dennis's rise, Lee Hadley was indicted for trading irregularities. Dennis was one of many in the firm who were interviewed by the government. He was one of several who were spared indictment in exchange for testifying against Lee. Lee did time in Allenwood, cushy enough, but his income flow stopped. Adrienne kept herself in the style to which she was accustomed in part by blackmailing Dennis with the threat of exposure."

Carmen asked, "Then he didn't tell the Feds everything?"

"No. He hid the extent of his own use of those tips. So he paid Adrienne."

I let out a long, shaky breath. Oh, yes, we had needed something like this, but the victory was bittersweet. What an awful disappointment. I remembered how I had felt learning about Adrienne alone. The disillusionment now was nearly as strong. "Then he wasn't a wunderkind at all."

"No."

Carmen touched my hand. "Are you all right?"

I pulled myself up and took a breath. "I'm fine."

"We could go to Selwey with this, but since it's untriable, he'll pass the buck. You'll have to raise it as a character issue with Jenovitz."

I nodded.

"Claire?"

"I will."

"You're having second thoughts. You're thinking of Dennis as your husband and feeling sad, even disloyal. Don't, Claire. This may be the strongest weapon you have in your fight for the kids."

With a conscious effort, I shrugged off those feelings of sadness, even disloyalty. It wouldn't do to think of what I had lost with Morgan's discovery, since so much of that had been illusory. I preferred to think of what I had gained. The more I thought about it, the better I felt.

Jenovitz didn't want to meet with me. I left message after message on his answering machine, but he didn't return my calls. Finally, after three days of calling, my perseverance paid off. He inadvertently picked up the phone when I was at the other end, and even then it took a whale of convincing.

"I don't know, Mrs. Raphael. My schedule is jammed."

"One more hour. That's all I want."

"To what end? I've already asked what I needed to ask. Time you take now is time taken from my writing up the final report. I thought you wanted this done quickly."

Oh, I had. I had also wanted it done in my favor. "I've just learned some things that I think you should know."

"The holiday is coming up. This is a bad time."

"One hour. You can bill me for three."

"Money is not the issue," he stated primly.

"I know. I'm sorry. But I'm a little desperate here. This is my life."

Whether he feared I would harm myself and thereby condemn him to a life of guilt, I didn't know, but he gave in with a marked lack of grace.

That lack of grace carried over to our meeting. He looked awkward and impatient. He was back to popping sourballs, and didn't sit for longer than ten minutes at a stretch before jumping up and leaving the office. I didn't know whether he was dashing out for illicit smokes, or whether he had the runs. Not that I cared, as long as he heard me out.

In an effort to be as gracious as I could, I thanked him profusely for giving me his time. Then I told him what Morgan had learned. I took time with the telling, tried to be as detailed as I could. I had read Morgan's report so thoroughly and often that I knew dates, places, and times by heart. When I was done, I set a copy of the report on his desk.

He looked at it, held up a hand to signal a break, and left the room. He was gone for several minutes. When he returned, he slid into his chair, sat back, and stared at me.

"So, what do you think?" I finally asked.

"I'm wondering why you hired an investigator. Why you didn't just ask your husband about this?"

"He's my estranged husband, and I did ask him. Fourteen years ago. He lied."

"Did you always suspect that?"

"I did at first. That was when I had the abortion. Then I put my suspicions aside for the sake of the marriage."

Jenovitz tapped a finger on the desk, nodded, stared.

"I'm surprised you aren't shocked," I said.

"Shocked? About what?"

"What Dennis did back then. He didn't tell you about it himself, did he?"

"No. We've been talking about his fathering abilities."

"And about my shortcomings. Like the abortion I had. You said it had direct relevance to the kind of person I was. Well, doesn't this?"

"Doesn't what?"

"Morgan Houser's report," I said with dwindling patience. "My husband is guilty of things that could have put him behind bars, if they'd come out at the time. But he hid it. He lied. *Under oath.* Doesn't that *bother* you? Won't you think twice about giving custody of two young children to a man capable of breaking laws that way?"

"Is he breaking laws now?"

"No. But this shows he has in the past. What's to say he won't again?"

"He's older now. More mature. He has more to lose. Back then he didn't have children. Now he does. Having custody of them gives him good reason to walk the straight and narrow."

His defense of Dennis left me dumbfounded. "But . . . but what about me?" I asked.

Jenovitz took a deep breath. His chair rocked every so slightly. No doubt about it, he did look bored.

Steadying my voice, I took a different tack. "Historically, the mother was considered the more appropriate parent to have custody. Why is my case any different?"

"You work, but your husband is free. He has the time, desire, and ability to parent the children."

"Did he tell you about his new business prospect? He's hoping to buy a vice-presidency in an up-and-coming company. It's in Springfield, halfway across the state. Between work time and travel time, how free will he be? I live ten minutes from my office, ten minutes from the kids—home, school, you name it. I have a second-in-command who runs the company for me when I'm not around. I'm the boss, so I don't have to ask permission to take time off. I have more flexibility than most working women, certainly than most working men."

Jenovitz swiveled in his seat, extracted a file from the pile on the credenza behind him, and tossed it open on the desk. He gestured toward it with a dismissive hand. "It's right there in black and white, the number of hours you work, the number of days you travel. It's also right there, the toll that takes—the missed rides and canceled appointments."

I didn't protest the charges. I had done it once too often. Instead, bluntly, I asked, "Do you think I'm a bad mother?"

"Do you think your husband is a bad father?"

"Bad?"

I barely had the word out, when Jenovitz signaled another break. He pushed himself up and left the room. By the time he returned, I had given his question some thought.

"Dennis isn't a bad father. I'm sure he loves the children. Do I think he's a better parent than I am? No. Do I think he understands what full-time parenting entails? I think he's beginning to, but two months is nothing."

"You think his patience will exhaust itself."

"I think his desire will, once the settlement is decided."

"He claims it won't."

"What else would he claim?" I asked. "If he admitted the truth at this stage, he would lose his edge in the negotiations."

"You make this sound like a game."

"Me?" My laugh was brittle. "I've taken this seriously from the start. It's everyone *else* who treats it like a game—this one feints, that one parries. Believe me, Dr. Jenovitz, the thought that the future of my children depends on bartering makes me sick, but that's the lesson I'm being taught. If regaining custody of them means playing a game, I'll play. My children mean more to me than anything in the world. That's one of the biggest differences between my husband and me."

"What means more to him than his children?"

"His image."

Jenovitz looked at the open file and shrugged. "It wasn't my impression that he cares much if he's viewed as a househusband."

Dennis had about as much intention of being a househusband as Valentino did. Jenovitz either hadn't heard a word I'd said, or was dense, or hopelessly biased. "Are you aware of what he's asking by way of a divorce settlement?"

"Children are my concern, not things."

"But one goes with the other in this case," I argued. "He's asking that I sell my business. He claims he wants the money, but that's only part of it. He wants me to lose WickerWise. Its success is a thorn in his side. It emasculates him."

"Emasculates?" Jenovitz asked dryly. "I doubt that." He frowned. "Right *there* is one of the reasons the children might be better off with their father. You're an angry woman. That kind of anger isn't good for children to see."

He was definitely stonewalling. It was the only explanation for the absurdity of his argument. I tried to let it go but couldn't. "My husband feels anger and more. He feels jealousy, he feels embarrassment, he feels the need for revenge. How healthy is *that* for the kids—not to mention a history of infidelity and dishonesty, not to *mention* a new top management position with new responsibilities and new pressures? If you think I'm gone a lot, how much will *he* be around?"

"He has his parents to fill in," Jenovitz said quietly.

I chose to think that the quietness was in deference to my mother's loss, but before I could see if it would linger, he was out of his chair and slipping out the door.

I fingered my watch. Time was running out. It was only then starting to hit me that I had played my ace and failed. Jenovitz didn't care about Dennis's past misdeeds. I half-suspected that if I could show him to be a *pedophile*, Jenovitz would simply pop in another sourball and sigh.

Brody was right. Something was very weird.

A sweet deal. That had to be it. A sweet deal between Selwey and Jenovitz.

After several minutes, I heard footsteps on the stairs. Soon after, the door opened. Jenovitz returned to his chair, looking freshened. This was my last, best chance.

"Can I talk about anger for a minute?" I asked.

He gave an indifferent wave. "Talk about anything you want."

I spoke from the heart. My appeal was personal, one human being to another. "When this all started, I was angry at Dennis. But the anger has shifted. Dennis wouldn't have been able to do what he did if the system hadn't allowed it. If the system was fair, I would have regained at least partial custody of my children after that first weekend, while Dennis and I reached a settlement. Please believe me, Dr. Jenovitz. I've never been a rebel. I've conformed. I've worked within the system. All my *life* I've done that. But I've never been—screwed, I'm sorry, that's the only word to describe it—by the system before. So, yes, I'm angry. I'm angry at a system—a system of *justice*, no less—that has made me be and do things that I don't want to be and do. It's made me fight people and suspect people and distrust people."

I wanted to think he was listening, wanted to think he was hearing. He was looking at me, and he didn't seem bored. Softly, I pleaded, "Injustice makes me angry. Unfairness infuriates me. You people are the ones who've created those conditions. Correct them, and there's no anger."

Jenovitz frowned. He gave a spasmodic shake of his head. "Give you what you want, let you have your way, and there's no anger. Is that what you mean?"

I sat forward. "It isn't." I held up a hand. "Okay. Here's the thing. I need your help. You're a psychologist. You deal in rationality. So please help me understand what's going on here. Nothing about this case rings true. There's no logic. There's no open-mindedness. I'm being viewed as a stereotype, but I'm not one. I've tried to convey that, but I'm not getting through."

"This case is about choices," he said. "We all have to make them in life. We get up in the morning and have to decide which shoes we're going to wear. We can't possibly wear three pairs at once. Same with jobs. We can't *be* everything at once, but that's what you want. Not only that, but you want us to tell you you're doing a great job. Choices, Claire, choices. Surely, that makes sense."

"Actually, no," I reasoned. "My children aren't babies. They spend most of the day in school. Afterward they need to be with their peers. I'd be stunting their emotional growth if I tried to prevent it. So I have time to do other things without taking time from them. Same thing with being with Brody. He complements my relationship with the kids. Same thing with WickerWise. Everyone benefits. No one's hurt. Some women choose to be full-time mothers. Some men choose to be absentee fathers. I choose to lead a multifaceted life. Isn't that a valid choice?"

"Not if you spread yourself too thin."

"But I don't."

He stood and looked down at me. "If you're thinking to change my mind with arrogance, you're mistaken. You have to make choices." He reached for the door.

"Where's the choice here?" I rushed out. "Nothing I've done or said in this room has mattered. You knew what you thought about me the first day you met me, and it hasn't changed. I haven't had any choice. It's been out of my hands from the start."

He closed the door behind him without argument.

I rose from my chair, paced to the side of the office, then back. I looked at my watch. I looked at Morgan's report, unheeded on top of my file. Oh, I had a choice, all right. I could go to the press and start yelling and screaming about the injustice of what I'd been through. Forget Hillary Howard. A local weekly was small potatoes. The *Globe* would love the story. The *New York Times* would love the story. So would Dan Rather and Barbara Walters. I could do the talk show circuit. I could become a spokeswoman for every woman who had ever been wronged. I could write a book.

But hell, I didn't want to do any of that. All I wanted was my kids.

Something was *very* weird here.

I gave Morgan's report a little push. Beneath it were the children's school records. Curious, I gave the records a little push.

I whipped my hand back and folded my arms at my waist. I wasn't a snoop.

Then it hit me that that file was mine. The court may have put Jenovitz to the task, but I was the one paying him to do it. Hadn't I just sent him a check?

Still, I listened. There was no sound on the outer stairs. If Jenovitz's two previous returns were any indication, I could expect to hear his footsteps for five, maybe six seconds before the door opened.

Alert for that sound, I flipped through the file. I didn't know what I was looking for, didn't know why I was looking at all. Curiosity, perhaps. Or defiance. Whatever, I saw Carmen's letterhead, and Art Heuber's letterhead. I saw court records, and Jenovitz's own typed notes. I saw a memo from the clinic where my abortion had been performed, pulled it out, skimmed it, fitted it neatly back in front of a piece of stationery with the official seal of the Essex County Probate Court at the top.

Something else was at the top, a handwritten note above the letterhead. To this day I don't know what made me look closer. But I did. I pulled it out and had read enough, when I heard Jenovitz's footfall on the stairs.

I hesitated for only as long as it took me to realize that I was stealing what was rightfully mine. Then I folded the paper, put it in my pocket, and slipped into my seat.

The door opened. I looked at Jenovitz in the same way I had every other time he had returned. I didn't look guilty, didn't feel guilty. If my heart was thudding, it could as easily have been from agitation as from elation or sheer and pervasive relief. Relief was what I felt, all right. I felt as though a band had been removed from my chest, a weight from my shoulders, cuffs from my wrists.

"We don't have much time left," Jenovitz advised me. "Is there anything more you want to say?"

I cleared my throat to keep my voice from shaking. "A question, actually. Out of curiosity. Was there anything I might have done differently in the course of this study to have earned your respect?"

He neatened the papers and closed the file. "You might have indicated that you wanted to change. But I never got that from you. You seem to feel that you're doing just fine, and that if there are problems in your life, they're caused by others. Sometimes, Claire, we have to take responsibility for our actions."

I couldn't have agreed with him more.

With my elation threatening to show, I mustered my composure, thanked him for his time, and left.

Ten minutes later, I unfolded the letter I had filched and spread it flat on Carmen's desk. It was a form letter assigning the Raphael matter to Dean Jenovitz. It gave dates and noted enclosures. There was nothing remotely personal in its body.

The personal note was at the top. It was a scrawl in the same blue ink as the judge's signature at the bottom. Knowing the letters in that name helped us decipher some of the less legible letters in the note.

"Dennis Raphael seems sincere," it said. "Let Father win this time."

Seventeen

Snow was falling when I returned to Reaper's Head, large flakes drifting steadily down to settle in clumps on the needled boughs of the pines. Though this wasn't the first snow of the season, it had that freshness. Dirt disappeared. Dusk sparkled. The artist in me saw things differently when they were reduced to white and green—or white and gray on pavement, or white and red on the rows of mailboxes I passed.

Then again, it could have been the woman in me seeing things differently now that I had found a method to the madness of the court.

I parked beside the keeper's cottage, scuffed my way to the door just for the joy of seeing the snow bunch ahead of my feet, let myself in, and set several bags on the kitchen counter. I was making dinner for Brody. We were celebrating, and though I would have liked to have had the children with us, it was enough to believe that they would be soon enough.

Brody called at six to say that he was going running, snow and all. He called at six-fifty to say that he was back, then again at seven-ten to say that he had just showered and would be heading over soon. He called again two minutes later to say we might well be snowed in, and could he pick anything up on the way.

I had shrimp and scallop risotto, a spinach salad, and a crusty Italian bread all set to eat, and didn't need anything else but him.

When he arrived at seven-thirty, I didn't need the food, either. Snow-flecked coat and all, he was food enough, hot, moist, filling. We partook of each other right there by the front door, and were licking each others' lips, contemplating seconds, when the phone rang.

"Let it ring," he whispered.

But the mother in me couldn't. With a promise to return—and laughter when we tripped over each other's unraveling arms, legs, and clothing—I made it, breathless, to the phone seconds before the answering machine would have clicked on. "Hello?"

"Meet us at the hospital," Dennis said in a voice I barely recognized. "Kikit's sick."

My breath caught. All laughter died. "Allergy sick?"

"Yeah. We're in the car. The driving's lousy, but it was faster than waiting for an ambulance."

I heard him swear, heard, muted, the prolonged blare of his horn and the awful, awful sound of Kikit wheezing. Clamping the phone to my shoulder, I threw Brody a frightened look and started pulling on my jeans. "Did you give her epinephrine?"

"That and antihistamine, but late. She didn't call me right away."

"Put the phone to her ear." The wheezing came louder. "Kikit? Sweetie, it's Mommy. You're going to be fine. Just relax and try to breathe slowly. Don't be scared. I'll be at the hospital soon after you get there, okay?" I was pushing at the buttons of my blouse. "Breathe slowly, slowly." I demonstrated with the cadence of my words. Calm was the last thing I felt but the best I could do for

Kikit just then. "Slowly and evenly. Don't try to take in too much air at once."

Her half-sobbed, half-wheezed, "Mah-mee," nearly broke my heart.

"Don't try to talk," I shoved my blouse into my jeans, "just breathe slowly and relax, okay, sweetie? You don't have to breathe deeply," I knew she couldn't, "you'll do just fine with shallow breaths, but don't be frightened. You've been through this before. You know how it goes. I'm going to hang up now and go out to the car. I'll meet you at the hospital. The doctors will make it better, they'll help you breathe, just like they always do. You'll be fine, baby, okay?" I had the jeans zipped and was hunting for my shoes. Brody produced them along with his own. "Be brave, just a little longer. You're such a good girl. Can you let me talk to Daddy?"

I pictured her nudging away the phone, which was all she would have the strength to do, what with itching and swelling and struggling to breathe. Dennis's "Yeah?" sounded scared.

"Keep her calm. I'm leaving now. I'll see you there."

Brody had my coat waiting when I hung up the phone. Within minutes we were on the road.

Between my fear for Kikit and the weather, the drive was a nightmare. The snow was mounting fast. Visibility was poor. Traction was iffy, with nary a snowplow in sight. That fear and the impotence I felt found expression in anger—at Dennis for letting her eat something she shouldn't have eaten, at the town crews that I imagined were sitting in the local diner chowing down lemon meringue pie until they deemed it time to plow, at whatever fate had set the snow to falling in the first place.

I'm not sure I would have made it had I been driving my own car. Even the Range Rover fishtailed around a corner or two, but Brody was an ace. We pulled up to the emergency room entrance and parked directly behind Dennis's car. His wipers had stopped mid-swipe on the windshield and were already spattered with snow.

Johnny was sitting straight in a chair in the waiting room. The instant he saw us he bolted up and ran across the room. He took my hand and started pulling me forward. "We were gonna eat supper out, but the lines were awful for Chinese and pizza, so we got take-out from Mad Mel's and brought it home, and Dad took all the nuts off the salad, so we don't know what it was. She just got up when we were done and went to her room."

We had reached a small cubicle. Brody put an arm around Johnny to hold him back while I slipped inside.

Kikit lay on the examining table. Had her face not been swollen, it would have been swallowed up by the oxygen mask that covered it. I couldn't tell if the wheezing had begun to ease; the mask muted the sound. I could see large hives on her bare chest and imagined, from the way she was squirming, that they were everywhere. One small hand had already been hooked up to needles. A blood pressure cuff was in place. Hovering close were two doctors and their stethoscopes, one nurse, two IV bags, and Dennis, who was holding her free hand, leaning in, talking softly. His tone was soothing, in stark contrast to the look of panic he sent me.

"Here's Mommy," he said. He moved aside to make room for me, but he didn't release Kikit's hand.

"Hi, sweetie." I stroked her hair. It was damp. Fresh tear tracks disappeared into her hairline, no doubt a product of the IV insertion. Her skin was flushed. "See, I told you I'd come. How do you feel, baby? Any better yet?"

Her eyes were small and frightened in her bloated face, opening to see me, then closing again. My own flew to the doctors.

"It may take a little while," the older of the two said. "She was well into the reaction by the time your husband gave her the first shot."

Dennis looked devastated. His voice was low and hoarse. "It would have been even longer if Johnny hadn't heard her wheezing. There were pine nuts on the salad. I combed through the damn thing and thought I got them all. She'd already eaten her hamburger by that time and didn't eat more than half of the salad when she said she was done. She must have started to feel lousy but not wanted to say anything."

Of course she hadn't wanted to say anything, I thought hysterically. Her last attack had immediately preceded our separation. No doubt, she connected the two.

"She must have thought I'd be angry," Dennis went on, "and no wonder, I've done it before." He leaned in again. "But I'm not, Kikit. I'm not. If anyone was at fault, it was me. I didn't do a good job getting rid of those nuts."

Her eyes remained shut. When a tiny tear escaped from the corner of one, Dennis made an anguished sound. "This isn't your fault, baby, none of it. Not even now. I should have checked up on you sooner, but I was trying to do all those things in the kitchen that Mommy always does. I love you, Kikit." Worriedly, he asked me, "Where's Johnny?"

"Outside with Brody."

"He blamed himself for not hearing her sooner."

I brushed the tear from Kikit's eye and kept my hand touching her, so she would feel me. "It wasn't his fault."

"It was my fault."

Damn right, it was your fault, a tiny voice inside me said. *She was in your custody. It was your job to see she stayed safe. Now it's twice that she's gotten sick when I haven't been around!*

But that angry voice died a quick death. "It wasn't your fault either. Allergic reactions happen. You tried to avoid it. At least this time we know its cause."

The doctor pumped up the blood pressure cuff and released it, listening to Kikit's pulse. Shifting the stethoscope to her chest, he listened there, then took the hypodermic needle the nurse offered. At the same time Dennis's hand tightened around Kikit's, I flattened my own on her forehead, bent low, and talked her through the shot. The fact that she made barely a sound said something about how sick she was.

"It was a candy bar last time," Dennis said close by my ear.

I looked at him fast and whispered, "What?"

"A candy bar," he repeated quietly enough that Kikit wouldn't hear. "I found the empty wrapper in her room a few days later. It was a kind of candy I'd never heard of. The list of ingredients included nuts, but I didn't think she would have deliberately eaten them. So I went out and bought a bar. It was smooth chewing. She wouldn't have detected anything if she hadn't read that list."

In a flash, I relived the agony of wondering what she had eaten and how we could protect her when we didn't know, not to mention the guilt of fearing that there *had* been something in the casserole I had made—all the while Dennis had known the truth.

I stared at him in disbelief.

To his credit, he didn't look away.

"Did she know it was the candy?" I asked.

Dennis's nod was superfluous. Of course she had known. That would explain why she hadn't been freaked out more than usual by the attack that she'd had. It would also explain the way she had cried and blamed herself that day when she learned we were separating.

She hadn't mentioned the candy to me. I wondered if Dennis had told her not to. But I wondered about something else more.

"What about the medicine?" I whispered.

He shook his head. "I couldn't find it. I swear."

A sound from Kikit, a small cry behind the mask, brought my attention back to her, but her eyes remained closed. "I'm here, baby. It's okay. Mommy and Daddy are here. The doctors will make it better. Just be cool, be cool, like a brave, brave little girl."

We continued to talk to her, taking turns, using the same encouraging tone. One IV bag came down and another went up. The doctors gave her another dose of antihistamine and, after a period of time had elapsed, another of epinephrine.

Usually the worst was over in an hour or two, and by the third, we were on our way home. This time was different. The wheezing went on.

Dennis left to check on Johnny. I glanced at the door when it opened a minute later to readmit one of the nurses. On the other side, Dennis had his arms around Johnny. Seconds after that, he returned. I actually felt better with him back, less alone.

The doctors conferred with each other at the far end of the cubicle. Their voices were muted, their faces grave. I knew what worried them. If Kikit didn't start responding to the medication soon, she would be in trouble. Much more swelling in her air passages and she would suffocate.

Dennis and I exchanged frightened looks.

The doctors returned. One held the oxygen mask more firmly in place. The other monitored Kikit's lungs with his stethoscope. The one holding the oxygen mask adjusted the speed of the drip. The one monitoring her lungs checked her blood pressure. With pale faces and anxious eyes, they listened and watched and waited, while we looked on in horror.

Do something, I wanted to cry, only I knew there wasn't anything more they could do. A tube in her trachea couldn't convey air if her lung capacity was too diminished to hold it. Nor could they risk an overdose of the medication and the potentially fatal complications that would cause.

Her eyes were closed. Her face had a bluish tinge. The doctors had begun to talk to her, too, but while we pleaded, they commanded.

I think I died ten deaths, standing there looking helplessly on while her breathing grew more and more shallow, more and more clipped. Tears streamed down my face. I felt Dennis's arm around me, heard his frantic, "Come on, Kikit, come on," then the doctors' more demanding urgings. I prayed silently, desperately, and put a hand to my mouth to stifle an anguished cry when the cutting sound of her breathing suddenly eased.

It was a minute before I heard the doctor's relieved, "There you go, sweetheart. That's better," and realized that she wasn't dead at all but over the hump. The downward spiral had stopped. I held my breath over the next few minutes until her color began to improve. Then I smiled through my tears and cried out sigh after thankful sigh.

It was only then that I saw Dennis. He was against the back wall of the cubicle, bent from the waist with his hands on his knees, making the same kind of relieved sounds I had, only deeper. I touched his shoulder. He hung his head lower, seemed to gather himself, then wiped his face with his palms. His eyes were red when he stood, but he was marginally composed. Still, I didn't object when he put his arms around me. We held each other for a minute of silent, shared relief before returning to Kikit.

The improvement was slow but sure. When I felt certain that Kikit was out of the woods, I went looking for Johnny. He was still with Brody, just outside Kikit's cubicle. Brody was sitting against the wall, Johnny sandwiched between his legs. Neither of them knew how bad things had been, yet when I appeared, two backs went ruler straight, two faces asked the same frightened question.

I knelt down, put a hand to Brody's knee for balance, and managed a tired smile. "She's holding her own."

"What does that mean?" Brody asked.

"It means she's starting to respond. We'll stay here for a while, though. They'll probably want to admit her."

Johnny's eyes were large and dark. "Why?"

"Because there's still some wheezing."

"She's had that before and they let her go home."

"This time, her blood pressure's low. They're giving her medication to raise it, but it's best given intravenously."

"Is she gonna be all right?"

"She's gonna be fine," I said, feeling weak with the knowledge. "She's gonna be fine," I repeated in a whisper, though I knew that I wouldn't breathe entirely freely myself until Kikit was up and running around.

I was thinking that I ought to return to her, when Johnny said in a rush, "Dad looked for all the nuts, he looked real hard. You should've seen him, he was shoving lettuce and tomatoes all over the place looking for them. He had a whole pile on the napkin."

I slid back to sit against the wall close beside Brody, and let the warmth of him renew me before I reached for Johnny. It was a minute until I had him transferred to the circle of my arms. Holding him tightly, I said against his hair, "I don't blame Daddy. Things happen sometimes, even in spite of the care we take so that they won't."

"You should've seen him on Halloween goin' through all the stuff. He was reading labels on everything. He even makes us eat oatmeal bread from the health food market."

I detected a note of distaste inadvertently tossed in with the praise.

I gave him a squeeze. "He's been a super dad about all those things, and he's being a super dad now. He hasn't left Kikit's side for anything other than to make sure you're okay. He's going to stay here with me to make sure she gets better. You, though, need sleep."

"I don't. I'm not tired."

"You have school tomorrow."

"I'm not going if Kikit's still here."

"Sure you are. Who else can tell her teacher, so that the kids will make cards? Who else can bring the cards home?"

"Why'll they have to make cards?" he asked quickly. "They

never did before. She comes home too fast and goes back to school too fast. Why'll they have to do anything this time? Is she sicker?"

I glanced at Brody. He slipped an arm around me and drew me closer.

"She was sicker," I told Johnny, "but she isn't now. She's getting better by the minute. But she may be out of school for a day or two."

"Us, too," he argued. "We won't have school if it keeps snowing. I want to be here with you guys."

"Know what would help most? Our knowing you're safe and sound at home. We'll be worrying about you if you're just sitting out here. Let Brody take you home now, before the snow gets much worse."

There was a pause. "To the house?"

That was what I had pictured. If a sense of normalcy was what I wanted for him, it seemed the best place.

Jenovitz said I was too controlling. Maybe he was right. Maybe normalcy wasn't what Johnny needed most just then. "Where would you like?"

Johnny thought for a minute and shrugged. "I dunno." He looked at Brody. "Where are you going?"

"I kind of thought I'd go to the lighthouse," Brody said. "There's good food there. And Valentino. Poor guy is alone. I don't know about you, but I don't feel like being alone. Not tonight. Not in the snow. Not after this scare."

There was another pause, then, to me, a nervous, "Will Dad be mad?"

I smiled. "Dad will be fine."

We spent another hour in the emergency room before Kikit was admitted. While immeasurably improved from that darkest point,

her breathing was still labored, and enough of the swelling remained for the doctors to want to keep her medicated and watched
through the night.

They settled her in the pediatric ward, in a double room
whose second bed was empty. The doctors and nurses left promising to be back. As soon as the door closed on them, I climbed
onto the bed and carefully resettled Kikit in my arms. After a few
minutes of close crooning, she fell into a fitful sleep, in effect
leaving Dennis and I alone for the first time since the night's ordeal had begun.

After several exchanged glances, he said, "So where's the
gloating?"

I drew a blank.

"She got sick under my care," he prompted. "After all I said
about you, you have a right to say a few things back. You were
angry enough at me without this. Where's the anger now?"

I had felt it earlier. If I delved into my psyche, I could probably
conjure it back up, but the effort didn't seem worth it. I had been
through the wringer and was feeling drained. It seemed best to
concentrate what energy I had left on helping Kikit.

By way of answer, I laid my head down on hers and closed my
eyes.

We took turns holding her, standing, sitting, walking around.
Doctors and nurses came and went, seeming content with the
improvement they saw. I couldn't see the improvement as easily,
being with Kikit constantly, not to mention being so emotionally
involved. But I watched them closely when they examined her
and took comfort in the gestures of satisfaction they made.

Somewhere around midnight, I began to feel lightheaded and
realized that I hadn't had dinner. When I mentioned it to Dennis, he offered to go out and get me something, but the worry in
his expression when he looked from Kikit to me and back said he

was reluctant to leave. I was impressed enough by his attentiveness not to make him.

I found cookies and juice in a machine at the end of the hall, and called Brody along the way to learn that he and Johnny had made it through six inches of snow and were safely ensconced at the lighthouse eating reheated risotto. I returned to Kikit revived.

That revival was a mixed blessing. While it gave me new strength to watch her, it also cleared my head. Strange, though, I didn't think of the twist my life had taken that day or what Dennis would say when he learned of it. Nor did I think of those awful, awful moments in the emergency room when we thought we might lose Kikit. Rather, I thought of another bedside vigil held less than a month before. Memory rushed back, hours of standing at my mother's bedside, listening to her breathe, watching the worry lines fade and her skin take on that terrible, peaceful sheen.

"Are you all right?" Dennis asked.

My eyes flew to his. "Yes."

"You're shaking."

I wrapped my arms around myself. "I've seen enough of hospitals lately to last a lifetime."

He was quiet for a time. Then he said, "I'm sorry about Connie. Was it difficult, waiting there?"

"Yes. No. Odd. Rona and I had a good talk. She's on the road for WickerWise as we speak."

"*Rona?*"

I smiled at his disbelief. I had started out that way, too. "Aside from one near-disaster when she threatened to fire an employee at one of our boutiques, she's doing a pretty good job. I should have thought of it sooner." I shifted my attention when Kikit opened her eyes. "Hi, baby."

"I'm itchy, Mommy." Her voice was a hollow rasp behind the oxygen mask.

Grateful for something to do, I got moisturizer from the nurse and began to rub it on. It would have been a perfect time for Dennis to take a break, but he stood right there, holding the bottle while I smoothed the cream on, handing me a towel when I was done. Kikit had fallen back to sleep by then. Midnight had come and gone.

"Why don't you go home," I suggested. "We don't both have to be here."

He shook his head. "You can. I don't want to take a chance of getting stuck in the snow. I'll stay here."

I wasn't leaving, of course, and it had nothing to do with the lack of a car. My child was sick. I wouldn't be anywhere else.

Neither, it seemed, would Dennis. As the hours passed, as I came to grips with remembering Connie's last days and separated those from the relative optimism here, I began to think more about Dennis. Whether he was sitting in a chair or on the edge of the second bed, or leaning over the rail, his eyes rarely left Kikit's face. Was it guilt? Love? What?

He looked different. Tired, yes. But older, too.

I remembered Rona saying that with Connie gone, she had finally become an adult. Dennis's situation was different. Kikit wasn't dying, for one thing. For another, he wasn't her child, but her parent.

For the first time, though, he looked it. For the first time, he looked like he was shouldering his share of the responsibility.

"Where are Elizabeth and Howard?" I asked.

He seemed startled by the question. "In New Hampshire."

"Do they know about this?"

"No. Should they?"

I shrugged. I knew that the children saw them once a week or so, which was no different from the way it had been before the separation. I also knew, from what the kids had said, that Dennis did most of the daily driving himself. I had often wondered, though, whether Elizabeth stole in during the week to do the laundry or fill the refrigerator with food.

"Have they helped out much since we split?" I asked.

"No. That wasn't the point."

"What was?"

He didn't answer right away. His eyes remained on Kikit. Finally he said, "It started out one thing and became another."

I thought about that, giving my own interpretation to the words while I waited for him to go on. We were on opposite sides of the bed, with Kikit's soft wheeze droning on between us.

Ten minutes must have passed before he said, "It started out as a challenge to you and ended up as a challenge to me. I'm not the world's worst father."

"I never said you were."

"You said it in court."

"My lawyer argued that I was in a better position to care for the kids."

"She said I wasn't fit to be a father."

"No, Dennis."

"Well, it felt that way."

"Not a good feeling, was it?" I remarked.

The look he shot me held a flicker of the old annoyance. Then he sighed, and it was gone.

Snow continued to fall. From the window in Kikit's room, we watched it blanket the parking lot, trees, nearby houses. Plows cleared the lot and the access roads, then, two hours later, did it again. Shortly before dawn, the snow finally stopped.

Soon after that, Dennis went home to shower and change. He returned in less than an hour, carrying Kikit's small flight bag stuffed with Travis, Michael, and Joy, her favorite teddy bear, a pair of pajamas, and her Barney slippers.

I was touched that he had thought to bring them, and that he had done it with a minimum of fanfare. Whether he did it because of lingering guilt or legitimate thoughtfulness didn't matter. We understood that the doctors wouldn't be releasing her yet, and that having her wake up with friends would help ease her disappointment.

Dennis took out the dolls and the teddy and arranged them on the bed. I took out the pajamas and slippers and put them on the bedside table. Then I reached back into the bag. Something was still inside. I could feel its weight.

The bag was a lightweight backpack, too large for school use, but perfect for travel. It still bore the airline ID that Kikit had made me affix to one of the back straps.

I felt around inside, but found nothing. I peered around inside, but saw nothing. I slid sandwiched hands over the nylon until I located the weight, unzipped a back pocket, and reached inside.

My heart skipped a beat seconds before my hand brought out the Epi-pen and antihistamine that "hadn't been packed" when the children had returned from Cleveland in October.

Dennis's gaze was riveted to them. For a second, I wondered if his astonishment was a cover for mortification at having been found out. Then his eyes rose to mine and I saw the kind of horror that said he honestly hadn't known. He closed his eyes, hung his head, ran a hand around the back of his neck.

"Christ," he finally said and raised his head. "What a fuckin' mess."

I had to ask, had to hear the words. "You didn't know?"

"I didn't know." With a look of disgust, he turned his head away. "What a *fuckin'* mess."

"Didn't you know it would be?" I cried. I wanted to think that the man I married and had stayed married to for so long wasn't as clueless as he sounded just then.

"I didn't," he confessed. "They made it sound clear. They made it sound simple. The judge was in agreement from day one. We didn't hit a single hitch."

I was grateful that Kikit chose that moment to wake up. If not, I might have told him about Selwey's note to Jenovitz, which wouldn't have been the best thing to do. We were still locked in a legal battle. Carmen had a sure-fire weapon in her hands. I had faith that she would use it wisely, and owed her that chance.

By the time Brody showed up with Johnny and takeout breakfast, I had bathed Kikit and put her in her own pajamas. With the swelling down and the oxygen mask replaced by nasal prongs, she was beginning to look more herself. She wasn't pleased with the continued presence of the IV needle, but the doctors promised that if she continued to improve, she might be released that afternoon.

Dennis was subdued. He hung back while Johnny and Brody sat on Kikit's bed telling jokes to cheer her up. I hung back, myself. I was starting to feel the lack of sleep.

My first impulse when Brody suggested driving me home for a nap was to refuse on the grounds that Kikit needed me there and that, if I was tired enough, I could stretch out on the room's second bed and doze. I went with my second impulse, which had to do with Kikit being out of the woods and needing to know that her father was there for her, too.

So Brody drove me to the lighthouse. I had barely made it out of the shower and into bed when Carmen called to say, with a satisfaction verging on glee, that we'd been granted a hearing on our new Motion to Recuse. Selwey would see us the following afternoon at two.

Not only that, she said, but we had the figures we needed on Jenovitz. In only two of twenty-three cases referred to him by Selwey in the last three years had his recommendation differed from Selwey's ruling. Of the twenty-one remaining, more than half had eventually been reversed.

I hung up the phone, grinned at Brody, and promptly fell into a sound sleep.

Kikit had started talking. Nonstop. She remained hoarse and neither the wheezing nor the hives were entirely gone, but either the doctors figured that she couldn't be too ill if she could chatter that way, or she simply wore them out. Whatever, by early afternoon she was back at the house that I had started to think of as Dennis's. I had a feeling Dennis would have let her come to the lighthouse if I had made an issue of it, but Kikit needed both of us, and, frankly, I didn't want Dennis at my place.

Dennis, on the other hand, had no objection to my being at his. He took an active role in getting Kikit settled on the sofa in the den and seeing that she had everything her little heart desired—bless her, she kept sending him on some little errand—but he remained subdued, pensive at times to the point of distraction. There was nothing about him to suggest smugness, arrogance, or flippancy. I wasn't sure whether the severity of Kikit's attack had shocked him or he'd had some other epiphany, but he was different. I sensed he was looking back on the last two months through different eyes.

At least, I hoped it. We weren't done with each other yet. Despite Carmen's unbridled optimism, I wasn't counting my chickens before they hatched. Even if I regained primary custody of the children, there was still the divorce itself to settle.

By mid-afternoon, Johnny was out sledding with friends, Brody was at the office, and I had sung Kikit to sleep. I dozed briefly there on the bed beside her and awoke smelling coffee. My nose led me to the kitchen. Dennis was at the window, holding a steaming mug between his hands.

"I'm impressed," I said. When he glanced at me, I gestured toward the coffee maker. Then my eye caught on a long Pyrex dish nearby, and I was doubly impressed. It contained chicken prepared Kikit's favorite way and ready to bake. The mixing bowl and utensils had been washed and lay drying against the edge of the sink. Everything else was neat and clean.

He grunted. "Amazing what a guy can do when he has to."

I filled a mug and leaned against the counter. He was looking out the window again. The snow in the backyard was blue-tinged as dusk approached.

"When will Johnny be back?" I asked.

"Soon, I'd guess. He almost didn't go."

"Why not?"

"Because you were here. He only left when I said you'd stay through dinner."

The admission startled me. Not so long ago Dennis would have died rather than let me know that the children wanted me around.

"Heuber called a few minutes ago," he said and brought the mug to his mouth.

Yes. About the new hearing.

I watched him swallow the coffee and lower the mug, watched him rub his thumb against its rim and purse his lips. His eyes held resignation when he raised them to mine. "Are you raising the Adrienne business?"

"Only if you make me. How could you have lived with that all this time? Weren't you afraid someone would find out?"

He shrugged. "There were times I was worried."

"About me? About my finding out?"

"That, too."

"Would it have been so awful to tell me, way back when I first asked?"

"I was afraid you'd divorce me." His gaze sharpened. "Be honest. You would have."

Maybe. Maybe not.

"You would have," he said. "You'll use it now."

"If that's the only way I can keep the kids. But that isn't what the hearing's about."

"What is?"

"We have evidence of something fishy going on between Selwey and Jenovitz. We want Selwey to leave the case."

Dennis didn't argue. He simply stood at the window, alternately studying his mug and the snow.

I sipped the coffee. It was stronger than I made mine but felt good going down.

"I fired Phoebe," he said without turning.

"Fired her?"

"Fired, broke up with, whatever. She didn't have any right to go after that medical file. If she'd asked me, I would have told her not to. That abortion was more my fault than yours."

I was so stunned that it was a minute before I could speak. *Thank you*, I might have said. Instead, I said, "Was it hard breaking up?"

"Not as hard as I thought it would be."

"Do you love her?"

"Nah. I thought I did at first. We worked everything out so I'd get custody of the kids and a neat divorce settlement after that. Then a funny thing happened. I found that I liked my kids." He looked at me. "Phoebe doesn't like kids."

"Ah. Has she met ours?"

"No. It never got that far."

"Just sex and law. No family."

He turned quickly, about to argue. I could see it in the flash of his eyes. Then the flash died, and he turned back to the window.

"What *was* it all about?" I asked. "I need to know."

"So do *I*," he said on a note of exasperation.

"Did you fall for Phoebe before or after you talked to her about getting a divorce?"

"After."

I felt an odd relief. If it had to be one or the other, after was preferable.

"She was so . . . on my side," he said, seeming far away. "She told me I was right and you were wrong. She told me I was smart. She loved my looks."

"I loved your looks."

"Yeah," he waffled, "but it's different when someone new says it. You *expect* your wife to say it. When another woman says it, one who is young and beautiful and powerful and has no obligation at all to do it, it's more exciting."

"Flattering."

"Yeah. So maybe it was a mid-life thing, at least, with her. But the other, the stuff about the business, it's been tough for a while. There was a time when I had the magic touch. But it's gone."

I might have reminded him that the magic touch hadn't been magic at all, but mere sleight of hand, thanks to the late Adrienne Hadley. But I didn't want to spoil the mood. He seemed to be feeling what I was—tired and mellow, benevolent now that Kikit was on the mend. We desperately needed to talk this way, for ourselves as much as the kids.

"You never really wanted WickerWise, did you?" I asked.

He snorted. "What would I do with it? I don't know the first thing about wicker."

"Then it's for the money? For Pittney?"

He nodded, drained his coffee, leaned against the window frame facing me. His stance would have been nonchalant, had it not been for the caution I saw on his face.

"Would you make me sell WickerWise?" I asked.

His smile was skewed. "Can't do that now, can I? You know about Hadley."

"But if I didn't, would you do it? Knowing how much the business means to me?"

He frowned, lowered his chin. "Probably not."

Well, that was something.

His expression was gentle when he looked at me. "I was listening when you sang Kikit to sleep. Your voice is as clear as it was twenty years ago. Can you believe it's been that long? Twenty years. I fell in love with that clarity." He lowered his eyes and studied his mug. "It was good when we sang."

"Yes."

"When we sang, we were in tune with each other. When we stopped, it went."

An oversimplification, perhaps. But I had thought it myself. "Singing was one of the good things. There were others. Certainly the kids. I don't regret our marriage, if for no other reason than them."

"So what happened to us?"

I had asked him that same question, way back when. His answer then had been accusatory. He had blamed our break-up on me. I had every right to turn the tables now, but I didn't. As exhausted as I was after Kikit's ordeal, I felt stronger than I had in months. I had been forced to do things I didn't like. Now I was taking back my life.

"We need different things," I said. "I'm wrong for you. You shouldn't have to compete with a wife. You shouldn't have to fight over who's the better worker or the better parent. You need someone who's vulnerable and will lean on you and look up to you and devour every word you say. Me," I gave a wry smile, "I'm an old hand when it comes to self-sufficiency. I've been at it since I was eight. So I needed other things from my marriage."

"Like what?"

"The security of knowing I'd never be left alone."

It was a while before Dennis said, "Guess I blew that."

I didn't respond at first. My mind was sorting things out. Much as I resented Dean Jenovitz, some of what he said rung true. "Maybe I'm too self-sufficient."

Dennis didn't say anything. Which was good. No hackles raised. I went on.

"Sometimes I don't listen. I find solutions and impose them. I jump in and take charge before others can, even when they want to, even when they need to."

When Dennis remained silent, I looked at him. He smiled gently. "I'm not arguing."

"Take Kikit," I went on, because this affected us both. "She can read. She knows how to spell all the things she's allergic to. We have to teach her how to look at labels and monitor herself. We have to give *her* the power, rather than keep it ourselves. That means letting go just a little." Quietly, I added, "I have to learn to do that."

It would be hard. I worried so about her. But if I had refused to put her on the floor as an infant, lest she fall and hurt herself, she would never have learned how to walk. So, now, I had to set her down. The trick would be in being there to prevent a fall while she learned. For Kikit, allergy-wise, falls could be fatal. But she had to learn that she could prevent them herself. She had to gain that self-confidence.

"Jenovitz accused me of not wanting to change. He's wrong," I vowed. But when I tried to apply the empowerment model to Dennis, I couldn't. I had let him be weak. I had let him lean on me. Now, he was too heavy. I no longer had the trust or respect to prop him up. I didn't want to catch him if he fell. "I'm just not sure I can change, where you and I are concerned."

And where Brody was concerned? Overpowering self-sufficiency had never been an issue with him. From the very first, I had been able to lean on him. He was a strong man.

Dennis was studying his mug again. When he raised his eyes this time, they held a vulnerability that did something to me. It brought back, in one swift instant, all the positive parts of our marriage, the feelings of warmth and affection and, yes, love, that had seen us through for years. In that swift instant, my heart ached for the potential that had been there and had gone awry. In that swift instant, I wanted to comfort Dennis.

"Is there any chance for us?" he asked.

With the passing of that first swift instant, came another. This one held all that I hadn't said about Dennis and our marriage, all that had come into focus only after Dennis himself had broken it up. It held things like rashness, lack of loyalty, and moral weakness. On the plus side, it held Brody.

I gave him an apologetic smile and a quick headshake. "It may be we'll be better friends than lovers. I'll try that, if you will. Want to?"

I stayed at the house until dinner was done and the children settled in, then left them in Dennis's care with a new sense of peace. I headed for the lighthouse, changed my mind and headed for Brody's, changed my mind again and headed for my workroom. By the time I got there, I was on an adrenaline high.

Setting the rocker and its table side by side on the workbench, I studied them. The reweaving was nearly complete, though I wasn't entirely satisfied with the job I had done. Often, working during the last few weeks, I had been tense and distracted, and it showed.

I was focused now. With infinite patience, I removed those reeds that I hadn't placed well, soaked new lengths, and wove them in. They fit smoothly. With similar ease, I wove replacement pieces into those spots previously empty. I had the touch tonight. My hands were magic.

Standing back, I admired my work. As jarring as the two pieces had looked filled with holes, now they looked mended. They weren't perfect yet. The new weavers had to dry before I could guarantee their alignment, and once that was done, there would be more cleaning and sanding, then priming and painting. I was hoping for a particular shade of green, something warm and lime. If I didn't get it right with the first coat, I would get it right with the second.

Had it not been for those still damp reeds, I might have started the priming right then, my energy level was so high. As fate had it, Brody appeared at the door and gave me another outlet.

Eighteen

A blustery wind blew me along Federal Street the following afternoon, but my shivering was as much emotional as physical. All too well I remembered the first time I was here, when Dennis had held all the cards. Now I held a few. But despite the change in circumstance, too much was at stake for complacency.

The chill left few people lingering on the courthouse steps. They crowded the lobby and, with the added bulk of overcoats thrown over bench backs, compounded the chaos in the courtroom. Otherwise, the scene was much as it had been in October. Lawyers and their clients huddled, uniformed court officers chatted, the judge moved up and down his bench, the radiators hissed.

Carmen and I sat at the back of the courtroom, waiting to be called. She had already handed Missy a copy of Selwey's letter, plus a statistical analysis of Jenovitz's reports, affixed to our Motion to Recuse. Since Dennis and Art Heuber sat several rows ahead of us, I couldn't see their expressions.

I had talked with Dennis briefly in the lobby, more by way of passing time while we waited for our lawyers than anything else. There was an awkwardness between us here. It didn't matter that we had come to an understanding of sorts at home. In this place, we were adversaries.

He had been at the house all morning, while I had been with Kikit. Then, as now, his manner had been quiet and conciliatory, his shoulders weighted.

"The Raphael matter," Missy called.

We took the same places we had in October—Dennis, Art, Carmen, and I, in that order. Selwey took Carmen's brief from Missy and stood swaying before us while he read it. I was acutely aware of the moment when the swaying stopped. Lips pursed, he read on a bit, then set the papers down and said to Carmen, "You are aware that your client has committed theft."

"No, your honor," Carmen dared say. "Since she is personally paying the guardian to conduct his study, we argue that the contents of that folder are hers. I don't expect that Dr. Jenovitz will press charges. He won't want us arguing our case in open court." She hitched her chin toward the papers Selwey held. "He won't want to risk those figures coming out. You may not mind."

Of course he would. His manner said it clear as day. Everything about him was small and tight and angry. "What, exactly, do you want?"

"It's stated in our petition," Carmen said, sparing him a public statement. We had asked him to excuse himself from the case, to reverse his orders against me, and dismiss the case.

In a huff, he said, "I was brought into this case on behalf of two young children. What about them?"

Art Heuber answered. "Your honor, my client is willing to drop his insistence on sole custody."

"Well, what about the original charges? I didn't dream them up, here. I didn't go looking for you. You came looking for me."

Again Heuber spoke. "My client has agreed to drop the original charges. The parents would like to determine custody of the children themselves."

"If the parents weren't able to do that two months ago, what makes them able to do it now?"

"A dialogue has begun," Heuber said.

Selwey moved his arms, black robes fluttering, feathers ruffled. "Well, what *happened* to those original charges?"

"There was a misunderstanding."

"A misunderstanding? You've wasted the time of this court and a GAL on a *misunderstanding*?" With a disdainful flourish, he made a notation on the paper he held. "This case is dismissed. Who's next, Missy?" he asked, turning his back on us as he walked our papers down the bench.

As quickly as that it was over.

I made it as far as the courthouse steps before my legs rebelled, this time from utter relief. I rested my weight against the stone wall and took breath after deep breath of the cold December air. With each one I felt stronger, freer, happier. With each one I stood straighter.

When Carmen joined me, her grin was as broad as mine.

"Nice work," I said.

Her lips quirked. "It's always nice when you can stand there like a lady and not say a word while the other guys squirm."

"Not that I'd have minded if you'd accused Selwey in a big loud voice of unethical conduct, the pompous jerk."

"The accusation's coming," Carmen promised. "That letter will make the rounds until Selwey is off the bench. My guess is it won't have to go past the first stop. That's the Judicial Conduct Commission. Trust me. Selwey's gone. Jenovitz will have to feed at another trough. And he'll find one. He'll get assignments from other judges. Maybe not enough to allow for the subsidized retirement he had in mind. But he won't starve."

"So he was in it for the money. What did Selwey get from the deal?"

"Ego. Control. Power. He'll lose all that now. As he should. What he did to you is not how our system of justice is supposed to work."

But he had nearly gotten away with it. A quiet exit was more than he deserved. In angry moments, I wanted to picket the courthouse, write the governor, call the media. In more rational ones, I simply wanted to leave this whole experience far, far behind.

Dennis emerged from between the stone pillars and stood on the top step looking around. He hesitated when he saw us, then pulled up his collar and started down. By the time he reached us, his hands were deep in his coat pockets. His expression was sober.

"Congratulations," he said to Carmen, then to me, "I didn't know about the note Selwey wrote. Neither did Art, or Phoebe. We knew he had a bias, but we didn't think it went that far." He paused. "So." His hands remained in his pockets, arms stiff. "What happens now?"

"We talk," I said. "The way we should have in October."

"I still want the kids."

Calmly, I said, "So do I."

"I still have more time for them than you do."

"Not if you buy into Pittney."

"What if I don't? What if I retire and live on alimony?"

"Will alimony give you enough to live the way you want?" I asked in a way that raised the Hadley business without my saying it aloud.

Carmen broke in. "I think we should discuss this when Dennis has counsel present. I'll call Art and set a date to meet."

Dennis nodded her way. Then, persistent as ever when he was onto a cause, he turned to me again. "I won't be kicked out of the house."

"You can have the house," I said, which took the wind from his sails for a minute, but only that.

"So. Who gets the kids?"

We opted for joint custody. It was the obvious solution. We lived close enough to each other so that Kikit and Johnny could go back and forth without any disruption to their everyday lives. They would stay with Dennis while I traveled and stay with me while he traveled, and for the rest of the time we would rotate weekly, with the assumption of added flexibility as the children grew older. We agreed to share all major decisions and responsibilities, and to consult with each other on all matters relating to the kids. Child support was never an issue. I was thrilled to be able to give my children a level of financial security that I had never had.

The divorce settlement was more thorny. Dennis held out for a large chunk of money. I simply held out longer. It took that long to convince him that I would use what I had against him if he went after WickerWise.

Would I? Really? Carmen asked me that more than once as we negotiated, and I thought about it long and hard. The woman I had been before all this would never have slandered her husband, but that woman had changed. She had been burned. The scars that had formed were tough. She might not take the offensive against her husband, but she would defend herself in a heartbeat if he ever again threatened what she held dear.

The final deal included my paying monthly alimony in an amount that would enable Dennis to live comfortably, plus a lump sum for the past year and each of the next four equal to twenty-five percent of the net profit of WickerWise.

For all of Dennis's complaints that I would thwart his ability to earn a decent living, he bought into Pittney Communications even without the larger share of WickerWise that he wanted. The first lump sum that I paid him, plus an advance on the second, plus a deal with Pittney that enabled him to pay for the rest with a portion of his monthly take, and that vice-presidency was his.

All things considered, it was more than he deserved.

But I was satisfied. I had made mistakes in the course of our marriage. I felt less guilty about those, knowing that Dennis would be all right. Besides, his ego was a major player in his life. The more satisfied that ego, the more agreeable the man. The more agreeable the man, the better a father he was. The better a father he was, the greater the well-being of my children. And that was the bottom line.

It always had been.

By the middle of January, we had our agreement in writing. By the first of February, we had a hearing in court. With Judge Selwey on an indefinite leave of absence, we stood before his replacement, Judge Collier. She granted the judgment *nisi* as a matter of course. Ninety days later, our divorce became final.

With the coming of May, the sun was high enough and strong enough to counter the chill of the Atlantic and warm Brody's back porch for a late Sunday brunch. It was a private affair, just Brody and me. The children were with Dennis in New Hampshire. Rona was with Valentino at the lighthouse.

Wrapped in a fleece blanket, I sat on my lime green rocker and, while its runners creaked to and fro on the weathered planks of the porch, I looked lazily out at my kingdom. The air held the salt smell that I loved, along with the sweeter one of the first tiny lilies of the valley to bloom at the foot of the porch. Later there would be morning glories and lilacs, and beach roses in the thickets where grass met rock. I was looking forward to watching the sun rise over them all.

Smiling, I fingered the pearls that wound around my throat and dipped under the blanket to fall between my breasts and rest in a gentle loop on my thigh. Connie had been right. My strand was long and ever-growing. In the last few months alone, I swear, a dozen new ones had appeared. There was one with a beaming Kikit posed prettily in her tutu at the dance recital, and one with Johnny's arms raised in victory when his basketball team won the league championship in double overtime. There was one at the joint birthday party we had thrown for the children, with thirty of their friends, one magician, Dennis and his parents, and Brody and Rona and I in amiable attendance. There was one for a newly signed WickerWise lease on Newbury Street in Boston, and another for the successful Alzheimer's Association benefit in Washington that Brody and I had supported.

There were pearls on my strand that were still half-formed but growing—Rona searching for the place in WickerWise that suited her best, she and I puzzling out a comfortable personal relationship, my memory of Connie that held not the withered figure she had been at the end but a more healthy woman in her prime.

I was working on other pearls, brushing at sand that stubbornly resisted my desire for perfection. Though Kikit had gone since December without an allergy attack, the last one had left her skittish about eating anything other than what we had checked and she had checked, and even then she searched for things as she ate. Johnny was still tussling with the divorce, still trying to figure out what the rules were, what position he played, and how he could score.

Divorce is never an ideal situation. For the sake of the greater good, something was always left behind. In our case, it was the intact family that the four of us had once been. As agreeable as Dennis was, I hated making arrangements about who would have whom when. As sensible as shared custody was, I never stopped wanting the children all the time.

On the positive side, Dennis had come to know the children.

And I had Brody.

Ahhh, Brody. So many pearls there, I couldn't begin to count them. Smooth and precious—best friend, lover, husband-to-be—my fingertips touched each. As I watched, the sun caught on the diamond he had given me. It was as multifaceted as our lives.

"You look like you're taking root," he mused, drawing up the rocker's matching table and setting down a tray. It held French toast, fresh strawberries, and a carafe of coffee.

I gave him a lazy smile and stretched under my blanket. "I might just."

Hunkering down before me, he opened the blanket, slipped his arms around my waist, and pressed a wet kiss to my bare middle. My fingers were in his hair by the time he looked up. I felt happier than I would have believed possible a few short months before.

Softly, I began to sing. It was another love song. I had sung more than my share of late.

He put his head down, cheek to my thigh. His pleasure was as warm as the breath on my skin. I stroked his hair. A sweet peace filled me as I hummed the rest of the song. Life didn't get much better than this.

Still softly but exuberant now, I shifted songs. This one was about wedding bells, chapels, and champagne, which was where we were headed.

Brody lifted his head and grinned. I was trying to figure out the devil in that grin, when he let out with a song of his own. It had to do with honeymoons and was slightly obscene.

Laughing, I wrapped myself over him to smother the sound. He might never carry a tune or be able to clap to a beat, but, Lord, I did love him.

Photo by Robert Clark

BARBARA DELINSKY, a lifelong New Englander, was a sociologist and photographer before she began to write. There are more than 30 million copies of her books in print. Readers can contact her c/o P.O. Box 812894, Wellesley, MA 02482-0026, or via the Web at www.barbaradelinsky.com

Barbara Delinsky

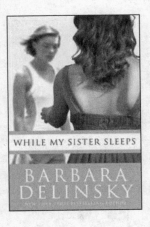